THE BICKERSONS SCRIPTS

The Bickersons Scripts

by Philip Rapp

Edited by

Ben Ohmart

Introduction by

Philip Rapp

The Bickersons Scripts

For information, address:

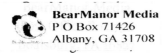

BearManor Media
P O Box 71426
Albany, GA 31708

bearmanormedia.com

Cover design by Lloyd W. Meek

Published in the USA by BearManor Media
ISBN 0-9714570-1-8

To Frances, Don, Lew and Phil

Table of Contents

J: Hey, Blanche — take it easy will you! Slow down!
You took that corner on two wheels!
Look out for that woman ahead!

B: John Bickerson! This is not the first time
I've pushed a shopping cart in a supermarket!

J: Well, you act like a Sunday pusher! Aren't we
thru yet? This whole cart is full.

B: I've got to get some ~~filet mignon~~ for Nature Boy.

J: Filet mignon! Let him eat cat food like
I do! We came in to buy some Coffee Rich
and that's all! ~~Now get some~~

B: ~~Here, the~~ ~~Here's the~~ ~~I'll take six~~
~~Se~~ Take out six cartons of Coffee Rich.

J: Six —! Where do you plan to put 'em?

B: Where I always do. On your cereal, fruit
and in your coffee. Coffee rich makes
everything taste better.

J: There's no more room in the cart. I'll
eat it right here.

A Bickersons script page in Philip Rapp's own hand.

Editor's Preface

"They fight, they yell, they squabble and squawk, but they love each other as much as any married couple in the world." The Bickersons also happen to be the most hilarious "man and wife" comedy team ever to hit radio. It's my sincere pleasure to have the honor of presenting these masterly crafted scripts to the world, for the first time in their original printed form.

These 13 scripts – 12 radio and 1 television – are laugh out loud funny. When reading, it's impossible not to recall the crazed inflections of Don Ameche's rants, or the shrew-like nagging of the relentless Frances Langford, or the broken man passion of Lew Parker. They were incredibly gifted performers.

But for those strange mortals who have never even heard a Bickersons recording, they too will be pleasantly surprised at the quick wit and sharpness of tongue that leap off the page at every turn.

Bickersons writer/creator Philip Rapp began his radio career writing for Eddie Cantor's radio show in the early 1930s, then moved on to write most of Fanny Brice's Baby Snooks material. In films, he wrote several hits for Danny Kaye, including *The Inspector General* and *The Secret Life of Walter Mitty*. Not to leave out the legitimate stage, he also penned the book of the musical *Springtime In Brazil* for Milton Berle, and wrote a Bickersons play entitled *Match Please, Darling*. He could, and did, do it all.

There would be no script collection without the continued assistance and guidance of Phil's son, Paul Rapp. He has contributed what few others would ever agree to: complete and unlimited access to a wealth of Phil Rapp papers (scripts, letters, photos, etc.). It was sheer joy to be able to run through these countless boxes of material in order to find out more about the Bickersons, for my upcoming biography on them, as well as assemble this collection of the Bickersons' "greatest quips." I'd also like to thank my father John for his Herculean support; N. Loganathan of India and Sheetal Chauhan for a lot of very helpful typing of scripts; Charles Stumpf for always being there to answer all radio questions; Frances Langford for opening the door to everything; and my mother Vickie for radiating enough love for twenty-two kids.

What you will find within these pages is the first of two volumes of scripts gathered from their various mediums. The Bickersons appeared on radio with Edgar Bergen and Charlie McCarthy, on *Drene Time*, on *The Old Gold Show*, and finally had their own series in 1951, *The Bickersons*. Their various TV appearances on variety programs, like *The Ed Sullivan Show*, were frequent, and the Bickersons sketches were the crown jewels in the 1950 series, *Star Time*. As all great writers do, Philip Rapp reused his material, whenever the Bickersons switched series, and sometimes within the same series. And of course when John and Blanche became big recording stars with Columbia Records, the best of the best of the scripts were re-edited again to create another laugh-a-minute package; which ended up selling millions of albums.

Even in this Volume One collection you'll find certain jokes and gags used several times. Rapp knew what worked, and he knew what the audience wanted to hear again.

Phil Rapp's introduction to this book isn't an introduction in the true sense. Philip Rapp died in 1996, six years before this book was published. However, I wanted the creator himself to have a hand in setting the stage on what to expect from our battling couple. In going through Phil's many works, I came across the following pitch for an animated Bickerson series that failed to fly (though a pilot script and storyboards were created). The opening pages of it will give Bickerson novices an immediate grasp of the characters and tone of John and Blanche and their surrounding bad luck. The synopses that follow it are incredibly interesting, and rare, in that they were never fleshed out into full scripts. Though Rapp had used some of these set-up situations before, they are now more visually oriented and often go to comic extremes that radio never would have dared!

I tried to keep to the original sense of the scripts, including layout, as much as possible, working from Phil Rapp's own broadcast drafts. Therefore, if you have any of these recordings, you may notice subtle or significant differences from these printed pages. Bonus cuts, you might say. And rather than edit out too much, I left in everything that would make sense to the whole of the book. My only warning is: beware all ye non-smoking readers. The cigarette sponsors are going to hit you heavy!

I hope you like, and will stick around for Volume Two, which will include the infamous Christmas episode, a routine from Edgar Bergen's show, and more surprises. Enjoy the squabbles!

Ben Ohmart
June 2002

Introduction

I am the master of my fate:
I am the captain of my soul.
— Invictus, W.E. Henley, 1872

Bullshit! You are a pawn in the hands
of women, children, pets and bosses,
relatives and "friends"– a target for
slings and arrows that Shakespeare
never dreamed about.
— The Honeymoon is Over, John Bickerson, 1972

It is to be assumed that anybody who reads this diatribe is familiar with "The Bickersons," the mismatched couple who, since 1946, have given us The Facts About Marriage As We Really Know Them.

They have survived radio, television, and even spilled blood on the legitimate stage. Now John and Blanche Bickerson are about to try animation.

Of course, everybody knows who the Bickersons are, and how funny they are, what their characters are like, how Blanche never lets John sleep because he snores, how John has to moonlight in three or four jobs at one time in order to keep body and soul together, and everybody knows about Blanche's sister Clara, the Constant Complainer, and her wispy, scrounging husband Barney, John's private bete noir, to say nothing of little Ernie, the seven-year-old enfant terrible and a smaller edition of his father, Barney, with larger talents for making John Bickerson's life miserable.

Borrowing shamelessly from the explanatory sleeve of one of Columbia's Bickerson albums, I must first inform the reader that John and Blanche yield not even to Tristan and Isolde or Abelard and Heloise in a love that transcends their constant caviling. Most students of connubial habits will agree the Bickersons are prime examples of what makes marriage work – hardships. The family that complains together remains together. In the proposed series life is not one long marital argument but rather a compendium of recognizable comic situations occurring in everybody's married life, deliberately exaggerated for maximum humor, situations of raucous desperation in what the Freudians call a love-hate relationship.

The mise-en-scene is a rather imposing apartment house in a large city. Various tenants may from time to time enter as part of the plot. John and Blanche live in this stylish condominium, but not in style. In fact, John is the superintendent (read Janitor), their free apartment resembles a goat's nest, and poor John is called upon to handle the most menial, if not degrading kind of odd job that can possibly be imagined. This is in addition to his outside part-time jobs which vary from week-to-week – his constant lack of sleep resulting in his inability to hold any position for any length of time.

Clara and Barney live elsewhere with their diabolical child but are constant spongers in the Bickerson ménage, which is barely large enough to hold the group. John's prime antagonist is Herb Trowel, a gigolo married to a rich and older woman, Birdie, the couple who occupy the palatial penthouse. Herb Trowel finds devious ways to irritate and frustrate the embattled John, is an intolerant swine to the point of bigotry, a swanking show-off, and seems to have one real mission in life – to get Bickerson fired. These people comprise the regular cast and all situations will be built around their relationships to each other. I have reserved the one character that John Bickerson hates most for last. This is Nature Boy, a huge tomcat that Blanche adores, who has the run of the tiny apartment and uses his demoniacal animal cunning to make Bickerson almost suicidal. John has a few ways of retaliation, at least overtly, but on many occasions has been violently assailed by Blanche for doing away with a couple of Nature Boy's predecessors. These attacks are invariably associated with John Bickerson's well-known bourbon fetish. And let us say here and now that Nature Boy loves bourbon and finds devious methods of raiding the precious Bickerson supply.

It is difficult to catalog the many small facets of John and Blanche's constant lack of the mythical syrup in conjugal life – her incessant references to Gloria Gooseby, a long forgotten and possibly invented former girl friend of John's – her constant demands to be told he loves his wife and is glad he married her – and the fact that he has somehow managed to outlive Blanche's culinary peculiarities – but they are many and funny which most married couples can identify.

Breakfast at the Bickersons is an unalloyed horror. In their kitchen debates a crisis which always develops. What on earth DOES John want for breakfast? He turns down such morning delights as stewed rabbit, enchiladas, chow mein – throwing the stuff to Nature Boy who promptly buries it in his sandbox. So he DOES want to poison the cat, after all! Now what kind of logic is that?

We may say without fear of successful contradiction that story lines for a half hour series are not too hard to come by, since all the elements are present, the characters are well-defined, and have a track record of twenty-five successful years.

Little concession will be made to comedy of a topical nature – a real virtue since the Bickersons are ageless and up to date – but the trials and tribulations concerning the NOW generation will not be avoided if they fit adequately into the plot.

"THE BICKERSONS"
FUTURE PROJECTION

The dramatic formula most susceptible to infinite variation is of course the triangle: playwrights and storytellers have been exploring its multiple facets since the days of Aeschylus and Sophocles. The classic components of the triangle consist of two men and a woman: when they are Oedipus, the father he slays, and the mother he marries, the result is stark tragedy. Take away one of the men and substitute a cat – not only is the dramatic formula converted to comedy, but the variations available are multiplied a hundred fold.

Naturally, the cat who replaces the man in the triangle cannot be just any cat. He has to be Nature Boy, the Bickerson cat who only thinks of himself as a man but has quite a few of the credentials. Spoiled rotten by the doting affection of Blanche Bickerson, displaying his feline cunning in involving his arch enemy John in hopeless predicaments, Nature Boy is not only one side of the triangle but its very apex. John Bickerson's other adversaries are many, all inhumanly human. As previously advertised there are Clara and Barney – the sponging in-laws, their brash devil-child, Ernie – the wealthy occupants of the penthouse where John janitors, Herb and Birdie – Bickerson's many bosses (he moonlights and can never hold a job over two weeks) – and the world in general. Even Dr. Hersey, the good and kind surgeon, must be considered an antagonist since his life seems devoted to forcing John to submit to an operation to cure his snoring. Comedy shares with tragedy the juxtaposition of great aspiration and inevitable failure – John Bickerson is a man who dreams large and is doomed mainly by a cat. Some of the chronicles of his frustration follow.

"GRAVE CONSEQUENCES"

John has secured a position with the Home of Eternal Peace selling cemetery plots to augment his meager income as janitor of the Venus Arms, a stylish apartment house. Herb Trowel, who occupies the penthouse with his wife Birdie, is caught in flagrante delicto dallying with a Playboy Bunny, but has had the forethought to give the unsuspecting girl the name of John Bickerson as his own. When the soiled Bunny confronts the absent John's wife, Blanche, hysteria reigns. Blanche's utter disbelief breaks down when the diabolical Nature Boy, cleverly using lipstick, drags in one of John's shirts bearing the incriminating marks of the collar. Enter Clara, Barney and little Ernie who add considerable fuel to the fire.

In the meantime John has had the good fortune to sell a vault, an entire crypt, to a Fraternal Order known as the Mysticrucians. They are going to use the vault as a retreat for meditation and prayer. They live in complete silence and John would dearly love to join them. He returns home in golden spirits which soon turn to dross as he is faced by the hostile group. Since the Bunny instantly declares that he is not the same John Bickerson, matters soon clear up. Blanche is not entirely convinced, however, and poor John is in for another classic Bickerson bout. "Keeping a Playboy Bunny," he screams," I can't even afford the Goddamn magazine!" When calm is restored, John is able to tell Blanche of his stroke of luck in the sale of the crypt, and visions of a huge commission. During all this Nature Boy is busy sniffing around the Mysticrucians, discovers they have installed twelve phones, and manages to lead the police who uncover the bogus friars as bookmakers.

John is charged with complicity and hauled off to jail. Herb's guilty conscience forces him to go bail for John and spring him, but not before swearing him to secrecy in the case of the Bunny.

"THE MELANCHOLY DANE"

From association with Nature Boy, John Bickerson acquires some of the cat's fiendish cunning. The man resolves to fight fire with fire. Why not bring home a pet of his own, he reasons, a dog! Thru the good offices of brother-in-law Barney, and separated from two weeks salary as a bowling ball salesman, he buys the largest and most perfectly trained Great Dane in the country. Naturally, the dog is not only marvelously trained but is guaranteed to reduce to cringing subservience any other animal alive. Opposed violently by Blanche and most of the tenants of the apartment house where he janitors, he brings home the Great Dane....and then finds that Nature Boy dominates the huge beast completely! Bickerson shrills commands, but the dog without his trainer is a ship without a sail, and he will do nothing but eat and lie down. The crowning blow comes when Nature Boy turns the Dane against John, Dr. Hersey is called in to minister to his wounds, and is forced to sell the dog back to his trainer at a tremendous loss ... which is how Barney and the trainer make a living.

"OPERATION UVULA"

John Bickerson snores because he has a long uvula and it flutters against his palate. At least that is Dr. Hersey's diagnosis and Blanche is convinced that an immediate operation is in order. A sleepless night, an exhausting morning at his janitorial duties and poor John's defenses are so weakened he finally consents to enter the hospital and have his uvula shortened. Nature Boy is gleeful at his distress, Clara and Barney agree to look after things when Blanche declares she's going to stay the pre-operative night with John in his hospital room to save on night nurses.

Under sedation John is relaxing beautifully in his Gatch bed (it cranks in all directions) until Blanche shows up with her overnight bag and proceeds to make him unbelievably uncomfortable. Unable to take any more, John flees in his hospital gown and takes refuge in an all night hamburger stand, frightening the fry cook half to death. All John wants to do is use the phone and get Barney to bring him some clothes. An all-points bulletin over the radio announces that a dangerous lunatic in a hospital gown has escaped — the counterman flies off on wings of terror. A cop enters, John quickly ties an apron on and proceeds to serve him. His inept attempts result in plastering the cop with a mélange of foodstuff, all wet, and causing the officer to remove his coat and hat to clean up. Seeing his chance, John dons the uniform and takes off. Another second and the cop is after him. Barney arrives with suitcase and clothes, finds nobody there, so helps himself to silverware and food, stuffing the bag with the loot.

Back at the apartment Dr. Hersey and Blanche are worriedly waiting for news, being "comforted" by Clara. John bursts in. Then the cop. Then Barney. In the ensuing scuffle the bag flies open and the silverware pops out.

Nature Boy views all this with happy detachment, meanwhile gorging himself on the stolen food and lapping at John's precious bourbon bottle. Dr. Hersey's explanations finally convince the second carload of police who have arrived and matters are brought to a head. But not before John Bickerson has promised to let the good doctor operate on his uvula in the near future.

"ANNIVERSARY BLUES"

John Bickerson's salary as janitor of the Venus Arms permits no extravagances, but Blanche has just reminded him that it is their eighth wedding anniversary and he is forced to take a job as a vacuum cleaner salesman in order to buy her a present. Needless to say he is a complete bust for all his high pressure selling, and weighed down by his sample and his other troubles he goes on the hook for a diamond ring — a bauble which Barney arranges for with a crooked jeweler — nothing down and ten dollars a week for life.

With the first payment on the ring coming up, John has still not made a commission on a sale – where to get the money? He finally decides to hock his samples and make the payment. As he enters a hockshop, the owner and a plain-clothes detective are going over a "hot sheet" – a cat burglar has been operating in the neighborhood, pilfering all sorts of household goods. TV sets, toasters, radios – and vacuum cleaners. John tries to explain how he came by the vacuum cleaner, but no dice. He winds up in the pokey.

A surprise party has been arranged for their anniversary by Blanche – Barney can't attend because he is going to a hard times party at his lodge at the United Nations Poolhall – and has borrowed John's best suit so he can go as bum. Of course, the ring is in the pants pocket.

Released from jail by Dr. Hersey, John returns home to find the anniversary party is over, the guests have all departed and Blanche is in tears. He tries to assuage her by telling her of the ring only to find Barney has it. Hysteria!

At the United Nations Poolhall John bursts in, finds a crap game in progress and learns Barney has blown the ring. A real donnybrook follows, John recovers the ring, returns to Blanche whose ecstasy and typical demands for professions of his deep love for her give poor Bickerson another sleepless night.

"SANTA BICKERSON"

It is nearly Xmas, the Bickersons are short of money as usual, and things look bleak. Even his menial job as janitor at the Venus Arms is hanging by a thread due to the machinations of the despicable Herb Trowel, the rich gigolo who lives in the penthouse. Brother-in-law Barney shows up with good news. For a slight fee he can get John an important job in a big department store, also owned by Mr. Flint, the landlord of the Venus Arms.

An interview with the manager of the store, a scene compounded of double-talk and double entendre, leads John to believe he has finally found a dignified job – supervisor of the toy department.

Back home to an overjoyed Blanche, who has squandered their meager bank account, anticipating great new fortunes, John displays remarkable constraint even while eating her idiot cooking. The landlord appears with a sheaf of complaints about John's janitorial work, mainly compiled by Herb Trowel – but John turns on him and tells him what he can do with his stinking job. So much for that.

Reporting for work at the department store to take over his new duties, Bickerson is handed a Santa Claus suit, beard and all, and told to go sit on the throne and minister to the little monsters and listen to their Xmas demands. Only temporary, the manager explains. John is caught in a trap and is forced to go thru with it. Of course, Clara and little Ernie show up – Ernie has brought Nature Boy for company – and between the boy, the diabolical cat and the appearance of the owner (the landlord), mayhem ensues.

The store becomes a shambles, Bickerson is finally unbearded by Nature Boy, and is revealed to the landlord as his erstwhile janitor.

Since it is the season for goodwill to all men the landlord relents, John gets his job back as janitor and a touching and tender scene between John and Blanche as they exchange gifts on Xmas Eve brings things to a happy ending.

Philip Rapp
1972

What you are about to read is the very first Bickersons script in the Philip Rapp collection. You'll see that they are introduced as "two new characters in a domestic vignette that we hope will provide you with excellent listening sport." Even though various books claim the Bickersons began on *The Chase and Sanborn Hour* around this time (1945 or 46), I've found no scripts or recordings that pre-date this first script in this collection. No doubt the first person who reads this book will disagree that this is indeed the premiere Bickersons episode; and if you can furnish me with proof or a recording, I'll give you a free copy of the second volume of scripts!

Until then, please enjoy at least the first *Drene Time* show, dated December 15, 1946. There are some interesting novelties in the Bickersons' characters here which are quite shocking to those who know the series as it progressed. This first show has the Bickersons married three years rather than their usual eight. And, it seems John has actually spent a lot of money on his own comforts, as Blanche lists his "double thickness sleep shade, lullaby musical pillow, toe mittens, electric pajamas and an automatic sheep counter." Quite a change from his later shouts of "I deny myself everything!"

In this opening script we also hear briefly about Blanche's pre-marital life: she was a schoolteacher. Of course, she's still as crazy as ever, dragging Gloria Gooseby into the late-night conversation whenever she can.

Don't forget to keep an eye out for the in-joke about Don Ameche's most famous role as Alexander Graham Bell!

PROCTER & GAMBLE

Present

DON AMECHE

In the

DRENE SHAMPOO SHOW

DECEMBER 15, 1946

MILLER: (ON CUE) The makers of Drene Shampoo are pleased to present the first in a series of new programs starring Don Ameche, Danny Thomas and Frances Langford.

THEME: (ESTABLISH AND FADE OVER FOLLOWING)

MILLER: In their earnest desire to provide a full half hour of quality entertainment the sponsors of this program have instructed me to employ great brevity while extolling the many virtues of Drene, spelled D-R-E-N-E. No adjectives, however, are to be spared in the description of our triad of star performers – stars who are as lustrous as your hair after using Drene Shampoo, spelled S-H-A-M-P-O-O. The delightful music trying desperately to obliterate that feeble jest is supplied by Carmen Dragon and his orchestra. Carmen will also add considerably to the zany songs of the irrepressible Danny Thomas, and accompany the thrush-like voice of the lovely and captivating Frances Langford. You can't call that sparing the adjectives. Now, here is your host for the evening – the amiable and talented gentleman who succeeds in rolling many facets into a career as an actor, singer, country squire, horse breeder, football impresario and family man – Don Ameche.
(APPLAUSE)

MUSIC: OUT

AMECHE: Thank you, ladies and gentlemen, and good evening. Let me add to Mr. Miller's imposing recital of my achievements that I also do my own paperhanging and am qualified to take a part-time job as a sand-hog.

MILLER: One might say that you're a jack of all trades and master of ceremonies.

AMECHE:	Yes, Marvin, one might say that. In fact, you said it.
MILLER:	No offense, Don. I didn't mean to be funny.
AMECHE:	Think nothing of it – you weren't. Well, we'd better --
CARMEN:	Er – pardon.
AMECHE:	Good evening, Carmen. Carmen, shake hands with Marvin Miller, our new announcer. Marvin, Carmen Dragon.
MILLER:	That's quite a remarkable name, Carmen. Carmen Dragon. Very curious.
CARMEN:	(COLDLY) Is it?
MILLER:	Wouldn't it be strange if my name were St. George? Then when Don introduced me to you I could tell you a joke that would make you laugh very hard and Don could say St. George slays the Dragon.
AMECHE:	I could, huh?
MILLER:	Of course, you have to know a bit of English mythology to appreciate that type of humor, besides, my name's not St. George, it's Miller. My throat hurts – anybody got any penicillin gum? (EXITS)
CARMEN:	That man is deranged.
AMECHE:	Nonsense, Carmen. He's just anxious to make good here. You can't say he isn't trying.
CARMEN:	On the contrary – I find him very trying. Say, what's all this talk about a new program? When does that start?
AMECHE:	It starts tonight, Carmen. It'll be an entirely different set-up.
CARMEN:	All musical numbers?
AMECHE:	Well, not exactly.
CARMEN:	Oh. Nearly all music?
AMECHE:	Er – no.
CARMEN:	Mostly music?
AMECHE:	To tell you the truth, Carmen, we're going to experiment. The plan is to start with as little music as possible and gradually work it up to where we have none at all.
CARMEN:	I see. Well, what am I supposed to do with this baton?
AMECHE:	Let's not expose ourselves to censorship, Carmen. I think there'll be plenty for you to do – accompanying Frances Langford and Danny Thomas, an occasional band number -- I daresay you'll get to like everybody pretty well.
CARMEN:	I don't think so. No, I don't think so. I already hate that announcer fellow – that St. George.
AMECHE:	His name is Miller – Marvin Miller.
CARMEN:	I don't care. I wish we were still with Drene.

AMECHE:	This is still the Drene Show, Carmen. Same sponsor.
CARMEN:	You mean I have to keep on using that stuff?
AMECHE:	It happens to be an excellent shampoo. And, Carmen, there's such a thing as loyalty to your sponsor, you know.
CARMEN:	Oh, brother, this is going to be a tough season. Carmen Dragon and his lustrous hair – no music. (AS HE LEAVES) We'll hear what Petrillo has to say about this.
AMECHE:	(CALLS AFTER HIM) Well, you needn't be so churlish about it!
LANGFORD:	What's the matter, Don?
AMECHE:	Oh, that Carmen, he's ---- Frances! Frances Langford! You had no business sneaking in like that. I was going to give you a wonderful introduction.
LANGFORD:	It's just as well. Who is that chap?
AMECHE:	He's the orchestra leader – Carmen Dragon.
LANGFORD:	Say, that's quite a remarkable name. Wouldn't it be strange if my name were St. George and you introduced me to Dragon and ----
AMECHE:	Frances! Who told you to say that?
LANGFORD:	I don't know – some man in the hall. Asked me if I had any penicillin gum.
AMECHE:	Oh, that Miller needs husking badly. I'm afraid he has a gift for childish puns, Frances – steer clear of him. It's Carmen that's worrying me.
LANGFORD:	What was the argument about?
AMECHE:	Not an argument, really. He somehow had the impression that the new Drene program would be all band numbers.
LANGFORD:	Didn't he know I was going to be on the show?
AMECHE:	Yes, but---
LANGFORD:	It's going to be all singing, of course, isn't it?....Isn't it?
AMECHE:	Well, you see, Frances ---
LANGFORD:	Mostly singing, anyway...Isn't it?
AMECHE:	Er......
LANGFORD:	Do I get to sing at all?
AMECHE:	Of course, darling!
LANGFORD:	That's good enough for me.
AMECHE:	You're wonderful! And as soon as you favor the customers with that bewitching smile of yours we'll let you hammer out a song. Turn it on.
LANGFORD:	(SMILING) It's on, Don.
AMECHE:	Beautiful! I wish I could describe to our listeners how that glittering smile lights up your face.

LANGFORD:	Just call it a flash in the pan.
AMECHE:	That's poetry. And just so you'll understand how I feel about you, Frances, I'll put all my sentiments into an old Spanish proverb...."El ojo del amo engorda el caballo".
LANGFORD:	How lovely. What does it mean, Don?
AMECHE:	(SERIOUSLY) The eye of the master fattens the horse!
LANGFORD:	(PUZZLED) What's this with horses?
AMECHE:	(EXAMINING HIS SCRIPT) I don't know. Looks like some of Miller's work. You sing, Frances, and I'll try to get to the bottom of this.
LANGFORD:	SONG
	(APPLAUSE)
AMECHE:	You swear you had nothing to do with that horse thing, Marvin?
MILLER:	Word of honor. I've been working on shortening this announcement about Drene. They want it brief, you know.
AMECHE:	Yes. Have you seen Danny Thomas yet?
MILLER:	No. I've got most of the essentials in but there are two or three very important things that I'd like to say if I had more time.
AMECHE:	Well, read it fast. You don't suppose he forgot about tonight, do you?
MILLER:	Who?
AMECHE:	Danny Thomas. I didn't want to say anything – but he didn't even show up for rehearsal this afternoon.
MILLER:	Oh, he'll be along. Listen to this, Don. A beautiful girl....dressed in her best....make-up just right....hair -- well, each soft tendril of her lustrous hair is an enchantment and a snare.
AMECHE:	He might have had a flat tire.
MILLER:	Don't be a flat tire – be glamorous. Girls, to be sure <u>your</u> hair gleams with all its natural beauty, try DRENE with hair conditioning action. Drene your hair and you bring out all its color brilliance....actually as much as 33 percent more lustre than any soap or soap shampoo. Drene your hair and you rid it of the drab, dulling film left by all soap and soap shampoos. Drene your hair and you remove unsightly dandruff flakes the very first time you use it. Drene your hair and you leave it soft...smoooooth...beautifully behaved. No other shampoo...only Drene Shampoo with hair conditioning action, leaves the hair so lustrous (HARP) yet so easy to manage. Well, what do you think, Don?
AMECHE:	I think he must have had an accident.

5

MILLER:	Who? Who must have had an accident?
AMECHE:	Danny Thomas.
CARMEN:	If he doesn't show up can I play a band number?
AMECHE:	I guess you'll have to, Carmen. Play something now.
MILLER:	Don, wait. What about the Drene Announcement?
AMECHE:	Make it shorter. I've gotta find Danny Thomas.
MUSIC:	BRIDGE.....FADES
AMECHE:	Where, son? Where did you say he was?
BOY:	In there, Mr. Ameche. He's been in there for over an hour.
AMECHE:	In <u>there</u>!
BOY:	Yes sir. Is there something wrong with him?
AMECHE:	Doesn't sound normal to me. Thanks a lot, son.
	SOUND: KNOCK ON DOOR
AMECHE:	Danny......
THOMAS:	Hello, Don.
AMECHE:	Come on out.
THOMAS:	No.
AMECHE:	Danny, the program's been on the air for fifteen minutes.
THOMAS:	I know it.
AMECHE:	Well, you can't sit there all night.
THOMAS:	I feel worse than you do.
AMECHE:	What's the matter, Danny boy?
THOMAS:	I'm ashamed of myself.
AMECHE:	First of all come out of that phone booth.
THOMAS:	No. No. Don, I'm scared. I've got mike fright. I don't wanna go on the radio.
AMECHE:	What are you talking about, Danny? You'll be a great hit.
THOMAS:	Is it a good audience? I mean do they laugh?
AMECHE:	Moderately. But we haven't said anything really funny – they're waiting for you.
THOMAS:	That settles it. I don't want that responsibility.
AMECHE:	Danny, you can't stay in that phone booth forever.
THOMAS:	Oh, yes I can. I'll put in a few sticks of furniture, maybe a picture or two to hang on the walls, some flowers--
AMECHE:	Oh, brother!
THOMAS:	After all it isn't so easy to get a room with a telephone these days. I like it here.
AMECHE:	Look, here, Danny -- I can understand and sympathize with your fear of the microphone, that's not too abnormal, but locking yourself up like this! It's a public phone booth – suppose someone wants to make a call?

THOMAS:	I can always step out for a minute – if it's a man.
AMECHE:	And if it's a woman.
THOMAS:	I'm married, I don't step out with women.
AMECHE:	I'm beginning to see why you don't want to go on the radio.
THOMAS:	Well, it's pretty stuffy in here – fellow's bound to lose his perspective. You go back, Don – you'll get along without me.
AMECHE:	Don't be ridiculous. Come on, Danny – I've got enough trouble with Carmen --
THOMAS:	Carmen? Who's she?
AMECHE:	It's a he. The orchestra leader – Carmen Dragon.
THOMAS:	Carmen Dragon. Say, that's quite a remarkable name. Wouldn't it be strange if my name were St. George and you –
AMECHE:	Did somebody ask you for some penicillin gum?
THOMAS:	Huh?
AMECHE:	Never mind. Would it help you any if we brought the microphone in here – away from the audience?
THOMAS:	No. It isn't the audience I'm afraid of, Don – it's the microphone itself. I can't explain it.
AMECHE:	Tell me a little bit about yourself, Danny. Your childhood.
THOMAS:	Oh, that psychiatric stuff won't work on me, Don. I've tried it. I've had a half a dozen psychiatrists probe my ego, expose my libido, and toy with my pocadilloes. I just get worse all the time.
AMECHE:	Perhaps I might catch something they missed.
THOMAS:	Well, all right. I was born in a small town near Toledo --
AMECHE:	What's the name of the town?
THOMAS:	You won't believe it.
AMECHE:	Of course I will. What was the name of the town?
THOMAS:	Pratt Falls, Ohio. Named after Chauncey Pratt, the founder. I told you you wouldn't believe it.
AMECHE:	Go on.
THOMAS:	As a kid I was crazy about the circus. Couldn't breathe till it came to town. It was even harder to breathe when it got there. But after all, we lived next door to a livery stable – and the camels were a breath of fresh air to me.
AMECHE:	Let's get on the lee side of this subject, Danny.
THOMAS:	Yes. Of course, I fell madly in love with the bareback rider --
AMECHE:	How old were you?
THOMAS:	Seven – but I was pretty big for my age. She was beautiful -- broke my heart when I found out she was married to the half-man half-woman.

7

AMECHE:	Just think how she must have felt. Did you get over it?
THOMAS:	Never. They came every year and when I was old enough I joined up with them. I was only a roustabout, but I secretly practiced sword swallowing every chance I got.
AMECHE:	Rather a dangerous profession, isn't it?
THOMAS:	I didn't know the meaning of fear – but I was completely lacking in caution. As a result of that I got into trouble.
AMECHE:	With the swords?
THOMAS:	Yes. A thirty-seven inch bayonet got lodged inside of me and I couldn't extract it. For weeks the doctors were unable to get it out.
AMECHE:	A thirty-seven inch bayonet! What did you do about eating?
THOMAS:	Oh, I managed, all right – but I scratched up an awful lot of chairs. It was finally removed by an itinerant tinker in Peapack, New Jersey, and I suffered no after effects.
AMECHE:	Well, that hardly sounds like it would cause mike-fright...but you never know. What did you do after that?
THOMAS:	I remained in Peapack and went to work for a botanist. He was an exponent of hydroponics. Raised orchids in water.
AMECHE:	I've heard of that.
THOMAS:	I was an apt student and in about six weeks I managed to produce a bouquet of goldenrods in a chest of drawers using nothing but water and a special root food.
AMECHE:	A root food?
THOMAS:	A root food with a weed seed. Won second prize at the Redband Horticulture show.
AMECHE:	Imagine that! I'll bet you were the only man who ever raised a goldenrod in his drawers.
THOMAS:	I would have gone on to bigger things – but I was cut down by hayfever. I'd – I'd rather not talk any more, Don.
AMECHE:	Well, come on back with me and I guarantee you'll feel right at home in two minutes. I know the people will love you.
THOMAS:	You think so?
AMECHE:	Certainly! That microphone isn't anything to be afraid of!
THOMAS:	Of course not! It's only a piece of metal on a pipe! It can't do me any harm! It hasn't got teeth!
AMECHE:	That's the way to talk!
THOMAS:	(MISERABLE) Yeah – but it's not the way I feel. You go back, Don – give me a few minutes to have it out with myself. Maybe I can lick it.
AMECHE:	Fine, Danny. Come as quickly as you can. (EXITS)

THOMAS:	Why should I be scared? What's a microphone? I'm not afraid to talk on the telephone. Hello? See, it's nothing. Someday I'll try putting a nickel in. Come on, Thomas – pull yourself together. Go out and face that microphone – you've got the courage – you can be a big radio star ----
MUSIC:	IN FOR THOMAS SONG
THOMAS:	SONG:
	(APPLAUSE)
LANG:	Did you find Danny Thomas, Don?
DON:	Yes, Frances. I had quite a talk with him. He's very neurotic...deathly afraid of a microphone.
LANG:	Would it do any good if I went to work on him?
DON:	I wouldn't recommend it. He's locked himself in a phone booth and if you got stuck in there with him there's no telling which line his neurosis would take.
LANG:	Sounds exciting. I'd like to try it.
DON:	Not right now, anyway. Suppose you sing something <u>sooth-ing</u>. I'll have the speakers turned up – maybe that'll have a therapeutic effect.
LANG:	All right. I have a --
MILLER:	Excuse me, Miss Langford.
LANG:	Oh, hello. Did you find your penicillin gum?
MILLER:	No, my throat doesn't hurt any more. (HE LOOKS AT HER FOR A SECOND) Yes – just as lovely as I thought it was! I'll bet you use Drene!
LANG:	Of course I use Drene. Is there anything else to use? (INTO COMMERCIAL)
DON:	Thank you, Marvin. Now, how about that song for Danny Thomas, Frances?
MUSIC:	LANGFORD SONG
	(APPLAUSE)
MILLER:	And now, ladies and gentlemen, you're about to witness the bringing to life of two new characters in a domestic vignette that we hope will provide you with excellent listening sport. Don Ameche and Frances Langford as the principals --- John and Blanche Bickerson in --- "The Honeymoon is Over."
MUSIC:	THEME: (SOFT AND PLAINTIVE)
MILLER:	(OVER MUSIC) The Bickersons have retired. Mrs. Bickerson tosses restlessly while her husband, John, lies in a profound, dreamless sleep composed of equal parts of bourbon and seconal.

MUSIC:	OUT
DON:	(SNORES)
LANG:	(SOFTLY) John.
DON:	(A SUSTAINED SNORE)
LANG:	John....John.
DON:	(GRUNTS) Mmmmm.
LANG:	Are you sleeping?
DON:	Mmm.
LANG:	Turn over on your side. You're snoring hideously.
DON:	Mmm.
LANG:	Why don't you get one of those snore balls at Eel & Conger's sleep shop? You've got everything else. Double thickness sleep shade, lullaby musical pillow, toe mittens, electric pajamas and an automatic sheep counter. I know you've got insomnia, but when you do fall asleep you snore so loud you sound like a Hotchkiss reciprocating force pump draining a peat bog in Clonakilty. Why don't you get a snore ball?
DON:	(VERY SLEEPY) Hmmm?
LANG:	If you'd take those wax corks out of your ears you'd be able to hear me.
DON:	(PLEADING) Why don't you let me sleep, Blanche?
LANG:	Well, get a snore ball.
DON:	(HALF ASLEEP) Wassa snore ball?
LANG:	It's a rubber thing you pin to your pajamas and when you roll over on your back it squeaks at you and wakes you up.
DON:	What do I need that for when I've got you?
LANG:	Don't be so funny.
DON:	Well, I wanna sleep. I have to get up in the morning and you know how long it takes me to fall asleep. I can't help it if I snore.
LANG:	But you keep me up half the night.
DON:	I don't snore anyway.
LANG:	(GASPS) John! How can you say that!
DON:	(DROPPING OFF AGAIN) 'S your imagination. All wives think their husbands ---- (DEEP SNORE)
LANG:	John!
DON:	Huh?
LANG:	Sit up. If you won't let me sleep I won't let you sleep either.
DON:	Okay. If that's how you want it. Turn the lights on.
LANG:	The lights are on. Take off that sleep shade.
DON:	Oh......all right, I'm awake. Now what do you want?

10

LANG:	I don't see how you can sleep anyway.
DON:	Who's sleeping?
LANG:	I mean I don't know how you could have fallen asleep in the first place. I've been waiting and waiting for you to say something but you never did. Do you know what day this is?
DON:	It's not day – it's night.
LANG:	(TEARFULLY) You've forgotten.
DON:	Blanche, that's one thing I will not be accused of. I have not forgotten how to tell day from night. Even if I do wear a sleep shade.
LANG:	How could you, John?
DON:	What's so terrible about it? It's just that I can't sleep if there's any light in the room ---
LANG:	Not that. How could you forget?
DON:	Forget what?
LANG:	It'd be different if we were an old married couple – but it's only three years and this is the first time you've ever forgotten our anniversary.
DON:	Anniversary?
LANG:	Today is our wedding anniversary.
DON:	(DEFIANTLY) Blanche, this is Sunday and our anniversary is Monday the sixteenth.
LANG:	I know it is.
DON:	Well, what are you beefing about?
LANG:	What time is it?
DON:	Time? It's twelve o'clock.
LANG:	It's one minute past. (TRIUMPHANTLY) That makes it Monday, and that's our anniversary and you completely forgot about it.
DON:	(CONTROLLING HIS TEMPER) How do you like that!
LANG:	(DEFENSIVELY) Well, you did.
DON:	Here I am suffering from insomnia, finally manage to fall asleep, and you're thinking up all sorts of weird excuses to wake me – lying there like an – an aardvark waiting to pounce on its prey!
LANG:	Aardvarks don't pounce on their prey.
DON:	What do I care!
LANG:	An aardvark is a South African edentate, that means no teeth, and it feeds entirely on ants.
DON:	(MUTTERS) Serves me right for marrying a school teacher.
LANG:	You're trying to make me forget that you forgot to remember not to forget our anniversary.

DON:	There must be a simpler way of saying that.
LANG:	(IN TEARS AGAIN) Well, I don't care. I always remember your birthdays, and if I didn't write to your folks they wouldn't know they had a ---
DON:	Blanche! I didn't forget our anniversary. In fact, I even bought a present for you today. I was going to give it to you in the morning – it's in the hall closet.
LANG:	No, it isn't.
DON:	It is, too. I put it there.
LANG:	I sent it back.
DON:	(STUNNED) What?
LANG:	That's not the kind of present a man buys for his wife.
DON:	You sent it back? That beautiful black nightgown?
LANG:	Why don't you give it to your girl friend, that harpy, Gloria Gooseby?
DON:	(SHOUTS) Gloria Gooseby is not my girl friend – she's yours! And she's not a harpy, she's a nice girl, and she doesn't wear black nightgowns! I mean, how do I know what kind of nightgowns she wears?
LANG:	(A LEER) Hmmm.
DON:	(FURIOUS) Don't you dare make those insinuating noises!
LANG:	Oh, go to sleep, silly.
DON:	Go to sleep? You woke me up to start this fight and now you tell me to go to sleep. You planned the whole thing just to get in a dig at Gloria Gooseby. Why do you keep asking her to dinner if you despise her so much?
LANG:	How can you say I despise Gloria Gooseby? What if she does cheat at cards? And of course she had me blackballed at her reading club and made a cheap copy of my wool sports dress – but I'm very fond of her.
DON:	I'm sure she feels the same way about you.
LANG:	As a matter of fact you're the one who doesn't like the Goosebys. You've told me a thousand times that Leo Gooseby is a heel.
DON:	I never said he was a heel. I said he was a toad. Besides, he's my best friend.
LANG:	Why, only last week you said you hated him.
DON:	I did, last week. Where's my sleepshade?
LANG:	That's right – go to sleep and let me suffer all night with the knowledge that you forgot our anniversary.
DON:	(SHOUTS) I didn't forget!
LANG:	You haven't even said happy anniversary.

DON:	(YELLS ANGRILY) Happy anniversary!
LANG:	(SHOUTS BACK AT HIM) The same to you!
DON:	Goodnight.
LANG:	Goodnight.......John.
DON:	Hmmm.
LANG:	I'm sorry.
DON:	I am too. Never mind, honey. Tomorrow we'll celebrate. Goodnight.
LANG:	Goodnight....John.
DON:	Mmmm.
LANG:	You don't have to buy me another present.
DON:	(HALF ASLEEP) Don't be silly. Buy you anything you want.
LANG:	Really, you don't have to. When I sent the nightgown back I ordered something else for myself. That'll be your present for me.
DON:	Good.
LANG:	You'll love it. It's the most adorable mink stole – and I got full credit for the nightgown. I simply couldn't resist it – it was a wonderful bargain. Six hundred and ninety-eight dollars.
DON:	Fine...(THEN, AS IF SHOT) Six hundred and ninety-eight dollars!
LANG:	Marked down from seven hundred.
DON:	You must be crazy! Six hundred and ninety-eight dollars!
LANG:	At that price the stole is a steal.
DON:	Now, look, Blanche ---
LANG:	I know what you're thinking, John Bickerson, but I'm not going to send it back. You've never bought me a piece of fur in all the years we've been married and you don't hesitate to spend anything on yourself. Every time I think of you paying eighteen dollars for a derby hat I get so indignant I could spit.
DON:	I bought the hat three years ago!
LANG:	And you've never even worn it.
DON:	It didn't fit!
LANG:	Well, if you can throw away money on a hat that doesn't fit I'm certainly entitled to a mink stole. Goodnight, dear.
DON:	(BEATEN) Ohhhh. Goodnight...(SETTLES DOWN AND MUMBLES)...What are you gonna do with a woman like that?...Oh, boy ---
LANG:	Shhh.
DON:	(FALLING ASLEEP) Six hunnerninetyeight dollars for a mink derby. Doesn't fit...(BREATHES DEEPLY THEN SNORES...A PAUSE...THE TELEPHONE RINGS)

DON:	(SNORES.)
LANG:	John. Answer the phone.
DON:	Hmm?
LANG:	The telephone. Answer it.
DON:	It's on your side. You answer it.
LANG:	I left my slippers in the bathroom and you know how susceptible I am to colds. Answer it, John.
DON:	Hello.
LANG:	Go to the phone and answer it!
DON:	Oh....(STRUGGLES OUT OF BED)..Don't know why you had it put so far away from the bed.
LANG:	It was next to the bed but you had the bed moved.
DON:	Well, I wanted to get away from the phone....I wish the darn thing had never been invented.
LANG:	Look who's talking.
DON:	(A CLANK AS HE STUBS HIS TOE AGAINST SOMETHING) Owww! What's that thing doing by the bed? How many times have I asked you to get rid of that tank helmet!... Put the lights on.
LANG:	The lights _are_ on. Take off your sleepshade.
DON:	Oh....Look how that phone keeps ringing. You'd think the guy would give up by now.
LANG:	Hurry up. It must be important.
DON:	(LIFTING RECEIVER) Hello.
THOM:	(FILTER...FULL OF GREAT CHEER) Jocko? This is Amos. Did I wake you?
DON:	(WITH MURDER IN HIS SOUL) Oh, no. I have to get up at seven anyway, and it's twelve thirty already.
LANG:	Who is it?
DON:	It's that half-witted brother of yours.
THOM:	(FILTER) Huh?
DON:	Nothing. What's the matter?
THOM:	(FILTER) Just thought I'd call and wish you and sis a happy anniversary. How about if I bring a few friends over for a fast drink?
DON:	How about if you'd drop dead and let me sleep?
	SOUND: SLAMS RECEIVER
LANG:	What did you do that for?
DON:	What right has that idiot got to call in the middle of the night? Where's my sleepshade? Put out the lights.
LANG:	Of all the ill-tempered creatures, John Bickerson, you're the

	vilest. You're just angry with yourself because he remembered our anniversary and you forgot it.
DON:	I didn't forget it!
LANG:	I just don't understand why you dislike my brother Amos so intensely. He may be a little tactless, but he's a darling underneath.
DON:	I never got underneath.
LANG:	He sent you a box of cigars on your birthday.
DON:	I know. And they tasted like a mixture of sheep dip and cracker dust. Let me sleep.
LANG:	No wonder we can't keep any friends. Your violent behavior is enough to drive anybody away.
DON:	Aaaaaahhh. (SETTLES DOWN AND TRIES TO SLEEP)
LANG:	I'm thoroughly ashamed of you. You have no right to humiliate me, even if it is my brother. You wouldn't act that way if your boss called.
DON:	(STARTS TO SNORE)
LANG:	Believe me, I'm not going to let you get away with it. You get right up and call Amos back and apologize...John!
DON:	Hmm?
LANG:	You go right to that telephone and call my brother and tell him you're sorry.
DON:	Oh, for heaven's sake!
LANG:	(IN TEARS) Go on, or I'll pack my things and--
DON:	Oh, all right...(STRUGGLES OUT OF BED. CLANK AS HE STUBS HIS TOE ON THE TANK HELMET) Oww! Why don't you put that thing under the bed where it belongs? Put on the lights.
LANG:	The lights <u>are</u> on. Take off your sleepshade.
DON:	Oh. (STARTS TO DIAL) Maybe I was a little short with him, but he knows I don't sleep very well and he should have thought twice before--
THOM:	(FILTER) (SLEEPY VOICE) Hello.
DON:	Amos? This is John.
THOM:	Who?
DON:	John. I want to thank you for your good wishes. If you like, you can bring your friends over for a drink.
THOM:	Drink? You know what time it is?
DON:	Sure, I thought--
THOM:	What's the idea of waking up a guy in the middle of the night? Go to sleep, you imbecile! (SLAMS RECEIVER)

DON:	Well, I'll be-- (HANGS UP) There you are, Mrs. Behaviorist. So I called him back just to please you, and-- Blanche.
LANG:	(LIGHT SNORE)
DON:	Hey!
LANG:	(SHE'S REALLY SLEEPING)
DON:	Aaahhh, nuts!
MUSIC:	THEME...UP FULL OVER APPLAUSE
NUMBER:	DRAGON & ORCHESTRA
	(FADE WHEN NECESSARY)
THOMAS:	(FADING IN) I can do it! I know I can do it! There's nothing to be afraid of! Why should I spend the rest of my life in a phone booth?
DON:	Danny!
THOMAS:	(STARTLED) Oh...hello. Hello, Miss Langford.
LANG:	Frances, Danny.
THOMAS:	Frances.
DON:	Well, have you made up your mind?
THOMAS:	Well --
LANG:	Come, Danny. Take my hand. We'll face the microphone together.
THOMAS:	All right. Let's go.
DON:	What about these three suits and the bundle of laundry?
THOMAS:	Leave everything in the phone booth. I might change my mind.
LANG:	Rubbish. I'll bet you feel better already. It's the first plunge that's so icy, that's all. Now here's the studio.
DON:	It's not so bad, is it, Danny? There's the microphone – walk right up to it and do what you feel like doing.
THOMAS:	Okay...(THREE STEPS AND A THUD)
LANG:	He did it, all right – he collapsed!
DON:	Quick – towels and plenty of hot water! Danny! Danny!...Marvin – tell the people about next week's show while I try to revive him.
	(INTO TAG AND HITCHHIKE)
	SIGNOFF

The first of the *Old Gold Show* scripts here is actually the 15th in the series. It's also the first of three consecutive shows, collected in order to give the reader an understanding of the show's formula, which did not alter considerably during its entire run. Singing commercial; announcer's show introduction; Frances Langford's song; commercial; Don Ameche's comedy with band leader Carmen Dragon, with guest's introduction; Frank Morgan enters, boasting and insulting the guest; commercial; the Bickersons; commercial.

Oddly, Frank Morgan was never given a part in the Bickersons section of the half hour show, as Danny Thomas was as brother Amos in *Drene*. It would be interesting to surmise just what sort of role Phil Rapp would have written for Morgan on *The Old Gold Show*.

THE OLD GOLD SHOW

Station CBS   Date 1-2-48   Time 6:00-6:30 PM   Studio El Capita

Cast	Music Routine
FRANK MORGAN	OPENING THEME
DON AMECHE	
FRANCES LANGFORD	"BETWEEN THE DEVIL AND THE DEEP BLUE SEA"
CARMEN DRAGON	MORGAN PLAYOFF
FRANK GOSS	"I WISH I DIDN'T LOVE YOU SO"
MARVIN MILLER	BICKERSON THEME
EVELYN SCOTT	BICKERSON PLAYOFF
HITS AND A MISS	CLOSING THEME

WRITTEN AND DIRECTED BY: Phil Rapp
PRODUCED BY: Mann Holiner

(ON CUE)	
MILLER:	From Hollywood – it's Old Gold Cigarette Time!
CHORUS:	Treat yourself....to Old Golds.
GROUP:	If you want a treat instead of a treatment.
CHORUS:	Treat yourself...to Old Golds.
GROUP:	If you want a treat instead of a treatment.
CHORUS:	Treat yourself... Treat yourself... Treat yourself....to Old Golds.
MILLER:	If you want a treat instead of a treatment..... TREAT YOURSELF TO A PACK OF OLD GOLDS! (PAUSE)
MUSIC:	THEME...ESTABLISH AND FADE UNDER FOLLOWING
MILLER:	This is Marvin Miller, ladies and gentlemen, speaking for the makers of Old Gold cigarettes who are pleased to present the fifteenth in a series of new programs with Carmen Dragon and his orchestra, starring Metro-Goldwyn-Mayer's lovable Frank Morgan, the genial Don Ameche and charming Frances Langford, who sings ---
MUSIC:	LANGFORD AND ORCH...."BETWEEN THE DEVIL AND THE DEEP BLUE SEA" (APPLAUSE) FIRST COMMERCIAL
MILLER:	Today's the day to find out about Old Golds. What a tasty cigarette it is...mellow...smooth....and so mild. An exclusive blend of the world's choice tobaccos...that's Old Gold. Smoke a pack today. Product of nearly two hundred year's experience with fine quality tobaccos...that's Old Gold. Smoke a pack...today. Because today's the day to find out about Old Golds. Like I say...if you smoke for the sheer wonderful pleasure of smoking...if you want a treat instead of a treatment...
CHORUS:	Treat yourself...to Old Golds.
GROUP:	If you want a treat instead of a treatment.
CHORUS:	Treat yourself...to Old Golds. (APPLAUSE)
AMECHE:	Thank you, ladies and gentlemen, and good evening.
DRAG:	Well, Don, I guess you don't have to look for a guest tonight, Boy.
AMECHE:	Don't I, Carmen? Why not?
DRAG:	You've got the greatest guest in town right under your nose.
LANG:	Who is he, Carmen?

DRAG:	The Game Warden that pinched Frank Morgan.
AMECHE:	What?
LANG:	What game warden?
DRAG:	It's all over the front pages. Frank was caught knocking off ducks ---
AMECHE:	Carmen! Your whole idea is in bad taste.
DRAG:	What?
AMECHE:	If Frank is guilty of some indiscretion, he probably has a good explanation. And I don't think we should air the case on this program.
DRAG:	Explanation? What is he gonna do – plead self-defense?
LANG:	Carmen, you're only making matters worse.
AMECHE:	Certainly. If we need a guest we can get a great golfer.
DRAG:	I still like the game warden.
AMECHE:	The 22nd Annual Los Angeles Open started today, and Jimmy Demaret shot sixty-six.
DRAG:	Was he arrested?
AMECHE:	Of course not.
DRAG:	Well, Frank only shot thirteen and they're gonna throw him in the can.
AMECHE:	Will you stop talking about that!
DRAG:	Sure.
LANG:	I think Jimmy Demaret would be a wonderful guest. Can we get him, Don?
DRAG:	That's one game I don't like – golf. No, sir. I took Eloise – that's Mrs. Dragon – over to one of those driving ranges and we tried to hit a bucket of balls.
AMECHE:	When was that?
DRAG:	New Year's Eve. Me and my wife stood there with the bucket, took three shots apiece, and got so stiff we couldn't walk.
MORG:	(COMING ON) Somebody must have slipped you a mickey, Herman. Three shots don't even wet my whistle!
AMECHE:	Frank!
	(APPLAUSE)
MORG:	Longest New Year's eve I ever spent. Feels like I've been going for days and here it is still Wednesday night.
DRAG:	It's not Wednesday, it's Friday.
MORG:	Nonsense. We're on the air every Wednesday night, aren't we?
AMECHE:	Not anymore, Frank. We switched to Friday. This is a Friday night.

MORG:	I don't believe it. It must be Wednesday because I had enough liquor to last me till Tuesday and that was gone on Monday. What's this about you drinking out of a bucket, Herman?
AMECHE:	No buckets, Frank. We're talking about golf.
MORG:	Oh, golf talk. Gets duller here every week.
LANG:	We thought it would be a good idea to get Jimmy Demaret, the golf champion as a guest.
MORG:	What a perfectly preposterous --- Oh, hello, my dear!
LANG:	Hello.
MORG:	What a pretty blossom! I had no idea Mr. Demaret employed such charming caddies! You look ravishing in those form-fitting plus-fours.
LANG:	What?
MORG:	Tell me, my dear, are you employed over the whole golf strip or do you just concentrate on the tees?
AMECHE:	Oh, stop fishing, Morgan! This is Frances Langford and she works for Old Gold – not Demaret.
MORG:	Err – Frances Goldfish. Not married. Yes. Well, that makes the path a little less thorny. As the witty French say "C'est aussi facile que possible"! (GIGGLES) Isn't that so, ma cherie?
LANG:	I'd love to.
MORG:	Who wouldn't? How long have you been interested in the Royal and Ancient sport, my pretty one?
LANG:	Ever since I got out of high school.
MORG:	Well! Started young, didn't you? Tell me, do you like golf, too?
LANG:	After a fashion.
MORG:	It's better after an old-fashioned. If you'd care to come over to my private golf course I'll be very happy to instruct you in the finer points of the game. What time can you come for a lesson?
LANG:	Well --
MORG:	Make it early. You'll find my links on Cuff Street right in back of the Lumper Mattress Factory.
LANG:	Mattress factory?
MORG:	Just another hazard. It won't take me any time to improve your niblick, straighten your wedge, and teach you to pet. Putt!
LANG:	Well, I don't think I can make it, but I'll be glad to send my husband over. He's wild about the game.
MORG:	Oh – husband's wild.
LANG:	Goodnight, Mr. Morgan.

MORG:	(LOOKING AFTER HER) Beautiful creature. Pity she won't let me instruct her. We'd make the perfect golf team.
AMECHE:	Perfect golf team?
MORG:	Yes. She looks so classy with a brassie and I'm so good in the woods.
AMECHE:	Why don't you stop, Morgan? You wouldn't know a three iron from a one-armed driver! You never saw a golf club and you know it.
MORG:	(LAUGH) Are you serious, Dodger!
AMECHE:	Yes, I'm serious! The only exercise you've had for thirty years is opening bottles! Now don't give off that you're an athlete!
MORG:	Athlete! Is that the way you talk to the greatest Olympic champion ever produced in America?
AMECHE:	Oh, no!
MORG:	Oh, yes! I smashed records in the discus and javelin throw, sixteen pound shot-put, running pole-vault, and by means of a special technique I made a standing broad jump forty-five feet! Furthermore, I won the Los Angeles Open for twenty-three years running.
AMECHE:	How could you win it twenty-three years running? It's only been in existence twenty-two years.
MORG:	Er -- twenty-two... Well, the first year I won in a walk! (That doesn't make sense, but'll confuse him.)
AMECHE:	You don't confuse me or anyone else, Morgan. There isn't a moron within a hundred miles who believes half the lies you tell.
DRAG:	I'm right here under your nose – and I believe all the lies he tells!
MORG:	My dear Herman, I find your selfless, albeit incoherent, devotion to me very touching. Each week my feelings become more pronounced until the early repugnance I felt at your sight has blossomed into a beautiful loathing. Go away!
DRAG:	How could a man be so sweet and so smart? What a pair of brains on him, huh, Don?
AMECHE:	What's the matter with you, Carmen? He just said he hates you!
MILLER:	I don't like to intrude, Don, but it seems to me you might treat Mr. Morgan with a little more respect.
MORG:	Well! What a pleasant interruption! You're Jimmy Demaret, the wizard of the greens, of course! I was delighted to hear you were 1947's leading money-winner.

MILLER:	Pardon?
MORG:	Haven't you had time to go to the bank, or do you always carry that pile under your vest? Why don't you take those golf balls out of your hip-pockets and sit down?
AMECHE:	Stop it, Frank! Now let's start the New Year right. All during 1947 you've been insulting Marvin Miller's physical appearance. Now, as a gentlemen don't you think an apology is in order?
MORG:	I suppose you're right, Dodger.
MILLER:	But it really isn't necessary, Mr. Mor-----
MORG:	You stay out of this, Fatty! If Mr. Mitchell thinks an apology is in order then let's say no more about it.
MILLER:	I'm sorry.
MORG:	I accept your apology. Now just run along and peddle your cigarettes like a good boy.
MILLER:	Mr. Morgan, I don't want to bother you ---
MORG:	Well, you do, you know.
MILLER:	I'm sorry. But I heard you discussing golf before and I swallow everything I can about the course. Right now I'm full of green data.
MORG:	You are? Don't they give you cramps? Who's your doctor, Mr. Castor?
MILLER:	Miller.
MORG:	Finest vet in town. Miller's Cat and Dog Hospital?
AMECHE:	More respect, eh, Marvin?
MILLER:	Please, Don. Mr. Morgan, you're jesting, of course. But lately I've been having trouble with my form and I need your advice.
MORG:	(BORED) Mmmm.
MILLER:	After five years of using a bent-over stance I've straightened my hook, taken a slice out of my cleek, but I still come too far back with my blaster.
MORG:	Well, if you wear loose knickers nobody'll notice it.
AMECHE:	Had enough, Marvin? Now will you believe he doesn't know what he's talking about?
MORG:	Don't be so childish, Mitchell. The Morgans have been golfers for generations, beginning with my grandfather Bunker Morgan, down to my Uncle Caddie and my Aunt Spoon.
AMECHE:	Your Aunt Spoon?
MORG:	A wooden-faced old stick – always hung from my Uncle's shoulder when she was bagged.
MILLER:	What a wonderful family.

MORG:	Yes. It was under their expert tutelage that I shot my first par. As soon as I was able to walk I could handle a putter with the skill of a professional, and while I was still in rompers my tee shots would average five hundred yards, split the fairways, and travel like bullets.
MILLER:	Bullets? What did you use?
MORGAN:	A gun. There was no limit to my ability.
AMECHE:	Just like shooting ducks, eh, Frank?
MORGAN:	Yes, just like --- Now you stop that, Dodger! I'm not going to stand around here and listen to those snide remarks ------
MILLER:	Please don't go, Mr. Morgan. I want to hear some more about the early days of golf.
MORG:	Very well. When I was still in grade school I applied myself to inventing various devices for cutting down the golfer's playing time, and before I was twelve I startled the Professional Golf Association by demonstrating an unorthodox grip for speeding up a slow dame. Game!
AMECHE:	What other improvements did you give to golf, Morgan?
MORG:	I don't suppose it's necessary to tell you, but I'm responsible for the eight ounce stroke iron.
AMECHE:	Eight ounce stroke iron? What's that?
MORG:	(PROUDLY) A half-pound putter, if you please.
AMECHE:	I'll take two quarts cream.
MORG:	Bottled?
AMECHE:	Curdled!
MORG:	That'll be eighty-five --- what are we talking about!
MILLER:	I wish you'd stop distracting him, Don. Did you ever make a hole-in-one, Mr. Morgan?
MORG:	Only once. It was during the British Open at Prestwick in 1903, and of course you know who won that. I was ---
AMECHE:	Yes. Harry Vardon won it. A new record – 300 for seventy-two holes.
MORG:	Oh. Harry holes. Hes, well – in 1907 at Hoylake --
AMECHE:	The Open was won by Massey from La Boulie.
MORG:	Err – one mass of bull.... but at St. Andrews in 1910 ---
AMECHE:	J. Braid from Walton Heath shot a two ninety-eight and stole the open.
MORG:	Uhh – he stole two-ninety-eight – in the open ---
AMECHE:	All right, Niblick! When did you win the championship?
MORG:	When?
AMECHE:	Yes, when?

MORG:	Err – when. Well, do either of you remember the winner of the Masters Tournament at Augusta in 1902?
MILLER:	I'm afraid I don't.
AMECHE:	I'm stuck, too.
MORG:	Well, I'm off the hook! (GIGGLES) I beat a field of the most spectacular golfers in history! My score was phenomenal, I shot thirteen birdies, nine eagles, four squirrels and a duck and injured two or three innocent bystanders. (I hope there's no game-warden in the house.)
AMECHE:	Frank, if you're such an expert golfer. How is it you didn't enter the L.A. Open this year?
MORG:	Not enough competition for me, my boy. I've already beaten Jimmy Demaret, Bobby Locke, Ben Hogan and ---
AMECHE:	Wait a minute – you beat Demaret, Locke and Hogan?
MORG:	I played left-handed using nothing but an umbrella handle and a weighted ping-pong ball. And even though they cheated in their scoring, I ----
SOUND:	PHONE RINGS
AMECHE:	Hold it! (RECEIVER UP) Hello?....Yes....Yes...Oh, the President of the Professional Golfers Association....Yes, he's right here.....It's for you, Frank.
MORG:	For me?
AMECHE:	The P.G.A. They've been listening to all your claims tonight. Here.
MORG:	Oh – listening.
AMECHE:	Go on – you can't stall. Take it.
MORG:	Oh – can't take it....Hello?...Yes, this is Frank Mor---- Oh! Well, you see, President....I -- er – oh – well – er Oh! Oh! Yes, your Majesty! But I -- No, sir!...Well, I was only --- Ohhhhh! Lie...big trap...Bunk...Yes, sir! ....No, sir!.....I promise. Goodbye. (HANGS UP)
MILLER:	What did he want, Mr. Morgan?
MORG:	Somebody's trapped in a bad lie and they demand an official ruling.
AMECHE:	Who's trapped?
MORG:	Me. So long, fellows, I gotta try out my irons.
MUSIC:	APPLAUSE
	COMMERCIAL II
CHORUS:	Treat yourself....to Old Golds.
GROUP:	If you want a treat instead of a treatment.
CHORUS:	Treat yourself...to Old Golds.

GROUP: If you want a treat instead of a treatment.

CHORUS: Treat yourself...to Old Golds.

MILLER: How long do you think it takes to find out that Old Golds are tastier...smoother...milder? Well, any Old Gold smoker will tell you...it takes a single pack to prove...that you simply cannot match the quality of an Old Gold.

WOMAN: Today's the day to find out about Old Golds.

MILLER: Yes. This is the time to discover Old Golds. Right now...compare any cigarette you know with an Old Gold....its unmatchable smoothness....its rich taste and aroma. See if it's not true that ... the quality of an Old Gold cannot be duplicated. Because no other cigarette in America has the quality traditions of an Old Gold. Listen ...

2ND ANNCR: Nearly two hundred years of fine tobacco experience stand behind every Old Gold you smoke. We're tobacco men...not medicine men. Old Gold cures just one thing...tobaccos...the world's choice tobaccos....to give you a milder smoke...a better-tasting smoke.

WOMAN: Today's the day to find out about Old Golds.

MILLER: Yes...by golly, you owe it to your sweet pleasure to get more smoking pleasure. Smoke a pack of Old Golds....Today. Because....if you want a treat instead of a treatment –

CHORUS: Treat yourself....to Old Golds.

GROUP: If you want a treat instead of a treatment –

CHORUS: Treat yourself....to Old Golds.

MILLER: Now here are Don Ameche and Frances Langford as John and Blanche Bickerson in "The Honeymoon is Over"!

THEME: (SOFT AND PLAINTIVE)

MILLER: The Bickersons have retired. Long past the witching hour Mrs. Bickerson writhes in bed as poor husband John, victim of recurrent insomnia or Muffler's syndrome, gives audible proof of his never-ending battle with the sleep-robbing ailment. Listen.

DON: (SNORES LUSTILY....WHINES....SNORES AND WHINES....BROKEN RHYTHM SNORE FOLLOWED BY A WHINE)

LANG: It's like being married to a Greyhound bus!

DON: (SNORES AND GIGGLES...SNORES AND GIGGLES AGAIN)

LANG: Wish I knew what was tickling him.

DON: (SNORES AND GIGGLES MERRILY)

LANG: John...John!

DON:	Mmmmm.
LANG:	What are you doing?
DON:	What are you doing, Blanche?
LANG:	Why don't you turn over on your side? John!
DON:	Wassamatter? What do you want, Blanche? Wassamatter?
LANG:	When are you going to stop it, John? It isn't bad enough you keep me awake all night but the neighbors are beginning to complain.
DON:	Mmm.
LANG:	The woman next door called up three times. She says she can't live in the same house with a man who snores like a foghorn.
DON:	What'd she marry him for?
LANG:	She means you!
DON:	Huh?
LANG:	You heard me. She claims she hasn't slept since she moved in and she's getting up a petition to have us thrown out.
DON:	Whaffor?
LANG:	Because she's stood for it long enough and now she's losing patience. She's revolting.
DON:	I know, I've seen her. Her husband's no bargain, either. Lemme sleep, Blanche.
LANG:	I will not! Not until you stop it!
DON:	Stop what? What are you talking about?
LANG:	You started snoring the minute your head touched the pillow and you haven't stopped once!
DON:	My head isn't on the pillow – my feet are on the pillow.
LANG:	Your feet! Is it any wonder you make those unearthly noises – you're sleeping upside down.
DON:	What difference does it make how I sleep?
LANG:	It makes a lot of difference. I wasted a whole bottle of nose drops.
DON:	Nose drops? So that's why my toes are all stuck together!
LANG:	Well, I just can't lie here night after night without any sleep, John.
DON:	What makes you think you'll sleep better if you put nose drops on my feet?
LANG:	I thought I was putting them in your nose. I did it in the dark.
DON:	Never heard of such a thing. Did it in the dark.
LANG:	Well, you always scream when I put the lights on – and Dr. Hersey said the nose drops would stop you from snoring.

DON:	Why do you keep running to that Dr. Hersey? I wouldn't trust that faker with a sick turtle.
LANG:	Don't you talk like that! Dr. Hersey knows his business and he knows what's wrong with you. He said all your trouble is caused by an aggravated lump and he promised to get rid of what's irritating you.
DON:	Where's he sending you?
LANG:	Very funny. Oh, you're so funny, John Bickerson.
DON:	I'm not funny – I'm sleepy. Blanche, do you know it's almost four o'clock in the morning and the holidays are over. I've gotta go to work in three hours.
LANG:	My work never ends. I didn't have any holiday.
DON:	Take one now.
LANG:	How can I take a holiday? Everything rests on my shoulders – who'll do the housework?
DON:	Shoulders.
LANG:	The place still looks like a pigsty after that New Year's Eve party. Believe me, John, that's the last time I'll let those drink-sodden friends of yours in the house. A bunch of bums!
DON:	My friends are not bums!
LANG:	You should be ashamed to be seen with them. They acted like a lot of maniacs.
DON:	They acted fine! A man's entitled to cut loose a little on New Year's Eve, isn't he? You're just narrow-minded.
LANG:	I am not! My mind's as thick as anybody's. I just can't tolerate that sort of behavior. How would you like me to associate with my inferiors?
DON:	I don't know – I never met any of your inferiors.
LANG:	Well, I'm warning you now, John – don't bring those horrible men around again. I'll just insult them.
DON:	You did insult them.
LANG:	It'll be worse next time. It's a funny thing, but as soon as we were married you made sure I gave up all my girl friends. Why don't you do the same?
DON:	All right – I'll give up your girl friends. Lemme sleep, Blanche.
LANG:	And what do you mean I insulted your friends? What kind of a crack was that?
DON:	Okay – you didn't insult them.
LANG:	No – I want to know why you said that.
DON:	Forget it, Blanche – I'm too tired.
LANG:	I suppose it was all right for that Al Homer, or whatever his

	name is, to pour bourbon into the goldfish bowl?
DON:	Didn't hurt the goldfish.
LANG:	They've been snapping at the cat since Wednesday. He wasn't too polite when I told him to stop it, either. But I put him in his place, all right. I may look timid but when it comes to a battle of tongues I can hold my own.
DON:	You say it but you won't do it.
LANG:	Well, I refuse to clean up that mess. The very thought of going into that kitchen gives me the shudders. Why can't I have a maid, John?
DON:	You had a maid. You had three maids. And you fired them all after one day!
LANG:	Well, they weren't clean. They never swept behind the door.
DON:	They did too. They swept everything behind the door.
LANG:	They wouldn't have stayed anyway. You can't expect to keep a servant when you only pay four dollars a week and make them work like a horse.
DON:	Get a horse.
LANG:	All our friends have help. Look at the Shaws. They have three servants and I'll bet Mel doesn't make half as much as you do.
DON:	Mel Shaw is the biggest idiot in town.
LANG:	He is not! He's a good husband.
DON:	And he's got the most stupid wife in the world!
LANG:	He's got a better wife than you have! There's nothing wrong with Louise Shaw at all. She's just the clinging vine type and Mel happens to be very indulgent.
DON:	Nobody indulges more than I do!
LANG:	That's no lie! I'll bet there are nine million empty bourbon bottles in the hall closet. Why don't you throw them out, John? What are you saving them for?
DON:	I'm waiting until I can afford a gold casket.
LANG:	A gold casket? For dead bourbon bottles?
DON:	I killed 'em – I might as well give 'em a decent burial.
LANG:	You'd better get rid of them in the morning. I'm not going to have my house cluttered up with bottles.
DON:	Okay.
LANG:	Maybe you can get something for them.
DON:	Mmm.
LANG:	There's no deposit, is there?
DON:	No.
LANG:	What about the second-hand clothes man?

DON:	What about him?
LANG:	He calls here every Monday.
DON:	Who does?
LANG:	The second-hand clothes man. He'll be here Monday. What shall I tell him?
DON:	Tell him I got all I need.
LANG:	I mean will he take the bottles?
DON:	Oh, Blanche, how do I know? Why don't you lemme sleep?
LANG:	I thought we were going to start the New Year differently, John. What happened to all those good resolutions you made?
DON:	What have I done now?
LANG:	It's what you haven't done. You haven't spoken a kind word to me since New Year's Eve. You haven't told me once you loved me. Go on -- say it!
DON:	Once I loved you.
LANG:	You see! That's what I mean! You don't care for me at all any more.
DON:	I do too.
LANG:	Then why do I have to goad you into saying it all the time?
DON:	Do I have to tell you I love you fifty thousand times a day?
LANG:	Yes. A woman has to be constantly reassured. And I like to feel that your love doesn't wane. That you'll always love me.
DON:	Blanche, I'll love you as long as the moon is glowing, as long as the stars are twinkling – I'll love you as long as the sun is shining! Satisfied?
LANG:	No. You'll only love me as long as the weather's nice.
DON:	What's the matter with you, Blanche? I never heard you carry on like this before!
LANG:	I should have known you'd be like you are. You were the same way on our honeymoon. I couldn't face the people on that train.
DON:	I don't wanna hear that all over again.
LANG:	I wasn't too surprised when you made me carry the luggage but you might have let me have the lower berth.
DON:	We tossed for it fair and square!
LANG:	I was so humiliated. A new bride and I had to scramble into the upper like an acrobat!
DON:	I gave you a boost, didn't I?
LANG:	You wouldn't have acted that way if you'd married Gloria Gooseby!

DON:	Now don't start with Gloria Gooseby!
LANG:	Believe me, before you'd get fresh with her you'd think of the consequences!
DON:	I always get fresh with her and I never think of the consequences! I mean I hate the sight of Gloria Gooseby and you made a resolution never to mention her name again!
LANG:	Oh, hush up and go to sleep.
DON:	Go to sleep she says...Keeps me up all night with Gloria Gooseby...Upper berths...Anything to steam me up...Now she tells me to go to sleep. I'll – never – sleep – another – wink as long -- as I -- (SNORES...PAUSE..PHONE RINGS)
LANG:	John!
DON:	Mmm.
LANG:	The telephone.
DON:	Who is it?
LANG:	How do I know? Answer it.
DON:	(STUMBLING OUT OF BED) Never saw it fail. The minute I --- (CRASHES INTO NIGHT TABLE) Owwww! (RECEIVER UP) Hello.
MAN:	(FILTER) This is Western Union. I have a telegram for Mrs. John Bickerson from New York, signed Clara.
DON:	Clara?
LANG:	Clara? That's my sister, Clara. What is it, John?
DON:	Go ahead, read it.
MAN:	"Expecting any minute. No one to take care of children. Big blizzard here. Will send kids out to you. Love"...Any answer?
DON:	Yes. Tell her to keep the kids and send the blizzard! (SLAMS UP RECEIVER) Where does she get the crust to saddle me with her overgrown --
LANG:	John! Stop that! Clara's going to have a baby!
DON:	What do I care?
LANG:	Help me pack, John. I'm going to take a plane to New York.
DON:	Are you out of your mind?
LANG:	She's my only sister and she needs comfort at a time like this. I'm going to fly there.
DON:	Why doesn't she fly here?
LANG:	She's probably in the hospital already. I wouldn't dream of letting her have the baby all by herself.
DON:	She's had fifteen babies all by herself!
LANG:	Twelve!
DON:	All right, twelve! Why are you making such a fuss over this one?

LANG:	I always make a fuss. A person doesn't have a baby every day in the week, you know.
DON:	Sure seems like you sister does. Twelve kids! And she wanted to ship 'em out here!
LANG:	Why do you hate children so much?
DON:	Because I can't bear 'em! Put that suitcase away, Blanche! You can't afford to spend all that money. The plane fare, and meals and ----
LANG:	I won't be gone over a week, John.
DON:	Gone a week?
LANG:	I know it'll be difficult for you all alone – but maybe the little separation will do us good. We've been fighting an awful lot lately.
DON:	A whole week?
LANG:	Oh, it won't be so bad, John. Of course, you'll have to eat out with those horrible friends of yours, and I won't be here to talk to you at night, and -- (HE GOES TO WORK FEVERISHLY ON THE SUITCASE) --- John! Stop throwing things into my suitcase!
DON:	You wanted me to help you pack, didn't you?
LANG:	Well, you needn't be so anxious to get rid of me.
DON:	I'm not anxious, darling. I'm just trying to pack your nightgown.
LANG:	You might wait till I get out of it!
DON:	Oh. I'm sorry. Do you wanna take along this bathing suit?
LANG:	In January? There's a blizzard in New York.
DON:	Well, you might want to stay a little longer.
LANG:	Why don't you come out and say it? You don't care if I never come back!
DON:	Now, Blanche, you know that I ---
LANG:	Go on! Pack me off to New York! Push me on a plane with no money and one measly suitcase.
DON:	Nobody's pushing you!
LANG:	Have me stay at some frowsy hotel – a tiny room with no sink -- no carpet on the floor – strange men tossing cigarette butts through the transom – the whole place will go up in flames and I'm trapped like a frightened animal --- no one to hear my screams ---
DON:	Blanche!
LANG:	Why don't you call the fire engines, John!
DON:	Why don't you stop getting hysterical?
LANG:	Well, I'm going whether you like it or not! All I want from you is the plane fare.

DON:	Oh, calm down, honey.
LANG:	Well, you get me all upset. I thought you'd be miserable if I left you.
DON:	I am. Let me call the airport and make a reservation.
LANG:	What about the money? The plane fare is over a hundred dollars.
DON:	Take the rent money. It's in the sugar bowl. (RECEIVER UP)
LANG:	No it isn't.
DON:	It is too. (STARTS TO DIAL) I looked there yesterday.
LANG:	You didn't look today.
DON:	(RECEIVER DOWN...STOPS DIALING) Blanche. Don't tell me you've done it again!
LANG:	Done what?
DON:	You haven't gone and spent that money on something foolish!
LANG:	Oh, no. I gave it to a bookbinder.
DON:	Bookbinder! What do we need with a bookbinder? Our book is in fine condition!
LANG:	Not that kind of a bookbinder. This man goes to the race track. He's a trout.
DON:	Trout! Racetrack! Blanche, did you bet that money with a bookmaker?
LANG:	Don't get excited, John. He said he'd give me a chance to get even.
DON:	How could you do that! How can you throw away a hundred dollars on a horse? I deny myself everything! I've been sewing buttons on onion sacks and wearing 'em for shorts! I took out my own appendix to save on doctor bills! And you bet a hundred dollars on a horse!
LANG:	I'm sorry, John. I'll stay home and let Clara have the baby by herself.
DON:	No. No. I'll suffer through it – I'll get the money somewhere. Clara needs you more than I need that hundred. You'll go, Blanche.
LANG:	I'd rather not, John. Honest, if you're going to miss me ---
DON:	Not another word. I'll call the airport and -- (PHONE RINGS ....RECEIVER UP) --- hello.
MAN:	(FILTER) This is Western Union. I have a telegram for Mrs. Bickerson.
DON:	We got it.
MAN:	No, this must be another one. It just came over the wire --- marked rush.

DON:	Huh?
MAN:	Here's the message. "It's a boy. Seventeen pounds, nine ounces. Feel fine. Love, Clara." Any answer?
DON:	No. Goodbye. (HANGS UP) Well, you don't have to leave, Blanche. She had a boy -- seventeen pounds, nine ounces!
LANG:	Oh, I'm so happy! The sweet little thing!
DON:	Little thing! It weighs more than her husband! And a premature baby at that!
LANG:	Who said it was premature?
DON:	Listen, any baby that stops you from going to New York is premature. Goodnight, Blanche.
LANG:	Goodnight, John.
MUSIC:	BICKERSON PLAYOFF
	(APPLAUSE)
MUSIC:	THEME
	CLOSING
AMECHE:	Well, that puts the lid on the fifteenth program of our new series for Old Gold Cigarettes, written and directed by Phil Rapp and produced by Mann Holiner. We hope you'll be on hand next Friday night for Frank Morgan, Frances Langford, and Carmen Dragon and the orchestra. This is Don Ameche saying goodnight and good smoking with Old Golds!
	(APPLAUSE)
MUSIC:	THEME
MILLER:	Frank Morgan appeared by arrangement with Metro-Goldwyn-Mayer, producers of Sinclair Lewis' "Cass Timberlane" starring Spencer Tracy, Lana Turner, and Zachary Scott. Remember next Friday at Old Gold Time it'll be Frank Morgan, Don Ameche, and Frances Langford with Carmen Dragon and his orchestra brought to you by P. Lorillard Company...a famous name in tobaccos for nearly two hundred years...makers of Old Gold Cigarettes...the treasure of 'em all...And listen... if you want a treat instead of a treatment....treat yourself to Old Golds. Buy 'em at your tobacco counters...Buy them in the cigarette vending machines...
	(APPLAUSE)

One of the odd quirks of *The Old Gold Show* was the caliber of guests which were a part of the first fifteen minutes each week. This episode has "the dean of Modern Architects," Richard Neutra, taking on the typical Morgan slurs. Often the guests (and sometimes there were none) would be regular workers at the top of their professions rather than the usual Hollywood and stage stars that occupied series like *Jack Benny, Eddie Cantor* and even *Amos & Andy*. Of course, as the guests were not much more than typical stooges for Frank Morgan's one-upmanship, had movie stars been available or requested, no doubt the whole structure for that individual show would have had to have been reworked.

THE OLD GOLD SHOW

Station CBS   **Date** 1/9/48   **Time** 6:00-6:30 PM   **Studio** VINE ST.

Cast   Music Routine

FRANK MORGAN   OPENING THEME
DON AMECHE
FRANCES LANGFORD   "DANCE AT YOUR WEDDING"
CARMEN DRAGON   MORGAN PLAYOFF
FRANK GOSS   "THESE FOOLISH THINGS"
MARVIN MILLER   BICKERSON THEME
                             BICKERSON PLAYOFF
EVELYN SCOTT   CLOSING THEME
HITS AND A MISS
RICHARD NEUTRA

WRITTEN AND DIRECTED BY: Phil Rapp
PRODUCED BY: Mann Holiner

MILLER:	From Hollywood – it's Old Gold Cigarette Time.
CHORUS:	Treat yourself......to Old Golds.
GROUP:	If you want a treat instead of a treatment.
CHORUS:	Treat yourself......to Old Golds.
GROUP:	If you want a treat instead of a treatment.
CHORUS:	Treat yourself...
	Treat yourself...
	Treat yourself......to Old Golds.
MILLER:	If you want a treat instead of a treatment......
	TREAT YOURSELF TO A PACK OF OLD GOLDS!
	(PAUSE)
MUSIC:	THEME....ESTABLISH AND FADE UNDER
	FOLLOWING
MILLER:	This is Marvin Miller, ladies and gentlemen, speaking for the makers of Old Gold cigarettes who are pleased to present the sixteenth in a series of new programs with Carmen Dragon and his orchestra, starring Metro-Goldwyn-Mayer's lovable Frank Morgan, the genial Don Ameche and charming Frances Langford, who sings ---
MUSIC:	LANGFORD AND ORCH......"I'LL DANCE AT YOUR WEDDING"
	(APPLAUSE)
	FIRST COMMERCIAL
MILLER:	For your own sweet pleasure's sake ... for the sake of good, honest, no-fooling-around smoking pleasure... smoke a pack of Old Gold cigarettes! Yes ... <u>today</u> ... find out about Old Golds! Light an Old Gold! Enjoy its taste ... that unique Old Gold taste. Don't you know? Nearly two hundred years' experience with fine quality tobaccos are behind every Old Gold you smoke. So ... today's the day to find out about Old Golds! Because like I keep saying ... if you want to smoke for the wonderful fun of it ... if you want a treat instead of a treatment ...
CHORUS:	Treat yourself ... to Old Golds.
GROUP:	... if you want a treat instead of a treatment.
CHORUS:	Treat yourself ... to Old Golds.
MILLER:	And here is your host for the evening, Don Ameche.
	(APPLAUSE)
AMECHE:	Thank you, ladies and gentlemen, and good evening. Tonight we have as a guest a gentleman whose vision and genius have made it possible for people of small means

35

	to enjoy a comfortable home. Winner of over two dozen awards in national and world-wide architectural competitions, author and lecturer – it's my pleasure to present the dean of Modern Architects – Richard Neutra. Mr. Neutra. (APPLAUSE)
NEUTRA:	Thank you.
AMECHE:	Before we begin, Mr. Neutra, I'd like you to meet some of the people on our show. This is Frances Langford.
LANG:	Mr. Neutra.
NEUTRA:	It's always a pleasure to meet a lovely lady.
LANG:	Thank you.
DRAG:	He may be an architect, but he's got the same old plans.
AMECHE:	All right, Carmen. This is Carmen Dragon, Mr. Neutra.
NEUTRA:	Mr. Dragon, as a member of the vast army of music-lovers may I say that I enjoy your orchestra very much.
DRAG:	Thanks. And as a member of the vast army of home-seekers I like your houses, too. You haven't got a two-family bungalow that I ---
AMECHE:	Stop that, Carmen. Mr. Neutra is an architect. He doesn't sell houses.
NEUTRA:	No, I design them, Mr. Dragon.
DRAG:	Oh. Well, my brother-in-law needs a new house. Right now he lives in a hot-water flat in Coldwater Canyon.
AMECHE:	A hotwater flat?
DRAG:	Maybe it's a cold-water flat in Hotwater Canyon. Anyway he wants to move out.
NEUTRA:	What's his address, Mr. Dragon?
DRAG:	You mean you'll design a new house for him?
NEUTRA:	No, but I've got a brother-in-law who'd like to move into his old one.
AMECHE:	That's that. Mr. Neutra, among our listeners tonight there may be many aspiring home-builders. How about a tip or two from an expert in Modern Architecture?
NEUTRA:	Very well. My advice to them is to think of a house not as just a place to live, but as a machine for living. The best modern architects design buildings according to the idea of functionalism.
LANG:	Functionalism?
NEUTRA:	Yes. It's a term signifying, in architecture, the adaptation of form to purpose, and to the nature of the materials used.

AMECHE:	You mean any architectural feature which serves no purpose but that of ornamentation is to be avoided.
NEUTRA:	Exactly. I, personally, will not waste my time with beauty if the proportions are not harmonious.
MORG:	(COMING ON) Neither will I. If they haven't got nice legs I never bother looking at their faces!
AMECHE:	Frank!
	(APPLAUSE)
MORG:	Of course, since the girls started wearing long dresses I've had to rely on my memory. But ---
AMECHE:	Frank! No girls! We're just chatting about houses.
MORG:	Err – girlhouses. What about it?
NEUTRA:	Mr. Morgan, I was about to give a few tips ---
MORG:	I'm sorry, my good man, but I never deal with touts. However, if you've got something hot in the fourth at Santa Anita ---
LANG:	Oh, please, Mr. Morgan! He's not a racetrack tout.
MORG:	Then why does he pester --- oh, hello, my dear!
LANG:	Hello.
MORG:	Aren't you the Barmaid at the Cock and Bull?
LANG:	Barmaid?
MORG:	I hardly recognized you without your padded apron and bungstarter. I haven't seen you since I drank a gallon of beer out of your dainty slipper.
LANG:	That's enough for me. Goodnight, gentlemen.
MORG:	What happened?
AMECHE:	Frank, that's Frances Langford! Every week for sixteen weeks you've met her and you still haven't made any headway. Are you losing your mind?
MORG:	Either that or I'm losing my touch. I've seen <u>you</u> before, haven't I? Your teeth look very familiar.
NEUTRA:	Mr. Morgan ---
MORG:	Don't rush me, son – I'll look at your scratch sheet later.
AMECHE:	Scratch sheet!
NEUTRA:	I'm sorry, Mr. Morgan, but I rather hoped you would recognize me. After all, I do have a sort of a name in my field.
MORG:	I know – Louie, the Owl, isn't it?
NEUTRA:	Louie the Owl?
MORG:	I don't know why you bother with such a hideous disguise. You should get rid of that false moustache – it wouldn't fool a Pinkerton man at thirty paces. I knew you were a horse-doper the minute I saw you.

NEUTRA:	Horse-doper?
MORG:	Pull out your racing form and let me have a look at your horse, dope. Have you just come from the stables?
AMECHE:	Frank!
MORG:	What?
AMECHE:	He doesn't come from the stables.
MORG:	Well, he's got that certain air about him. Who is he?
NEUTRA:	I'd like to explain, Mr. Morgan. I get an income by advocating a certain type of house.
MORG:	Well, it's nothing to be ashamed of unless the dice are crooked. I had an uncle who ran a shell game in an oyster bar. That is, until they clamped down on him.
AMECHE:	Frank, this gentleman ---
MORG:	Poor old codger fell into the lobster pot and was shipped to the cannery with two tons of sea food. Our whole family gave up eating chowder after that. How long have you been steering the suckers?
AMECHE:	Frank, he doesn't steer anybody! He's a designer.
MORG:	Not really? Are you responsible for the New Look?
NEUTRA:	In a way.
MORG:	Well, I wish you'd do something about the new evening gowns. Either give the women lower necklines or give me higher heels.
AMECHE:	Oh, this has gone far enough. Frank, have you ever heard of California's leading Modern Architect, Richard Neutra?
MORG:	Heard of him? My dear Dodger, it was mainly through my efforts that he is where he is today. By the way, where is he?
NEUTRA:	Right here in California, the last I heard of him.
MORG:	Well, I wish I heard the last of him. Most incompetent architect I ever met. Crooked, too. I thought he got bumped off.
NEUTRA:	Bumped off?
MORG:	A very distasteful matter. He stole the sketches for the City Dog Pound and got caught with his plans down. He made a good target for the watchman's buckshot and ---
AMECHE:	Frank! Don't say another word! This gentleman is Richard Neutra, the architect!
MORG:	Oh -- err -- you – I --- rich gentleman.
AMECHE:	Yes. He's Neutra and he didn't get bumped off! He's very much alive, you goose!
MORG:	Err -- he's a live goose. Well, I'm a dead duck. I think I'd better ---

AMECHE:	Come back here, you faker. Apologize to Mr. Neutra and tell him you invented that whole string of lies!
NEUTRA:	That isn't necessary, Don. I know Mr. Morgan by reputation and I'm certain he was just joshing me.
MORG:	Why, bless your heart, of course! I recognized you instantly, Mr. Goiter......
NEUTRA:	My name is Neutra. N – E – U – T – R – A.
MORG:	Yes. That's Nature spelled sideways, isn't it?
AMECHE:	You see, Mr. Neutra! You can't be polite to a windbag like --
MILLER:	I don't like to intrude, Don. But it seems to me you'd serve better as a host if you would show Mr. Morgan a little more courtesy.
MORG:	Well, what a timely distraction! You're that plump young chef from the Pig 'n Whistle. Pull up a pig and whistle.
MILLER:	Pardon?
MORG:	How thoughtful of you to bring us a snack before dinner. I see your hip pockets are just bulging with ground round.
AMECHE:	Why don't you stop, Frank! You know very well he's our announcer.
MORG:	He is? He doesn't look like that obnoxious lardbucket, Marvin Miller.
MILLER:	That's me. I'm that obnoxious lardbucket, Mr. Morgan.
MORG:	My apologies, sir. Allow me to introduce you to America's greatest Modern Architect. Mr. Gumboil, this is Mr. Lardbucket.
MILLER:	Mr. Gumboil.
NEUTRA:	Mr. Lardbucket.
AMECHE:	Frank, where did you get that Gumboil and Lardbucket?
MORG:	I don't know – but I'd like to get rid of them.
MILLER:	Mr. Morgan, I don't want to bother you ---
MORG:	Well, you do, you know.
MILLER:	I'm sorry, but I heard you discussing architecture and I've been studying ancient buildings for years. Right now I'm all wrapped up in Gothic pillars.
MORG:	Oh, is that what it is? I thought you had a mattress stuffed in your pants.
AMECHE:	I can't stand any more of this! Mr. Neutra, I'm sorry you've had to put up with all of Morgan's foolishness.
NEUTRA:	Don't be ridiculous, Don. Why, I'll wager Mr. Morgan knows as much about Modern architecture as I do.
MORG:	I do? I mean I do! As it happens, the Morgans have been architects for generations, beginning with my grandfather

39

	Blueprint Morgan, down to my Uncle Stucco and my Aunt Rafter.
AMECHE:	Your Aunt Rafter?
MORG:	A hefty old buttress. Always hung from the ceiling when she was plastered.
MILLER:	What a wonderful family.
MORG:	Yes. Their plans and esquisses were masterpieces of perfection, and to this day, if you visit the British Museum, you may see my gaffer's famous hanging portico and protruding rotunda. It was mainly through his efforts that I received my first architectural assignment.
NEUTRA:	You were quite young, I suppose.
MORG:	I suppose so. At the age of twelve I designed a building for an Italian Nobelman that was two miles long and a half inch wide.
AMECHE:	Two inches long and a half inch wide! What did he keep in it?
MORG:	Spaghetti. Before I reached manhood I astounded the American Institute of Architects by laying the foundation of Vassar University, using nothing but two iron stays and a large girdle. Girder! No doubt you've heard of the Morgan Foundation?
AMECHE:	Oh, of corset.
MORG:	Of corset. You should get a good lacing for that, Dodger. Don't you think so, Mr. Tolstoy?
NEUTRA:	Neutra.
MORG:	Yes.
NEUTRA:	Did you ever go beyond the Vassar foundation, Mr. Morgan?
MORG:	Unfortunately I was forced to abandon the project because of a minor disagreement with the Dean of Women. She approved my plans for the main buildings, but didn't like my designs on the girls dormitory. It was then I decided to conquer the field of modern construction.
AMECHE:	You gave up the old-fashioned entirely?
MORG:	No, but I cut down to nineteen a day. In no time at all I designed and executed an ultra-modern bungalow employing an early principle of heat pressure on lumber and using a flank of scorefied supports.
AMECHE:	A flank of scorefied supports? What's that?
MORG:	A side of baked beams.
AMECHE:	I'll have an order of fried peas.
MORG:	Ketchup?
AMECHE:	Just a barrel!

MORG:	That'll be thirty-five --- what are we talking about! Well, I'm not going to stand around here and ---
NEUTRA:	Please don't go, Mr. Morgan. I want to hear more about your experiments in architecture.
MORG:	Oh, well – all right. It was almost twenty-five years ago that I entered into competition with twelve of America's greatest architectural engineers who were bidding for the privilege of building a bridge over the widest portion of the Potomac River. I was awarded the contract, naturally, and ---
AMECHE:	What was your bid?
MORG:	Pretty low. I ---
AMECHE:	How low?
MORG:	Well, I agreed to furnish my own material and build a bridge across the Potomac for two hundred and forty dollars.
NEUTRA:	Incredible!
MORG:	I don't believe it myself.
MILLER:	I do. How long did it take you to accomplish the task?
MORG:	Operations began on the ninth of June, 1923. By the tenth it was obvious I had made a bad bargain, but a Morgan's word is his bond. No matter what it cost me I was determined to finish the bridge.
AMECHE:	Uh-huh.
MORG:	Single-handed, I dredged and filled, built coffer dams and riveted steel. The massive span lengthened day by day, and three months later, during a heavy fog, the city fathers gathered for the opening ceremony.
NEUTRA:	This is exciting.
MORG:	To the mayor went the honor of crossing my bridge in his official car. With a great flourish the ribbon was broken and the mayor and his entourage started on their way across the Potomac, while I watched with bated breath.
AMECHE:	I'll bet I know what your breath was baited with.
MORG:	Silence! The whole town turned out in a triumphal procession of automobiles and for five hours a steady stream of traffic passed the toll gate. Since I had been promised a percentage of the toll my happiness knew no bounds.
NEUTRA:	And you've been collecting for twenty-five years?
MORG:	No – after the first day the receipts dwindled to nothing.
AMECHE:	Didn't the public like your bridge?
MORG:	They liked it all right – but there was one thing wrong with it.
AMECHE:	What was that?

MORG:	It didn't quite reach the other side. Well, so long fellows, I gotta play with my Erector.
MUSIC:	MORGAN PLAYOFF (APPLAUSE) SECOND COMMERCIAL
MUSIC:	INTRO "THESE FOOLISH THINGS" DOWN UNDER
MILLER:	(OVER THEME) Francis Langford sings "These Foolish Things."
MUSIC:	ORCH AND LANGFORD....."THESE FOOLISH THINGS" (APPLAUSE)
CHORUS:	Treat yourself....to Old Golds
GROUP:	....if you want a treat instead of a treatment
CHORUS:	Treat yourself....to Old Golds
GROUP:	....if you want a treat instead of a treatment
CHORUS:	Treat yourself....to Old Golds!
MILLER:	(A LITTLE EXCITEMENT) Whatever you smoke ... today ... buy a pack of Old Golds! See if they're not the tastiest cigarette you ever enjoyed ... smoother ... milder. See if it's not true that ... you simply cannot match the quality of an Old Gold!
WOMAN:	Today's the day to find out about Old Golds!
MILLER:	Yes! This is the time to discover the sheer pleasure of smoking an Old Gold. Today ... compare any cigarette you know with an Old Gold ... its taste and fragrance. You'll surely agree that ... the quality of an Old Gold cannot be duplicated! Because no other cigarette in America has the quality traditions of an Old Gold. Listen.
2ND ANNCR:	Nearly two hundred years of fine tobacco experience are behind every Old Gold you smoke. We're tobacco men ... not medicine men. Old Golds cure just one thing ... tobaccos ... the world's choice tobaccos ... to give you a milder smoke ... a better-tasting smoke!
WOMAN:	Today's the day to find out about Old Golds!
MILLER:	Yes, yes, yes! You owe it to your sweet pleasure's sake to get more smoking pleasure. So smoke a pack of Old Golds today! Because if you want a treat instead of treatment...
CHORUS:	Treat yourself...to Old Golds.
GROUP:	...if you want a treat instead of a treatment.
CHORUS:	Treat yourself...to Old Golds!
MILLER:	Now here are Don Ameche and Francis Langford as John and Blanche Bickerson in "The Honeymoon Is Over."

THEME:	SOFT AND PLAINTIVE
MILLER:	Three o'clock in the morning finds Mrs. Bickerson and Dr. Hersey at the bedside of poor husband John, victim of undulant insomnia, as he reaches the crisis during an acute attack of the dread ailment.
DON:	(SNORES LUSTILY...WHINES...SNORES AND WHINES...BROKEN RHYTHM SNORE FOLLOWED BY A WHINE)
DOC:	Mmm-hmm. Whiner's Syndrome.
LANG:	It's like being married to a meat-grinder.
DON:	(SNORES AND GIGGLES...SNORES AND GIGGLES AGAIN)
DOC:	Tickleberry's Reflex.
DON:	(SNORES AND GIGGLES MERRILY)
LANG:	Did you ever hear anything like that, Doctor?
DOC:	Never. Let's step outside a minute, Mrs. Bickerson.
DON:	(CONTINUES TO SNORE UNTIL THE DOOR CLOSES)
LANG:	He's getting worse, isn't he?
DOC:	Sounds to me like a post-pharyngeal flaccidity accompanied by cogwheel breathing. Some people acquire the habit because of too rapid feeding during infancy. Was your husband a bottle baby?
LANG:	If he was he's never been weened.
DOC:	I see. And when did he first start to snore like that?
LANG:	Right after our honeymoon. I couldn't hear the Falls on the last day.
DOC:	Very unusual. I still don't understand why you waited so long before consulting a physician, Mrs. Bickerson.
LANG:	Oh, my husband doesn't trust physicians, Dr. Hersey. He said the only cure for snoring was two aspirins and a sip of bourbon every night.
DOC:	Does he take that? Regularly?
LANG:	Well, he's six months behind on the aspirin but he's two years ahead on the bourbon.
DOC:	Obviously it's not much of a remedy.
LANG:	Well, he won't take it anymore. When he went to sleep tonight I hid his last three bottles in the chandelier.
DOC:	I think you'd better persuade him to come down to my office, Mrs. Bickerson, and I'll give him a through examination.
LANG:	I hope he'll go. I haven't had a good night's sleep for so long I'm a nervous wreck.

DOC:	Well, if you'll walk out to my car with me I'll let you have a couple of sleeping pills.
LANG:	All right, Doctor. One second till I look in and see if John's still sleeping...(DOOR OPENS)
DON:	(SNORES LUSTILY...HUMS AND CLUCKS)
LANG:	He's still going strong...(DOOR CLOSES)
DON:	(SNORES...HUMS AND CLUCKS...SNORES, THEN SUDDENLY BREAKS OFF WITH A STRANGLING SOUND) Huh? What'd you say, Blanche?...Wassamatter?...O kay, don't answer me. Woman's got more ways of waking me up...Blanche! Why don't you say something?...I know you're there – I can hear you keeping quiet!...Oh, Blanche, that's a dirty trick. I'm so tired and you know I can't go to sleep unless you nag me...Blanche! Where's the light? (CLICK) What's the idea of – she's gone! (SCRAMBLES OUT OF BED) Blanche! Maybe some prowler – oh dear heaven! If somebody broke in and carried off -- (CLOSET DOOR OPENS) Oh, this is the end! (RECEIVER UP...DIALS OPERATOR) How could such a thing happen to me!
OP:	(FILTER) Number, please?
DON:	Get me the police department. (CLICKING)
MAN:	(FILTER) Police department!
DON:	Officer! This is John Bickerson, 224 Clump Street. Send a squad car over right away!
MAN:	What's the trouble?
DON:	Somebody stole my bourbon! Three bottles...Oh yes. My wife's gone too.
MAN:	Uh huh. Can you supply a description?
DON:	Yes. They were four years old, bottled in bond – they all had green labels and one of the corks was chipped right where the revenue stamp --
MAN:	No, no, no. I mean a description of your wife.
DON:	Oh. Well, she's kind of – er – she's got – er – I'll mail you her picture in the morning.
MAN:	Never mind, we'll look for the bourbon.
DON:	Thanks. (HANGS UP) I gotta lie down. What have I done to deserve this? Oh, I hope she's all right. She's gotta be all right. Maybe she walked out on me. I should have been more considerate...I've been keeping her awake for years...while I snore my head off...I'll never sleep --- another -- wink -- as long as I -- (SNORES...PAUSE...DOOR OPENS)

LANG:	John!
DOC:	Mmm.
LANG:	Why are you lying there with the lights on and a big smile on your face?
DON:	Is that you, Blanche?
LANG:	Yes, it's me.
DON:	I'm not smiling any more. Put out the lights.
LANG:	I won't put out the lights. Who sent for that squad car full of policemen?
DON:	I did.
LANG:	Well, you'd better do something – they just arrested Dr. Hersey.
DON:	Dr. Hersey? What are you talking about?
LANG:	Somebody complained about a prowler and they started searching us both before I could convince them I lived here.
DON:	What were you doing with Dr. Hersey?
LANG:	I went to his car with him to get some sleeping pills. He was here listening to you snore for two hours.
DON:	Well, they should arrest him!
LANG:	They didn't, really. But they asked a lot of nasty questions and it was very embarrassing. Why did you send for the police?
DON:	Honey, I woke up and saw your bed was empty. I thought somebody broke into the house and I went crazy. You can imagine how I felt when I found my precious joy had disappeared – my very life had gone; I searched everywhere!
LANG:	Did you look in the chandelier?
DON:	Oh, so that's where you hid 'em! Okay, now I can sleep in peace. Goodnight, Blanche.
LANG:	I made an appointment for you to see Dr. Hersey tomorrow.
DON:	Mmm.
LANG:	You'll go, won't you?
DON:	Where?
LANG:	To see Dr. Hersey. He wants you in his office at nine o'clock.
DON:	Whaffor?
LANG:	He's going to examine you for twenty dollars.
DON:	If he finds it I want half.
LANG:	Don't be funny, John.
DON:	I'm not being funny, I'm sleepy. I went to bed late, Blanche.
LANG:	It's your own fault. Nobody told you to stay up till two o'clock fiddling around in the kitchen.
DON:	I wasn't fiddling around. You wanted me to fix the electric iron and the vacuum cleaner, didn't you? Well, I fixed 'em both.

LANG:	Do they work?
DON:	They work fine. Except the vacuum cleaner burns holes in the rug. I think I must have got the wires crossed.
LANG:	I can imagine the mess you must have left in that kitchen.
DON:	There's no mess.
LANG:	Did you lock the porch door?
DON:	Mmm.
LANG:	All the lights out?
DON:	Lights out.
LANG:	Did you water the plants?
DON:	Yes.
LANG:	Are you sure you watered the plants?
DON:	Blanche, I watered the plants, I grained the canary, I boned the dog and I milked the cat! Why don't you let me sleep?
LANG:	Because somebody has to see that things are taken care of in this house. If I didn't check on you nothing would get done. Every time you leave the kitchen I find the ice box door open, or the cupboards, or the breadbox. It's no use! I'll just have to follow behind you shutting up all the time.
DON:	You say it but you won't do it.
LANG:	Whether you like it or not I'm going to talk. There's a lot of things I want to get off my chest.
DON:	Oh, dear.
LANG:	You're tired of me, aren't you, John?
DON:	No, I'm just tired.
LANG:	Seeing the way you act now, I can't believe you ever loved me.
DON:	Oh, Blanche --
LANG:	Well, you're never sweet or solicitous and you just hate the sound of my voice. If you'd only give me the least attention.
DON:	I give you the least attention I ever gave anybody. That's not what I mean.
LANG:	Then why don't you ever tell me you love me?
DON:	I always tell you.
LANG:	But I have to goad you.
DON:	That's because you want me to say it fifty thousand times a day.
LANG:	Maybe I do. That's the only way I can be sure that you'll never stop loving me.
DON:	Blanche, I'll love you as long as the moon is glowing, as long as the stars are twinkling – I'll love you as long as the sun is shining. Satisfied?
LANG:	No. You'll only love me as long as the weather is nice.

46

DON:	I will not. I'll love you in rain, I'll love you in snow, I'll love you in hail. What more do you want? Do I ever ask you to tell me you love me?
LANG:	That's another thing that upsets me. Why don't you ever ask me?
DON:	All right. Do you love me?
LANG:	No. That'll teach you not to take me so much for granted. Other men think I'm pretty attractive, you know. I could tell you plenty.
DON:	Not tonight.
LANG:	Believe me, there's better fish in the ocean than the one I caught.
DON:	There's better bait, too.
LANG:	All right, John Bickerson, just for that I'll never do another thing for you. No more cooking.
DON:	Good.
LANG:	No more laundry.
DON:	Wonderful.
LANG:	Maybe you won't be so smug if you don't get a clean tablecloth.
DON:	I can eat without a tablecloth.
LANG:	I'm not talking about eating.
DON:	What do you mean?
LANG:	What do you think you're sleeping on?
DON:	What? What happened to the bedsheets? Why do I have to sleep on a tablecloth?
LANG:	Well, it was too soiled to use on the table but not dirty enough to go to the laundry.
DON:	Now listen to me, Blanche, I work hard for a living and I want to sleep on a bedsheet.
LANG:	That's too bad! From now on I'm not going to do a lick of work in this house unless I get paid for it.
DON:	You get paid plenty!
LANG:	I mean I want a regular salary. Just like you get.
DON:	Okay, I'll pay you a salary. I'll pay you exactly what you're worth.
LANG:	I won't work that cheap! I want fifty dollars a week and I want a maid.
DON:	You had a maid!
LANG:	Yes, but how long was she with us?
DON:	She was never with us – she was against us from the start! And I can't afford to pay you fifty dollars a week. I only make sixty myself!
LANG:	Then why don't you ask for a raise! You said you were going to ask for one. Did you do it?

DON:	Did I do what?
LANG:	Ask for a raise.
DON:	I refuse to discuss my business with you!
LANG:	Just answer my question. Did you or didn't you ask for a raise?
DON:	Blanche, when the time is propitious, I'll ask for a raise. And what's more, I'll get it!
LANG:	No, you won't.
DON:	All right – so I won't.
LANG:	I happen to know you won't get a raise.
DON:	How do you know?
LANG:	Because I called your boss and asked for one.
DON:	You what?
LANG:	I called your boss and asked for a raise.
DON:	Blanche – you didn't! How could you have the – what did he say?
LANG:	He turned you down.
DON:	Ohhh! Now, look, Blanche!
LANG:	He said you're not worth what you're getting now. He said your mind wasn't on your work and you spend half the day at the office sleeping.
DON:	That's because you keep me awake all night! Oh, what am I gonna do? No woman calls her husband's boss for a raise! How will I face the man tomorrow?
LANG:	You don't have to – I quit for you.
DON:	How could you do such a thing? I been working there sixteen years. I started as an office boy – I worked my way up to ship-ping clerk – then bookkeeper – finally sales manager – and you quit for me!
LANG:	Oh, don't get hysterical. It's not the only job in the world. Besides, you never made enough to keep me decently clothed. I haven't got a rag to my name.
DON:	You've got a closet full of rags! I'm the one who hasn't got anything.
LANG:	You've got much more than I have.
DON:	What's the matter with that fur coat? A twelve hundred dol-lar bald mink. And last week I bought you a muff – genuine plucked skunk. And who paid for your formal bed-jacket?
LANG:	Don't scream at me.
DON:	I deny myself everything. My clothes are in shreds! I'm the only man in town with a midriff shirt and bareback

	pants! I use leg-paint to save on socks! I've been making over your old bloomers -- (PHONE RINGS RECEIVER UP IMMEDIATELY) DROP DEAD!
MAN:	(FILTER) Hello, Bickerson?
DON:	What do you want?
MAN:	This is your boss, Mr. Guernsey. I know this is an unearthly hour to call, but I haven't been able to sleep.
DON:	Oh?
MAN:	I'm afraid I was a bit hasty when your wife called me, and I've been thinking it over.
DON:	You have?
MAN:	Yes, she's a pretty sensible woman and more than fair. I want you to come back to work, and I'm going to give you a twenty-five dollar raise.
DON:	Oh, I don't think you ---
MAN:	All right, fifteen. You'll be in tomorrow, won't you, Bickerson?
DON:	I certainly will. Goodnight. (HANG UP)
LANG:	Who was it, John?
DON:	That was my boss. You know, I ought to clout you -- but I think I'll kiss you instead.
LANG:	Oh, John.
DON:	Of all the blundering troublesome stumblebums you're the worst, Blanche. But somehow you get lucky. I don't know what you said to the old crab, but he's giving me a fifteen dollar raise.
LANG:	If you'd have kept your big mouth shut, you'd have got the whole twenty-five. Goodnight, John.
DON:	Goodnight, Blanche.
MUSIC:	BICKERSON PLAYOFF (APPLAUSE)
MUSIC:	THEME
CLOSING	
AMECHE:	Well, that puts the lid on the sixteenth program of our new series for Old Gold Cigarettes, written and directed by Phil Rapp and produced by Mann Holiner. We hope you'll be on hand next Friday night for Frank Morgan, Frances Langford, and Carmen Dragon and the orchestra. This is Don Ameche saying goodnight and good smoking with Old Golds! (APPLAUSE)
MUSIC:	THEME
MILLER:	Frank Morgan appeared by arrangement with Metro-Goldwyn-

Mayer, producers of Sinclair Lewis' "Cass Timberlane" starring Spencer Tracy, Lana Turner, and Zachary Scott. Remember next Friday at Old Gold Time it'll be Frank Morgan, Don Ameche, and Frances Langford with Carmen Dragon and his orchestra brought to you by P. Lorillard Company...a famous name in tobaccos for nearly two hundred years...makers of Old Gold Cigarettes...the treasure of 'em all...and listen...if you want a treat instead of a treatment...treat yourself to Old Golds. Buy 'em at your tobacco counters...Buy them in the cigarette vending machines.. Don't forget every Friday night on C.B.S. it's "Fun For The Family." Stay tuned now for "The Adventures of Ozzie and Harriet" which follow immediately over most of these stations. This is Marvin Miller speaking.
(APPLAUSE)
THIS IS....CBS....THE COLUMBIA BROADCASTING SYSTEM.

John Bickerson hates kids. When once asked why that was so, he replied to Blanche, "Because I can't bare them." And yet, everything he loathes and despises worst in the world will happen to him – if it's what his wife wants. She is overpowering, but obviously a lonely person at heart. The only time she has to talk with John is late at night, and his snoring is the perfect excuse to start a conversation. No wonder she never let him have the operation to cure it.

In this episode, Blanche's sister Clara and her huge kid George are staying with the unfortunate couple in their small apartment. Wistful even for a child who's the size of a man, Blanche would like a baby, thinking it might curb the amount of fights they have. She might also think that that would keep John awake more, to talk, though most likely it would require him having a second job to support the increased family. But as always, in the end, our unhappy couple remain happily the same, week after week, year after year.

THE OLD GOLD SHOW

Station CBS   Date 1/16/48   Time 6:00-6:30 PM   Studio VINE ST.

Cast	Music Routine
FRANK MORGAN	OPENING THEME
DON AMECHE	"TRUE"
FRANCES LANGFORD	MORGAN PLAYOFF
CARMEN DRAGON	"SO FAR"
FRANK GOSS	BICKERSON THEME
MARVIN MILLER	BICKERSON PLAYOFF
EVELYN SCOTT	CLOSING THEME
HITS AND A MISS	
TONI MATT	

WRITTEN AND DIRECTED BY: Phil Rapp
PRODUCED BY: Mann Holiner

(ON CUE)

MILLER:	From Hollywood – it's Old Gold Cigarette Time.
CHORUS:	Treat yourself...........to Old Golds.
GROUP:	If you want a treat instead of a treatment.
CHORUS:	Treat yourself...........to Old Golds.
GROUP:	If you want a treat instead of a treatment.
CHORUS:	Treat yourself...
	Treat yourself...
	Treat yourself...........to Old Golds.
MILLER:	If you want a treat instead of a treatment......
	TREAT YOURSELF TO A PACK OF OLD GOLDS!
	(PAUSE)
MUSIC:	(THEME....ESTABLISH AND FADE UNDER
	FOLLOWING)
MILLER:	This is Marvin Miller, ladies and gentlemen, speaking for the makers of Old Gold cigarettes who are pleased to present the seventeenth in a series of new programs with Carmen Dragon and his orchestra, starring Metro-Goldwyn-Mayer's lovable Frank Morgan, the genial Don Ameche and charming Frances Langford, who sings ---
MUSIC:	LANGFORD AND ORCH.................."TRUE"
	(APPLAUSE)
MILLER:	The <u>best</u> way to smoke is to smoke for pleasure. And the best way to get your smoking pleasure is through an Old Gold. Today ... why not start enjoying the wonderful pleasures of an Old Gold... its taste...its smoothness and mildness. After all ... Old Golds are an exclusive blend of the world's choice tobaccos ... product of nearly two hundred years' experience with fine quality tobaccos. So ... today ... find out about Old Golds! Because listen
	... if you want to smoke for the wonderful pleasure of it
	... if you want a treat instead of a treatment....
CHORUS:	Treat yourself ... to Old Golds
GROUP:	... if you want a treat instead of a treatment
CHORUS:	Treat yourself ... to Old Golds!
MILLER:	And now here is your host for the evening, Don Ameche.
	(APPLAUSE)
AMECHE:	Thank you, ladies and gentlemen, and good evening. Our guest tonight ---
LANG:	Don, do you mind if I don't meet the guest tonight? I want to be gone before Frank Morgan gets here.

AMECHE:	What's wrong, Frances?
LANG:	Well, you know how he keeps mistaking me for a waitress or a chambermaid – or whatever ... I don't mind for myself so much, but my husband listens in and he's very sensitive.
DRAG:	I don't blame him. I'll be darned if I'd stand idle and listen to my wife be insulted over the radio. No, sir.
AMECHE:	What would you do, Carmen?
DRAG:	I'd stop listening.
AMECHE:	Oh, fine. Frances, I've been begging you for weeks to tell Morgan off and tonight you should really do it.
LANG:	Oh, I can't do that. He's such a nice man.
AMECHE:	Well, stick around and meet our guest, anyway. Ladies and gentlemen, beautiful Sun Valley in Idaho is rapidly becoming the world's garden spot for winter sports and rivalling Europe's famous St. Moritz for its ski runs. Making a special trip to appear on our program, and here tonight, is the Head ski instructor – the only man ever to win the much-coveted Gibson trophy competition more than once – holder of a speed record that's never been approached – the internationally celebrated ski expert – Toni Matt! Toni. (APPLAUSE)
MATT:	Thank you.
AMECHE:	Toni, how are skiing conditions up at Sun Valley?
MATT:	Just perfect. All the slopes are covered with snow, and there must be about thirty-eight inches on Mount Baldy.
AMECHE:	Mount Baldy. That's eleven thousand feet high, isn't it?
MATT:	That's right. I climb up to the top every morning.
DRAG:	What for?
MATT:	Pardon?
DRAG:	What do you climb up there for?
MATT:	Well, I get a kick out of it. When I get to the top of Mount Baldy I stand there for an hour, looking down into the valley below. That valley is the most beautiful thing in the world.
DRAG:	If it's so beautiful in the valley why do you keep climbing up the mountain?
MATT:	Good evening, Mr. Dragon.
AMECHE:	How do you know his name?
MATT:	I've been listening to this program and nobody else could ask such a question.
AMECHE:	That takes care of Carmen. Now I'd like you to meet Frances Langford, Toni.

MATT:	How do you do, Miss Langford?
LANG:	How do you do?
AMECHE:	I'm sorry Frank Morgan isn't here yet, Toni, but you'll meet him later.
MATT:	Oh, I saw Mr. Morgan in Sun Valley last weekend.
AMECHE:	You saw our Frank Morgan in Sun Valley? Was he skiing?
MATT:	Oh, no – he could hardly stand up. On skis, I mean.
AMECHE:	I know what you mean.
MATT:	I don't know why he came down there, he spent practically the whole weekend in his room, probably resting or something.
AMECHE:	Probably something. Why did he try to ski, Toni?
MATT:	Well, for one half hour he was in Mr. Hennig's Nursery Class.
LANG:	Nursery class?
MATT:	Yes. That's for children, beginners, dubs and impossibles.
AMECHE:	What was Morgan?
MATT:	Impossible. After falling on his back ten times Mr. Morgan finally tied the skis to his coat-tails.
AMECHE:	What happened?
MATT:	He fell on his face.
AMECHE:	So Morgan went to Sun Valley?
DRAG:	You can have just as much fun skiing at Big Bear and it's only a couple of hours drive. I took Eloise – that's Mrs. Dragon – and the kids up there last Sunday.
LANG:	I didn't know you could ski, Carmen.
DRAG:	Well, I can't. But my three kids ski like eagles. Boy, you should have seen 'em.
AMECHE:	They were good, huh?
DRAG:	Wonderful. We've had a lot of fun with our kids – but I was really a proud father when Big Bear came along!
MORG:	(COMING ON) Congratulations, Herman! How's Mrs. Dragon feeling since she had the new cub?
AMECHE:	Frank!
	(APPLAUSE)
MORG:	Hello, fellows. I hope I'm late this evening.
AMECHE:	You hope you're late! Why?
MORG:	Well, I understand it's become your custom to engage Herman in a bit of fatiguing banter that's well worth missing. So I come as late as possible.
DRAG:	Hiya, Frank!
MORG:	Oh – I'm still too early. Well, I guess I'll be –
AMECHE:	Now just a minute, Frank --

MORG:	Oh, hello, Dodger. I trust your health is a good deal better than your debauched appearance indicates.
AMECHE:	My health is just as debauched as your appearance.
MORG:	Remarkable how much the human body can stand. You're well along in years, aren't you, Mitchell?
AMECHE:	Moderately.
MORG:	It's amazing how your birthdate is practically impossible to guess. I'll wager you could pass for a man twice your age.
AMECHE:	You think so, huh?
MATT:	I don't think so. He doesn't look old enough to be my father.
MORG:	(GIVING HIM THE EYEBROWS) Oh. Is this hulking dollop your son, Mitchell?
AMECHE:	He's not my son.
MATT:	I'm not related to him at all.
MORG:	Well, it's a fortunate thing for both of you. What is it you want, my lad?
MATT:	Mr. Morgan, I just arrived from Idaho ---
MORG:	Well, I'll look at your potatoes later. Just leave ten pounds in my dressing room and I'll see that Mitchell gets the sack.
MATT:	I don't understand.
AMECHE:	Frank, what's the matter with you tonight?
MORG:	Well, I'm a little distrait. I had an awful wreck in my car on the way to the studio. Luckily I managed to crawl out unscathed.
AMECHE:	What did you do with the wreck?
MORG:	I left her sitting in the car. Never saw a woman with a temper like that in my life!
AMECHE:	I thought you had an accident.
MORG:	I did. While I was driving along I thought it might be a good idea to warm up my car – and my new-found friend – so I reached for the heater button and turned on the radio by mistake. Dodger, have you heard the foul entertainment they're foisting on the American public lately?
AMECHE:	What program did you hear?
MORG:	I don't know. Some awful comedian with a fake Austrian accent was palming himself off as a ski expert, and a horrible master of ceremonies named Meecher, or something, kept asking some stupid questions. There was a girl-singer, too, with a gravel-throated voice who bleated through a few off-key bars of "True." Then ---
LANG:	Gravel-throated singer!

MORG:	Well, you should -----Oh, hello, my dear!
LANG:	Well, hello. Aren't you the substitute cook at Barney's Beanery?
MORG:	Cook?
LANG:	I knew your face was familiar, but I couldn't place your pot. If you're so fond of the culinary art, why don't you visit my restaurant?
MORG:	What?
LANG:	You'll find my kitchen on La Brea Boulevard right in back of the Chinese Hand Laundry. Bring your own hands....pans! Two hours of cooking with me and I'll baste your bones, trim your fat and cook your goose. Goodnight, Mr. Morgan. (SHE GOES)
MORG:	What happened?
AMECHE:	Serves you right, Morgan. You've been embarrassing that poor girl for months by not recognizing her, and she finally paid you back.
MORG:	Well, who is she? Isn't she the Pin-Girl at the Sunset Bowling Alleys?
AMECHE:	You know very well who she is. She's Frances Langford, our featured singer.
MORG:	Oh, Frances Longfeet. Singers midgets. Yes.
MATT:	Mr. Morgan, can't I talk to you for a minute?
MORG:	I'm sorry, my boy – we buy all our vegetables at the Farmer's Market. Some other time.
AMECHE:	Frank – no market.
MATT:	I'm afraid I won't be around much longer, Mr. Morgan. I have to rush home and pack my bags.
MORG:	Well, be sure you put the large potatoes on top. Come back when you get your pushcart loaded.
MATT:	I have no pushcart.
AMECHE:	Stop making him a peddler! He's a friend of mine. I invited him here -- and he's leaving town tomorrow.
MORG:	Splendid! I'm always happy to see a friend of yours leave town. Where are you going, young man?
MATT:	I'm going to Sun Valley. I have an undying interest in skiing.
MORG:	Consider it dead, son. You're much too clumsy for the graceful sport. However, if you read up on the Morgan method for the downhill slide you'll have something to fall back on. Did you say you were going to Sun Valley?
AMECHE:	That's what he said.

MORG:	What a strange coincidence! It's been my custom to spend my weekends down there during the month of December and January. As a matter of fact, I was there last Sunday.
AMECHE:	Yes, we heard about that.
MORG:	Really? Well, I go down there more or less as a favor to the management. I've been teaching their instructors a new technique.
AMECHE:	Oh, brother.
MORG:	Most incompetent bunch of dubs I ever saw. Particularly the head instructor. Fellow by the name of Hatrack or Mattress or something.
MATT:	Toni Matt.
MORG:	That's him. They won't let him in the cocktail lounge since he tripped over an ice cube and broke his leg. Do you know him?
MATT:	I'm Toni Matt.
MORG:	Ohhhh....He's.....
AMECHE:	Yes, Morgan – he's Matt!
MORG:	He's Matt. Well, I'm a little sore myself. Why do you trap me into these things, Dodger! If you knew this was Matt why did you let me wipe my feet on him?
AMECHE:	Why don't you give up, Frank? We heard all about your falling on your face at Sun Valley.
MORG:	Well, I had an ill-fitting pair of skis and the bindings --
AMECHE:	Oh, stop it! You couldn't bellywhop over three feet of sherbet if you had a toboggan strapped to your nose.
MILLER:	I don't want to intrude, Don, but it seems to me Mr. Morgan deserves a little more respect.
MORG:	Well! What a pleasant interruption! You're that fat young clerk from Ralph's meatmarket. Pull up a chair and rest your hamburger.
MILLER:	Pardon?
MORG:	Now, now, you needn't try to hide those choice cuts of meat from me. I can see at a glance you've got a side of beef concealed in your pants.
MILLER:	Oh, Mr. Morgan, you're pulling my leg.
MORG:	Is that what it is? I thought it was a pot-roast.
AMECHE:	Cut it out, Frank. You know he's our announcer.
MORG:	He is? He doesn't look like that overgrown beanbelly, Marvin Miller.
MILLER:	That's me. I'm that overgrown beanbelly, Mr. Morgan.
MORG:	My apologies, sir. Allow me to introduce you to the world's champion skier. Mr. Pratfall, this is Mr. Beanbelly.

MILLER:	Mr. Pratfall.
MATT:	Mr. Beanbelly.
AMECHE:	What's going on here! Frank, why must you always make fun of Marvin's size. I like him!
MORG:	Well you can have him, I don't want him, he's too fat for me.
MILLER:	Mr. Morgan, I don't want to bother you ---
MORG:	Well, you do, you know.
MILLER:	I'm sorry, but I heard you discussing skiing and I've been addicted to the alpine sport for years. Just recently I've combined the Arlburg Method with my own system for skiing.
MORG:	(BORED) Mmmmmmm.
MILLER:	I've managed to get a Telemark and Gelandespring into my system but I can't get my feet to handle a Herringbone.
MORG:	Why don't you try eating with a knife and fork?
AMECHE:	Had enough, Marvin? I told you this faker doesn't know anything about skiing.
MORG:	Have a care, my pippy young squeak. It might interest you to know that the Morgans have excelled in Winter Sports for generations, beginning with my Grandfather Snowshoe Morgan, down to my Uncle Dogsled, and my Aunt Husky.
AMECHE:	Your Aunt Husky?
MORG:	A fuzzy old beast. Always snapped at my uncle when she was mushed.
MILLER:	What a wonderful family.
MATT:	Why didn't they teach you to ski, Mr. Morgan?
MORG:	Teach me! My dear man! I was born with skis on my feet, a rucksack on my back, and an alpenstock in my hand. There was no doctor in the village and I was delivered by a hardware salesman.
AMECHE:	What village was that, Morgan?
MORG:	It was the Swiss hamlet of Grundewaald. A little east of Untervesche, and forty miles from Schtunkwasser. Naturally, I spent most of my childhood frolicking at the bottom of the Jungfrau.
AMECHE:	That's for sure.
MORG:	By the time I was five I was traversing the Alps, rocketing over the great slopes with perfect volage, doing gelande-sprungs, christianias and telemarks with the speed of an antelope and the grace of a butterfly.
AMECHE:	Is that ski talk, Toni?
MATT:	It sure is.

MORG:	It is? I mean it is! Since we lived in very modest circumstances my equipment was pitiful – my skis were nothing but barrel staves strapped on my bare feet – and I'll never forget how overjoyed I was the day I got my hands on a pair of soft-skinned Italian beauts. Boots!
MILLER:	I knew you meant boots, Mr. Morgan.
MORG:	Oh, you did. Well, the boots gave me new confidence and I was determined to become the first man in history to ski down the Matterhorn.
MATT:	The slalom course.
MORG:	Of course. At that time I was not aware of the dangers that lay ahead, and had never heard of the terrible hairpin turn that became the graveyard for many an intrepid skier. The harrowing double return!
AMECHE:	Double return? What's that?
MORG:	A tight two-way stretch.
AMECHE:	I'll take a loose uplift.
MORG:	Lace edges?
AMECHE:	Just burlap!
MORG:	Well, try this on for si-------what are we talking about!
MILLER:	Please, Don! Go on, Mr. Morgan.
MORGAN:	No! I refuse to continue if this overweening young fop persists in making sport of me!
MATT:	Please don't stop, Mr. Morgan! I find you most interesting.
MORG:	All right, then. The day finally came when I felt confident enough to attempt to set a record on the Matterhorn – and the cheering spectators gave me heart as I stood poised at the top.
MILLER:	Uh-huh.
MORG:	As the starter's pistol rang out I began my hazardous descent -- my speed at times reaching a hundred miles an hour. I safely negotiated the double return – but imagine my horror when I saw straight in my path what looked to me like a chasm. A dark, yawning abyss!
AMECHE:	Was it yawning before you got there?
MORG:	I told you I won't continue unless you ---
MILLER:	You cut that out, Don! What was it, Mr. Morgan?
MORG:	Well, it wasn't a chasm at all. Somebody had spilled an enormous quantity of fountain pen fluid on the ice – where it froze solid.
AMECHE:	What of it?
MORG:	What of it? It's one thing to ski over frozen water – which is nothing but iced water -- but what is frozen ink?

AMECHE:	Iced ink.
MORG:	That's what everybody says, Dodger! So long – I'm gonna buy a frigidaire.
MUSIC:	MORGAN PLAYOFF
	(APPLAUSE)
	SECOND COMMERCIAL
MUSIC:	INTRO "SO FAR" DOWN UNDER
MILLER:	(OVER THEME) Frances Langford sings "So Far."
MUSIC:	ORCH AND LANGFORD......"SO FAR"
	(APPLAUSE)
CHORUS:	Treat yourself ... to Old Golds.
GROUP:	... if you want a treat instead of a treatment.
CHORUS:	Treat yourself ... to Old Golds.
GROUP:	... if you want a treat instead of a treatment
CHORUS:	Treat yourself ... to Old Golds!
MILLER:	There's only one way to find out if Old Golds are tastier, smoother, milder than any cigarette you know! And that is ... to smoke a pack of Old Golds. And then you'll know ... that you simply cannot match the quality of an Old Gold!
WOMAN:	Today's the day to find out about Old Golds!
MILLER:	Yes! Of course ... today ... discover the wonderful pleasures of smoking an Old Gold! Find out what it really means to smoke a cigarette that's tastier...smoother ... milder! Actually ... the quality of an Old Gold cannot be duplicated! Because no other cigarette in America has the quality traditions of an Old Gold. Listen ...
2ND ANNCR:	Nearly two hundred years of fine tobacco experience are behind every Old Gold you smoke. We're tobacco men ... not medicine men. Old Golds cure just one thing ... tobaccos ... the world's choice tobaccos ... to give you a milder smoke ... a better-tasting smoke!
WOMAN:	Today's the day to find out about Old Golds!
MILLER:	Yes, yes, yes! You owe it to your sweet pleasure's sake to get more smoking pleasure. So smoke a pack of Old Golds .... to-day! Because if you want a treat instead of a treatment ...
CHORUS:	Treat yourself ... to Old Golds.
GROUP:	.... if you want a treat instead of a treatment
CHORUS:	Treat yourself ... to Old Golds.
MILLER:	Now here are Don Ameche and Frances Langford as John and Blanche Bickerson in "The Honeymoon is Over."
THEME:	(SOFT AND PLAINTIVE)

60

MILLER:	The Bickersons have retired. Mrs. Bickerson writhes in sympathetic anguish as poor husband John, victim of progressive insomnia, or Thumper's disease, enters the critical stage during an acute attack of his chronic ailment. Listen.
DON:	(SNORES LUSTILY…WHINES…SNORES AND WHINES… BROKEN RHYTHM SNORE FOLLOWED BY A WHINE.)
LANG:	It's like sleeping with a buzz saw.
DON:	(SNORES AND GIGGLES…SNORES AND GIGGLES AGAIN)
LANG:	I'm dying and he's laughing.
DON:	(SNORES AND GIGGLES MERRILY)
LANG:	Oh, I can't stand it any more! John! John!
DON:	Mmm.
LANG:	Turn over on your side. Go on!
DON:	(A PROTESTING WHINE) Mmmmmmmm.
LANG:	John! Stop it!
DON:	Stop it, Blanche…wassamatter? What time is it? Wassamatter, Blanche?
LANG:	It's twenty to four and you haven't stopped that hideous snoring since nine o'clock. You promised you'd quit but I think you're making a deliberate campaign to keep me awake.
DON:	Campaign promise.
LANG:	None of my girl friends has a husband who draws all the cats in the neighborhood because he yowls like an old tom! Do we know anybody with such trouble? Do we?
DON:	Tom Dewey.
LANG:	Very funny. Oh, you're so funny, John Bickerson.
DON:	I'm not funny, Blanche – I'm sleepy.
LANG:	You're always sleepy. I wouldn't care if you slept thirty-six hours a day but I'm not going to stand for that snoring any longer.
DON:	It's just your imagination. I never snore and you know it.
LANG:	Never snore? The second day of our honeymoon I couldn't hear the Falls!
DON:	What are you beefing about? A lot of brides never even see 'em – not everybody goes to Niagara, you know.
LANG:	You better change your habits, John, or I'm warning you some day you'll wake up and find yourself sleeping in an empty bed.
DON:	What?
LANG:	You know what I mean. I'm not going to spend another night suffering through this kind of torture.

DON:	Oh, stop magnifying it. Maybe I do breathe a little heavy --
LANG:	You don't breathe. You giggle, you grunt, you whine and you rasp. How can I sleep?
DON:	Put your head under the covers.
LANG:	I did, but there's a hole in the blanket and your snores leak through.
DON:	Well, go sleep in the other room.
LANG:	You know very well I can't sleep in the other room. What about Clara and the baby?
DON:	Let 'em go to a hotel. What right has your broken down sister got to drag that kid of hers from New York and steal my bedroom? Why must I sleep in the kitchen?
LANG:	It's little enough to ask. Even if she wasn't my sister you should have more consideration for a mother with a poor little eight-day old infant.
DON:	Little! He's a monster! That kid weighs forty-one pounds – you told me so yourself!
LANG:	That's with his clothes on.
DON:	He only wears a diaper! There isn't another eight day old kid in the world who'd weigh forty-one pounds soaking wet!
LANG:	He's a perfectly healthy, normal child. He can't help it if he's big – his mother and father are big.
DON:	Big what?
LANG:	I think he's adorable. And if you'd only break down and be human you'd love him, too.
DON:	Ahhhhh.
LANG:	You're the most stubborn man in the world, John. I'm ashamed to tell Clara you won't even look at George.
DON:	Who's George?
LANG:	The baby.
DON:	George? Is that his name?
LANG:	Certainly. It's a wonderful name. Sounds so mannish.
DON:	Nobody calls a baby George! That's for Pullman porters. What kind of a baby is called George? I never heard of such a thing!
LANG:	Well, I like it. And I'm going out tomorrow and buy him a whole layette.
DON:	What for?
LANG:	Because Clara can't afford it. He's my nephew and it doesn't look right for the child to sleep in your shirt.
DON:	My shirt! Is that elephant sleeping in my shirt? It's the only clean shirt I've got! How do you expect me to wear it in the morning?

LANG:	George is very neat – he won't wrinkle it.
DON:	I swear, Blanche, I don't know why I let you push me around like this. I'm a good husband and I work hard for a living – I don't ask for any luxuries – and you sacrifice my last bit of comfort for your sister!
LANG:	Well, sisters are thicker than husbands.
DON:	You can say that again! Nobody's thicker than your sister Clara! She's got as much shape as a boxcar! Why doesn't her husband make her go on a diet?
LANG:	Because he likes her the way she is – in one big lump.
DON:	Well, I'm telling you now, Blanche. This is the last night I sleep in the kitchen.
LANG:	Are you threatening me?
DON:	I'm not threatening you. Just put out the light and lemme go to sleep.
LANG:	No. I want to talk to you.
DON:	I don't feel like talking.
LANG:	You mean you don't feel like talking to me. But I'll bet the minute you get down to the office you'll jabber your head off. I'd give anything to know what you men talk about.
DON:	The same as you women.
LANG:	Oh, you horrible things! And I thought it was all business.
DON:	It is business.
LANG:	No wonder you don't get anywhere. Everybody makes a good salary except you. Why don't you get a paying job?
DON:	Now, don't go maligning my job! I got a fifteen dollar raise only last week.
LANG:	Well, it isn't enough. The minute I ask you for an extra few dollars you jump down my throat.
DON:	Listen, last month you went to the doctor three times, you got fitted for glasses, you had two teeth pulled – seventy dollars for your own private pleasure! You think I'm made of money?
LANG:	You're the one who wastes it. You throw it away on silly things.
DON:	What silly things?
LANG:	Didn't you spend twenty-five dollars on that fire-extinguisher?
DON:	Certainly.
LANG:	Well, you've had it a whole year and never used it once!
DON:	I'll set fire to the house in the morning. Goodnight.
LANG:	If you had any ambition we'd have had a home of our own long ago – and not have to live in these two skimpy rooms.

DON:	Mmm.
LANG:	You'd better get yourself a new set of friends, John – instead of hanging around with those shiftless people at your office. How would you like it if I associated with my inferiors?
DON:	I don't know – I never met any of your inferiors.
LANG:	That's a very nice thing to say, John.
DON:	Well, I'm sleepy.
LANG:	If you'd have spoken to me like that while we were engaged I never would have married you.
DON:	Now she tells me.
LANG:	Believe me. I'm finding out plenty. The things you told me when I first met you. Such promises! Before we were married you told me you were well-off.
DON:	I was, but I didn't know it. Blanche, why don't you let me get some sleep? Whether you like my job or not I still have to get up in the morning and go to work.
LANG:	Well, you've got to promise to get acquainted with some nice people. You should belong to a lodge, or something. Why don't you join the Elks, John?
DON:	I'll join next week.
LANG:	You say it, but you won't do it. Why don't you join now?
DON:	What?
LANG:	Go on – get up and join the Elks.
DON:	Are you out of your mind! It's almost four o'clock in the morning!
LANG:	You'd join the Elks soon enough if Gloria Gooseby asked you to.
DON:	Now, don't start with Gloria Gooseby!
LANG:	If you were married to her she'd scream so loud you'd give up in a hurry.
DON:	She always screams and I never give up! I mean I hate Gloria Gooseby and I forbid you to mention her name again! Do you hear me!
LANG:	Keep quiet – you'll wake the baby.
DON:	What do I care!
LANG:	You'll only have to rock him to sleep.
DON:	I'll be glad to – where's a rock?
LANG:	John!
DON:	Well, stop driving me crazy with that Gooseby dame! And why do I have to put the kid to sleep if he wakes up? Where's his mother?

LANG:	She couldn't stand your snoring so she went to an all-night movie. Is it four o'clock yet?
DON:	It's five after.
LANG:	The baby has to be fed.
DON:	Well, what are you looking at me for?
LANG:	Get up and fix his formula. Everything's on the stove. Just put the light under the presto cooker.
DON:	I don't know how to feed him. Let him come in and eat it out of the pot.
LANG:	He doesn't eat – he drinks. And he uses an old-fashioned nursing bottle. Fix it, John.
DON:	Okay – where's the bourbon?
LANG:	Bourbon? What do you want the bourbon for?
DON:	To make the old-fashioned.
LANG:	What's the matter with you, John? How can you give a child bourbon? It's only eight days old!
DON:	It is not! It's over six months and aged in the wood! Look at the label.
LANG:	I'm talking about the baby.
DON:	Oh. Well, what do you want me to do, Blanche?
LANG:	Just light the stove and let the formula get warm. You don't even have to get off the cot. Just reach behind you.
DON:	Okay. You better watch it – I gotta get some sleep. Goodnight.
LANG:	John.
DON:	Mmm
LANG:	I wish you'd go in and look at George. He's really very sweet.
DON:	Mmm.
LANG:	You couldn't possibly be angry, or short-tempered if you spent a little time with him.
DON:	Tomorrow.
LANG:	Maybe that's why we're not too happy, John.
DON:	We're happy.
LANG:	No, there's something missing. All of our friends have such fun with their children, I mean. The Goosebys have a baby – the Shaws have a baby – and now Clara has a baby. Everybody has a baby.
DON:	Blanche, it's four o'clock in the morning. Can't you tell me about it tomorrow?
LANG:	Oh, don't be so irritable. There was a time when you could listen to me all night.

DON:	I'm still doing it.
LANG:	Well, it's your own fault. I wouldn't talk so much if you were a little more attentive to me. You never take me out dancing, or to a show – or even to a restaurant for dinner.
DON:	Ohhh.
LANG:	Before we were married you used to take me to nightclubs and buy me champagne and caviar. Why don't you do it any more?
DON:	No good.
LANG:	Why?
DON:	It's like buying oats for a dead horse.
LANG:	How can you talk like that? But it doesn't surprise me the way you've been acting lately. You probably can't stand the sight of me. It's true, isn't it?
DON:	I wouldn't say that.
LANG:	Why not, John?
DON:	I'd be up for the rest of the night.
LANG:	I know how you feel just the same. You don't love me.
DON:	Blanche, I do!
LANG:	You do not! You don't love me half as much as you used to.
DON:	Blanche, I do!
LANG:	Then say it!
DON:	I love you half as much as I used to! Now will you let me sleep?
LANG:	John, if I'm to blame because we fight so much I wish you'd tell me.
DON:	You're not to blame.
LANG:	They why don't we get along? You used to be so crazy about me. You used to call me the light of your life.
DON:	Put the light out.
LANG:	No! I'm not going to let you sleep until you come in and look at the baby. That'll change your attitude.
DON:	Well, I guess I have no alternative. Come on. (THEY GET OUT OF BED) Do you want me to take his grub in?
LANG:	Yes. Turn off the stove. I'll fix his bottle...(DOOR OPENS)
DON:	Where is he?
LANG:	Shhh. Right there in the crib. Don't let the light shine on him. Isn't he a doll?
DON:	He looks just like Clara. Turn him over and let me see his face.
LANG:	That is his face.
DON:	Oh.

LANG:	Look at him lying there like a little cherub. So innocent in sleep. Soon he'll be walking and in a little while he'll begin to talk – he'll say such cute things... Then his first day at school – he'll be so scared -- maybe he'll be a wonderful scholar or a great athlete. He'll grow into manhood – handsome and strong. He might be a doctor, or a lawyer -- he might even grow up to be the president of the United States. It makes you wonder, doesn't it?
DON:	(ABSENTLY) Uh-huh.
LANG:	What are you thinking of, darling?
DON:	How can they make a crib like that for three-ninety-eight?
LANG:	Goodnight, John.
DON:	Goodnight, Blanche.
MUSIC:	THEME
	(APPLAUSE)

CLOSING

AMECHE:	Well, that puts the lid on the seventeenth program of our new series for Old Gold Cigarettes, written and directed by Phil Rapp and produced by Mann Holiner. And, say, did you know that that snappy Marine Corps uniform is being worn by civilians these days -- civilians who are members of the new Citizen Marine Corps. Their membership is purely voluntary. They share the pride and prestige of the nation's proudest military organization. They benefit themselves and help guarantee peace for America by being in the Citizen Marine Corps. And, they can earn, while they learn, as civilian Marines. Any Marine Corps activity center has the details. Well, we hope you'll be on hand next Friday night for Frank Morgan, Frances Langford, and Carmen Dragon and the orchestra. This is Don Ameche saying goodnight and good smoking with Old Golds!
	(APPLAUSE)
MUSIC:	THEME
MILLER:	Frank Morgan appeared by arrangement with Metro-Goldwyn-Mayer, producers of Sinclair Lewis' "Cass Timberlane" starring Spencer Tracy, Lana Turner, and Zachary Scott.

CLOSING

MILLER:	Remember next Friday at Old Gold Time it'll be Frank Morgan, Don Ameche, and Frances Langford with Carmen Dragon and his orchestra brought to you by P. Lorillard

Company...a famous name in tobaccos for nearly two hundred years...makers of Old Gold Cigarettes...the treasure of 'em all...and listen... if you want a treat instead of a treatment...treat yourself to Old Golds. Buy 'em at your tobacco counters...Buy them in the cigarette vending machines...Don't forget every Friday night on C.B.S. it's "Fun For The Family." Stay tuned now for "The Adventures of Ozzie and Harriet" which follow immediately over most of those stations. This is Marvin Miller speaking.
(APPLAUSE)
THIS IS....CBS....THE COLUMBIA BROADCASTING SYSTEM.

The Old Gold Show
*Don Ameche, Frances
Langford and Frank
Morgan.*

As a rule, the Bickersons don't go out much. Mostly they keep to their one-bedroom flat, either fighting in the bedroom or sleeping in the kitchen. Occasionally they'll venture out to a wedding or the doctor's office. This time, the lovebirds are just coming back from a late movie.

The movie: *Sleep My Love*, from 1948, which starred Don Ameche as the conniving husband of Claudette Colbert. Another in-joke to keep an eye out for in this script is the mention of Jon Hall, who happened to be Frances Langford's husband at the time.

THE OLD GOLD SHOW

Station CBS   Date 2-27-48   Time 6:00-6:30 PM   Studio   El Capita

MUSIC:	(ON CUE) OPENING FANFARE
MILLER:	(ON CUE) From Hollywood.
CHORUS:	(ON CUE) It's Old Gold Cigarette Time.
	If you want a treat instead of a treatment
	Smoke Old Golds.
	We're tobacco men, not medicine men.
	Pleasure is what we pack,
	Oh, Old Gold cures Just one thing
	The world's best tobacco!
	So, if you want a treat instead of a treatment
	Smoke, smoke, smoke, smoke – Smoke Old Gold.
	(PAUSE)
MARVIN:	The treasure of 'em all, gives the most pleasure of 'em all.
MUSIC:	THEME …. (ESTABLISH AND FADE UNDER FOLLOWING)
MILLER:	This is Marvin Miller, Ladies and Gentlemen, speaking for the makers of Old Gold Cigarettes who are pleased to present the twenty-third in a series of new programs with Carmen Dragon and his orchestra, starring Metro-Goldwyn-Mayer's lovable Frank Morgan, the genial Don Ameche and charming Frances Langford, who sings –

MUSIC:	LANGFORD AND ORCH......"THE STARS WILL REMEMBER"
	(APPLAUSE)
	FIRST COMMERCIAL
MILLER:	We're tobacco men.......not medicine men. Old Gold cures just one thing...the world's best tobacco. And the one thing we sell is ...tobacco pleasure...pleasure...as real and solid as the Old Gold you put between your lips. After all...nearly two hundred years of quality tobacco experience are behind every Old Gold you smoke. And friends...you simply cannot match that quality tradition in any other cigarette. Nor can you match the finer taste...the smooth, mild pleasure of an Old Gold.
CHORUS:	So....if you want a treat instead of a treatment
	If you want a treat instead of a treatment
	Smoke, smoke, smoke, smoke
	Smoke...Old Golds.
MILLER:	Now here is your host for the evening, Don Ameche.
	(APPLAUSE)
AMECHE:	Thank you, ladies and gentlemen, and good evening. Last night after four days of record-breaking attendance ---
DRAG:	Pardon, Don.
MILLER:	Carmen, why must you keep interrupting Don week after week?
DRAG:	Just trying to keep the show moving, Marvin. It gets awful tiresome listening to Don wade through a long introduction for some guest who doesn't mean anything. By the way, who's the guest, Don?
AMECHE:	Nobody.
DRAG:	See what I mean?
AMECHE:	What do you mean?
LANG:	Carmen, if you've got a better way of opening the program I'm sure Don would like to hear it.
DRAG:	Well, I just thought that since this is a comedy program we ought to have a joke in it. Right, sister?
LANG:	Right, brother.
DRAG:	Fine. Don, do you mind if I crack a joke I made up out of my own head?
AMECHE:	I don't care if you crack your head.
DRAG:	Let's just watch your temper or you'll be looking for a new boy, boy.
AMECHE:	Carmen, what are you talking about?

DRAG:	Never mind, boy. You know what I mean, boy.
AMECHE:	No, I don't, boy.
MILLER:	Please, Carmen, will you tell us the joke?
DRAG:	Okay. A bachelor skunk married a widow skunk and they're expecting a little stinker in the spring. Anything?
AMECHE:	Nothing.
DRAG:	All right, smart guy, what were you going to say before I interrupted you?
AMECHE:	Simply that the famous Freedom train, containing the greatest collection of historical documents ever assembled in America, left Los Angeles last night.
DRAG:	Well, what's so funny about that?
LANG:	It's not supposed to be funny, Carmen. You know about the Freedom train, don't you?
DRAG:	Sure. I took the wife and kids to see it yesterday.
MILLER:	Did the wife like it?
DRAG:	Yare, she never saw a streamliner before. The kids liked it, too. The little one is only two years old, but he was crazy about the Declaration of Independence. We had to stop him from eating it.
AMECHE:	Smart kid, the little one.
DRAG:	Yare, but he's awful stubborn. Just before we got thrown off the train he locked himself in the washroom and wouldn't come out. The conductor was pounding on the window, but that was locked, too.
LANG:	Well, what happened to him?
DRAG:	Oh, we found him later walking around under the train. Still can't figure out how he got there.
AMECHE:	I can see the whole project was wasted on you, Carmen. Didn't you get to see any of the documents at all?
DRAG:	Sure. I read that letter that Columbus wrote to Isabella. Pretty hot stuff, boy.
AMECHE:	Hot stuff? That letter is priceless. It was written in sheer desperation to Isabella, and I'd give anything to have it.
MORG:	(COMING ON) You would? Did your wife find out about it, Dodger?
AMECHE:	Frank! (APPLAUSE)
MORG:	I once wrote a letter to a fan dancer who turned out to be a shakedown artist.
AMECHE:	What?

MORG:	I've stopped paying – but she's still shaking. How'd you get mixed up with this expensive dame, Dodger.
AMECHE:	No dame. We're talking about the Freedom train.
MORG:	Oh, free dame. No talking. Well, what about it?
LANG:	Nothing, Mr. Morgan. Don simply mentioned seeing a copy of the letter Columbus wrote to Queen Isabella.
MORG:	Well, if he'd like to see the original, I ----- Oh, hello, Miss Langford.
AMECHE:	Miss Langford?
LANG:	Hello.
MORG:	Before we go any further, I'd like to apologize for embarrassing you in front of your husband last week. I had no idea you were married, and I have a great deal of respect for Jon Hall. Is he here tonight?
LANG:	No.
MORG:	Well, forget the whole thing. What are you doing after the broadcast, my dear?
LANG:	Well, my husband ---
MORG:	Never mind your husband. What he doesn't know won't hurt me. Where can I meet you, darling?
LANG:	Well, I ---
MORG:	Make it at my office at eight o'clock – I'm not there just leave your name with the bartender.
AMECHE:	Why don't you stop that, Frank? You're only embarrassing Frances.
LANG:	I think I'd better run along. Goodnight.
MORG:	(LOOKING AFTER HER) What a beautiful creature! I should be making those jungle pictures with her instead of her husband.
AMECHE:	Jungle pictures?
MORG:	She's such a cute little coconut and I love to monkey around.
AMECHE:	Frank, haven't you got a serious thought in your head?
MORG:	Why?
AMECHE:	Aren't you interested in the Freedom Train? The American Heritage? Wouldn't you like to see those documents?
MORG:	My dear boy, I'll see them soon enough when they're returned to my private collection. No use me running ---
AMECHE:	<u>Your</u> private collection? Are you trying to give off that all those priceless documents belong to you?
MORG:	Every single one of them. The Morgan Collection is loaded with rare items worth a king's ransom.

AMECHE:	What are you loaded with?
MORG:	King's Ransom. Over a period of years I've collected every important historical document from the Constitution to Lincoln's Gettysburg Address and Betsy Ross's phone number.
AMECHE:	What!
MORG:	It was crocheted on the bottom of the flag.
AMECHE:	Betsy Ross's phone number?
MORG:	A very rare item. I picked it up ---
AMECHE:	But they didn't have telephones in those days.
MORG:	That's what makes it so rare. When I first started collecting –
AMECHE:	What's all this talk about collecting? You couldn't collect a hatful of bone meal from a turnip field with a hopped-up vacuum cleaner.
MORG:	How would you like to see the original letter Columbus wrote to Queen Isabella?
AMECHE:	I saw it on the Freedom Train.
MORG:	That was only a copy. I happen to have the original in my pocket.
AMECHE:	Let's see it.
MORG:	It's been insured by Lloyd's of London for over five million ---
AMECHE:	Where's the letter?
MORG:	Right here. Handle it carefully, my boy.
AMECHE:	Let's see. (READS) Dear poopsie – I haven't heard a penny from you since last ---
MORG:	Wrong letter! Let me have that, Dodger. That's a memo from the Trustworthy Finance Company. (GIGGLES) I wish she was a little more trustworthy.
AMECHE:	I wish you were, too. Morgan, why don't you stop wasting your time? Only a fat-headed dope from the backwoods would believe what you're saying.
MILLER:	I don't like to intrude, Don – but I believe Mr. Morgan.
MORG:	Well, what a pleasant interruption. It's that fat-headed dope from the backwoods. Pull up some wood and rest your fat-back, dopey.
MILLER:	Pardon?
MORG:	Merely a figure of speech – but you've got the figure for it, my boy.
MILLER:	Mr. Morgan, I don't want to bother you ---
MORG:	Well, you do, you know.
MILLER:	I'm sorry, but I heard you discussing your collection and I'm a dilettante myself. Mostly American Indian hieroglyphics and skins.

74

MORG:	(BORED) Mmm.
MILLER:	I've got a large accumulation of hide that goes way back.
MORG:	It's beginning to bulge in the front, too.
MILLER:	You're joking, of course ---
AMECHE:	Of course.
MORG:	Of course.
MILLER:	Of course. I'd like your advice on an Indian finger painting about four hundred years old. I'm not sure whether it's the work of a Cherokee from the Great Lakes or a Creek from the upper West.
MORG:	Er – up the creek. Cherry coke.
AMECHE:	What are you asking him for, Marvin? He doesn't know anything about finger painting or any other kind of painting!
MORG:	Nonsense! The Morgan's have been artists for generations, beginning with my grandfather, Smock Morgan, down to my Uncle Watercolor and my Aunt Canvas.
AMECHE:	Your Aunt Canvas!
MORG:	A blank old square. Always stretched out on the easel when she was oiled.
MILLER:	What a wonderful family.
AMECHE:	All of a sudden he's a painter!
MORG:	Under their tutelage I became known as the greatest draughtsman since Davinci, the finest master of the palette knife since Rubens – and unsurpassed with charcoal.
AMECHE:	How were you with the brushes?
MORG:	The best man Fuller ever had.
AMECHE:	Fuller is right.
MORG:	Oh, well – if he's gonna ---
MILLER:	Cut that out, Don... Go on, Mr. Morgan – tell us about your career as a painter.
MORG:	I'll never forget my first commission. I was struggling in a garret on the Left Bank, when I received fifty thousand francs to paint a portrait of the lovely Countess de la Bourge.
AMECHE:	Know her well.
MORG:	This beautiful woman came to my tiny studio every day for three months, and I caught her in a variety of charming poses – my brushes flying over the canvas with lightning. After that I bought some paint.
AMECHE:	Well, what were you doing for three months, Morgan?
MORG:	Looking for the right angle. It finally came – and before the portrait was even completed, the Countess fell madly in love with me.

MILLER:	What kind of technique did you use?
MORG:	Well, I started by telling her I was lonely, and --- oh! You mean painting technique! My method was to use contrasting colors, dark to produce light and vice versa.
AMECHE:	How'd you do that?
MORG:	Very simple. A little number, a touch of ochre, a few drops of burnt sienna ---
AMECHE:	A jigger of gin ---
MORG:	A dash of Angosture – and pour into a ten ounce glass. Finest drink since – you stop that, Dodger!
MILLER:	Yes. What happened to the countess, Mr. Morgan?
MORG:	I'd rather not discuss it. Suffice it to say that after that first commission, things broke badly for me.
AMECHE:	Serves you right! I'll bet you made overtures to all your models!
MORG:	I resent that, Dodger! I had three models on my very next picture, and I never even kissed them!
AMECHE:	Who were they?
MORG:	An apple and two bananas! It was a brilliant still life, but I could never sell it. In despair I turned to sculpture, and for the first two years I worked in every medium, including marble, granite and cherry wood which was always finished in white.
AMECHE:	Plastered?
MORG:	Most of the time – but my spirits were low. Inevitably, I wound up making a bust of myself. (That whole paragraph has a double meaning).
AMECHE:	I only got one of them.
MILLER:	Never mind, Mr. Morgan. Did you make any famous statues?
MORG:	What a question! Surely you've heard of the famous bronze "Mercury in Flight!"
MILLER:	Oh, sure!
MORG:	Oh, sure, he says. Well, I ---
AMECHE:	The bronze Mercury was done by Gionanni de Bologna, and it reposes in the Uffize in Italy!
MORG:	Oh, Bronze baloney...Uffizi...well, there's the famous couple in alabaster – "Le Baiser" or "The Kiss" that I ---
AMECHE:	That you never even saw! That's Rodin's greatest piece of sculpture outside of The Thinker.
MORG:	Er – Thinker...Think, think, think. I wish I could. Dodger, are you familiar with heroic sculpture on mountain sides?
AMECHE:	Well, in Washington there's ---

MORG:	In Australia?
AMECHE:	No.
MORG:	Well, that's where I did my greatest work! The entire history of the Antipodes carved on the side of Mount Adelaide.
MILLER:	Is that a cliff?
MORG:	No, it's just a bluff. The mouth of the principal figure took four days to carve and ---
AMECHE:	How big was the mouth?
MORG:	It compared favorably with yours, Dodger! To give you a rough idea of the size of the head, each tooth was a foot, each foot was ten yards, and I had my office in his left ear.
AMECHE:	Cozy spot.
MORG:	To make the figure realistic I used hundreds of pounds of cotton for the eyebrows ---
AMECHE:	Cotton.
MORG:	Yes. Constant battering wind hampered my work on top of the mountain, and in order to facilitate my efforts I was forced to lash myself to a couple of heavy babes. Bales!
MILLER:	I knew you meant bales, Mr. Morgan.
MORG:	Did you really! Well, the most startling feature of my masterpiece was the realism of the hair. They insisted on perfect detail – and they got it.
AMECHE:	The cotton again.
MORG:	Oh no! I scoured the vast sheep lands of Australia until I had corralled fifty thousand young sheep.
AMECHE:	Young sheep?
MORG:	Yes. With my own hands I sheared the wool from their bodies, fashioned it into a huge wig, and spent nine months with secret formulas dying it black!
AMECHE:	Well, what of it?
MORG:	What of it? Aside from being a great sculptor it proves that I'm the world's biggest lamb dyer! So long, fellows, I gotta buy a chisel.
MUSIC:	MORGAN PLAYOFF (APPLAUSE) SECOND COMMERCIAL
MUSIC:	INTRO "THE MAN I LOVE."
MILLER:	(OVER THEME) Frances Langford sings "The Man I Love."
MUSIC:	ORCH AND LANGFORD...."The Man I Love" (APPLAUSE)
CHORUS:	If you want a treat instead of a treatment Smoke Old Golds.

If you want a treat instead of a treatment
Smoke Old Golds.

MILLER: I think there's much wisdom in that little chorus. Yes ... give yourself a treat – in the cigarette that can't be matched for smooth mildness and wonderful taste, Old Gold. Yes – Old Gold – the treasure of 'em all .. with a quality tobacco tradition unmatched by any other cigarette. You know – nearly two hundred years of fine tobacco experience and knowledge are in back of Old Golds – helping us bring you, in every Old Gold, the ripest, mellowest, best-tasting tobacco a cigarette can hold. That's something real ... something you taste and enjoy when you smoke an Old Gold. And that's the whole point. Listen –

2ND ANNCR: We're tobacco men – not medicine men. Old Gold cures just one thing ... the world's best tobacco.

MILLER: That's right. Fine, choice, ripe tobaccos – that make Old Gold so much smoother and mellower, so much tastier and more pleasing. Tonight or tomorrow morning, get a pack of Old Golds. Then, as you smoke them, compare the downright enjoyment an Old Gold gives you with anything else you ever smoked. Do – just – exactly – that, won't you?

CHORUS: So ... if you want a treat instead of a treatment
If you want a treat instead of a treatment
Smoke, smoke, smoke, smoke
Smoke, Old Golds.

MILLER: Now here are Don Ameche and Frances Langford as John and Blanche Bickerson in "The Honeymoon is Over!"

THEME: (SOFT AND PLAINTIVE)

MILLER: It is a little past midnight and the Bickersons are just returning from a late movie. Poor husband John, who suffers from cinephobia, or a morbid dread of talkies – mainly because they interfere with his sleep – drags his weary feet up the stairs to the Bickerson apartment as the wide-awake and stimulated Blanche follows. Listen.
SOUND: FOOTSTEPS

LANG: (OVER FOOTSTEPS) Never been so humiliated in my life! Once a year you take me to a movie and you had to start snoring the minute you sat down!

DON: Wasn't snoring.

LANG: Not much! You snored so loud you blew the hat off a woman five rows away.

78

DON:	Lemme sleep, willya, Blanche?
LANG:	Sleep? What's the matter with you, John? We're not in bed – we're walking up the stairs!
DON:	Oh, I'm dead. Should have gone right to bed after work.
LANG:	I don't see why you're complaining anyway. You slept all thru the picture.
DON:	What picture?
LANG:	Sleep My Love.
DON:	Okay – Goodnight darling. (NO FOOTSTEPS)
LANG:	John! Stop undressing in the hall! No man can possibly be as tired as you make yourself out to be!
DON:	I am. Honest, Blanche. How much further we got to go?
LANG:	It's the next landing. Come on, get up!
DON:	Okay.
	SOUND: FOOTSTEPS
LANG:	Just once I'd like to be able to sit thru a whole picture without having you embarrass me. I was dying to see the finish of this one – it was such an exciting mystery.
DON:	Mmm.
LANG:	Now I'll never find out if the man killed the woman.
DON:	Were they married?
LANG:	Certainly.
DON:	He killed her. (NO FOOTSTEPS) Open the door – I can't stay awake another minute.
LANG:	I didn't take a key. I left mine on the dresser. Where's your key?
DON:	I haven't got a key.
LANG:	You have, too. I gave you one on your last birthday.
DON:	Oh, (SEARCHES HIMSELF) Hmm. That's funny....Oh, brother – I can't find it.
LANG:	Did you look in your change pocket?
DON:	Yeah.
LANG:	How about your pants pocket?
DON:	It's not there. It's not in my breast pocket --- my hip pocket – let's see. Oh, dear. Blanche, I can't find the key!
LANG:	Have you looked everywhere?
DON:	Everywhere except my bourbon pocket.
LANG:	Bourbon pocket!
DON:	In my coat. That's the only place I haven't looked.
LANG:	Well, why don't you look in your coat?
DON:	I'm afraid.

LANG:	What are you afraid of?
DON:	If it isn't there I'll drop dead!
LANG:	Oh, let me look, you silly thing. Stand up straight!
DON:	Is it there?
LANG:	Sure it is – here.
DON:	That's a corkscrew! Must have fell out of my wallet.
LANG:	Well, don't stand there! Try and pick the lock with it.
DON:	Oh, you can't pick the lock. Go down and wake up the janitor – he's got a pass-key.
LANG:	It's almost one o'clock in the morning. I wouldn't wake the man up at this hour.
DON:	You never think of the hour when you wake me up.
LANG:	Well, you're my husband.
DON:	I wish I was the janitor.
LANG:	Well, what are we going to do? We can't stand here for the rest of night. John!
DON:	Mmm.
LANG:	Stop dozing off like that! There must be some way to open the door! Why don't you use your head?
DON:	Won't fit in the keyhole. Goodnight, Blanche.
LANG:	How can you sleep standing up? If you ever move away from that wall you'll fall flat on your face.
DON:	Can't fall.
LANG:	Why not?
DON:	I got my suspenders hooked over the light bracket.
LANG:	Stop hanging there like a sack of wash! Why don't you do something, John? Why don't you call a locksmith, John?
	SOUND: DOOR OPENS
MAN:	(SLEEPY AND ANGRY) Why don't you hire a hall, John?
	SOUND: DOOR CLOSES
LANG:	Who was that?
DON:	John Hall.
LANG:	You see what you've done! You've awakened all the neighbors. Now, you listen to me, John Bickerson – pull yourself together and start thinking how we can get into the apartment.
DON:	I'm thinking.
LANG:	You're sleeping! You get right over to that door and see if you can't break it down quietly. Go on!
DON:	Okay. (TAKES TWO STEPS....THEN A TERRIFIC THUD AS HE FLIES BACK AGAINST THE WALL) Owwwwwwwww!

LANG:	What happened?
DON:	I forgot to unhook my suspenders. Ohhh, my back. Get me off of here, Blanche.
LANG:	Serves you right. Bend your head a little. There.
DON:	Thanks. Now, let's see. Wonder how strong this lock is. (TRIES IT AND THE DOOR OPENS) Well, I'll be -------
LANG:	It was open all the time. (DOOR CLOSES) I don't remember leaving the door open. You must have done it.
DON:	Okay, I done it. Just let me get to bed.
SOUND:	A SHOE DROPS
LANG:	Well, don't throw your things on the floor. Why don't you hang your clothes in the closet? I'll bet there isn't another man in the world who's as careless as you are.
DON:	Mmm.
LANG:	No wonder you have to buy a new suit every two months.
DON:	New suit! I've only got one measly suit to my name!
LANG:	How can you say that! What about your blue suit – and your grey suit, and your brown suit!
DON:	That's it – on the floor.
LANG:	What are you talking about?
DON:	It's the same one – I keep on painting it. I've had it dyed so often I look like an Easter egg when it rains. I'm the only guy in town who's got a second-hand clothes man for a tailor.
LANG:	Oh, don't be so funny!
DON:	I'm not funny – I'm sleepy. Put out the light, Blanche.
LANG:	You're always crying poverty and your clothes are as new as anybody's. If you didn't throw them on the floor every night they'd last longer.
DON:	I take better care of my clothes than you do!
LANG:	You do not! Look at your pants – rolled up in a ball. How do you expect them to keep their shape?
DON:	I'll have 'em rebagged in the morning.
LANG:	You get out of that bed and pick your things up!
DON:	Please, Blanche.
LANG:	Come on – get up, get up, get up!
DON:	(A PROTESTING WHINE) Mmmmmmmmmmmm!
LANG:	I won't have you turning this room into a pigsty! Your hat's on the chandelier – your shirt's on the night-table – your shoes are sitting on the radio. Where are your socks?
DON:	Standing in the corner. I told you a hundred times not to starch the bottoms.

LANG:	Well, have some new soles put on your shoes. Now, come on – get out of bed and pick up your things, John. I mean it.
DON:	Okay. Can't get a minute's rest. Work like a horse all day and then have to clean the house at night. Here – what do you want me to do with it?
LANG:	Hang it up. Now, take all your soiled linen and put it in the laundry basket. Your shirt, too, John.
DON:	All right – all right.
LANG:	Well, don't roll up that dirty stuff in those lace curtains!
DON:	What lace curtains – these are my shorts! All right – now everything's picked up. Is there anything else?
LANG:	No.
DON:	Are you sure you don't want the windows washed – or the closet painted? It's only one o'clock in the morning, Blanche – I got nothing to do until seven!
LANG:	Don't be so sarcastic. It doesn't kill a man to help with the housework. Every husband does it.
DON:	(GETS INTO BED) Ahhhh!
LANG:	Louise Shaw is the lucky one, believe me. She's got a real husband.
DON:	Oh, sure.
LANG:	He has the house clean as a pin by the time she gets home from work.
DON:	Who has?
LANG:	Mel Shaw.
DON:	Mel Shaw is a bum!
LANG:	Well, he's a neat bum! That's more than I can say for you!
DON:	Blanche, why don't you put out the lights so I can sleep?
LANG:	Some day you'll be more considerate of me and then we'll get along a lot better. I'd die from surprise if you ever offered to make the bed with me – or polish the furniture with me. I've been waiting for six years for you to mop up the floor with me.
DON:	Don't put ideas in my head.
LANG:	Are you threatening me, John Bickerson?
DON:	I'm not threatening you. Didn't I dry the dishes tonight?
LANG:	You cracked half of them.
DON:	Well, the oven was too hot. Goodnight.
LANG:	I knew I never should have left you alone in the kitchen. I'll bet you didn't clean out the breadbox?
DON:	I cleaned out the breadbox.
LANG:	Did you cover the birdcage?

DON:	Mmm.
LANG:	What about the cat?
DON:	Cat's sleeping.
LANG:	Where?
DON:	In the birdcage.
LANG:	In the birdcage! Where's the canary?
DON:	In the cat.
LANG:	John Bickerson!
DON:	Oh, the canary's all right! And I took care of the cat!
LANG:	Did you brush his coat?
DON:	I brushed his coat, I pressed his pants, I washed his drawers and I hung him up to dry! I hate that cat!
LANG:	It's a pretty fair indication of a man's character when he doesn't like animals. I love that cat!
DON:	Good.
LANG:	I wish he was married and had twelve kittens!
DON:	Mmm.
LANG:	Why don't you introduce him to some nice tabby, John?
DON:	I'll introduce him in the morning.
LANG:	You say it but you won't do it. Do it now.
DON:	What!
LANG:	Go on – get up and find the cat a wife!
DON:	Blanche, what do you want from me? Why don't you come to bed? You're all undressed, you've got your hair in crimpers, you've creamed your elbows and you've rolled your neck!
LANG:	I haven't finished my face yet.
DON:	Finish it in the morning.
LANG:	Oh, don't be so impatient. I have to let this greasepack set for ten minutes otherwise it has no effect.
DON:	Greasepack?
LANG:	It's a new cream and it cost me fifteen dollars. It's guaranteed to make you beautiful in five treatments. This is my fourth.
DON:	It is, huh?
LANG:	Yes.
DON:	Boy, that fifth treatment must be a pip.
LANG:	Oh, that's too bad about you, John Bickerson. Maybe your other girl friends don't have to use face cream.
DON:	Oh, put out the lights.
LANG:	I notice you never complain about Gloria Gooseby's make-up?!
DON:	Now don't start with Gloria Gooseby.

LANG:	She has to struggle out of twelve pounds of cosmetics before you can even get close to her!
DON:	I always get close to her and she never struggles! I mean I can't stand the sight of Gloria Gooseby and you know it.
LANG:	Then why are you always making comparisons?
DON:	I didn't make any comparisons. I just wanna sleep, that's all.
LANG:	What a fool I am. I go thru torture to look good for you and you reward me with insults.
DON:	Well, why must you do it at night, Blanche? You know I have to get up so early.
LANG:	I just wish you had to spend a whole day under a permanent wave machine – or have your eyebrows done.
DON:	Why do you have to wave your eyebrows?
LANG:	I don't wave my eyebrows. I have them plucked.
DON:	What for?
LANG:	Because it sets off my eyes and improves the lines of my face.
DON:	Your eyes are offset enough – and you've got plenty of lines in your face! You don't have to pluck your eyebrows for me.
LANG:	Yes, I do!
DON:	You do not! I like 'em the way they are – nice and bushy!
LANG:	That's a left-handed compliment if I ever heard one!
DON:	Well, I'm left-handed. Why don't you put out the lights, Blanche?
LANG:	As soon as I read the paper.
DON:	Read the paper!
LANG:	Go to sleep. I just want to glance thru it.
	SOUND: RUSTLES PAPER
DON:	Never heard of such thing! I'm so exhausted.
LANG:	Shh. I can't read when you're mumbling like that.
DON:	Mumbling.
LANG:	How do they get away with these burlesque ads? This Cuddles Laverne is built like a truck-horse.
DON:	Mmmm.
LANG:	I can't imagine what the men see in her.
DON:	She's got two beautiful legs.
LANG:	How would you know?
DON:	I counted 'em. Put away the paper, Blanche.
LANG:	Just a minute. Here's a story about –
DON:	I read the whole thing – every word of it! Why don't you let me get some rest?
LANG:	I'll bet you didn't read this. It's about a woman who recovered her voice in an airplane accident.

DON:	How much is her husband suing the company for?
LANG:	Don't be so smart. Oh, here's what I was looking for. I heard about this on the radio. The Museum of Art just received Carot's famous painting. Look at it.
DON:	I can't – my eyes are closed.
LANG:	Well, this'll open them. It's the world's greatest masterpiece – Circus Maximus. Just look at this awful savagery, John.
DON:	Where?
LANG:	Here.
DON:	What are those lions doing?
LANG:	Devouring innocent wives. Listen to what it says. (READS) In the fourth century the barbarous Roman emperors indulged their blood-thirsty appetites in the cruelest sport known to mankind. Wives of villagers would be herded into an arena where ferocious and hungry lions were turned loose.
DON:	(SYMPATHETICALLY) Uh-huh.
LANG:	Carot's painting depicts the grinning, hideous faces of the spectators, the ravenous yawning jaws of the lions, and the plight of the wives about to be devoured.
DON:	What a shame!
LANG:	Why, John – you've got tears in your eyes. I didn't think you'd be so touched.
DON:	It's awful.
LANG:	Why are you so upset?
DON:	That little lion in the corner isn't getting any. Goodnight, Blanche.
LANG:	Goodnight, John.
MUSIC:	BICKERSON PLAYOFF
	(APPLAUSE)
MUSIC:	THEME
CLOSING	
AMECHE:	Well that puts the lid on the twenty-third program of our new series for Old Gold Cigarettes, written and directed by Phil Rapp. We hope you'll be on hand next Friday night for Frank Morgan, Frances Langford, and Carmen Dragon and the orchestra. This is Don Ameche saying goodnight and good smoking with Old Gold.
	(APPLAUSE)
MUSIC:	THEME
MILLER:	Frank Morgan appeared by arrangement with Metro-Goldyn-Mayer producers of "High Wall" starring Robert

Taylor, Audrey Totter, and Herbert Marshall. Remember next Friday at Old Gold Time it'll be Frank Morgan, Don Ameche, and France Langford with Carmen Dragon and his orchestra brought to you by P. Lorrillard Company....a famous name in tobaccos for nearly two hundred years.....makers of Old Gold Cigarettes....the treasure of 'em all...and listen... if you want a treat instead of a treatment.... Treat yourself to Old Golds... Buy 'em at your tobacco counters....Buy them in the cigarette vending machines. Don't forget every Friday night on CBS it's "Fun For The Family." Stay tuned now for "The Adventures of Ozzie and Harriet" which follows immediately over most of these stations.

This is Marvin Miller speaking.

(APPLAUSE)

THIS IS CBS....THE COLUMBIA BROADCASTING SYSTEM.......

(Don Ameche co-starred with Claudette Colbert, can now be seen in their new picture, "Sleep My Love".)

Probably the farthest the Bickersons ever traveled in their lives was to Niagara Falls. Twice. This time Blanche has dragged sleepy John in for a second honeymoon. As she stated in another script, on their honeymoon Blanche couldn't hear the falls after the third day due to John's snoring. Nothing has changed.

This is one of the few routines that wasn't used often in other TV or radio Bickerson programs. It definitely wasn't used in the 1951 series, though it contains the usual Rapp brilliance of tight comedy and sharp jokes.

THE OLD GOLD SHOW

Station CBS   Date 3-12-48   Time 6:00-6:30 PM   Studio VINE ST.

Cast	Music Routine
FRANK MORGAN	OPENING THEME
DON AMECHE	"THOUGHTLESS"
FRANCES LANGFORD	MORGAN PLAYOFF
CARMEN DRAGON	"TIME ON MY HANDS"
FRANK GOSS	BICKERSON THEME
MARVIN MILLER	BICKERSON PLAYOFF
HITS AND A MISS	CLOSING THEME

WRITTEN AND DIRECTED BY PHIL RAPP

MUSIC:	(ON CUE) OPENING FANFARE
MILLER:	(ON CUE) From Hollywood.
CHORUS:	(ON CUE) It's Old Gold Cigarette Time
	If you want a treat instead of a treatment
	Smoke Old Golds
	If you want a treat instead of a treatment
	Smoke Old Golds.
	We're tobacco men, not medicine men
	Pleasure is what we pack
	Oh, Old Gold cures just one thing
	The world's best tobacco!
	So, if you want a treat instead of a treatment
	If you want a treat instead of a treatment
	Smoke, smoke, smoke, smoke – Smoke Old Gold!
	(PAUSE)
MARVIN:	The treasure of 'em all, gives the most pleasure of 'em all.
MUSIC:	THEME...(ESTABLISH AND FADE UNDER FOLLOWING)
MILLER:	This is Marvin Miller, Ladies and Gentlemen, speaking for the makers of Old Gold Cigarettes who are pleased to present the twenty-fifth in a series of new programs with Carmen Dragon and his orchestra, starring Metro-Goldwyn-Mayer's lovable Frank Morgan, the genial Don Ameche and charming Frances Langford, who sings ---
MUSIC:	LANGFORD AND ORCH...."THOUGHTLESS" (APPLAUSE) FIRST COMMERCIAL
MILLER:	We're tobacco men...not medicine men. Old Gold cures just one thing...the world's best tobacco. And the one thing we sell is...tobacco pleasure...pleasure...as real and solid as the Old Gold you put between your lips. After all... nearly two hundred years of quality tobacco experience are behind every Old Gold you smoke. And friends...you simply cannot match that quality tradition in any other cigarette. Nor can you match the finer taste...the smooth, mild pleasure of an Old Gold.
CHORUS:	So...if you want a treat instead of a treatment
	If you want a treat instead of a treatment
	Smoke, smoke, smoke, smoke
	Smoke....Old Golds.
MILLER:	Now here is your host for the evening, Don Ameche. (APPLAUSE)

AMECHE:	Thank you, ladies and gentlemen, and good evening. Tonight we're very fortunate ---
DRAG:	Pardon, Don, but I'd like to help you.
AMECHE:	Help me?
DRAG:	Yare. I noticed a few people yawning when you started to talk so I thought I might snap 'em out of it with a yocker.
AMECHE:	A yocker?
DRAG:	Yare, a yocker.
AMECHE:	Some other time, Carmen. We have a very interesting guest tonight and we need every minute.
DRAG:	Same old story. Well, I guess I don't need a building to fall on my head to see what's going on.
AMECHE:	What are you talking about?
DRAG:	Never mind, boy. You know what I mean, boy.
AMECHE:	What do you mean, boy?
DRAG:	Well, since you became the head of the comedy department I'm always the butt of your jokes.
AMECHE:	I'm not the head!
DRAG:	Well, I'm sick of being the butt. I might as well go home.
LANG:	You can't go home, Carmen. What about the music?
DRAG:	What do I care about the music? Let Don get some other dope to play it.
AMECHE:	Now be reasonable, Carmen – where am I going to find another dope at this late hour?
LANG:	Oh, let him tell his joke, Don. Go on, Carmen, tell it.
DRAG:	Not unless Don asks me.
AMECHE:	Oh, you and your yockers! Is it anything like the one you told a couple of weeks ago – about the two married skunks who were expecting a little stinker in the spring?
DRAG:	Oh, no. This is about two rabbits. A friend of mine in New York mailed me two rabbits, how many do you think there were by the time they got here?
AMECHE:	How many?
DRAG:	Two. One came by American Airlines and the other came by Greyhound Bus. Yocker?
AMECHE:	Stinker!
DRAG:	Okay, jealous. Introduce your broken-down guest.
LANG:	Carmen!
AMECHE:	Ladies and gentlemen, in our search for unusual guests we've literally scaled the highest mountains and combed the deepest ocean. This week we went so low we came up with a deep-

sea diver. May I present the director of the Sparling School of Deep-Sea Diving – a former Navy man – and a veteran of fourteen years of under-ocean exploration --- Mr. E. R. Cross. Mr. Cross.

(APPLAUSE)

CROSS: Thank you.

AMECHE: Before we plunge into deep-sea diving, Mr. Cross, I'd like you to meet some of the people on our show. This is Frances Langford.

CROSS: Hello, Miss Langford, I'm an old fan of yours. While I was diving in the Navy I always listened to your records.

LANG: Why, thank you.

DRAG: Oh, sure! He had a phonograph that played under water. Oh, sure!

CROSS: I beg your pardon?

DRAG: What'd you use for a needle, buddy – a barracuda?

AMECHE: Cut it out, Carmen. Mr. Cross, this is Carmen Dragon, our orchestra leader.

CROSS: I figured it was.

DRAG: What kind of a crack is that?

CROSS: Never mind, boy. You know what I mean, boy.

DRAG: Say, this fellow's all right, boy – he talks my language.

LANG: Mr. Cross, are there any lady deep-sea divers?

CROSS: Not to my knowledge, Miss Langford. I don't think the man-eating sharks would stand for it.

DRAG: Get it, Don? I told you he was all right, boy.

AMECHE: What's the greatest descent you've ever made, Mr. Cross?

CROSS: Around three hundred feet. It's practically impossible to work at that depth, though.

AMECHE: I suppose a great deal depends upon the cooperation you get from the tender on the surface. Does he control your air supply?

CROSS: No, that's up to the diver himself. He regulates it according to the extent of the pressure – and decreases it through an exhaust in his helmet.

LANG: What does a diving suit consist of?

CROSS: We call it a diving dress.

DRAG: New Look, hah?

CROSS: Not exactly. As a rule it consists of a copper helmet and breast-plate, lead belt and lead-soled shoes with the suit itself usually being made of canvas and rubber.

AMECHE: Must be a pretty heavy outfit.

CROSS: Well, I wouldn't want to wear it to a dance.

AMECHE: I guess not. Mr. Cross, according to my notes you've been a deep-sea diver for fourteen years and among your many salvage jobs was the raising of the famous Normandie. Would you mind telling us about that?

CROSS: Well, there's not much to tell, Don. She had been tipped for three days when I went to work. I took one look at her and realized that the only way to get her beam out of the water was to seal her ports and inflate her holds.

MORG: (COMING ON) You did! Why didn't you just slap her face and pump up her girdle!

AMECHE: Frank!
(APPLAUSE)

MORG: I once tried to rescue a couple of fat ladies and had my hands full for hours. How do you break their hold when they're going down for the third time and ----

AMECHE: Frank – what are you talking about?

MORG: Isn't he the life-guard at the Bimini Baths?

AMECHE: No! He was never with any Baths. What do you take him for!

MORG: Oh, never takes a bath.

LANG: Please, Mr. Morgan. He's our guest for tonight, and we were discussing deep-sea diving.

MORG: Well, if there's anything you want to know about --- Oh, hello, my dear!

LANG: Hello.

MORG: Well! You look just like a mermaid in that fishtail evening gown. Have you finished singing, or would you like me to run over your scales?

LANG: Scales?

MORG: I had no idea you were interested in under-water exploration. If you'll meet me in my bathysphere I'll be glad to plumb the depths with you. I'm a pretty good plumber too. (GIGGLES)

LANG: Well, I ---

MORG: You'll find my Diving School on Spring Street, right underneath Hoagy's fishmarket. Bring your own nose – hose – and we'll get tanked together. What time can you come for a dunking?

LANG: Well, I can't make it, but I'll be glad to send my husband. He loves to plunge in the water.

MORG: Oh, her husband's a plunger. Well, I'll send for him the next time the drain is stuck.

91

LANG:	Goodnight, gentlemen.
MORG:	Tantalizing creature. That girl affects me like a shot of bourbon.
AMECHE:	She affects you like a shot of bourbon?
MORG:	Yes, she's always so straight and I just love to chaser. I think I will!
AMECHE:	Come back here, Morgan! How can you rush off and on here every time without so much as a hello or a goodbye to our guest.
MORG:	Oh. My dear guest, I can assure you it requires a minimum of effort for me not to say hello to you ---
CROSS:	What?
MORG:	But I'll be happy to say goodbye to you anytime. Goodbye.
AMECHE:	Wait a minute! You don't even know who he is.
MORG:	Who is he?
AMECHE:	He's an instructor from the Sparling School of Deep Sea Diving.
MORG:	A very worthy institution. I believe they were the first advocates of the Neufeldt and Kuhnke aluminium alloy diving dress and the Siebe-Gorman two cylinder double-acting reciprocating pump with the valves on the breastplate and the Tender behind. Isn't that so?
CROSS:	Huh?
AMECHE:	Morgan! Are you a diver?
MORG:	In a belly-flopping sort of a way.
CROSS:	He sounds pretty good to me.
MORG:	I do? I mean I do! If you'll check with the authorities at your diving school, my boy, you'll find that all the instructors follow the Morgan method.
CROSS:	Is that so?
MORG:	All except one. He was an unmanageable young toad with a nose like a barnacle.
AMECHE:	What was his name, Frank?
MORG:	I believe it was Earwig or Horsecar, or something.
CROSS:	E. R. Cross?
MORG:	That's him. Most timid diver I ever saw. Fellow gets the bends every time it rains.
AMECHE:	He does, huh? What else, Frank?
MORG:	I could tell you plenty about that little sinker. I supervised his first descent, and manned the pump. Every time he went down there was a jerk at the end of the line.
CROSS:	What did you do?

MORG:	I pulled the jerk up and put him in the decompression chamber. The school finally got wise to him and fired him for incompetency.
CROSS:	Mr. Morgan, I'm Cross.
MORG:	Well, they were pretty mad, too ----- Oh, he's -- Cross!
AMECHE:	Yes, he's Cross! E. R. Cross! And he wasn't fired – he's the Director of the school. Now you apologize to this gentlemen!
MORG:	Take your grubby paws off me, Dodger!
MILLER:	I don't want to intrude, Don, but I think you should treat Mr. Morgan with a little more respect.
MORG:	Well! What a timely interruption. You're that fat young busboy from Barney's Beanery. Pull up a bus and rest your pot.
MILLER:	Pardon?
AMECHE:	Why don't you stop trying to change the subject! You know very well he's our announcer.
MORG:	He is? He doesn't look like that overfed lardbucket, Marvin Miller.
MILLER:	That's me. I'm that overfed lardbucket, Mr. Morgan.
MORG:	My apologies, sir. Allow me to introduce you to the world's greatest deep-sea diver. Mr. Crosseyed, this is Mr. Lardbucket.
MILLER:	Mr. Crosseyed.
CROSS:	Mr. Lardbucket.
AMECHE:	What's going on here!
MILLER:	Mr. Morgan, I don't want to bother you ---
MORG:	Well, you do, you know.
MILLER:	I'm sorry, but I heard you discussing deep-sea diving ---
AMECHE:	Oh, stop it, Marvin. What does he know about diving?
MORG:	Now see here, Dodger ---
AMECHE:	Go on! You couldn't dive to the bottom of a washtub full of soapsuds if you had Jack Benny's wallet strapped to your nose!
MORG:	Poppycock! The Morgans have been divers for generations beginning with my grandfather Whale Morgan down to my Uncle Octopus and my Aunt Crab.
AMECHE:	Your Aunt Crab.
MORG:	Poor thing was half-cracked. Always turned red when she was boiled.
MILLER:	What a wonderful family.
MORG:	Yes. This amazing trio performed some of the greatest underwater salvage operations in maritime history.
CROSS:	Did they have good equipment in those days?

93

MORG:	Only the crudest. But it wasn't long before my grandfather invented a diving suit made entirely of granite and persuaded my Uncle to try it.
CROSS:	Your uncle went down in a diving suit made of granite?
MORG:	With a manhole cover for a face-plate. My grandfather had a fortune in his grasp, but the insurance company refused to pay off and the whole experiment was a dismal failure.
AMECHE:	What were you doing all this time?
MORG:	I was hard at work inventing rescue devices – and before I was twelve years old I demonstrated a method for putting new life into a half-conscious diver by hooking him up with a simple wench. Winch!
AMECHE:	Never mind that. When did you start diving, Morgan?
MORG:	Well, it was while I was in Naval Intelligence on the Cocos Islands that I had my first experience.
MILLER:	What was it?
MORG:	I got orders from Washington to locate thirty million dollars in sunken gold bullion with a specially constructed undersea divining rod.
CROSS:	Divining rod?
MORG:	It's a sensitive device that registers the presence of gold by vibrating sharply. My divining rod was attached to two heavy wheels, somewhat like a motorcycle, and was weighted for undersea work by means of an auxiliary receptacle.
AMECHE:	Auxiliary receptacle? What's that?
MORG:	A large sidecar.
AMECHE:	I'll have a small old-fashioned.
MORG:	Angostura?
AMECHE:	Just a bunch.
MORG:	That'll be forty --- what are we talking about!
MILLER:	Cut it out, Don! Go on, Mr. Morgan.
MORG:	Yes. Where was I?
AMECHE:	In a dive.
MORG:	Yes. Two of the B-girls came over and tried ---- I'm going home!
MILLER:	No, Mr. Morgan. I'm dying to hear about the sunken bullion.
MORG:	Well, all right. We cruised in the deep waters around Flugel Bay, and the divining rod showed no signs of life. As we got close to an uncharted reef, however, the thing began to shake. Instantly I dove overboard with the heavy mechanism – plummeting right to the bottom of the ocean like so much granite.

AMECHE:	He was wearing his grandfather's suit.
MORG:	Silence! As I touched bottom, I became aware of a dreadful clicking sound – and at once I realized that I was surrounded by the deadliest enemies of the deep-sea diver. A school of fierce, hungry abalone!
MILLER:	Abalone?
CROSS:	Abalone?
AMECHE:	Ah, baloney!
MORG:	I knew he'd make something of that. Well, it's no use – I'm not gonna---
MILLER:	Please, Mr. Morgan. What about the sunken treasure?
MORG:	Well – in the inky blackness of the ocean I could see nothing – but the divining rod began to quiver uncontrollably. I tried to move to the left but the instrument pulled me to the right.
AMECHE:	Why was that?
MORG:	As I told you, the rod was so sensitive it reacted that way in the presence of gold – no matter how small a quantity. Soon I came upon the hulk of a sunken vessel. I hacked my way through to the cabin and what I saw convinced me that the divining rod had not failed.
MILLER:	It was the bullion!
MORG:	No – it was a pack of Old Golds.
AMECHE:	So you got a treat instead of a treatment and came right to the surface.
MORG:	Not yet, my boy. Nine hundred feet below the surface my air supply got choked, my exhaust refused to function, and I couldn't get the lead out of my shoes.
MILLER:	How did you get to the surface?
MORG:	Fortunately, my telephone was still in order and I called the tender up above. The line was busy, so I got my nickel back and cut my way out of my diving suit. I lost consciousness immediately, and when I came to I found myself on board ship with the doctor trying to force brandy down my throat.
AMECHE:	He was forcing, huh?
MORG:	I told you I was unconscious.
MILLER:	Did you get the bends?
MORG:	Only at the elbows. For my heroic feat I was awarded every decoration for bravery and only yesterday I got a message from the Navy Department to salvage a -- (PHONE RINGS)

AMECHE:	Just a minute, Frank – the phone...Hello?
MORG:	Oh, that's the last straw! You can't interrupt an Admiral when he gives a report of his activities! It's downright discourteous – and it's not good, by George!
AMECHE:	The Navy Department?
MORG:	Goodbye, George!
AMECHE:	Hold him, Marvin!...Hello...Yes, sir...Mr. Morgan? One moment, please...It's for you, Frank.
MORG:	For me?
AMECHE:	Navy Department. Been trying to reach you for ten minutes.
MORG:	Ohh – navy bean...
AMECHE:	Here – take the phone.
MORG:	Hello .....yes, this is Frank Mor---yes, but I---ohhh! Well, you see, I --- no, I didn't -- but I never --- oh, Admiral! Well, if you – I -- no, sir! Yes, sir...Imposter.. Pirate...Walk the plank...Yardarm...Yes, admiral. No, admiral...Yes, admiral. I won't. Goodbye. (HANGS UP)
MILLER:	What did he want, Mr. Morgan?
MORG:	They cancelled my salvage orders on account of a sinking.
AMECHE:	Sinking? Who's sunk?
MORG:	I am! So long, fellows, I gotta buy a lifebelt.
MUSIC:	MORGAN PLAYOFF (APPLAUSE) SECOND COMMERCIAL
MUSIC:	INTRO "TIME ON MY HANDS"
MILLER:	(OVER THEME) Frances Langford sings "Time On My Hands."
MUSIC:	ORCH AND LANGFORD..."Time On My Hands" (APPLAUSE)
CHORUS:	If you want a treat instead of a treatment Smoke Old Golds If you want a treat instead of a treatment Smoke Old Golds.
MILLER:	Friends, our little choral group here is singing to no one else but you. Yes...give yourself a treat – in the cigarette that can't be matched for smooth mildness and wonderful taste, Old Gold. Yes – Old Gold – the treasure of 'em all...with a quality tobacco tradition unmatched by any other cigarette. You know – nearly two hundred years of fine tobacco experience and knowledge are back of Old Golds – helping us bring you, in every Old Gold, the ripest, mellowest, best-tasting tobacco a cigarette can hold. That's something real...something you

taste and enjoy when you smoke an Old Gold. And that's the whole point. Listen ---

2ND ANNCR: We're tobacco men – not medicine men. Old Gold cures just one thing...the world's best tobacco.

MILLER: Now here are Don Ameche and Frances Langford as John and Blanche Bickerson in "The Honeymoon is Over."

THEME: (SOFT AND PLAINTIVE)

MILLER: Like most married women Blanche Bickerson is a romanticist. Having talked poor husband John into taking her on a second honeymoon, three o'clock in the morning finds Mrs. Bickerson in the lobby of a small hotel at Niagara Falls. Exhausted and bleary-eyed from the long drive, John Bickerson unloads the luggage outside as his wide-awake wife talks to the night-clerk. Listen.

LANG: It doesn't really matter about the room as long as we have a nice view of the Falls.

CLERK: Yes, ma'am.

LANG: I'll bet you don't remember me.

CLERK: No, ma'am.

LANG: I wouldn't expect you to, with all the honeymoon couples you meet. I was here seven years ago.

CLERK: Is that so?

LANG: Yes.

CLERK: Well, better luck this time.

LANG: Oh, we're still married to each other. We're just having a second honeymoon. Do many people do that?

CLERK: No ma'am.

LANG: I wonder why.

CLERK: I wouldn't know, ma'am.

LANG: Are you married?

CLERK: No, ma'am.

LANG: Oh.

CLERK: Arthritis makes me walk like this. Would you please sign the register, ma'am?

LANG: Oh, I'm sorry. Last time we were here we had to wait two days for a room. We stayed in a motel in Buffalo. Here you are.

CLERK: Thank you. Is that – Bickerson?

LANG: Yes. Did I sign it right?

CLERK: Yes, Ma'am. Mrs. John Bickerson and husband. Here's a key – room 318. There's the automatic elevator over there. We don't have any bellboys at night.

LANG:	Oh, that's all right. I'll go out to the car and get my husband. (RAPID FOOTSTEPS) John! Where is he? He's not in the car. I wonder if he took the luggage out of the trunk compartment. (OPENS TRUNK OF CAR)
DON:	(SNORES LUSTILY)
LANG:	Good heavens!
DON:	(WHINES...SNORES AND WHINES)
LANG:	The man is positively insane.
DON:	(SNORES AND GIGGLES...SNORES AND GIGGLES MERRILY)
LANG:	John!
DON:	Mmmm.
LANG:	Get out of that trunk, you darn fool!
DON:	(A PROTESTING WHINE)
LANG:	John, John, John!
DON:	Blanche, Blanche, Blanche. Wassamatter? Shut the door, there's a draft.
LANG:	Come out of that thing.
DON:	All right, all right – don't pull. (BANGS HIS HEAD) Ohhh, my head!
LANG:	Serves you right. Pick up that luggage and straighten yourself up. I don't want you to go into that nice hotel looking like a ragamuffin.
DON:	(SLEEPY) Nice muffins. Grab a couple of these bags, will you, Blanche?
LANG:	No. It wouldn't look right on our honeymoon...Come on. (THEY WALK IN)
DON:	Ohh. my back! Where's the bellboy?
CLERK:	We don't have any at night.
DON:	Are you the clerk?
CLERK:	Yes, sir.
DON:	Where's the register – I want a room with a bed.
LANG:	I've already signed it. You've got a room.
DON:	Good. Where are <u>you</u> gonna sleep?
LANG:	Don't pay attention to him, mister – he's sleepy.
CLERK:	Yes, ma'am.
LANG:	Come on, John. Stop dragging your feet!
DON:	Drove two thousand miles for a second honeymoon. Didn't have enough with the first. Lead me to my room. (THEY WALK TO THE ELEVATOR)
LANG:	You had to talk like that in front of the clerk.

DON:	Lemme sleep, will you, Blanche?
LANG:	I'd just love to go one place with you that you don't embarrass and humiliate me. You've been unbearable since we left home. Keep going.
DON:	In here?
LANG:	Yes. Pull the bags in so I can close the door. (DOOR SLIDES CLOSED)
DON:	No windows – no nothing! How much do they get for this broken-down room?
LANG:	This is the elevator.
DON:	Oh. Well, push the button or something and get it started. I can't keep my eyes open another minute. (THE ELEVATOR STARTS UP)
LANG:	I was afraid this would happen. I prayed and prayed that you'd act differently – I was hoping that going on a second honeymoon would bring us closer together.
DON:	Can't get closer than this. Not unless you throw the luggage out.
LANG:	Every time I want you to be romantic you're so distant, John. What is it that's keeping us apart?
DON:	The brown suitcase. What floor are we on?
LANG:	The third. I don't suppose it means anything to you – but we have the same room we had when we were here before.
DON:	Is it the same price?
LANG:	Is that all you can think of? Haven't you got an ounce of sentiment in your body? Must you constantly act like an old married man?
DON:	I'm not acting. I'm sleepy.
LANG:	You're always sleepy. And when you're not sleepy you're humiliating me. I'll never be able to face that night clerk in the morning.
DON:	You won't have to.
LANG:	Why not?
DON:	There'll be a day clerk. (ELEVATOR STOPS. THE DOOR SLIDES OPEN) Which way is the room?
LANG:	I don't know and I don't care. I'm going to stay in the elevator.
DON:	Oh, come on, willya, Blanche?
LANG:	Well, say you're sorry.
DON:	I'm sorry. Now, where's our room?
LANG:	Right in front of you – 318.
DON:	Well, open the door before I collapse...(KEY IN DOOR...DOOR OPENS)...Thank heaven. (DROPS LUGGAGE) Gotta get some sleep.
LANG:	Well, put the lights on. Don't stumble around in the dark!

99

DON:	Don't wanna open my eyes. Just aim me at the bed and give me a shove.
LANG:	Am I supposed to unpack all these bags? Open them up so I can get a nightgown.
DON:	In the morning. (FALLS ON BED) Oh, this is a wonderful bed. Goodnight.
LANG:	I'm not going to let you sleep until you undress properly and unpack the luggage.
DON:	Oh, Blanche! Why did you have to bring so much stuff?
LANG:	You've got as much stuff as I have.
DON:	I have not! All I brought was my toothbrush and my overnight bottle.
LANG:	You and that bourbon! You wouldn't take five steps away from home without it.
DON:	Well, I still remember what happened when we got snowbound in that cabin.
LANG:	It wasn't so terrible.
DON:	Not much. I had to live for two weeks on nothing but food and water.
LANG:	Don't throw my things around like that.
DON:	There's no closet. Where shall I put these dresses?
LANG:	In the drawers.
DON:	Where do you want these drawers?
LANG:	In the dresser. Fold up your pants neatly and put them under the mattress.
DON:	Okay. (DIVES INTO BED)
LANG:	Well, take them off first, John!
DON:	Oh. Listen, Blanche, can't we do this in the morning? I wanna sleep.
LANG:	What a fool I was to think that you'd change. This second honeymoon was just as big a mistake as our first one.
DON:	Oh, no, it wasn't.
LANG:	I'm so sorry you made me go on this trip, I could die!
DON:	I made you go? You shanghaied me! You even tried to get me to marry you again.
LANG:	Is that such an unreasonable request?
DON:	Get married to you again? Yes. It isn't legal.
LANG:	Why not?
DON:	A man can't be punished twice for the same crime.
LANG:	Oh, that's too bad about you. How you shamed me in front of all my friends – after I sent out the invitations, too.

DON:	Well, I wasn't going to have any formal wedding and put out a lot of dough to feed your hungry friends and their squalling brats.
LANG:	There wouldn't have been any brats there at all.
DON:	How do you know?
LANG:	Because it said plainly on the invitation. Mr. and Mrs. John Bickerson will be married March 9th. No children expected.
DON:	Put out the lights.
LANG:	I'm never going back to that horrible apartment we live in. I'm just going to sit here and stare at the falls forever. Wouldn't hurt you to look at them.
DON:	I see 'em every day on a Shredded Wheat Box.
LANG:	How can you be so cynical? I'm glad I have a little romance in my soul. Just the sight of those Falls brings back memories.
DON:	Mmm.
LANG:	Sit up, John. Look at that sight. Doesn't it remind you of something?
DON:	Yeah.
LANG:	What, John?
DON:	I think I left the water running in the bathtub.
LANG:	John, you didn't!
DON:	Okay, I didn't. Goodnight, Blanche.
LANG:	I never should have trusted you to lock up. Now I'm really worried. Did you close all the windows?
DON:	Closed the windows.
LANG:	You didn't leave any lights burning, did you?
DON:	Mmm.
LANG:	Did you leave food for the cat?
DON:	Left enough for a week.
LANG:	What did you leave him?
DON:	A six pound tin of corned-beef.
LANG:	Did you empty it into a plate?
DON:	No.
LANG:	Well, how do you expect the cat to eat it?
DON:	I left a can-opener on top. Why don't you stop worrying about the cat?
LANG:	We should have taken all the animals with us. The poor little canary is locked in the cage – the cat can't get out of the house – and who's going to feed the goldfish? I'll bet they're terribly unhappy.
DON:	Oh, they're not unhappy. They're having a fine vacation.
LANG:	They are not.

DON:	They are, too. When I left the cat was fishing.
LANG:	Fishing? Where?
DON:	In the goldfish bowl – and he was using the canary for bait!
LANG:	John Bickerson!
DON:	Oh, go to sleep. The canary and the goldfish are fine – and I wish that cat would drop dead.
LANG:	Don't talk like that. I love that cat. When I get home I'm going to enter him in a cat show.
DON:	What for? He couldn't win anything.
LANG:	Maybe not – but he'd meet a lot of nice cats.
DON:	Blanche, do me a favor. Put out the lights and come to bed. If I stay awake another minute I'll fall asleep from exhaustion.
LANG:	I'm not sleepy. Why don't you sit up and talk to me?
DON:	Blanche – people don't talk at four o'clock in the morning.
LANG:	You talked till five o'clock on our first honeymoon. You kept reciting poetry, and telling me how beautiful I was. Do you remember what you said, John?
DON:	No.
LANG:	You told me your love for me was like a raging inferno. You said you had a fierce fire blazing in your breast, like a live coal. It's gone, isn't it, John?
DON:	What's gone?
LANG:	The live coal.
DON:	It's still there, but it's only a clinker now.
LANG:	How can you say such terrible things to me?
DON:	Blanche, I'm so sleepy I don't know what I'm saying.
LANG:	I've known all along you don't love me and you never did.
DON:	I did, too. I mean I do, too!
LANG:	You don't, you don't, you don't.
DON:	Blanche, I love you.
LANG:	You're lying. Swear you love me.
DON:	I hope I choke on a quart of bourbon if I'm lying.
LANG:	I'd like to hear you say things like that to Gloria Gooseby.
DON:	Can't I even go to Niagara Falls without Gloria Gooseby?
LANG:	The only reason you didn't was because she wouldn't have you.
DON:	What!
LANG:	You proposed to her fifteen times before you proposed to me. You big second fiddle, you!
DON:	I never proposed to Gloria Gooseby, and you know it! I can't stand the sight of that woman. And the next time I see her I'm going to punch her husband, Leo, right in the nose!

LANG:	What have you got against Leo? He's a better husband than you are.
DON:	And I'm sick of hearing that, too. Leo Gooseby is a cheap, chiselling bum.
LANG:	He is not. He's more generous than you.
DON:	Would Leo Gooseby give you a new dress? No. Would he give you a new hat? No. Would he give you a mink coat? No.
LANG:	Would you give me a mink coat?
DON:	No – why should I give you anything Leo wouldn't give you!
LANG:	Stop screaming, you'll wake up the whole hotel.
DON:	Well, stop goading me. You want to do nothing but fight, fight, fight.
LANG:	No, I don't. All I do is ask for proof that you love me and you go into a tantrum.
DON:	Blanche, what more proof do you want? I tell it to you a thousand times a day! I raised a new crop of warts to spell out "I love you" – I painted it on all the Burma Shave signs! (LIGHT KNOCK AT DOOR)
LANG:	Shhh!
GIRL:	(OFF) Honey?
LANG:	(WHISPERS) Somebody's at the door, John. (LIGHT KNOCK)
GIRL:	(OFF) Honey? Honey? Honey?
DON:	Madam, this is not a beehive – it's my bedroom! What are people wandering around in the halls at this time of night for? Broken-down hotel!
LANG:	Oh, don't be so crabby. It's probably some little bride who can't find her husband. He may be lost.
DON:	He isn't lost – he's hiding! Put out the lights, Blanche. I've got a vile headache.
LANG:	Well, nobody told you to yell your brains out.
DON:	Goodnight.
LANG:	If you just stand here and look at the Falls for a few minutes your headache'll go away and you'll sleep fine.
DON:	Mmm.
LANG:	Where does all that water come from? I once read that it goes over at the rate of three hundred and forty six thousand gallons a second. John.
DON:	Mmmm.
LANG:	Are the Falls higher on the American side or the Canadian side?
DON:	I dunno.

LANG:	I'll have to find out in the morning. What a majestic spectacle. I'm convinced there's nothing in the world like Niagara Falls.
DON:	Except you, Blanche.
LANG:	Really, John? Why do you say that?
DON:	Because you never dry up either. Goodnight, Blanche.
LANG:	Goodnight, John.
MUSIC:	BICKERSON PLAYOFF
	(APPLAUSE)
MUSIC:	THEME
CLOSING:	
AMECHE:	Well, that puts the lid on the twenty-fifth program of our new series for Old Gold Cigarettes, written and directed by Phil Rapp. We hope you'll be on hand next Friday night for Frank Morgan, Frances Langford, and Carmen Dragon and the orchestra. This is Don Ameche saying goodnight and good smoking with Old Gold.
	(APPLAUSE)
MUSIC:	THEME
MILLER:	Frank Morgan appeared by arrangement with Metro-Goldwyn-Mayer producers of the Technicolor movie "Three Daring Daughters" starring Jeannette MacDonald, Jose Iturbi, and Jane Powell. Remember next Friday at Old Gold Time it'll be Frank Morgan, Don Ameche, and Frances Langford with Carmen Dragon and his orchestra brought to you by P. Lorrillard Company...a famous name in tobaccos for nearly two hundred years....makers of Old Gold Cigarettes..... the treasure of 'em all...and listen...if you want a treat instead of a treatment...treat yourself to Old Golds...Buy 'em at your tobacco counters...Buy them in the cigarette vending machines. Don't forget every Friday night on CBS it's "Fun For the Family." Stay tuned now for "The Adventures of Ozzie and Harriet" which follows immediately over most of these stations.
	This is Marvin Miller speaking.
	(APPLAUSE)
	THIS IS CBS...THE COLUMBIA BROADCASTING SYSTEM...
	(Don Ameche co-starred with Claudette Colbert, can now be seen in their new picture, "Sleep My Love.")

Though this is not a complete *Old Gold Show*, I wanted to include it for the simple reason that it gets John and Blanche out of the house. It's also amusing to "see" Leo Gooseby's incredulous reaction to John's snoring.

THE OLD GOLD SHOW

Station CBS   Date 4-9-48   Time 6:00-6:30 PM   Studio VINE ST.

MILLER: Now here are Don Ameche and Frances Langford as John and Blanche Bickerson in "The Honeymoon is Over."

THEME: (SOFT AND PLAINTIVE)

MILLER: In an unguarded moment John Bickerson allowed himself to be inveigled into a dinner invitation to the Gooseby's tiny country home. A heavy fog which washed out a bridge has forced John and Blanche to remain for the night in the sadly unequipped cabin, and the sleeping arrangements leave much to be desired. So, the Bickersons have retired....John is bunking with Leo Gooseby while Blanche spends the night with Gloria. Listen....

LANG: Are you asleep, Gloria?

GLOR: No. What time is it, Blanche?

LANG: It's after two o'clock. Are you sleepy?

GLOR: No. I'm just lying here thinking. I don't see much of the old crowd since I got married. Do you ever run into Louise Shaw?

LANG: Once in awhile. She looks wonderful. She's putting on a little weight.

GLOR: I wish I was blessed with an appetite like Louise. She eats like a pig, doesn't she?

LANG: What else has she got to do, poor thing. Her husband works day and night. Louise deserves a lot of credit, though. If she didn't hound him all the time he'd probably never have a job. Poor girl makes his life miserable.

GLOR: You know, Mel thought he'd get away with plenty when he married her. He thought she was dumb just because she has such a stupid face.

LANG:	Dumb, nothing. Louise is plenty well-informed. Not many women are clever enough to be as nosey as she is, Gloria.
GLOR:	Yes?
LANG:	Lots of people don't understand Louise Shaw. What do you think of her?
GLOR:	I think she's one of the most intelligent, thrifty, and honest women I've ever met.
LANG:	I don't like her either.
GLOR:	We'd better not talk any more – Leo's such a light sleeper and these walls are like paper.
LANG:	I'm sure John's not sleeping, anyway. He's got the most awful condition, Gloria. It's some rare kind of insomnia and it keeps us both awake all night. I can just see him lying in that strange bed with Leo, tossing and struggling --(FADES)-- to get a little rest.
DON:	(FADES IN SNORING LUSTILY...WHINES PITIFULLY...SNORES AND WHINES...BROKEN RHYTHM SNORE FOLLOWED BY RINGING SOUND)
LEO:	Oh, he must be kidding.
DON:	(SNORES, GIGGLES)
LEO:	Oh, brother.
DON:	(SNORES AND GIGGLES MERRILY)
LEO:	That's enough for me. Hey, Bickerson...John...John...JOHN!
DON:	Mmm. Yes, dear?
LEO:	Sit up. What's the matter with you, John?
DON:	Matter? Wassamatter? What's the matter with you, Blanche – you look horrible.
LEO:	I'm not Blanche, I'm Leo.
DON:	Oh. Go to sleep, Leo.
LEO:	I can't sleep. The only reason I'm in here is because I had a beef with Gloria. But if I had known that you snore like---
DON:	Sssshh. Not so loud, Leo, you'll wake up the dames.
LEO:	I didn't even start the beef. All I said to Gloria tonight was that somebody ought to give that kid sister of hers a good spanking.
DON:	Kid sister.
LEO:	Yes.
DON:	How old is she?
LEO:	Eighteen. Do you think it does any good to spank her?
DON:	I don't know, but I imagine it's a lot of fun. Goodnight, Leo.
LEO:	If I was that girl's mother---
DON:	(HAS STARTED TO SNORE)

LEO:	Oh, nuts! I'm getting out of here. I'm gonna sleep in my own room. (GETS OUT OF BED...DOOR OPENS AND CLOSES... FOOTSTEPS...KNOCK ON DOOR)
GLOR:	(OFF) Who is it?
LEO:	It's me, Leo. (DOOR OPENS) I wanna sleep in here.
LANG:	Won't it be too crowded?
LEO:	You better go in with your husband, Blanche. He's blasting my ears off.
LANG:	Well, turn around while I put my robe on. I knew this setup was no good. Goodnight. (DOOR CLOSES...FOOTSTEPS... DOOR OPENS)
DON:	(SNORES...HUMS...CLUCKS)
LANG:	John! John Bickerson! Cut it out!
DON:	(A PROTESTING WHINE) Mmmmm.
LANG:	Stop it, stop it, stop it.
DON:	Stop it! What the devil is the matter with you, Leo? You keep waking me up like that nagging wife of mine.
LANG:	What!
DON:	You're even beginning to look like her. What are you wearing that pink nightgown with the---BLANCHE! What happened? Where's Leo?
LANG:	You blasted him out of here. The poor man's a nervous wreck.
DON:	Huh?
LANG:	He said he couldn't stand another minute of it. Rather than stay in the room with you he said he'd face the worst kind of torture. So he went to sleep with Gloria.
DON:	What kind of torture is that?
LANG:	Don't you be so smart, John Bickerson.
DON:	I'm not smart, I'm sleepy. Put out the light.
LANG:	I will not. I haven't closed my eyes.
DON:	Close 'em.
LANG:	I don't see why we had to spend the night here, anyway. That bridge wasn't so bad that we couldn't have crossed it. And I'm sure there was another way home.
DON:	No other way.
LANG:	I spent the most miserable three hours in that room with Gloria. She talked so much I got hoarse listening.
DON:	Mmmmm.
LANG:	She kept trying to pry into our private affairs, but I told her off in no uncertain terms. Believe me, I was outspoken.
DON:	I don't believe it.

LANG:	What do you mean?
DON:	Nobody can outspeak you.
LANG:	Well, I have to talk sometime. You do plenty of talking. You sure jabbered away with Gloria. I'd give anything to know what you were talking about.
DON:	Blanche, they can hear you in the other room.
LANG:	I don't care. I saw you two at the dinner table playing footsies.
DON:	Footsies!
LANG:	Yes, footsies!
DON:	I wasn't playing footsies! I was reaching for my shoes under the table and I accidentally brushed against Gloria's calf.
LANG:	What were you doing with your shoes off?
DON:	I had a bottle of bourbon strapped to my leg and I was trying to pull the cork out with my toes! Are you satisfied?
LANG:	No. And the gown that woman wore tonight! She ought to be arrested! But you loved it, didn't you?
DON:	Now, don't start that!
LANG:	Every night in the week she wears dungarees, but the minute I bring you here she has to put on that strapless gown!
DON:	It wasn't strapless. It had two big buttons on it!
LANG:	What buttons – those were your eyes!
DON:	Why don't you put out the lights and let me sleep?
LANG:	You never pay any attention to me. Do you ever compliment me on my clothes? No. Do you ever say I have a pretty figure? No. Do you ever tell me I have a schoolgirl complexion?
DON:	No.
LANG:	Why not, John? Don't you think I have a schoolgirl complexion?
DON:	Maybe you had one – but it graduated.
LANG:	Keep it up. Keep tearing me down. You wouldn't have dared to talk that way before we were married. You were the meekest little jellyfish in the world.
DON:	Ahhh.
LANG:	Even when you proposed to me you almost lost your nerve. Didn't you? Admit it!
DON:	I admit it. I almost lost my nerve.
LANG:	I'll never know what saved you.
DON:	Nothing saved me – I went ahead and proposed, didn't I?
LANG:	And you never even gave me a wedding ring. You told me you couldn't afford one. No, of course not. All your money went for bourbon, bourbon, bourbon!
DON:	Did not. Some of it went for soda.

LANG:	Don't I know it! When we stood at the altar you slipped a bottle opener on my finger.
DON:	Well, it was a gold one. And it's the same one my father got married with. It's a family superstition and all Bickersons get married with a bottle opener.
LANG:	Why?
DON:	It's a long story and I don't wanna go into it now.
LANG:	Because it's a lie! You lied to me about everything. You told me you were independently wealthy, and you told me you had a great big car. What happened to that big car, John?
DON:	I washed it and it shrunk. Goodnight, Blanche.
LANG:	I can just see Leo talking to Gloria the way you talk to me. He's such a nice little man and she really takes advantage of him. It's a funny thing, the biggest shrews always marry the nicest men.
DON:	That's the first time you ever paid me a compliment.
LANG:	Don't try to twist it around. Look at the way Gloria spends Leo's money. She buys more clothes in a week than I do in a year. And I always have to hunt for bargains.
DON:	You never bought a bargain in your life.
LANG:	I did, too. Last week I bought five pair of shoes for twelve dollars and they're only three sizes too small for me.
DON:	Well, what good is that! You can't wear them!
LANG:	That has nothing to do with it. They're the latest style. You can't expect me to walk around this year with last year's shoes.
DON:	Why not? You've got last year's feet, haven't you?
LANG:	Oh, what do you know.
DON:	You just throw money away, that's all. Why don't you trade the shoes to Gloria for one of her dresses? Get that low one, with the buttons.
LANG:	You've got the worst taste of any man I ever met. A brazen gown like that would look awful in the best places.
DON:	Oh, I don't know. I thought it looked pretty good in the best places. Blanche, it's almost three o'clock and I've gotta get some sleep. Please put out the light.
LANG:	Well, aren't you going to kiss me goodnight?
DON:	Sure. (KISS) Goodnight.
LANG:	Tell me you love me.
DON:	I love you.
LANG:	Am I beautiful?

DON:	Mmm.
LANG:	Am I?
DON:	Yes!
LANG:	Well, say it!
DON:	Blanche, you're beautiful!
LANG:	How beautiful? As beautiful as a sunset?
DON:	Yes.
LANG:	As beautiful as a painting by Rembrandt?
DON:	Yes.
LANG:	Now you say one.
DON:	You're as beautiful as a bathtub full of bourbon.
LANG:	No – say something pretty.
DON:	Blanche, you're the most stunning woman in the world. Your hair fascinates me so I can't work, your eyes hypnotize me – so I can't think, and your mouth bothers me so I can't sleep. Goodnight.
LANG:	Now I'm happy. And I think you're the most wonderful husband in the world. I'll confess something to you, John.
DON:	Mmm.
LANG:	I think I was lucky to get you.
DON:	I know.
LANG:	I'm the envy of all the girls. Sometimes, I just can't believe we're married.
DON:	We're married.
LANG:	I mean it. I keep thinking about it and I can't sleep.
DON:	Neither can I.
LANG:	To think you chose me instead of all those girls that chased you! John, I swear, I have to keep pinching myself! I can't believe we're married!
LEO:	(OFF) Hey, Bickerson!
DON:	What?
LEO:	For heaven's sake show her the license so we can all get some sleep!
DON:	Goodnight, Blanche.
LANG:	Goodnight, John.
MUSIC:	(BICKERSON PLAYOFF)
	(APPLAUSE)
MUSIC:	(THEME)

Not quite the Bickersons: Mary and Phil Rapp, circa 1948.

In 1951 the Bickersons finally got their own half hour series. No more sharing time with other comedians. Frances Langford still opened with a song, requested by a serviceman's letter. The series ran from June 5th to August 28th.

When Lew Parker took over the John Bickerson role, a new element was added. Though the scripts were almost exactly the same as previous Don Ameche *Old Gold Show* sketches, Lew brought a real working man's demeanor to the role. Perhaps it was his Brooklyn accent that distinguished this Bickerson as a sleepy fighter, ever pushing his shoulder to the grindstone and his nose to the wheel.

The series only lasted 13 episodes, but it contained some of the best writing on the air.

THE BICKERSONS

PRODUCER: PHIL RAPP
PRODUCT: PHILIP MORRIS
AGENCY: BIOW
BROADCAST: JULY 3, 1951

HOLBROOK: Ladies and gentlemen, Mr. Les Damon.
(RECORDING)
DAMON: Good evening, ladies and gentlemen. Haven't you often wished, as you listened to a radio commercial – that the announcer would stop pounding, stop pressing, stop making up your mind for you – in fact, that he would just stop and allow you the simple privilege of deciding for yourself whether you liked his product or not? And haven't you often thought how refreshing it would be if the sponsor, especially the cigarette sponsor, would only skip the jingles, the wild claims and fancy phrases – and simply give you the facts and explain that there's only one way for you to really find out whether you like his cigarette better than the other brands -- and that's for you to test his cigarette against any other cigarette... and then decide for yourself which one you like better? Wouldn't

it be wonderful if a sponsor put it to you on that basis? There is such a sponsor. That Sponsor is...PHILIP MORRIS. In a moment I know you will hear a PHILIP MORRIS program. It has no singing commercials, no dancing cigarettes, no ballyhoo. But it extends an invitation for you to make the only test that makes any sense – an invitation to compare, match, and judge PHILIP MORRIS against any other cigarette. And the decision as to which cigarette you prefer will be left entirely up to you.

I think this is an invitation you will welcome.

Thank you.

END OF RECORDING

MUSIC:	UP AND UNDER
HOLBROOK:	And now....PHILIP MORRIS presents Frances Langford and Lew Parker, starring in Philip Rapp's humorous creation, "THE BICKERSONS," produced and broadcast, from Hollywood.
MUSIC:	THEME
JOHNNY:	CALL.... FOR....PHILIP....MORRIS! CALL...FOR... PHILIP......MORRIS!! (APPLAUSE)
MUSIC:	(THEME UP TO FINISH)
HOLBROOK:	And now, here is John Bickerson as his other self --- Lew Parker. (APPLAUSE)
PARK:	Thank you, ladies and gentlemen and good evening. You know we've reserved these first few minutes of the program especially for the men in the service and it's here that Frances Langford becomes the beloved Purple Heart Girl before she puts on the cloak of Blanche Bickerson. So Fran ---
LANG:	Yes, Lew? (APPLAUSE)
PARK:	Let's catch up on some of the mail. Here's a letter from Camp Pendleton Hospital at Oceanside, and the boys want to hear "Just One of Those Things." Okay?
LANG:	You bet it's okay. So with the help of Tony Romano and his orchestra, this is for you, fellows.
LANG:	SONG (APPLAUSE)
HOLBROOK:	Now, here are Frances Langford and Lew Parker as John and Blanche Bickerson in "The Honeymoon is Over!"
THEME:	(SOFT AND PLANTIVE)

LANG:	(CALL) John!
PARK:	(OFF) What do you want, Blanche?
LANG:	Hurry up and have your breakfast or you'll be late for work.
PARK:	I'm hurrying! I just can't find my clothes in this dark bedroom. Where's my jacket?
LANG:	How do I know? Did you look under the chair?
PARK:	The cat's under the chair.
LANG:	Well, look under the cat.
PARK:	I got it…. Wish that broken down cat would stop sleeping on my clothes.
LANG:	Oh, he doesn't hurt them any.
PARK:	Not much. My pants have been shedding for three days… Have you seen my tie?
LANG:	Look on my dresser.
PARK:	Where's your dresser?
LANG:	What's the matter with you, John? Why don't you put on the light?
PARK:	The light is on – it only makes it darker! Blanche, why do you have to buy these nine-watt bulbs?
LANG:	They're fifteen watts, and it's plenty light in there. If you can't see, you need glasses.
PARK:	Then the cat needs glasses, too.
LANG:	He does not.
PARK:	He does, too. He just tripped over a mouse.
LANG:	Oh, stop it, and come in for your breakfast.
PARK:	I'm coming. (FADING IN) Blanche, I've got to get a new tie – the bowtie I'm wearing is so big I had to wrap it around my neck twice.
LANG:	John Bickerson! Take off my garter.
PARK:	I told you I couldn't see what I was doing.
LANG:	Take it off. Hurry up.
PARK:	Don't rush me. Every time I open my jacket, it snaps up at my chin.
LANG:	Here. Put on your tie. You've only got five minutes to eat breakfast.
PARK:	Okay, okay. Where's my breakfast?
LANG:	What do you want to eat?
PARK:	What do you mean, what do I want to eat! You've been yelling at me for a half an hour to come and get it!
LANG:	Well, you never eat anything in the morning, anyway. All you ever have is coffee.

PARK:	All right, give me my coffee.
LANG:	It'll be ready in a minute. Wait till I put the pot on.
PARK:	Never mind, Blanche. I haven't time. Is this all the mail there is?
LANG:	Yes. Don't bother with that now – we've got a million things to do today.
PARK:	This one's for you.
LANG:	Throw it away.
PARK:	Aren't you going to read it?
LANG:	I did read it, it's from Gloria Gooseby.
PARK:	How could you? The envelope isn't even open.
LANG:	I though it was addressed to you, so I held it up to the light and read it.
PARK:	Serves you right .... What's the May Company writing me letters for? (TEARS OPEN ENVELOPE.. RUSTLE OF PAPER)
LANG:	Here's your coffee, John.
PARK:	Ohhhhh!
LANG:	Is the coffee too hot?
PARK:	Never mind the coffee, Blanche! What's the idea of spending 57 dollars for an evening gown? You know we can't afford it.
LANG:	Now take it easy, John. That gown isn't costing you a penny. I got it for nothing on an exchange.
PARK:	Exchange of what?
LANG:	A fifty-seven dollar coat I bought the day before.
PARK:	Take it back. Do you hear me? Take it back.
LANG:	I can't take it back. I'm going to wear it to the wedding to-night.
PARK:	What wedding?
LANG:	Don't you remember? My cousin Eunice is getting married. I told you about it three weeks ago.
PARK:	You did not.
LANG:	Yes, I did. I told you about it at the same time I asked for money to buy a new dress.
PARK:	Why did you trick me that way? You know I never listen to you when you ask for money!
LANG:	Well, we're going anyway.
PARK:	What for, Blanche? I don't even know the girl and I hate those broken down weddings your cheap relatives are always having.
LANG:	This isn't one of my cheap relatives. Eunice's father is very wealthy and he's invited all the guests to go on a cruise after the ceremony.
PARK:	A cruise!

LANG:	Yes. I think he's the President of a steam-ship line, or something. Anyway, he's giving the groom a boat for a wedding present
PARK:	Poor guy. First they stick him with the anchor, then they give him the boat.
LANG:	Never mind – he's doing a lot better than you did. They've even got a picture of Eunice in the paper. Did you see it?
PARK:	I don't wanna see it.
LANG:	It's right here on the society page. (RUSTLES PAPER) See – there's a picture of Eunice in her bridal gown.
PARK:	I see it.
LANG:	And look, they gave her a three-column spread.
PARK:	Well, she can use it. She's bulging into the Help Wanted Section. Look at the clock – I've gotta get out of here.
LANG:	Wait a minute, John. You haven't told me what you're getting Eunice for a present.
PARK:	I'm not getting her anything! We can't afford it, and with her wealthy parents she doesn't need anything.
LANG:	Well, I'm not going to the wedding without a present.
PARK:	Why do we have to go at all?
LANG:	Because it means a lot to me, John. To a woman a wedding is a beautiful and sacred thing. It's the joining together of two souls in everlasting love and devotion. And you ask "Why do we have to go?" Have you no sentiment?
PARK:	No.
LANG:	Neither have I, but you can't go around offending rich relatives!
PARK:	Goodbye, Blanche.
MUSIC:	BRIDGE
LANG:	What do you mean you're not going to the wedding, Clara?
CLARA:	I've got no one to leave the kids with. Barney's going alone. That's what I came over to talk to you about. Listen, if cousin Eunice asks you about me, say we didn't get any invitation.
LANG:	But you did get one.
CLARA:	How do they know? Maybe it got lost in the mail. I want them to think I'm sore about not being invited.
LANG:	Why?
CLARA:	Because I'm not giving them a present.
LANG:	Won't they know you got the invitation when Barney shows up?
CLARA:	Of course not. Since when does Barney need to be invited anywhere? And Blanche --- act very indignant when you tell them about me.

LANG:	But Clara, I don't think I ---
CLARA:	My own sister, and she's on their side! If they invited one of us they had a right to invite the other! Are you going to take my part or theirs?
LANG:	All right, Clara. Help me move these cartons.
	SOUND: BOXES SLIDING ON FLOOR
CLARA:	What are you rummaging through this storage closet for?
LANG:	Oh, I told John three weeks ago to get a present for Eunice's wedding and he forgot. Maybe I can find something here that would make a nice gift.
CLARA:	Why don't you just give her what's in all these cartons. It looks like a complete set.
LANG:	It is, but who wants empty bourbon bottles? There must be something here that could be cleaned up and made suitable.
CLARA:	Say, what's this doing in your closet? This is a gorgeous statue. If you could just find the arms and glue them back on it'd look brand new.
LANG:	It never had arms, silly. That's a copy of the Venus de Milo.
CLARA:	Even so it'd make a very expensive looking gift. And how would cousin Eunice know it's only a copy?
LANG:	Well for one thing, the original Venus doesn't have a clock in her stomach.
CLARA:	Then this one is more useful!
LANG:	Well, I haven't any use for it. Wait a minute, Clara, maybe you're right. I might be able to sell it to a curio shop and get enough to buy Eunice something nice. Give me a hand with it, will you?
CLARA:	Have you got a coat to throw over it?
LANG:	A coat? What for?
CLARA:	Well, you can't drag that big thing through the streets as it is.
LANG:	Why not?
CLARA:	Every man that passes will stop and ask you the time. Here – use mine.
MUSIC:	BRIDGE
LANG:	Oh, clerk—would you wait on me, please?
CLERK:	(OFF) Certainly. (FADING ON) Now then, which of you ladies is first?
LANG:	This is a statue. Wait – I'll take off the coat.
CLERK:	Oh. Yes, of course. Lovely, isn't it? Do you wish to have her clock repaired, Madam?
LANG:	No, I want to sell it.

CLERK:	To us?
LANG:	Naturally.
CLERK:	I'm afraid there isn't much of a market for this type of item.
LANG:	The sign on your window says you buy and sell everything.
CLERK:	Well, that's always been Bludgeon and Pruett's policy, but –
LANG:	Then what'll you give me for this statue?
CLERK:	Well – how about a dollar and a half?
LANG:	A dollar and a half? I lug this piece of junk all the way down here and that's all you have the nerve to offer me?
CLERK:	I'm sorry, madam.
LANG:	All right, I'll take it. At least, it'll pay my cab fare home.
CLERK:	Very well.
	SOUND: CASH REGISTER ...SELECTING COINS...COINS ON COUNTER
CLERK:	Here we are. A dollar-fifty.
LANG:	Thanks. Mind if I use you phone?
CLERK:	(CLOSES REGISTER) Help yourself. (FADING) Yes, madam, can I help you?
	SOUND: RECEIVER OFF...DIALS NUMBER...RING FILTERED...RECEIVER OFF
PARK:	(FILTERED) Hello....
LANG:	Is that you, John? This is Blanche.
PARK:	Yeah?
LANG:	John, I've tried everything I could think of. Now it's up to you to get a gift for cousin Eunice's wedding.
PARK:	What'll I use for money?
LANG:	Get a loan on you car.
PARK:	A loan on my --- Blanche, how much are you figuring on spending?
LANG:	They're rolling in money, and I'm not going to be embarrassed giving them a cheap gift.
PARK:	But a loan on my car!....After all, it's a '32 Essex! I might get as much as twenty bucks on it!
LANG:	It's a good investment, John. If Uncle Gilvert is pleased, he might even offer you a part time job on one of his steamships.
PARK:	How can I work part time on a steamship, Blanche? What do you want me to do – swim home for lunch?
LANG:	Well, then a full time job. You might make a lot of money working on a boat. It's steady. Some of those cruises last for six months.
PARK:	(SLIGHT PAUSE) They do?

LANG:	On second thought, that's an awfully long time for us to be separated.
PARK:	Yeah. Well I'll rush right out and see what I can get on my car. (HANGS UP)
LANG:	John! (JIGGLES HOOK) John!
MUSIC:	BRIDGE
CLERK:	Is somebody waiting on you, sir?
PARK:	No. I'm looking for something extra special. It's a wedding gift for a very important party.
CLERK:	Well you came to the right place, Bludgeon and Pruett have a complete selection of fine gifts. Something in silver? Tea service, perhaps?
PARK:	N-no. I want something expensive looking and impressive. Something that catches your eye and ---- Saaaaay, how much is this statue?
CLERK:	This --- statue?
PARK:	Yeah, it's beautiful! And what a spot for a clock!...... How much?
CLERK:	Well, I'm not sure. It just came in. That is, we only recently acquired it from an estate. I don't believe it's been appraised yet.
PARK:	Well get out your eye-piece and start sniffing around it, I'm in a hurry. And if it's over thirty-five dollars you can forget it – that's all I've got.
CLERK:	Well, now, let me see...hmmmmm.......It's worth a good deal more, but I suppose we could let it go at thirty-five for someone who really appreciates fine things.
PARK:	Now you're talking. Wrap it up!
MUSIC:	BRIDGE
SOUND:	PARTY NOISES B.G.
LANG:	Oh John, wasn't it a lovely ceremony?
PARK:	Mmmmmm?
LANG:	Wake up, John! Doesn't cousin Eunice look beautiful in her veil?
PARK:	Yeah, but sooner or later she's gonna have to take it off.
LANG:	Look at the groom – isn't he handsome?
PARK:	Poor bum looks drugged.
LANG:	Oh stop it, John!......Let's go over and watch – Eunice is starting to open the presents.
PARK:	All right.
LANG:	I still can't understand why you wouldn't tell me what you sent.
PARK:	I told you, I want it to be as much of a surprise to you as it is to your cousin.

LANG:	You're sure it's nice?
PARK:	Oughta be. Set me back thirty-five bucks. Wait'll you see it, it'll knock your eye out!
LANG:	Not so loud, she'll hear you.
CAST:	MURMUR OF EXCITEMENT....OOHS AND AHS
EUNICE:	(FADING IN) Oh that's lovely, thanks so much, aunt Margaret. Now let's see – this one is from Blanche and John Bickerson. Oh there you are, Cousin Blanche!...I'm so excited, I can't wait to unwrap it, and see what it is.
LANG:	Me, too, I mean, let me help you, dear. Get the scissors, John.
EUNICE:	I remember how excited you were at your wedding, Blanche, when you opened daddy's gift.
LANG:	We adored it. Didn't we, John?
PARK:	Huh? Oh yes – beautiful. (SOTTO) What the devil was it, Blanche?
LANG:	(SOTTO) How do I know?
PARK:	Here's a knife.
LANG:	I'll cut the strings.
EUNICE:	I'm glad you liked it, Blanche. (CONFIDENTIAL) Just be-tween us, I tried t talk daddy into getting you something else. I've always felt that daddy's taste was – well, you know!
LANG:	I'm afraid I don't.
EUNICE:	I mean if you like that sort of thing it's all right, but after all, drilling holes in statues to install a clock – well, really!
PARK:	Did you say a statue with ----
EUNICE:	Well, the strings are all cut. (UNWRAPPING PRESENT) Now let's see what Cousin Blanche and John ----- Ohhhh!
LANG:	Ohhhhhhh!
PARK:	I gotta make a phone call.
EUNICE:	A statue with a clock in the middle of – (GRIMLY) Lovely, isn't it?
LANG:	Yes. We're so crazy about ours, we wanted you to have one just like it!
MUSIC:	PLAYOFF
	INSERT COMMERCIAL
HOLBROOK:	(CHUCKLES) In a moment, we'll join the "happy" Bickersons. Right now, it's time to join our roving reporter, <u>Jay Jackson</u>, for the story of his interview with an actual smoker in Central Park, New York City. Okay, Jay Jackson! (SWITCH TO INTERVIEW)
	RECORDING:

JACKSON:	Hello there. This is Jay Jackson. While we've been arranging our microphones here at the entrance to Central Park of Fifth Avenue, New York City, my assistant has located a volunteer to take the Philip Morris Nose Test. Are we all set, Frank?
FRANK:	All set, Jay. Jay, I'd like you to meet Mr. Benjamin Yasky from New York City, Mr. Yasky is not a Philip Morris smoker.
JACKSON:	Thank you, Frank. How do you do, Mr. Yasky?
YASKY:	How do you do.
JACKSON:	Now about this test, I'd like to ask you one favor. Please don't refer to your present brand by its brand name. OK? All right, Mr. Yasky. Now let me offer you a Philip Morris cigarette. Here we are. Now do you have one of your own brand handy?
YASKY:	Right, sir.
JACKSON:	Would you take that out too, please. Fine, Mr. Yasky. Now which of the two cigarettes would you like to light first? It makes no difference. Take your choice.
YASKY:	My own brand.
JACKSON:	You'll try your own brand first. All right, sir. Let me light it for you. And I want you to take a puff, do not inhale, and let the smoke come slowly through your nose. That's the idea. That was your own brand first, right? Now, sir, let's try exactly the same test with the Philip Morris cigarette. I'll light it for you. Take a puff, do not inhale, and let the smoke come slowly through your nose. There we are. Now sir, you've tried exactly the same test with both cigarettes. Your own brand first, and then, the Philip Morris. Right? Tell me, Mr. Yasky, what difference, if any, did you notice between the two cigarettes?
YASKY:	Philip Morris is much milder.
JACKSON:	You found the Philip Morris much milder. Well, Mr. Yasky, you've just confirmed the judgment of thousands of other smokers, who have also found that Philip Morris is milder. Thank you so much, Mr. Yasky. END OF RECORDING
HOLBROOK:	Remember this … the test you just heard is entirely voluntary and no payment whatsoever is made for any statement in the interview. Yes, try this test – BELIEVE IN YOURSELF – and you too will believe in PHILIP MORRIS, America's FINEST Cigarette!
ANN:	Now back to Frances Langford and Lew Parker as John and Blanche Bickerson in "The Honeymoon Is Over"!
THEME:	(SOFT AND PLAINTIVE)

ANN:	Well, the Bickersons are among the select few who have been invited by Blanche's cousin Eunice to be guests on her honeymoon cruise. The happy little group embarked right after the reception, and we find them now breasting one of the worst squalls in maritime history.
	SOUND: POUNDING SURF...WIND HOWLING... FAINT BOAT WHISTLES...FADE
ANN:	In their none too spacious cabin, Mrs. Bickerson squirms in the darkness as poor husband John, afflicted with a type of insomnia which is aggravated by storms and salt air, reaches the agonizing crisis of his dread ailment... Listen.
PARK:	(SNORES LUSTILY...WHINES...SNORES AND WHINES... BROKEN RHYTHM SNORE FOLLOWED BY A WHINE)
LANG:	It's like sleeping with a motorcycle.
PARK:	(SNORES AND GIGGLES.)
LANG:	I wish this boat would sink!
PARK:	(SNORES AND GIGGLES MERRILY)
LANG:	John! John!
PARK:	Mmm.
LANG:	Turn over on your side! Go on.
PARK:	(A PROTESTING WHINE) Mmmmmmmmmmmmmmm!
LANG:	Stop that silly noise! Cut it out!
PARK:	Cut it out, Blanche. Wassamatter? Wassamatter, Blanche?
LANG:	It's bad enough getting tossed around in mid-ocean without listening to that whining and snoring and rasping. It's been going on for there hours. I wish you could hear it.
PARK:	I hear it. Must be that fat guy in the next cabin.
LANG:	It isn't any fat guy at all. It's you! You've been snoring like a man choking to death.
PARK:	Not me. Never snore. Put out the light, Blanche.
LANG:	I will not! When am I going to get some sleep, John? You don't know how I've been suffering. I've been lying here for hours on end.
PARK:	Bad position. Turn over.
LANG:	Don't be so funny, John Bickerson.
PARK:	I'm not funny, Blanche. I'm sleepy.
LANG:	You've been sleeping like you were chloroformed.
PARK:	Me? I haven't slept a wink all night.
LANG:	Not much! You snored so loud they stopped the boat twice.
PARK:	Whaffor?
LANG:	They thought the bilge pumps were clogged with seaweed.

PARK:	Go to sleep, Blanche.
LANG:	I'm so sorry I came on this trip I could cry. Why did you make me go?
PARK:	I made you go? You were the one who didn't want to offend your Cousin Eunice. I thought you said she was wealthy, Blanche.
LANG:	She is – she's heir to her father's steamship line.
PARK:	She's a hostess on a live bait boat! Fine honeymoon cruise, on a fishing scow.
LANG:	Well, anyway, it was nice of her to invite us.
PARK:	What do you mean – invite us? They're charging us four dollars a couple – and we had to bring our own worms! And on top of that I had to throw away thirty-five dollars for a wedding present.
LANG:	It's your own fault. You had no business buying the same broken down statue I sold the man.
PARK:	You and your cheap cousin's wedding have cost me a fortune. Why did you have to squander 57 dollars for that evening gown? Spend! Spend! Spend!
LANG:	You're a fine one to talk. You're the one who squanders money! Only two weeks ago you had your life insured for ten thousand dollars.
PARK:	What about it?
LANG:	You're always thinking of yourself!
PARK:	Thinking of myself? What kind of idiotic talk is that, Blanche? If I die you get the ten thousand!
LANG:	You know perfectly well you have no intention of dying! You only got your life insured to tantalize me!
PARK:	I'll drop dead in the morning!
LANG:	You say it, but you won't do it.
PARK:	Blanche, what's the matter with you?
LANG:	Well, I'm so sick of this boat trip I don't know what I'm saying. I wish we'd have stayed home.
PARK:	Well, we didn't. So put out the light and let's get some sleep.
LANG:	Did you feed the canary before we left?
PARK:	Fed the canary.
LANG:	How about the cat?
PARK:	Fed the cat.
LANG:	What'd you feed the cat?
PARK:	The canary.
LANG:	John Bickerson!

PARK:	Oh, stop blowing your cork! The cat won't starve – I left him a whole six pound tin of salmon.
LANG:	Did you open it?
PARK:	No.
LANG:	Well, how do you expect the cat to eat it?
PARK:	I left the can opener on top. Now will you please go to sleep?
LANG:	I can't sleep. I've been worried since we left the house. I don't remember whether I locked the back door.
PARK:	I locked it.
LANG:	Did you put the porch light out?
PARK:	I put the porch light out.
LANG:	I'll bet you didn't leave a note for the milkman.
PARK:	Yes, I did.
LANG:	What did you say?
PARK:	Dear Milkman – having wonderful time, wish you were here, love, John!
LANG:	What kind of a note is that?
PARK:	Oh, how do I know what I said? I told him not to leave anything.
LANG:	Well, if he leaves anything I won't pay for it.
PARK:	Mmm.
LANG:	Not with food prices what they are today.
PARK:	Please, Blanche! Don't talk about food! Just let me sleep.
LANG:	Well, I have to talk about something or I'll go out of my mind. Why does this thing rock so much?
PARK:	I don't know.
LANG:	I'm getting scared, John. When are we supposed to get to Catalina?
PARK:	Yesterday afternoon. I'll be surprised if we get there at all.
LANG:	Suppose the boat sinks, John?
PARK:	Oh, it won't sink.
LANG:	Suppose it does.
PARK:	Then it'll sink.
LANG:	I can't swim. Will you save me?
PARK:	Yes, I'll save you.
LANG:	Why?
PARK:	Look, Blanche – I've got a terrible neuritis in my legs. All I want to do is lie quietly so it doesn't pain too much.
LANG:	Who told you to get neuritis?
PARK:	Nobody told me to get neuritis!
LANG:	Serves you right for catching fish in your shorts.

PARK:	I didn't catch fish in my shorts! I used a rod! And if you'll just ---
	SOUND: THERE IS A ROAR OF SURF AND A BIG WAVE HITS THE BOAT MAKING IT CREAK AND GROAN
LANG:	What was that, John?
PARK:	Guess it was a wave. Must be a pretty rough sea.
LANG:	John.
PARK:	Mmm.
LANG:	I don't feel so good.
PARK:	Lie still.
LANG:	Will you tell me what to do if I get seasick?
PARK:	It won't be necessary to tell you.
LANG:	It's awfully close in here, John. And this is the most uncomfortable thing I ever slept in. Are you comfortable?
PARK:	Mmm.
LANG:	Why don't you change with me?
PARK:	Oh, please, Blanche! I purposely sacrificed my own comfort just so you wouldn't squawk. I took this bed with only one mattress. I gave you my pillow – what more do you want?
LANG:	I want to change. I'm not comfortable.
PARK:	You are, too! There's nothing in the world more comfortable than a hammock!
LANG:	It swings too much. I keep rolling back and forth.
PARK:	Tie your feet to the wall!
LANG:	There isn't even any room to turn over. Why did you have to put your fishing tackle up here?
PARK:	It won't fit on the floor.
LANG:	Well, I don't see why I should have to sleep with a fifty-five pound halibut!
PARK:	I couldn't get it off the hook and you know it! Besides it isn't a halibut – it's a white sea bass.
LANG:	I don't care if it's a mackerel – I'm not going to have it in my hammock! It bothers me.
PARK:	It can't bother you – it's been dead for eleven hours. Turn the fish over on his side and go to sleep.
LANG:	No. You change places with me.
PARK:	Blanche, you're just being contrary. You know as well as I do that it's more restful in a hammock – there's more air and it's ten times as good as this bed. You'll only suffer down here.
LANG:	I don't mind suffering.
PARK:	Well, I do – and I'm not gonna get up there.

LANG:	Then throw this fish out! What are you saving it for?
PARK:	I told you I want to take it home and stuff it. Settle down and go to sleep.
LANG:	No. You're going to change places with me or I'll keep talking all night.
PARK:	Okay. Let's change.
LANG:	Help me down.
PARK:	Come on. (THEY FUMBLE AROUND CHANGING PLACES) All right – so now you've got the bed…How do you climb into this darn thing? It won't stop swinging – I can't get the other leg in! Blanche! Look out! (CRASH AND THUD)
LANG:	Ohh! John – John. Are you hurt? Your face is all cold and clammy – your mouth is cut from ear to ear! John – speak to me.
PARK:	I'm up here – that's the sea bass.
LANG:	Why do you scare me like that? Get this fish out of my bed!
PARK:	He's used to you, Blanche – leave him alone.
LANG:	John!
PARK:	Mmm.
LANG:	I've got to have some water – quick!
PARK:	Wassamatter with you?
LANG:	I'm getting squeamish again. Oh, John! I need air!
PARK:	She needs water – she needs air. You want me to check your oil, too?
LANG:	Don't be funny! I can hardly breathe.
PARK:	Reach up and open the porthole.
LANG:	Porthole? What porthole?
PARK:	That little round thing with the iron handle.
LANG:	Is that a porthole? I thought it was a wall safe.
PARK:	Well, I hope you didn't put any valuables in it.
LANG:	No. Just those eight bottles of liniment.
PARK:	Liniment? Blanche, those bottles were full of bourbon! You threw them in the ocean! Why did you do it?
LANG:	Serves you right for trying to camouflage the stuff!
PARK:	I wondered why that school of sardines was chasing a shark! My bourbon! Now I'm really sick! (THE WAVES CRASH AND THE BOAT GROANS)
LANG:	(WEAKLY) Oh, John.
PARK:	(WEAKLY) Oh, Blanche.
LANG:	(SICK AS A DOG) John, do you love me?
PARK:	I love you, Blanche.

LANG:	Would you die for me?
PARK:	Gladly! I wish I was dead now. Ohhh, Blanche – I wanna leave everything to you – my will is in the desk drawer – the stocks are in the safe deposit vault – and listen, Blanche, when we get to Catalina bury me there. I couldn't stand the trip back alive or dead!
LANG:	Wait a minute, John. I think the storm is letting up.
PARK:	It is? Oh. Well, here – you can have one of these lifebelts.
LANG:	John Bickerson! You've been wearing two lifebelts all the time and I didn't have any!
PARK:	There's ten of 'em under the bunk!
LANG:	I don't believe it! You deliberately took my only ---
PARK:	Why don't you stop getting hysterical, Blanche? Every night you ---- (KNOCK AT DOOR)
LANG:	Some body's at the door. Open it, John.
PARK:	(FUMBLING AROUND) That's the last straw! Sick as I am. (KNOCK AT DOOR) I'm coming! (TERRIFIC CRASH AND THUD) Owww!
LANG:	What happened?
PARK:	I forgot I was in the hammock! (DOOR OPENS) What do you want, Eunice?
EUNICE:	John, you'd better hurry and get dressed.
PARK:	What for?
EUNICE:	There's a big run of barracuda off the port bow.
PARK:	Let 'em run. I'm not fishing anymore.
EUNICE:	Well, most of the passengers are up on deck and they've used up all of my squid. Would you let us cut up your sea bass for bait?
PARK:	Go ahead and take it. There it is – on the bunk. It's the one without the nightgown,
EUNICE:	Thanks a lot. If you want breakfast you'll have to come and get it now. There won't be any more food served until we reach Catalina.
PARK:	Oh, go away. (DOOR SLAMS) What a trip! Borrowed money on my car – threw away thirty-five dollars on a wedding gift – I'm losing two days pay – I'm sick as a dog – you won't let me sleep…There's only one thing to do.
LANG:	John – where are you going with that fishing rod?
PARK:	I'm going fishing.
LANG:	At four o'clock in the morning you're going fishing for Barracuda?
PARK:	Barracuda, nothing – I'm going to try and catch my bourbon! Goodnight, Blanche.

LANG:	Good luck, John.
MUSIC:	PLAYOFF
	(APPLAUSE)
HOLBROOK:	In a moment Frances Langford and Lew Parker will return for a curtain call; but first may I make a friendly suggestion. You've heard the PHILIP MORRIS nose test. You've heard that PHILIP MORRIS is less irritating. Why not try that test? We believe you'll find the PHILIP MORRIS is not only less <u>irritating</u> but also <u>more</u> <u>enjoyable</u>, smoother, better tasting than any other cigarette! And now once again here are John and Blanche Bickerson as Frances Langford and Lew Parker.
LANG:	Say, Lew – what are you and Mrs. Parker going to do over the Fourth?
PARK:	Well, she wanted to go away for a little vacation – but I've decided to stay home and invite some friends over for dinner.
LANG:	That's nice.
PARK:	Listen – why don't you and your husband drop over, too? You'll get a big kick out of the fireworks.
LANG:	Wonderful. When do the fireworks start?
PARK:	When my wife finds out how many people I've invited for dinner. Goodnight, Frances.
LANG:	Goodnight, Lew...Goodnight, everybody.
	(APPLAUSE)
MUSIC:	ON THE TRAIL (SNEAK)
HOLBROOK:	Thank you, Frances and Lew for the curtain call. And for America's FINEST Cigarette, here's another call well-worth remembering...
JOHNNY:	CALL....FOR..PHILIP...MORRIS...CALL...FOR...PHILIP MORRIS
MUSIC:	THEME UP
HOLBROOK:	Be sure to listen next Tuesday night when PHILIP MORRIS again will present The Bickersons. And don't miss the PHILIP MORRIS Playhouse this coming Thursday night over this same station when PHILIP MORRIS will present PAULETTE GODDARD, starring in "Mr. and Mrs. Smith." That's Thursday night for the PHILIP MORRIS Playhouse, over CBS. In the meantime, don't forget to...
JOHNNY:	CALL...FOR...PHIPIP...MORRS!
MUSIC:	UP
	(APPLAUSE)
HOLBROOK:	The Bickersons came to you, from Hollywood, California.

John Holbrook speaking.
The is CBS....THE COLUMBIA BROADCASTING

This script and the previous one both claim July 3, 1951 as its air date, though most likely this "Gooseby Vacation" script is from the following week, July 10. In it, we're treated to one of the few rare times Gloria Gooseby has an on-microphone role. While the second half of this script replicates a previous *Old Gold* script, there are major differences and I include it here to give the reader a chance to appreciate the distinction between the sketch and the full half-hour show.

Blanche and Gloria seem to be friends, but the only person to which Blanche is really honest face to face seems to be poor John who really could care less. One begins to wonder whether or not Blanche is actually jealous of Gloria, or if she just uses it as an excuse to keep the conversation going. Blanche doesn't ever seem to be threatened by others; she does the threatening! But deep down, it's obvious to both John and Blanche that they will never part. The word "divorce" or "separation" is never used. Couples in the '50s often worked through insurmountable problems in a marriage, even through the clucking of unearthly snoring.

THE BICKERSONS

CAST

FRANCES LANGFORD
LEW PARKER
BENNY RUBIN
JOHN BROWN

PRODUCER:	PHIL RAPP
PRODUCT:	PHILLIP MORRIS
AGENCY:	BIOW
TAPED:	JUNE 29, 1951
BROADCAST:	JULY 3, 1951

ANN:	They're married – they're miserable – but they love each other. That's Frances Langford and Lew Parker as the hilarious couple in Phillip Rapp's humorous creation – THE BICKERSONS! And here is John Bickerson himself – Lew Parker! (APPLAUSE)
PARK:	Thank you, ladies and gentlemen, and good evening. First I want to thank those of you who wrote in complimenting me on being able to portray a henpecked husband so accurately. I appreciate it, but my wife doesn't. She read some of the letters and didn't talk to me for a week. But it's always easy to give a good performance when you're able to work opposite an able actress – here she is, gracious and lovely – Frances Langford. (APPLAUSE)
LANG:	Thank you.
PARK:	Frances. I've been meaning to ask you. How do you go about answering all those requests from GI's for a song?
LANG:	Well, I've been working it on a first-come first-served basis, Lew. For instance, this week the first letter received was from a Marine – PFC Frank Sanchez at the U.S. Naval Hospital Joseph H. Pendleton in Arizona.
PARK:	What did he ask for, Frances?
LANG:	Well, he wanted to hear " ." So with the help of Tony Romano and his orchestra, this is just for you Frank.
LANG:	SONG
SOUND:	LIGHT CLINKING OF HAMMER ON METAL
LANG:	John!
PARK:	(OVER HAMMERING) Wait a minute.
LANG:	Come on out from under that car, I want to talk to you.
SOUND:	HAMMERING GETS LOUDER
LANG:	John!
PARK:	What do you want, Blanche?
LANG:	I haven't seen the cat all morning. I think he's lost.
PARK:	He's not lost. He's under the car.
LANG:	Where?.......That black alley cat isn't ours. Nature Boy has a golden coat.
PARK:	That's him. I've been petting him.
LANG:	You mean you've been wiping your hands on him! You ought to be ashamed of yourself, John Bickerson.
PARK:	Well, he had no business to come sniffing around while I was changing the brake fluid. Now if you'll leave me alone for five minutes, I'll be all through.
LANG:	A fine way you've picked to spend your vacation – under a car.

PARK:	I'm trying to fix it so we can go for a ride.
LANG:	I don't want to ride in this thing. You've got a whole week off. Why don't you do something with it?
PARK:	What do you want me to do?
LANG:	Go down and collect your unemployment insurance.
PARK:	I can't do that. You know I'm getting paid while I'm on my vacation.
LANG:	Well, you're not getting as much as you'd get from the Unemployment Bureau.
PARK:	I can't help it.
LANG:	Why can't you quit your job for a week and collect?
PARK:	If I quit for a minute they'd never take me back! Vacuum Cleaner salesmen are a dime a dozen.
LANG:	Stop waving that oil can around, it's pouring all over the seat.
PARK:	I'll wipe it up. Hand me that cat.
LANG:	You leave him alone...How much longer you going to be, John?
PARK:	I'm almost finished.....Grab hold of that wire, will you, Blanche?
LANG:	This one?
PARK:	Yeah....Feel anything?
LANG:	No, why?
PARK:	Nothing – I just wanted to see if it was connected to the battery.
LANG:	John Bickerson!
PARK:	Oh, take it easy – the battery is dead, anyhow.
LANG:	Well, you're not going to get a new one. You've squandered enough money on this car.
PARK:	What are you talking about? The only things I've bought in the last two years are a windshield wiper and a crank handle.
LANG:	If you didn't throw money away on all those fancy accessories we could afford a decent car.
PARK:	Nothing wrong with this car. Anybody'll tell you 1932 was a great year for Essex.
LANG:	Then why do you have to fool with it so much?
PARK:	I'm not fooling. You always have to make these minor adjustments till the car gets broken in.
LANG:	How can a broken down car be broken in?
PARK:	You'd better move, Blanche, unless you wanna get this paint over you.
LANG:	Are you going to paint the tires?
PARK:	I have to – the tubes are showing thru.
LANG:	John, if you take my advice you'll trade this thing in.
PARK:	I'm not making any trades unless I can get a good deal.

LANG:	How do you know you can't? Have you tried the Smiling Irishman?
PARK:	I tried the Smiling Irishman.
LANG:	What did he say?
PARK:	He didn't say anything – he laughed out loud.
LANG:	That's because you're not a good business man. I'll bet my brother-in-law, Barney, could make a good trade for you.
PARK:	Barney.
LANG:	Barney's a shrewd business man. He can get things from people.
PARK:	He got plenty from me, all right!
LANG:	I wish you were more like him. Barney makes good everywhere he goes. Even when he was in the Army he worked himself up to a Field Marshal.
PARK:	He worked himself up to a Buck Private!
LANG:	How can you say that? You know very well we got word that they made him a Field Marshal!
PARK:	He was a private – and he was court-martialed! Not Field Marshal!
LANG:	Well, what's the difference? Court Marshal – Field Marshal. Stop wasting your time with that pile of junk and come in and have your lunch.
PARK:	Later.
LANG:	But your creamed anchovies are getting cold.
PARK:	I don't want any creamed anchovies! Throw 'em away.
LANG:	I will not! I've got a good mind to eat them myself.
PARK:	Fine.
SOUND:	FOOTSTEPS....SCREEN DOOR OPENS
LANG:	(UP) If I get indigestion, it's your fault!
SOUND:	SCREEN DOOR CLOSES
BARNEY:	Hy'a Blanche.
LANG:	Barney! How did you get in here? The front door was locked.
BARNEY:	I had a key made.
LANG:	What did you do that for?
BARNEY:	For your own protection, Blanche. I always check my friends' apartments for prowlers when they're not home.
LANG:	Prowlers?
BARNEY:	Yeah. Let me warn you – never hide money in the sugar bowl when you're not in the house, Blanche. That's the first place a crook looks.
LANG:	How do you know I hid money in the sugar bowl?
BARNEY:	I just guessed it.
LANG:	Well.... It's only four dollars.

BARNEY:	Three sixty-five. Listen, Blanche, have you decided where you're gonna spend John's vacation?
LANG:	Not yet. Why?
BARNEY:	Well, I'm in the real estate business now, you know.
LANG:	No, I didn't know that.
BARNEY:	Just a few exclusive summer rentals. I'm the sole agent for Leo Gooseby's summer cottage. Have you ever seen it?
LANG:	No.
BARNEY:	It would be perfect for you and John. Every modern convenience....Wood stove, oil lamps, and you don't have to go very far for water. It's right on the edge of a swamp.
LANG:	A swamp! I heard it was near a lake.
BARNEY:	It was, but it dried up and they got the most beautiful cactus there now! Leo Gooseby wouldn't even consider giving up the place if he didn't have to come into town to get treated for snake-bite.
LANG:	Barney, I don't think......
BARNEY:	You can have the dump for twenty-five dollars and I'll waive my commission.
LANG:	That is a bargain.....But I don't know – John hates the country.
BARNEY:	He don't know what's good for him. The country's healthy, and the altitude might cure his snoring.
LANG:	Do you think so? I haven't slept a single night in four months.
BARNEY:	You sure look it. Believe me, I'm thinking of your health – I won't make a dime on the deal.
LANG:	I know it would be good for John if he'd only try it. But how can I get him up there?
BARNEY:	That's easy. Get him to give you a driving lesson – and while you're driving – keep driving right up to the Gooseby's.
LANG:	Barney, you've got the most wonderful conniving brain.
BARNEY:	Oh, it's nothing. I'll notify Leo you're going up there.... So long, Blanche.
SOUND:	DOOR OPENS
LANG:	Thanks, Barney.
BARNEY:	Oh, by the way, Blanche. As long as you're going to be away for a week, do you mind if I use your apartment?
LANG:	What for?
BARNEY:	Well, you see, I'm throwing a big poker party tonight for the gang from the United Nation's pool-hall.
LANG:	Well, why don't you use your own apartment?

BARNEY:	I can't…. Clara won't let me. You know how fussy she is about the furniture and everything ….What do you say, Blanche? I'm in a spot.
LANG:	Well, I don't think John would like it.
BARNEY:	Blanche, what he don't know won't hurt him. Besides, I'll cut you in on my poker winnings.
LANG:	Well… I could use the money….But how do you know you'll win?
BARNEY:	We're using my cards.
MUSIC:	BRIDGE
SOUND:	CAR DOOR OPENS
LANG:	Here, John – put these in the back seat.
PARK:	Blanche, you're only going to drive around the block – what do you want with three suitcases?
LANG:	I am taking them to the laundry.
PARK:	What for? They're not dirty.
LANG:	The laundry's inside. Well, are you going to teach me to drive, or aren't you?
PARK:	Get in.
SOUND:	CAR DOOR CLOSES
LANG:	All right – what do I do?
PARK:	Just relax. I want to explain a few things first. Teaching a wife to drive requires a great deal of patience and understanding, and we'll get along fine if you'll just listen to me and do as I tell you. If I tell you to put out your hand and slow down, don't step on the gas and speed up. If I say pull over to the right, do it now – not later. If I say there's a yellow light – come to a stop – don't step on the gas and try to beat it – because if you get away it, from then on you'll be speeding – going thru lights – reckless driving – I'll get a ticket! It's all your fault, Blanche! GET OUT OF THE CAR!
LANG:	John! I haven't done anything.
PARK:	You better not! Now start the motor, shift it to first, let out the clutch and feed the gas slowly. Have you got that?
LANG:	Yes.
PARK:	Start the car.
LANG:	The seat is too far back.
PARK:	It's not too far back.
LANG:	But I can't see the radiator cap.
PARK:	Why do you want to see the radiator cap?
LANG:	How else can I aim it?
PARK:	You steer it, you don't aim it – it's not a weapon ….Let's go.

LANG:	Don't rush me. Now let's see....Put the clutch in....Shift to first.....Let the clutch up – easy – and feed gas....There. Well, why aren't we moving?
PARK:	You didn't start the motor.
LANG:	What motor?
PARK:	The one that comes with the car! What do you mean – what motor!
LANG:	Don't snap at me.
PARK:	I'm not snapping! Start the car.
LANG:	Oh, all right.
SOUND:	WHIRRING OF STARTER
PARK:	(OVER SOUND) Wait a minute …. Stop ….. stop …..stop!
LANG:	(OVER SOUND) What's wrong? Am I going too fast?
PARK:	You're not moving – take your foot off! (SOUND OUT) The motor won't start unless you turn on the ignition.
LANG:	Where's the ignition?
PARK:	On the dashboard there – the key is in it.
LANG:	Why do you have to lock it? – Nobody's going to steal your ignition.
SOUND:	MOTOR TURNS OVER
LANG:	How's that?
PARK:	Wonderful…..Now put it in first, let the clutch out easy and you'll roll slowly and smoothly.
LANG:	All right ……Easy ……Easy.
SOUND:	CAR ACCELERATES BUCKING WIDELY….THEN RUNS SMOOTHLY
LANG:	There – how was that? John – where are you?
PARK:	In the back seat!…Make a right turn here.
LANG:	I don't think I'm ready for it yet. When do you shift this thing into second, John?
PARK:	Well, sometimes you shift into second to pick up speed, and sometimes you shift into second to go up or down a steep hill, but you never shift that thing you're holding into second BECAUSE THAT'S THE EMERGENCY BRAKE!…Step on the clutch, I'll do it for you.
SOUND:	GEAR SHIFT … MOTOR CONTINUES SOFTLY UNDER
PARK:	There….Now make a right turn.
LANG:	John, I'm doing so well this way…Why can't I keep driving straight?
PARK:	Because you'll be on the highway in two minutes.
LANG:	Well, that's all right. I know a good wide driveway I can turn around in.
PARK:	What driveway?

LANG:	At the Gooseby's summer cottage!
PARK:	Are you out of your mind! They're a hundred miles from here.
LANG:	Forty-seven. I looked it up on the map.
PARK:	I don't care if they're around the corner – I'm not ruining my vacation by visiting the Gooseby's!....Move over, I'll turn the car around.
LANG:	Wait a minute, John...I'm only doing this for you.
PARK:	What are you talking about?
LANG:	Well, it's business. The Gooseby's need a vacuum cleaner.
PARK:	You know I hate ---- They need a vacuum cleaner, huh?
LANG:	Yes, and this is your chance to sell them one.
PARK:	Well, why didn't you tell me right away?
LANG:	I didn't think of it till now. Aren't the Gooseby's fortunate to have a summer cottage?
PARK:	It serves them right.
LANG:	I wish we had a place in the country – it's so nice and healthy.
PARK:	Not for me – the altitude is bad for my sinus.
LANG:	What do you mean?
PARK:	It makes me snore like the devil!
MUSIC:	BRIDGE
SOUND:	CLINKING OF DISHES
GLORIA:	Leave the dishes on the sink, Blanche, you can wash them after we have our coffee.
LANG:	All right, Gloria.
GLORIA:	Well, how does John like the idea of renting our cottage?
LANG:	I haven't told him yet.
GLORIA:	Let's go tell him.
SOUND:	DOOR OPENS...HUM OF VACUUM CLEANER
LANG:	(OVER SOUND) John! Take that vacuum cleaner off the table! You're sucking up the sauerkraut! (SOUND OUT)
PARK:	I'm just trying to show Leo how it picks up breadcrumbs.
LEO:	I'm convinced. Now I suppose you folks are anxious to see the rest of the house.
PARK:	Not particularly. Now this cleaner has a ---
GLORIA:	Come on, Blanche, I'll show you around ... (FADING) You'll love the bathroom, it's just a short way down the road.
LEO:	Well, John, what do you think of my place?
PARK:	Lots of insects, huh?
LEO:	Just mosquitoes. But when the rain stops they go outside. You know, they don't build places like this anymore. This interior is solid beaver board.

PARK:	Where's the wall plug? I'd like to show you how this thing ---
LEO:	Oh, please, not again, Bickerson! You're acting like a man that's trying to sell me a vacuum cleaner.
PARK:	Huh?
LEO:	You're a little late, old man. Last Friday your brother-in-law sold me one wholesale.
PARK:	He did? Wait here a minute, Leo ... (DOOR OPENS ... CLOSES) (CALLS) Blanche! Blanche!
LANG:	(FADING IN) What's wrong, John?
PARK:	Where did Barney get a vacuum cleaner?
LANG:	He borrowed ours last Thursday. Why?
PARK:	He sold it to Leo on Friday.
LANG:	Wonderful! Are you going to give him a commission?
PARK:	I'm gonna fracture his skull! ... Blanche – why did you tell me the Gooseby's needed a vacuum cleaner?
LANG:	Well, it was the only way I could get you up here.
PARK:	What did I wanna get up here for?
LANG:	John, I just wanted you to see the place. We're going to rent it for a week.
PARK:	Get in the car.
LANG:	Wait a minute, John – we can't leave now.
SOUND:	CAR DOOR OPENS.
PARK:	Are you coming with me or not?
LANG:	John ---
SOUND:	CAR DOOR SLAMS ...MOTOR STARTS
LANG:	Listen to me, John! You can't drive home now!
PARK:	I wouldn't stay here for a million dollars!
LANG:	You said yourself the tires were so thin you could see the tubes.
PARK:	Who cares? I've got a spare in the trunk.
LANG:	No you haven't. I took it out to make room for the vacuum cleaner.
PARK:	Blanche, you didn't! We're fifty miles from home. Do you re-alize what could happen without a spare tire?
SOUND:	BLOWOUT
LANG:	What was that?
PARK:	I don't know – but I hope I'm shot!
MUSIC:	PLAYOFF
	INSERT COMMERCIAL
MUSIC:	(SOFT AND PLAINTIVE)
ANN:	Well, Blanche Bickerson's well-meant plan to spend a week in the country has turned into a nightmare. After wasting three hours trying to fix a blowout on his car, poor husband John has graciously accepted the Gooseby's snarling invitation to spend

the night. Unfortunately, the sadly unequipped cabin leaves much to be desired in the way of sleeping accommodations. So the Bickersons have retired...John is sleeping with Leo Gooseby on the porch, while Blanche doubles up with Gloria. Listen .....

LANG:	Are you asleep, Gloria?
GLOR:	No.
LANG:	I hate to impose on you this way. Are you sure you wouldn't rather double up with Leo?
GLOR:	I'd sooner see Leo double up by himself.
LANG:	I wish you hadn't lost your temper, Gloria. I hate to see married people squabble.
GLOR:	But he's such an ingrate, Blanche. I only suggested renting this house to you to get him out of this miserable hole.
LANG:	Well, that isn't what got him mad. It was after John turned him down and you mentioned moving in with your folks.
GLOR:	He hates my family, you know, Blanche.
LANG:	Sure.
GLOR:	It's a shame. I've been dying to get back into town. I don't see much of the old crowd since I got married. Do you ever run into Lorraine White?
LANG:	Once in a while. She looks wonderful. She is putting on a little weight.
GLOR:	I wish I was blessed with an appetite like Lorraine. She eats like a pig, doesn't she?
LANG:	What else has she got to do, poor thing. Her husband works day and night. Lorraine deserves a lot of credit, though. If she didn't hound him all the time he'd probably never have a job. Poor girl makes his life miserable.
GLOR:	You know, Lester thought he'd get away with plenty when he married her. He thought she was dumb just because she has such a stupid face.
LANG:	Dumb, nothing. Lorraine is plenty well-informed. Not many women are clever enough to be as nosey as she is. Gloria.
GLOR:	Yes.
LANG:	Lots of people don't understand Lorraine White. What do you think of her?
GLOR:	I think she's one of the most intelligent, thrifty, and honest women I've ever met.
LANG:	I don't like her, either.
GLOR:	We'd better not talk any more – Leo's such a light sleeper and these walls are like paper.
LANG:	I'm sure John's not sleeping anyway. He's got the most awful

	condition, Gloria. It's some rare kind of insomnia and it keeps us both awake all night. I can just see him lying in that strange bed with Leo, tossing and struggling – (FADES) – to get a little rest.
PARK:	(FADES IN SNORING LUSTILY....WHINES PITIFULLY... SNORES AND WHINE...BROKEN RHYTHM SNORE FOLLOWED BY A WHINE)
LEO:	Oh, he must be kidding.
PARK:	(SNORES AND GIGGLES)
LEO:	Oh, brother.
PARK:	(SNORES AND GIGGLES MERRILY)
LEO:	That's enough for me. Hey, Bickerson...John...John...JOHN!
PARK:	Mmm. Yes, dear?
LEO:	Sit up. What's the matter with you, John?
PARK:	Matter? Wassamatter? What's the matter with you, Blanche – you look horrible.
LEO:	I'm not Blanche, I'm Leo.
PARK:	Oh. Go to sleep, Leo.
LEO:	I can't sleep. The only reason I'm in here is because I had a beef with Gloria. But if I had known that you snore like ---
PARK:	Sshh. Not so loud, Leo, you'll wake up the dames. First thing you know you'll have Blanche in here and then nobody'll sleep.
LEO:	What's the matter? Don't you two get along, either?
PARK:	Get along fine.
LEO:	I don't know. My whole marriage is one big beef. John, do you ever have words with your wife?
PARK:	Lots of 'em but I never get a chance to use 'em. Goodnight. (STARTS TO SNORE)
LEO:	Oh, nuts! I'm getting out of here. I'm gonna sleep in my own room. (GETS OUT OF BED...DOOR OPENS AND CLOSES...FOOTSTEPS...KNOCK ON DOOR)
GLOR:	(OFF) Who is it?
LEO:	It's me, Leo. (DOOR OPENS) I wanna sleep in here.
LANG:	Won't it be too crowded?
LEO:	You better go in with your husband, Blanche. He is blasting my ears off.
LANG:	Well, turn around while I put my robe on. I knew this set up was no good. Goodnight.
SOUND:	DOOR CLOSES....FOOTSTEPS...DOOR OPENS
PARK:	(SNORES...HUMS...CLUCKS)
LANG:	John! John Bickerson! Cut it out!
PARK:	(A PROTESTING WHINE) Mmmm.

LANG:	Stop it, stop it, stop it!
PARK:	Stop it! What the devil is the matter with you, Leo? You keep waking me up like that nagging wife of mine.
LANG:	What!
PARK:	You're even beginning to look like her. What are you wearing that pink nightgown with the ---- BLANCHE! What happened? Where's Leo?
LANG:	You blasted him out of here. The poor man is a nervous wreck.
PARK:	Huh?
LANG:	He said he couldn't stand another minute of it. Rather than stay in the room with you he said he'd face the worst kind of torture. So he want to sleep with Gloria.
PARK:	What kind of torture is that?
LANG:	Don't you be smart, John Bickerson.
PARK:	I'm not smart, I'm sleepy. Put out the light.
LANG:	I will not. I haven't closed my eyes.
PARK:	Close 'em.
LANG:	I can't. I'm worried about the animals at home. I hope you locked the back door. The cat got out three times last week.
PARK:	Cat won't get out tonight.
LANG:	Where'd you put him?
PARK:	In the bird-cage.
LANG:	In the bird-cage? Where's the canary?
PARK:	In the cat!
LANG:	John Bickerson!
PARK:	Oh, stop knocking yourself out! Nothing happened to the canary and the cat's fast asleep in the oven.
LANG:	Well, don't scare me like that. Are you sure all the animals are taken care of?
PARK:	I'm sure.
LANG:	How about the fishbowl? Did you heat up the water for the new baby goldfish?
PARK:	I heated his water, gave him his pabulum, burped him twice and changed his diaper! Now will you put out the lights and let me sleep?
LANG:	You'd have been asleep long ago if it hadn't been for your snoring.
PARK:	Can I help it if I snore?
LANG:	Yes you can. Dr. Hersey says you snore because you have a long uvula and it flutters against your palate.
PARK:	Mmm.
LANG:	He says he can fix it with a simple operation. Why don't you let him fix it, John?

PARK:	I'll go see him next week.
LANG:	You say it but you won't do it. Do it now.
PARK:	What!
LANG:	Go on – get up and let Dr. Hersey pull out your uvula.
PARK:	Are you out of your mind, Blanche! It's three o'clock in the morning and I'm not gonna let that broken-down horse doctor hack off my uvula!
LANG:	He doesn't hack – he snips.
PARK:	I don't care if he knocks it off with a hockey stick! Nobody's gonna fool around with my uvula! Put out the lights!
LANG:	Wish I hadn't come up here in your broken down car. It's all your fault.
PARK:	My fault! You had some scheming plan to rent this place. I said I didn't want to come!
LANG:	Sure. You said you didn't want to come so I would think that you didn't want to see Gloria Gooseby, but I knew you knew I would expect you to say you didn't want to come, so I asked you and you said no and here you are.
PARK:	What?
LANG:	Never mind, you know what I mean. And I spent the most miserable three hours in that room with Gloria. She talked so much I got hoarse listening.
PARK:	Mmm.
LANG:	She kept trying to pry into our private affairs, but I told her off in no uncertain terms. Believe me, I was outspoken.
PARK:	I don't believe it,
LANG:	What do you mean?
PARK:	Nobody can out speak you.
LANG:	Well, I have to talk sometimes. You do plenty of talking. You sure jabbered away with Gloria. I'd give anything to know what you were talking about.
PARK:	Blanche, they can hear you in the other room.
LANG:	I don't care. I saw you two at the dinner table playing footsies.
PARK:	Footsies!
LANG:	Yes, footsies!
PARK:	I wasn't playing footsies! I was reaching for my shoe under the table and I accidentally brushed against Gloria's calf.
LANG:	What were you doing with your shoes off?
PARK:	I had a bottle of bourbon strapped to my leg and I was trying to pull the cork out with my toes! Are you satisfied?
LANG:	No. And the gown that woman wore tonight! She ought to be arrested! But you loved it, didn't you?

PARK:	Now don't start that!
LANG:	Anybody could look pretty with the money she spends on clothes. Every time Leo wants a kiss he has to buy her a dress! Believe me, you're lucky you've got a cheap wife like me.
PARK:	Oh, dear.
LANG:	If you were married to Gloria Gooseby you'd have to pay for her kisses!
PARK:	I'm not married to her and I get 'em for nothing! I mean I hate Gloria Gooseby!
LANG:	I go out of my way to make myself attractive for you but it's just a waste of time. It's been years since you paid me a compliment.
PARK:	Blanche, you're the most charming, gifted beautiful and sensible wife in the whole world.
LANG:	But you don't love me.
PARK:	I must love you – who else would put up with you?
LANG:	The way you talk you'd think you saved me from being an old maid. I had more boy friends than any of the girls in our crowd. I could have married any six of them.
PARK:	Yep.
LANG:	I had my pick.
PARK:	And they had their shovels.
LANG:	They did not! They were the wealthiest, handsomest, most intelligent boys in town.
PARK:	Then why did you marry me?
LANG:	For spite.
PARK:	What'd you have to spite me for?
LANG:	It wasn't you. It was another man.
PARK:	Well, you killed two birds with one stone.
LANG:	All those promises you made. Before you married me you told me you were well off.
PARK:	I was but I didn't know it.
LANG:	I knew it. You're sorry you married me. I can see it in every word you utter. You hate me.
PARK:	Oh, I don't hate you.
LANG:	Well, you don't love me.
PARK:	You know I do.
LANG:	You never say it!
PARK:	I say it a million times a day! What do you want me to do – carry a sign?
LANG:	Yes!

PARK:	Okay – I'll take my next week's salary and hire a skywriter to write the words in the sky!
LANG:	Honest, John?
PARK:	No -- Madman Bickerson! Now leave me alone and go to sleep!
LANG:	I can't sleep.
PARK:	Why not?
LANG:	I'm never able to sleep in a strange place. I'll be up all night.
PARK:	All right! (GETS OUT OF BED…OPENS BUREAU DRAWERS)
LANG:	John! What are you doing?
PARK:	I'm packing. Get dressed – we're going home.
LANG:	Home? We can't go home!
PARK:	Why can't we?
LANG:	We have a flat tire and there's no spare.
PARK:	What do I care! We'll ride home on the rims…Come on, Blanche.
LANG:	Wait a minute, John…You're so tired, you can't see straight --- you might fall asleep at the wheel!
PARK:	(HOPEFULLY) Yeah ….. It's worth a try!
MUSIC:	BRIDGE
SOUND:	AUTOMOBILE CLUMPING ALONG ON THREE TIRES AND A RIM …. IT COMES TO A STOP
PARK:	We made it. Now we can get some sleep.
SOUND:	CAR DOOR OPENS AND CLOSES
LANG:	Wait, John…Before you go in the house, just answer one question…Do you love me?
PARK:	Oh, Blanche!
LANG:	Please, I've got to know…Do you love me, John?
PARK:	Yes, I love you…Now get the bags and let's go in!…Wait a minute – who left that light burning in the living room?
LANG:	I didn't. It must be prowlers.
PARK:	Prowlers?
LANG:	Yes –we'd better not go in there, John! Let's go to a hotel and sleep. They might be gone by the time we get back.
PARK:	If there's anyone in there, I'll take care of them…Give me that jack-handle.
LANG:	No….Wait, John. I might as well confess – I loaned the apartment to Barney for a poker game with a bunch of his pool-room friends.
PARK:	What did you do that for?
LANG:	Don't scream at me. I didn't want to lend it to him – Barney talked me into it.
PARK:	He did, huh? Well, I'll take care of Barney and that bunch of bums.

SOUND:	KEY IN LOCK
LANG:	What are you going to do, John?
PARK:	I'm going to throw 'em out, one by one. Stand here and start counting as they come flying out.
SOUND:	DOOR OPENS AND CLOSES...PAUSE...DOOR OPENS... BODY THUD
LANG:	One!
PARK:	Stop counting, Blanche – it's me!
LANG:	Get up, John.
PARK:	In the morning...Goodnight, Blanche.
LANG:	Goodnight, John.
MUSIC:	BICKERSON PLAYOFF
	(APPLAUSE)

COMMERCIAL

HOLBROOK:	Now once again here are John and Blanche Bickerson as Frances Langford and Lew Parker.
LANG:	Lew, before I forget...I've been meaning to invite you out to our house. Why don't you come over tomorrow and spend the day with us?
PARK:	Thanks, Frances, but I can't make it tomorrow. I've got a club meeting.
LANG:	How about Thursday or Friday?
PARK:	Sorry. Club meeting.
LANG:	Every day?
PARK:	Except Sunday and Monday.
LANG:	What sort of a club is it, Lew?
PARK:	Oh just a bunch of fellows who get together, pay our dues, and go home.
LANG:	Sounds weird. But if you pay dues every day, you must have some beautiful clubhouse.
PARK:	You should see it...It's called Hollywood Park. If you're ever in the neighborhood drop in and see us.
LANG:	Goodnight, Lew.
PARK:	Goodnight, Frances. Goodnight everyone.
	(APPLAUSE)
	CLOSING COMMERCIAL

If any further proof were needed of the power of Blanche Bickerson over poor husband John, the following script from August 7, 1951 provides it. John, as tired and exhausted as he is, is egged on to take on a second job, to pay for Blanche's tonsil operation. This John willingly embarks upon, through a combination of a love to be dominated (probably) and a love for his wife. Blanche meanwhile is more than happy to have an operation. In fact, she's thrilled to death there's something wrong with her, since it's only in times of crises that she can pull out just a little more sympathy and time from her sleepy husband. Yes, the Bickersons love each other, though it's not the most obvious thing in the world to spot sometimes.

THE BICKERSONS

PRODUCER: PHIL RAPP
PRODUCT: PHILIP MORRIS
AGENCY: THE BIOW CO., INC.
BROADCAST: AUGUST 7, 1951

OPENING

HOLBROOK: PHILIP MORRIS presents...from Hollywood..."The Bickersons".....starring Frances Langford and Lew Parker.
MUSIC: THEME
JOHNNY: CALL...FOR...PHILIP...MORRIS!
MUSIC: (MUSIC UNDER)
VOICE: BELIEVE...IN...YOURSELF!
HOLBROOK: Yes, BELIEVE...IN...YOURSELF!! Compare PHILIP MORRIS, match PHILIP MORRIS-----judge PHILIP MORRIS against any other brand! Then...decide for YOURSELF which cigarette is milder...tastier...more enjoyable. BELIEVE IN YOURSELF...and you'll believe in PHILIP MORRIS, America's FINEST CIGARETTE!
JOHNNY: CALL...FOR...PHILIP...MORRIS!
MUSIC: (THEME UP TO FINISH)

HOLBROOK: They fight, they yell, they squabble and squawk, but they love each other as much as any married couple in the world – that's Frances Langford and Lew Parker – stars of Philip Rapp's humorous creation – THE BICKERSONS. (APPLAUSE)

HOLBROOK: Friends, in a moment we'll have a look-in at the Bickersons... but first, I'd like to have a word with the <u>most important person in the world</u> when it comes to choosing a cigarette. That person, of course, is <u>YOU</u>. We of PHILIP MORRIS believe that no one's taste is more important to <u>YOU</u> than <u>YOUR</u> taste – no one's <u>judgment</u> is better than YOUR judgement. That's why we ask you to...BELIEVE IN YOURSELF. That's why – unlike others – we of PHILIP MORRIS <u>never</u> ask you to test our brand alone. That's <u>no test</u> because it gives you <u>no choice</u>. We say...<u>compare</u> PHILLIP MORRIS...<u>match</u> PHILIP MORRIS...<u>judge</u> PHILIP MORRIS against ANY OTHER CIGARETTE. Then make your <u>own</u> choice according to your <u>own</u> taste. Your <u>own</u> judgment. In short, BELIEVE IN YOURSELF.
Later, you'll hear an interview with an actual smoker – not an actor, not a paid performer, but a real person – who will make the only fair cigarette test, the PHILIP MORRIS nose test. I know you'll be interested—so stay with us won't you? (PAUSE) Now, light up a PHILIP MORRIS...and let's join Frances Langford and Lew Parker as John and Blanche Bickerson in "The Honeymoon is Over."

THEME: (SOFT & PLAINTIVE)

PARK: Blanche! Are you going to be in that bathroom all day? I've gotta go to work.

LANG: (OFF) Well, since when are you working in the bathroom?

PARK: I want you to come out of there and give me my breakfast!

LANG: I'll be out in a minute – as soon as I finish gargling.

PARK: Gargling! Is that what you're doing? I thought the plumbing had busted. Hurry up, Blanche – I'm starved.

LANG: Your breakfast will be ready by the time you're dressed. Put a small light under the popcorn and take the sour cream out of the icebox.

PARK: Popcorn and sour cream! I won't eat it, all I want is coffee.

LANG: What?

PARK: Never mind, I'll get it myself. (FOOTSTEPS...REMOVES POT FROM STOVE...POURS LIQUID) I work like a dog all day and have to cook my own breakfast.

SOUND:	DOOR OPENS
LANG:	John.
PARK:	Mmm.
LANG:	Stop drinking for a minute and listen to me.
PARK:	It'll get cold. What do you want, Blanche?
LANG:	My throat doesn't feel any better. Do you think I should go to see Dr. Hersey?
PARK:	What for? The minute you put your foot in that thief's office he charges five dollars. It isn't worth it. There's nothing wrong with you but a slight cold.
LANG:	Well, what shall I do for it?
PARK:	Cough! That's what I do!...Now will you let me finish this coffee before it gets cold?
LANG:	How did you make coffee so fast?
PARK:	I didn't make it. I just poured it out of that new electric coffee pot on the stove.
LANG:	Electric coffee pot? That's my inhalator! John Bickerson, you've been drinking my tincture of benzoin!
PARK:	Well, it tastes better than your coffee.
LANG:	Every time I don't feel well you lose your temper.
PARK:	I do not. Blanche, darling, I don't mind you having a sore throat – if it makes you feel better, have it. It's just that I can't keep giving Dr. Hersey five dollars every time he tells you to take two aspirin.
LANG:	I'd hate to have my friends hear about this. Look at Louise Shaw – in the last six months she's had her appendix removed and two goiter operations.
PARK:	Well, she's lucky. Her husband can afford it.
LANG:	We could afford it, too, if you made a decent salary.
PARK:	Nothing wrong with my salary.
LANG:	You better look for another job, John.
PARK:	What good would that do? I'm barely making a living now! If I quit this job I'm liable to make less on a new one.
LANG:	You don't have to quit.
PARK:	What are you hinting at, Blanche? You want me to have <u>two</u> jobs?
LANG:	Why not? A little extra work won't kill you. Dr. Hersey says you're healthy as a horse.
PARK:	What does that horse doctor know? I gotta go, Blanche...Wait a minute – who stole my pants?
LANG:	Nobody stole your pants.

148

PARK:	They're not here. I distinctly remember draping them over the canary's cage last night.
LANG:	Well, the cat dragged them under the bed this morning.
PARK:	He wouldn't dare!
LANG:	Well, he did. See – there he is, under the bed sitting on your pants.
PARK:	I'll kill that cat! What right has he got to sit on my pants?
LANG:	Nature Boy is one of the family and he has as much right to sit on your pants as you have.
PARK:	He has not! I don't go sitting in his sandbox, do I? (FOOTSTEPS) Give me that broom....Get off of there, you! Get off! Scat!
LANG:	Stop poking that cat, you'll hurt him.
PARK:	He can't even feel it, he's got his head in my pocket...There – I got 'em.
LANG:	You didn't have to make such a fuss. The cat didn't hurt them any, did he?
PARK:	Not much! Look at the way he shed his fur all over 'em – I feel like I'm wearing mohair pants. Give me my jacket, I'm late already.
LANG:	Here. Your lunch is in your breast pocket.
PARK:	Okay.
LANG:	I wrapped it in the Help Wanted Section, you can read it while you're eating.
PARK:	Now don't start that again. Here – I'll go without lunch.
LANG:	But John, there are so many wonderful opportunities and we can use the money. Listen to this ad ---
PARK:	I haven't time, Blanche.
LANG:	It might lead to big money, John. It says "Learn To Be A Pilot In Your Spare Time At Home."
PARK:	I haven't got any spare time at home.
LANG:	You have, too. You spend hours every morning in the shower.
PARK:	Well, what do you want me to do – fly around the bathroom? (OPENS DOOR)
LANG:	That's right – run away and leave me helpless.
PARK:	Oh, what's the matter now?
LANG:	My throat is itching again.
PARK:	Well, I can't stay here and scratch it – I'll be late for work.
LANG:	How can you be so unsympathetic?
PARK:	Because there's nothing wrong with you. I've examined you ten times.

149

LANG:	You did not. I didn't show you my throat.
PARK:	You didn't have to – you've had your mouth open all morning. Listen, Blanche, it's all in your imagination – there isn't a thing wrong with you – you're in perfect health. I'll see you later.
LANG:	Aren't you going to kiss me goodbye?
PARK:	What – and catch your sore throat? Goodbye, Blanche.
MUSIC:	BRIDGE
SOUND:	DOOR OPENS
LANG:	Dr. Hersey -----
HERSEY:	(OFF) Oh hello, Mrs. Bickerson.
LANG:	Would you step out here in the hall for a minute?
HERSEY:	(FADING ON) Why, yes. Certainly. (DOOR CLOSES) What's the trouble?
LANG:	Nothing. Just happened to be in the neighborhood, Dr. Hersey, so I thought I'd drop in to see you.
HERSEY:	Fine. But – why out here in the hall?
LANG:	I don't want to make this an office call.
HERSEY:	I don't charge people for just dropping in to say hello.
LANG:	Oh. Well while I'm saying hello could you take a look at my throat?
HERSEY:	(OPENS DOOR) Stop being silly and come into my office.
SOUND:	(DOOR CLOSES)
LANG:	John didn't want me to come here at all. He says it's nothing.
HERSEY:	I'm glad it isn't hurting him much. Sit down and let's have a look at it.
LANG:	Never mind the stick, I'll hold my tongue down myself. Ahhhhh!
HERSEY:	That's fine. Breathe through your mouth. Hmmmm. When did this start to bother you?
LANG:	(ANXIOUSLY) This morning. What is it?
HERSEY:	There's a lot of it around.
LANG:	There is? What is it?
HERSEY:	Had two patients yesterday with the same thing.
LANG:	You did? What is it?
HERSEY:	Yes, there's a lot of it around.
LANG:	Dr. Hersey, I don't want to pry, but what have I got?
HERSEY:	Calm yourself, Mrs. Bickerson. It's merely a slight inflammation – nothing really.
LANG:	Well for something that's nothing there's certainly a lot of it around!

HERSEY:	Just take two aspirin and you'll be fine in the morning.
LANG:	Oh. Just two aspirin? No gargle?
HERSEY:	It isn't necessary.
LANG:	How about a shot of penicillin?
HERSEY:	You don't need any penicillin.
LANG:	Well it can't hurt me, can it?
HERSEY:	What's the matter with you? You sound positively dejected that your condition isn't serious.
LANG:	Well, John's always saying there's nothing the matter with me, and just once I'd like to show him how wrong he is!
HERSEY:	Oh come now, Mrs. Bickerson.
LANG:	If only I didn't have to see that smug look on his face when he finds out I've got the healthiest throat in town.
HERSEY:	Well, now, I wouldn't say that. Matter of fact, those tonsils of yours are going to have to come out one of these days.
LANG:	Tonsils? I had them out six years ago.
HERSEY:	Really? Let's have another look.
LANG:	Ahhhhhhh.
HERSEY:	Well, they've grown back. Clumsy job. Big pieces left. Who removed them?
LANG:	You did.
HERSEY:	Hmmmm. Well, they're not too bad. There's no hurry. We can talk about removing them again next winter.
LANG:	Oh, next winter. Well...Thanks for everything, Dr. Hersey.
HERSEY:	Not at all, Mrs. Bickerson.
LANG:	And I must say it's been a pleasure visiting you this way--- socially, that is.
MUSIC:	BRIDGE
SOUND:	PHONE...RECEIVER UP
MAN:	Fulbright Employment Agency...Quibble speaking. No, you have to have a personal interview here at the office. That's right. Bye. (<u>HANGS UP</u>) Now then, you're next Mr. Bickerson. Sit down please.
PARK:	Can you make it fast? It's taken most of my lunch hour just to fill out this questionnaire.
MAN:	We'll do the best we can, but let us bear in mind that the race is not always to the swift. Haste makes waste, and waste makes want, and want makes strife between the good man and his wife.
PARK:	Well, that's about two minutes of waste right there, now suppose we try a little haste.

MAN:	Hmm – testy this morning, aren't we? Well, let's see if we've filled this out correctly. Name, address, telephone number, age, previous experience --- Mr. Bickerson – you've had seventeen jobs in the last six months?
PARK:	No exactly, I left out the ones that didn't last all day.
MAN:	Not very steady, are we?
PARK:	I don't know about you, I haven't had a drink all morning.
MAN:	No need to get personal, Bickerson. I was referring to your job record.
PARK:	If we're going to look down noses, buddy, I've got as good a runway as yours.
MAN:	I'm only trying to help you. Now how do you account for this frequent change of jobs?
PARK:	I was in a rut. What's that got to do with you?
MAN:	Our reputation as an employment agency has been built on a careful screening of all job applicants. Now then, it says here that you're employed at present. Why do you need an extra job?
PARK:	I don't need it. I'm only taking it to avoid starving to death.
MAN:	Mr. Bickerson......
PARK:	Just put down that my wife needs a tonsil operation.
MAN:	Oh I'm sorry to hear it. How soon will she be up and around?
PARK:	What difference does that make?
MAN:	Well I have an excellent opportunity here for a couple---gardener and cook – pays two hundred and seventy-five a month and ---
PARK:	I'm not a domestic! I've indicated the type of work I desire right there on the questionnaire.
MAN:	Oh, yes. Executive position??
PARK:	That's right.
MAN:	Don't you feel that's sort of starting at the top?
PARK:	What's wrong with starting at the top? I've tried the bottom – it's nothing!
MAN:	But your present job is as a salesman. Don't you think you'd do best in that line of work?
PARK:	If I did best as a salesman, I wouldn't need an extra job, would I? Now look – you've wasted my whole lunch hour with your silly questions – do you have a job for me or don't you?
MAN:	Why yes, I believe we have a very fine job here for a man of your caliber. Here – go to this address. Hours are from seven PM till one in the morning, and the pay is thirty dollars a week.

PARK:	Thirty dollars a week for a man with my qualifications! Why, I'm a college graduate!
MAN:	Better not mention that – they're only giving them twenty-five.
MUSIC:	PLAYOFF
HOLBROOK:	(CHUCKLES) In a moment, we'll join the "happy" Bickersons. Right now, it's time to join our roving reporter, Jay Jackson, for the story of his interview with an actual smoker in Memphis, Tennessee.
	Okay, Jay Jackson!
	(SWITCH TO INTERVIEW)
	(RECORDING)
JAY:	Hello there, this is Jay Jackson. While we've been arranging our microphones here, on the banks of the Mississippi in Memphis, Tennessee my assistant has located a volunteer to take the PHILIP MORRIS nose test. How are we doing, Frank?
FRANK:	All set Jay. Jay I'd like you to meet Mrs. Marion Schnapper from New York City. Mrs. Schnapper is not a PHILIP MORRIS smoker.
JAY:	Thank you Frank. How do you do Mrs. Schnapper.
SCHNAPPER:	How do you do.
JAY:	Now about this test, I'd like to ask you one favor first. For obvious reasons, let's not refer to your present cigarette by its brand name. All right?
SCHNAPPER:	Right.
JAY:	All right Mrs. Schnapper, now let me offer you a PHILIP MORRIS cigarette. Here we are, and do you have one of your own brand handy?
SCHNAPPER:	Yes, I do.
JAY:	Would you take that out too please. Now Mrs. Schnapper, which of the two cigarettes would you prefer to light first, PHILIP MORRIS or your own brand?
SCHNAPPER:	Either one.
JAY:	Well, the choice is up to you, so…
SCHNAPPER:	I'll try the PHILIP MORRIS.
JAY:	The PHILIP MORRIS first. All right. Now I'm going to light it for you, then I want you to take a puff, do not inhale and let the smoke come slowly through your nose. That's the idea, and that was the PHILIP MORRIS first, right?
SCHNAPPER:	Yes.

JAY:	Now Mrs. Schnapper let's try exactly the same test with your own cigarette which I see is also one of the leading brands. I'll light it for you, want you to take a puff, do not inhale and let the smoke come slowly through your nose. There we are. Now Mrs. Schnapper, you tried exactly the same test with both cigarettes, PHILIP MORRIS first, then your own brand. Tell me please what difference, if any, did you notice between the two cigarettes.
SCHNAPPER:	Well I found that the PHILIP MORRIS was much milder, it didn't bite as much as the cigarette that I usually smoke.
JAY:	You found that PHILIP MORRIS was milder and didn't burn as much as the one you've been smoking.
SCHNAPPER:	That's right.
JAY:	Well Mrs. Schnapper, you've just confirmed the judgment of thousands of other smokers all over the country who've also found that PHILIP MORRIS is milder. Thank you so much.

(END OF RECORDING)

LEAD OUT FROM COM. #2

HOLBROOK:	Remember this...the test you just heard is entirely voluntary and no promise of any kind, no payment whatsoever, is made for any statement in the interview. Friends, the PHILIP MORRIS nose test is the only <u>fair</u> test for it allows you to compare, match, judge PHILIP MORRIS against ANY OTHER CIGARETTE. Yes, try this test---BELIEVE IN YOURSELF – and you too will believe in PHILIP MORRIS, America's FINEST Cigarette! (Pause) And now...The Bickersons.
THEME:	(SOFT AND PLAINTIVE)
ANNCR:	Well, John Bickerson has finally succumbed to his wife's nagging demands that he earn enough money to pay for her tonsil operation. To this end he has taken on another job and one o'clock in the morning finds the weary John returning home from his new position. Listen.
SOUND:	KICKING ON DOOR
LANG:	Just a minute. (GETS OUT OF BED...OPENS DOOR)
PARK:	Took you long enough to get to the door. What were you doing – sleeping?
LANG:	Of course I was sleeping. It's one o'clock in the morning. Did you lose your key?
PARK:	No. It's in my pocket – I was too tired to reach for it.
LANG:	How's the new job, dear?
PARK:	I hate it. Is the kettle on the stove?

LANG:	No. I didn't know what time you were coming home. Are you going right to bed?
PARK:	I'm gonna make some hot tea and bathe my feet.
LANG:	Can't you bathe 'em in plain water?
PARK:	I am gonna bathe 'em in plain water. I want some hot tea to drink. You go to sleep.
LANG:	Not yet. I have a lot of things to discuss with you.
PARK:	Blanche, you're gonna have your tonsils out at eight in the morning, why don't you give 'em a rest for a while?
LANG:	I don't see any reason for you to be so disagreeable, John. I haven't done anything to you.
PARK:	No, you haven't done anything. It isn't bad enough I work like a slave on one job – you force me to take another one! I'm so tired I can't see!
LANG:	Is it my fault if you have no initiative? Other men with twice your brains earn half as much as you do.
PARK:	Ahhh!
LANG:	That's the thanks I get for – (DOOR OPENS – CLOSES) – don't walk out on me when I'm talking to you, John! (PHONE RINGS...RECEIVER UP) Hello.
DOC:	(FILTER) Mrs. Bickerson, this is Dr. Hersey.
LANG:	Oh, hello, doctor.
DOC:	I got a message from my exchange to call you whenever I got in. Is something wrong?
LANG:	Well, I was worried about that throat gargle you gave me today.
DOC:	What about it?
LANG:	Do I gargle before or after meals?
DOC:	It doesn't matter, Mrs. Bickerson. It's to be used any time in case of irritation.
LANG:	Oh. Well, I'm plenty irritated right now.
DOC:	What's irritating you?
LANG:	My husband. I swear I don't know what's come over the man, doctor. He tears around here in a fury and he keeps picking on me. I wish you'd talk to him.
DOC:	Well, have him drop into my office tomorrow mor------
LANG:	He can't come to your office. He took on an extra job three days ago, and doesn't have the time.
DOC:	You say he has two jobs?
LANG:	Yes. This new one is from seven to twelve at night. He starts work at the other place at seven in the morning and quits at six in the evening. Sort of eats up the whole day.

DOC:	Yes. Well ---
LANG:	He doesn't seem to like his new job very much – he just start-ed today. He's working for the street-car company. It's really a wonderful position.
DOC:	I imagine it is. Well, Mrs. ---
LANG:	(DOOR OPENS) I can't understand why he resents it so much. It pays very well and ---
PARK:	(OVERRIDING HER, ANGRILY) Why don't you stop yap-ping about my business, Blanche!
LANG:	Excuse me a minute, Doctor…(WHISPERING TO JOHN)… Keep quiet – it's Dr. Hersey and I don't want him to hear you yelling!
PARK:	Well, get off the phone and stop blabbing about my private affairs.
LANG:	Oh, Dr. Hersey – here's John now. He wants to talk to you… Here, John.
PARK:	I don't wanna talk to him.
LANG:	(BETWEEN HER TEETH) John! You better take this phone or I'll—
PARK:	Oh, all right…Hello.
DOC:	Yes, Bickerson?
PARK:	Yes, what?
DOC:	I understand you're not feeling too well. You're not in bad shape, physically, but your mental attitude could be im-proved.
PARK:	It could, huh?
DOC:	I think so. Mrs. Bickerson isn't too well, you know, and you're not helping her any. I understand you've been very short-tem-pered. How long have you been nursing that grouch?
PARK:	Ever since she got sick.
DOC:	I beg your pardon?
PARK:	Nothing. I'm just tired.
DOC:	Bickerson, I'm afraid you're working too hard. If I were you I'd go out and have a good time with my wife.
PARK:	Okay. Where does your wife live?
LANG:	John!
DOC:	What's that?
PARK:	I said I'll think about it, doctor. Goodnight. (HANGS UP) What's the idea, Blanche? Why must you tell everybody ev-erything that goes on in my life?
LANG:	What's wrong with telling people you have another job?

PARK:	Just don't do it, that's all. I'm not too proud of slaving seven years as a bowling ball salesman without having you tell everybody I work for the streetcar company!
LANG:	It's nothing to be ashamed of.
PARK:	Well, don't do it!
LANG:	Oh, stop yelling. Just take off your conductor's uniform and go to bed.
PARK:	I've never been so embarrassed in all my life.
LANG:	Well, what's wrong with being a streetcar conductor?
PARK:	Nothing's wrong with it! I just don't like your friends getting on at every corner and staring at me! How come all your friends suddenly decided to ride on the streetcar? And why do they wait for mine?
LANG:	Are you crazy, John? I told them to ride with you!
PARK:	What for?
LANG:	Don't you want to do a good business? Why should they patronize some rival streetcar conductor who they don't even know?
PARK:	What?
LANG:	And you shouldn't throw your uniform down like that. Fold up the pants so you'll look nice for tomorrow's run. Where are the nickels, John?
PARK:	Nickels? What nickels? I've got fifteen cents in my pocket.
LANG:	Fifteen cents? I sent you over forty customers myself.
PARK:	You don't think I keep that money, do you? I have to turn it in to the company!
LANG:	All of it?
PARK:	Yes, all of it! What are you hinting at, Blanche?
LANG:	I didn't say anything, did I?
PARK:	No, but I know what you're thinking! And you'd better get those ideas out of your head!
LANG:	Ideas?
PARK:	I'm beginning to understand how that no-good uncle of yours can travel all over Europe on a bank janitor's salary.
LANG:	He isn't a janitor at all! He's one of the wealthiest bachelors in Canada. How do you think he got his title?
PARK:	What title?
LANG:	You know as well as I do my uncle was knighted for his operations in the stock market.
PARK:	It was the black market! And he wasn't knighted –he was indicted!.....Knighted!

LANG:	Well, whatever it was. He's got money and that's all that counts. You don't have to go dragging my family in every time you get upset.
PARK:	Just don't upset me, and I won't drag your family. I don't like your hints, that's all.
LANG:	What hints?
PARK:	About me keeping the streetcar company's money.
LANG:	I only asked you a civil question and you took it the wrong way.
PARK:	Well, let me get some sleep so I can get up in the morning! I've been working my brains out just so you can have your tonsils out.
LANG:	I don't see how you can go to sleep without kissing me good-night.
PARK:	I can do it.
LANG:	I guess you can. Well, don't leave your pants on the chair – hang them up.
PARK:	Okay...I'll hang 'em up...(THERE IS A SHOWER OF COINS ON THE FLOOR....PAUSE) Well, what are you staring at, Blanche?
LANG:	Where did all those nickels come from, John?
PARK:	If you must know I hit the jackpot on a slot machine! Are you satisfied?
LANG:	Yes, dear.
PARK:	What do you mean, yes dear! What kind of talk is that?
LANG:	I said yes dear.
PARK:	Well, you don't have to say it like that! I swear I won it in a slot machine. Don't you believe me?
LANG:	Of course I believe you.
PARK:	That's the last straw! If you're going to accuse me of stealing ---
LANG:	John! I'm not accusing you of anything. Why don't you hush up and go to sleep?
PARK:	Go to sleep she tells me...Stumble around form one job to another...Work like a horse...Then she thinks I'm snagging nickels...My whole body aches...Go to sleep she says...I'll never – sleep – another wink as – long a I ---(SNORES LUSTILY ...WHINES...SNORES AND WHINES)
LANG:	Sounds like he brought the trolley home with him.
PARK:	(SNORES AND GIGGLES)
LANG:	Oh, dear.
PARK:	(SNORES AND GIGGLES MERRILY)
LANG:	John! John!

PARK:	(A PROTESTING WHINE) Mmmmmmmmmmmm!
LANG:	Stop it, stop it, stop it!
PARK:	(SLEEPY AND CONFUSED) We don't stop at this corner… Move to the rear of the car, please…Fares, please…One for me and one for you.
LANG:	John!
PARK:	Mmmmm! Wassamatter? Wassamatter, Blanche?
LANG:	Get that streetcar off your mind. You're not only snoring and whining, you're talking in your sleep.
PARK:	Blanche, do you begrudge me those few words?
LANG:	If you want to talk why don't you sit up and talk to me?
PARK:	Don't wanna talk. Wanna sleep.
LANG:	Well, then don't make so much noise, I'd like to sleep, too.
PARK:	Mmmm…
LANG:	Did you put the light out in the kitchen?
PARK:	Mmmm…
LANG:	I think I see a light under the door.
PARK:	No light.
LANG:	Did you put the cat out?
PARK:	I put the cat out.
LANG:	What about the doors and windows?
PARK:	What about 'em?
LANG:	Is everything shut up for the night?
PARK:	That depends on you --- everything else is. Put out the lights.
LANG:	Aren't you going to kiss me goodnight?
PARK:	Again? I kissed you goodnight last night, didn't I?
LANG:	You did not. I was sleeping when you came home.
PARK:	Well, I kissed you twice the night before. That's four times I kissed you this month.
LANG:	What of it? It's no shame to kiss your wife. Look at that couple who just moved in next door. They've been married as long as we have and he kisses his wife right under my nose.
PARK:	Well, it's shady there.
LANG:	He kisses her when he leaves for work, he kisses her at lunch-time, and he kisses her when he comes home for dinner! Why don't you do that, John?
PARK:	Oh, Blanche – I hardly know the woman. Put out the lights.
LANG:	How can you be so mean to me?
PARK:	Blanche dear – I'm not being mean. I have to get up early in the morning and I'm so exhausted I could die. If you just let me sleep a few hours I'll kiss you till you're blue in the face.

159

LANG:	I'm sorry, John. I won't bother you anymore.
PARK:	Mmmmm.
LANG:	Just say something nice to me before you go to sleep.
PARK:	Mmmmm.
LANG:	You really love me more than anything in the world, don't you?
PARK:	Mmmmm.
LANG:	And I'm the prettiest girl you ever saw, aren't I?
PARK:	Mmmmm.
LANG:	The world would end for you if you ever lost me, wouldn't it, John?
PARK:	Mmmmm.
LANG:	See! You can say the sweetest things when you want to. Tell me some more.
PARK:	That's all I could think of.
LANG:	Will you love me as much after my tonsils are out?
PARK:	Blanche, why don't you let me sleep? I'll be dead on my feet all week – then you'll complain because I'm too tired to go out on my day off.
LANG:	You won't be too tired if Gloria Gooseby calls up.
PARK:	Now don't start with Gloria Gooseby.
LANG:	Believe me, if you were married to her, you wouldn't get away with anything.
PARK:	I'm not married to her and I get away with plenty. I mean I hate the sight of Gloria Gooseby and I wouldn't have anything to do with Gloria Gooseby or anybody else!
LANG:	You'd better not. I'd just like to catch you flirting!
PARK:	That's the way you caught me!
LANG:	That's right! Now malign my character!
PARK:	All right, all right.
LANG:	Maybe if I had shopped around a little more I wouldn't have got such a bad bargain.
PARK:	Mmmmm.
LANG:	I should have known how you felt about me when I read the inscription you had engraved on my wedding ring.
PARK:	What's the matter with that inscription?
LANG:	It says "Faithful To The Last!"
PARK:	Well, what of it?
LANG:	You told me I was the first!
PARK:	You are the first! And the last? Now will you please let me sleep?

LANG:	That's right – sleep your life away. Don't try to work out our difficulties. Don't pay any attention to the fact that I'm so sick that I won't last another month.
PARK:	What's the matter now?
LANG:	Nothing.
PARK:	Is it your tonsils?
LANG:	No. I keep getting dizzy spells. I get them every five minutes.
PARK:	How long do they last?
LANG:	About a half hour.
PARK:	How can they last a half hour when you get them every five minutes?
LANG:	Don't hound me, help me. Call the doctor, John.
PARK:	Oh, you don't need any doctor.
LANG:	You don't care how I feel – all you care about is the expense.
PARK:	Listen, last month you had a broken rib fixed, then you had your appendix out – three weeks ago you had two teeth pulled – two hundred dollars for your own private pleasure! You think I'm made of money?
LANG:	Sick as I am! I bet I'll have to have an operation – an ambulance will come in the middle of the night and take me away. An emergency.
PARK:	There's no emergency.
LANG:	I might not survive – and if I do I'll lie there in the hospital, in a charity ward – nobody to visit me – no calls ---
PARK:	Blanche!
LANG:	Why don't you send some flowers, John?
PARK:	Blanche, all you want to do is keep me awake! You're not sick and you know it! And on top of that you accuse me of stealing! Just for that, I'm not going back to that broken down streetcar company – and I'm not giving them their nickels back.
LANG:	What!
PARK:	I mean their uniforms! I'm so tired I don't know what I'm saying! Why don't you let me sleep, Blanche? You can sleep all day tomorrow, but I've got to get up at eight in the morning and take you to the hospital so you can have your tonsils lopped off!
LANG:	I've changed my mind. I'm not going to the hospital.
PARK:	Fine. Keep your broken-down tonsils. Just give me back the fifty dollars I gave you for the operation.
LANG:	Well, I was just thinking --
PARK:	The money, Blanche.

LANG:	Yes. Well, I have an opportunity to get a sweet little hat. You can wear it with the brim up or you can turn it down. It's fifty dollars.
PARK:	Turn it down.
LANG:	Well, I was thinking --
PARK:	Blanche, stop thinking so much. Where's my fifty dollars?
LANG:	I haven't got it, John.
PARK:	What! Blanche, don't tell me you spent it on something foolish!
LANG:	Oh no. I gave it to a bookbinder.
PARK:	Bookbinder! What do we need with a bookbinder? Our book is in perfect condition.
LANG:	Not that kind of a bookbinder. This man goes to the race track. He's a trout.
PARK:	Trout? Racetrack! Oh, Blanche! Did you bet that money with a bookmaker?
LANG:	I was doing it for you, John – I wanted to make enough money so you could buy me a new fur coat for my birthday.
PARK:	Doing it for me! How can you squander my money like that? I deny myself everything! I've been sewing pockets on your old girdles and wearing 'em for vests! I don't even drink my bourbon anymore – I just chew on the cork and hit myself over the head with the bottle! I never spend a penny on myself.
LANG:	You bought a tie last week.
PARK:	It wasn't a tie! It was a rope to hold my jacket together! Now you listen to me, Blanche – things are going to be different around here. From now on I'm gonna spend the money and you can do the working!
LANG:	What?
PARK:	I'm gonna squander every penny on myself – buy all the things I've always longed for...New pants – with zippers instead of paper clips! Real shaving cream instead of Duz! I'm even gonna buy three silver faucets for the bathtub!
LANG:	Three faucets?
PARK:	Hot, cold and bourbon! And if you want to bet on the races I'll give you something to bet on. You're going to buy me a race-horse.
LANG:	John! You're out of your mind! I can't get you a race-horse.
PARK:	Yes, you can – they sell 'em at the race-track. Do you hear me?
LANG:	All right. I'll go in the morning.
PARK:	You say it, but you won't do it. Do it now.

LANG:	What?
PARK:	Go on! Get up and buy me a horse!
LANG:	(CRYING) You stop yelling at me like that, you big –
PARK:	Well, don't steam me up. You had it coming to you for a long time,
LANG:	I've never been so unhappy in all my life. To think I had to meet a man with such an awful disposition. I wish I had known that you were such a terrible low-down character before I married you.
PARK:	Go on – you knew it. And so did everybody else.
LANG:	How any man could have such a savage temper! I was raised in an atmosphere where everything was pleasant – no arguments. My father never has words with my mother.
PARK:	Your father has words all right, but he doesn't get a chance to use 'em.
LANG:	That's not true. They've never quarreled since the first day they married. Believe me, John Bickerson, I'd pack up and go home to my mother if it wasn't for one thing.
PARK:	What's that?
LANG:	My mother packed up and went home to <u>her</u> mother.
PARK:	Listen, Blanche, do you think I enjoy sitting up all night fighting like this? Have you ever asked yourself the reason why we argue so much?
LANG:	I can't understand it.
PARK:	Well, just think for a minute. Why is it that an easy-going fellow – a guy who would run a mile to avoid a fight – why is it that I turn into a demon every night of my life?
LANG:	You've got me, John.
PARK:	That's the reason. Goodnight, Blanche.
LANG:	Goodnight, John.
MUSIC:	BICKERSON PLAYOFF
CLOSING	
	(APPLAUSE)
HOLBROOK:	Frances Langford and Lew Parker are standing by for a curtain call. In the meantime, for America's FINEST cigarette, here's another call well-worth remembering...
JOHNNY:	CALL....FOR...PHILIP MORRIS.
MUSIC:	"ON THE TRAIL" THEME
HOLBROOK:	Remember: PHILIP MORRIS is definitely less irritating, definitely <u>milder</u> than any other leading brand. Remember: NO CIGARETTE HANGOVER means MORE SMOKING PLEASURE – so...

JOHNNY:	CALL...FOR....PHILIP...MORRIS!
HOLBROOK:	And now, here are John and Blanche Bickerson as Frances Langford and Lew Parker.
LANG:	Lew, before I forget...I'd like you to bring your wife over to our place for dinner Sunday.
PARK:	I'd love to, Frances, but I can't. I promised to take her to the movies Sunday to see "Sirocco." She's crazy about Humphrey Bogart, you know.
LANG:	Oh, really?
PARK:	Yeah. I guess that's why she married me. You know, the strong forceful type usually attracts the weak delicate individual.
LANG:	I didn't know you were the strong, forceful type, Lew.
PARK:	I'm not – my wife is.
LANG:	Goodnight, Lew.
PARK:	Goodnight, Frances...Goodnight, everybody. (APPLAUSE)
MUSIC:	"ON THE TRAIL" THEME
HOLBROOK:	Thank you Frances and Lew for the curtain call. And for America's finest cigarette, here's another call well worth remembering.
JOHNNY:	CALL.... FOR... PHILIP .... MORRIS. CALL.... FOR... PHILIP .... MORRIS.
MUSIC:	"ON THE TRIAL" THEME.
HOLBROOK:	Be sure to listen next Tuesday night when PHILIP MORRIS again will present The Bickersons. And don't miss the PHILIP MORRIS Playhouse this coming Thursday night over this same station when PHILIP MORRIS will present _____ _____. That's Thursday night for the PHILIP MORRIS Playhouse, over CBS. In the meantime, don't forget to....
JOHNNY:	CALL ...FOR ...PHILIP...MORRIS!
MUSIC:	OUT (APPLAUSE)
HOLBROOK:	The Bickersons came to you from Hollywood, California. John Holbrook speaking. This is the CBS ....RADIO .....Network! (This is the new System Cue – use no other).

Poor husband John only makes 1.5 cents commission per bowling ball that he attempts to sell door to door. It hardly seems worth it. But in this episode, he has the hope of a big order waiting for him at the post office in the guise of a letter with 28 cents postage due...

Alas, what the letter contains only leads John Bickerson into the hospital, finally to have his snoring cured. And even in the hospital, the poor man can't get one night of rest.

This and "The Anniversary Party" are probably the two most performed routines in the Bickerson repertoire. However, the ending here differs slightly from the sentimental Ameche-Langford version in other scripts.

But alas again, it seems no matter how many times Blanche drags him into the hospital, John will never be cured.

THE BICKERSONS

PRODUCER:	PHIL RAPP
PRODUCT:	PHILIP MORRIS
AGENCY:	THE BIOW COMPANY, INC.
BROADCAST:	AUGUST 21, 1951

OPENING

HOLBROOK: PHILIP MORRIS presents "The Bickersons" produced, broadcast and transcribed, from Hollywood...starring Frances Langford and Lew Parker.
MUSIC: THEME
JOHNNY: CALL...FOR...PHILIP...MORRIS!
MUSIC: (MUSIC UNDER)
VOICE: BELIEVE...IN...YOURSELF!

HOLBROOK: Yes, BELIEVE...IN...YOURSELF!! <u>Compare</u> PHILIP MORRIS, <u>match</u> PHILIP MORRIS-----<u>judge</u> PHILIP MORRIS against <u>any</u> <u>other</u> <u>brand</u>! Then...decide for YOURSELF which cigarette is milder...tastier...more enjoyable. BELIEVE IN YOURSELF...and you'll believe in PHILIP MORRIS, America's FINEST CIGARETTE!

JOHNNY: CALL...FOR...PHILIP...MORRIS!

MUSIC: (THEME UP TO FINISH)

HOLBROOK: They fight, they yell, they squabble and squawk, but they love each other as much as any married couple in the world... that's Frances Langford and Lew Parker – stars of Philip Rapp's humorous creation – THE BICKERSONS. And here is John Bickerson himself—Lew Parker!
(APPLAUSE)

PARK: Thank you, ladies and gentlemen, and good evening. Before we don the gloves for our weekly Bickerson bout I'd like to present my marital sparring partner in another role – here she is, your purple heart girl friend – Miss Frances Langford.
(APPLAUSE)

LANG: Thank you.

PARK: Frances, the first request received this week from servicemen came from the Oak Knoll Hospital in Oakland. The fellows would like to hear you sing "Beyond The Blue Horizon."

LANG: It's my pleasure, Lew. So with the help of Tony Romano and the orchestra – this is for you, boys.

LANG: SONG

HOLBROOK: Friends, in a moment we'll have a look-in at the Bickersons... but first, I'd like to have a word with the <u>most important person in the world</u> when it comes to choosing a cigarette. That person, of course, is <u>YOU</u>. We of PHILIP MORRIS believe that no one's taste is more important to <u>YOU</u> than <u>YOUR</u> taste – no one's <u>judgment</u> is more important <u>YOU</u> than <u>YOUR</u> judgment. That's why we ask you to...BELIEVE IN YOURSELF. That's why – unlike others – we of PHILIP MORRIS <u>never</u> ask you to test our brand alone. That's <u>no test</u> because it gives you <u>no choice</u>. We say...<u>compare</u> PHILLIP MORRIS... <u>match</u> PHILIP MORRIS...<u>judge</u> PHILIP MORRIS against ANY OTHER CIGARETTE. Then make your <u>own</u> choice according to your <u>own</u> taste, your <u>own</u> judgment. In short, BELIEVE IN YOURSELF.

Later, you'll hear an interview with an actual smoker – not an actor, not a paid performer, but a real person – who will make the only fair cigarette test, the PHILIP MORRIS nose test. I know you'll be interested—so stay with us, won't you? (PAUSE) Now, light up a PHILIP MORRIS…and let's join Frances Langford and Lew Parker as John and Blanche Bickerson in "The Honeymoon is Over."

THEME:	(SOFT & PLAINTIVE)
SOUND:	KITCHEN NOISES…POTS AND PANS BEING MOVED
LANG:	Every morning it's the same thing.…Rush – rush – rush… Get up at seven and make breakfast for you, then clear the things away, straighten the house, make the beds, do the shopping, do the laundry. Why can't I have a maid, John? John!
PARK:	Mmmm?
LANG:	John Bickerson! How can you fall asleep at the breakfast table?
PARK:	It ain't easy with all that talking going on. Wake me in five minutes, Blanche.
LANG:	Take your face out of the oatmeal and sit up straight.
PARK:	Oh dear.
LANG:	I don't know why I bother to make breakfast for you, anyway – you never eat it. What's wrong with the oatmeal, John?
PARK:	Too lumpy.
LANG:	How do you know? You didn't taste it.
PARK:	Didn't have to taste it – I got a lump on my head.
LANG:	You've got it all over your clothes, too. You can't go to work looking like that – go in and change your suit.
PARK:	What for? My other suit looks worse.
LANG:	No, it doesn't. I had it cleaned.
PARK:	Cleaned? You had no right to do that! Who told you to have that suit cleaned?
LANG:	What's wrong with you, John? There was a big stain on the lapel. It was filthy.
PARK:	What do you mean – filthy? That was a bourbon stain! I've been saving it for months.
LANG:	What for?
PARK:	In case there's liquor rationing, I don't wanna be caught short. Where's my hat, Blanche?
LANG:	Look in the sandbox.
PARK:	What's my hat doing in the sandbox? I'll kill that cat!
LANG:	Don't be like that, John. I think the poor thing's going to have kittens.

PARK:	Well, it's not gonna have 'em in my hat! Wait a minute, Blanche – Nature Boy can't have kittens – he's a male!
LANG:	That's not Nature Boy, silly – the pet shop loaned us another cat while ours is being wormed.
PARK:	I never heard of such a thing!
LANG:	Anyway, I want you to take this cat back and pick up Nature Boy before you leave for work.
PARK:	I can't do that, Blanche – I'll be late. I've got a big day ahead of me and I'm so tired I can't keep my eyes open.
LANG:	Well, it's your own fault if you're tired every morning. Your snoring keeps you awake.
PARK:	You keep me awake!
LANG:	It amounts to the same thing…Your snoring wakes me up and I wake you up to stop it. Why don't you have an operation?
PARK:	What are you talking about? There's no operation to cure snoring.
LANG:	Yes, there is. I cut an article out of the paper about a snore doctor. His name is Dr. Rasper.
PARK:	Dr. Rasper!
LANG:	He was the head of surgery at a goat clinic in Salzburg.
PARK:	Goats don't snore!
LANG:	I know they don't. He just used them for experiments. It can't hurt you to let him try it, can it?
PARK:	Blanche, I can't afford any operations. I haven't had a single order in three weeks. The only reason I've still got a job is because my boss has forgotten I'm working for him!
LANG:	Maybe there's an order in that letter that came for you.
PARK:	What letter?
LANG:	It arrived yesterday – it was in a big fat official looking envelope.
PARK:	Well, why didn't you tell me yesterday?
LANG:	I wasn't talking to you yesterday.
PARK:	Where is it? Where's the letter?
LANG:	I sent it back to the post-office.
PARK:	Blanche, that letter might contain a big order! What did you send it back for?
LANG:	There was 28 cents postage due and I didn't want to break a dollar.
PARK:	Oh, how could you do such a thing! For a measly 28 cents you're liable to cost me my job!
LANG:	Don't get excited. You can pick it up on your way to work.

PARK:	This may be the break I've been waiting for...I sent our catalogue to the National Bowling Association – they have two million members – yes, that's it! Blanche, I'm made. I can retire and live on my income! A man with my money doesn't have to work.
LANG:	Oh, John – hurry and get that letter!
PARK:	Lend me twenty-eight cents for the postage-due!
LANG:	Here...Now John, you've got to promise me that you'll go through with the operation to cure your snoring.
PARK:	Oh, forget about that quack doctor.
LANG:	He's not a quack. Just listen to what the newspaper ---
PARK:	I haven't time.
LANG:	It'll only take a minute. Listen. "Dr. Hugo Rasper, eminent respiratory surgeon has accepted a residency at Parkhaven Hospital. The doctor, a former goat specialist, attained national prominence through his many experiments on snoring. Among his most celebrated patients were the late Lord Nubsan, the late Charles Canterbary, and the late Countess------" John, where are you going?
PARK:	I'm getting out of here before you make me the late John Bickerson!
MUSIC:	BRIDGE
SOUND:	DOOR OEPNS AND CLOSES
CLARA:	It's me, Clara. Are you home, Blanche?
LANG:	(OFF) I'm getting dressed. Be right in.
CLARA:	I was down at the market shopping. I never saw such prices! Can you lend me some eggs, Blanche?
LANG:	(FADING IN) If you were down at the market, why didn't you buy some?
CLARA:	At ninety-three cents a dozen?
LANG:	That's what <u>we</u> pay – I don't lay them myself, you know. Even though you're my own sister, Clara, I must say you have some awful chiseling habits, and frankly, I don't know where you learned them.
CLARA:	Forget about the eggs. What are you putting on those old rags for?
LANG:	I've got to see a doctor. Why should I dress up and get a big bill?
CLARA:	She doesn't know where I learned them she says. What's wrong with you?
LANG:	It's not me, it's John. Clara, does Barney ever disturb you in the middle of the night?

CLARA:	Terribly! He sleeps with a smile on his face. If I ever find out who he's dreaming about, I'll kill him.
LANG:	Well John snores, and it's driving me mad. I'm going to arrange to have him operated on.
CLARA:	Who you going to – Dr. Hersey?
LANG:	No, Dr. Rasper. He's a surgeon who just arrived in town, and there's a whole article in today's paper about his new operation to cure snorers.
CLARA:	Dr. Hersey will be terribly hurt. All these years you've sort of been promising him John's nose, and here you are giving it to a perfect stranger.
LANG:	Well, Dr. Rasper's a specialist. Dr. Hersey can have any other part of John he wants. I just want this snoring operation to be perfect.
CLARA:	It doesn't sound good to me.
LANG:	Listen, Clara – in case I get detained at the hospital, would you kind of look in on our animals?
CLARA:	What do you feed them?
LANG:	Well the canary gets tomato juice, the goldfish gets hamburger, and the cat a can of Puss and Boots.
CLARA:	You give that to the cat? I've been feeding it to Barney.
LANG:	Does he like it?
CLARA:	Loves it. And you oughta see the way his eyes shine in the dark.
LANG:	Well, I've go to go and make arrangements with the doctor now.
CLARA:	Blanche, I don't want to mix in, but do you think John'll agree to be operated on? You know how he always screams about money.
LANG:	Yes, but there's a special delivery letter for him at the Post Office and John seemed to think it was a big order. He gets a commission on every bowling ball he sells, you know.
CLARA:	But an operation might cost hundreds of dollars.
LANG:	Well, Dr. Rasper has a convenient credit plan and the way it works is that you're completely healed the day you make your last payment.
CLARA:	Uh-huh.
LANG:	Now suppose this big order is for, say – twenty bowling balls a week. How long would it take John to make three hundred dollars, if his commission is a cent and a half a ball?
CLARA:	I don't know, but it seems like an awful long time for a man to have his nose in a sling!

MUSIC:	BRIDGE
SOUND:	PARCEL POST PACKAGE BEING STAMPED A FEW TIMES THEN THROWN ON FLOOR
CLERK:	Next.
PARK:	You've got a special delivery letter here for John Bickerson.
CLERK:	You want the dead letter window. You're on the wrong line.
PARK:	I've been on <u>six</u> lines! Dead letters, Stamps, Parcel Post, Registered letters, Money Orders, and Complaint Department! I've been kicked back and forth in this building like a used Republican! Now I realize you've got a nice going business here that doesn't depend on good will, but don't you think it time you hopeless incompetents got yourselves organized??
CLERK:	(COOLY) Would you mind lowering your voice? You see, part of our civil service examination is a hearing test.
PARK:	Oh, is that so?
CLERK:	Yes, it is. I happen to be a government employee, you know.
PARK:	I don't care if you're Margaret Truman, I'm a taxpayer! And while we're on the subject, you can tell the people you work for, I haven't received my <u>refund</u> yet! ... I can just see them waiting six months for <u>their</u> money!
CLERK:	This is not the Bureau of Internal Revenue.
PARK:	There's a lot of things it's not, including a post office! But there's a special delivery letter here for me, (POUNDS FIST ON COUNTER FOR EMPHASIS) and I'm gonna get it!
SOUND:	TWANG OF BROKEN SPRING. FEW SMALL METAL PARTS TINKLE TO FLOOR
CLERK:	(SOFTLY AND WITH GREAT COMPASSION) Why did you break our weighing scale?
PARK:	I didn't break it, it must have been weak.
CLERK:	Worked fine this morning. I'm afraid that's going to set you back thirty-two dollars and sixty-five cents.
PARK:	I haven't got any thirty-two dollars and sixty-five cents.
CLERK:	Sign here, please, and then just forget the whole ugly incident.
PARK:	(SIGNING) If I had a few witnesses, I'd fight this thing!... Now where's my letter? And don't tell me you haven't got it or I'll have you arrested for robbing the mails!
CLERK:	I'm looking for your letter now.
PARK:	Wasted a whole morning in this broken down post office.
CLERK:	Here we are – Homer Fickett.
PARK:	Bickerson's the name! John Bickerson!
CLERK:	Sorry, nothing with that name.

PARK: What about that one on top – that looks like my name – let me see it. It <u>is</u> mine! John Bickerson! Can't you read?

CLERK: Is that "B – I"? Looks to me like "Q – W"

PARK: Show me one name in the world that starts with "QW!" Go on, show me and I'll give you ----

CLERK: Twenty-eight cents, please.

PARK: Here. (DROPS COINS ON COUNTER. TEARS OPEN ENVELOPE. OPENS LETTER) If I've lost out on a big order on account of your stupidity --- What the devil is this?

CLERK: Looks like an advertising circular.

PARK: (STUNNED, READS) "Dear fellow sufferer, Dr. Rasper can end your snoring forever."

MUSIC: BRIDGE

HOLBROOK: (CHUCKLES) In a moment, we'll join the "happy" Bickersons. Right now, it's time to join our roving reporter, Jay Jackson, for the story of his interview with an actual smoker in Memphis, Tennessee. Okay, Jay Jackson!
            (SWITCH TO INTERVIEW)
            (MRS. F. MARSHALL)
            (RECORDING)

JACKSON: Hello there. This is Jay Jackson. While we've been setting up our microphones here in the beautiful lobby of the Hotel Peabody in Memphis, my assistant has been talking to some of the guests and has located a volunteer to take the PHILIP MORRIS nose test. Are we all set, Frank?

FRANK: All set, Jay. Jay, I'd like you to meet Mrs. Frank Marshall of Memphis, Tennessee. Mrs. Marshall is not a PHILIP MORRIS smoker.

JACKSON: Thank you, Frank. How do you do, Mrs. Marshall?

MARSHALL: Fine, thank you.

JACKSON: Now, about this test, I'd like to ask you one favor first. For obvious reasons, don't refer to your present cigarette, please, by its brand name. All right?

MARSHALL: All right.

JACKSON: All right, Mrs. Marshall, now let me offer you a PHILIP MORRIS cigarette. There we are. Do you have one of your own brand handy?

MARSHALL: Yes, I do.

JACKSON: Good. Now which of the two cigarettes would you prefer to light first?

MARSHALL: Oh, it doesn't make any difference.

JACKSON: Well, suppose you make the choice.

MARSHALL: All right. I'll light the PHILIP MORRIS first.

JACKSON: The PHILIP MORRIS first. All right, I'll light it for you, then I
             want you to take a puff, do not inhale and let the smoke come
             slowly through your nose. That's the idea. And that was the
             PHILIP MORRIS first, right?

MARSHALL: That was.

JACKSON: Now, Mrs. Marshall, let's try exactly the same test with
             your own cigarette – which I notice is also one of the lead-
             ing brands. I'll light it for you, I want you to take a puff, do
             not inhale and let the smoke come slowly through your
             nose. There we are. Now, Mrs. Marshall, you've tried exactly
             the same test with both cigarettes – first with the PHILIP
             MORRIS and then your own brand.

MARSHALL: Right.

JACKSON: Tell me, please, what difference, if any, did you notice be-
             tween the two cigarettes?

MARSHALL: Well the PHILIP MORRIS seemed much milder.

JACKSON: You found that PHILIP MORRIS milder than your own ciga-
             rette.

MARSHALL: Yes, I did.

JACKSON: Well Mrs. Marshall, you've just confirmed the judgment of
             thousands of other smokers all over the country who've also
             found that PHILIP MORRIS is milder. Thank you so much.
             (END OF RECORDING)

HOLBROOK: Remember this…the test you just heard is entirely volun-
             tary and no promise of any kind, no payment whatsoever,
             is made for any statement in the interview. Friends, the
             PHILIP MORRIS nose test is the only fair test for it allows
             you to compare, match, judge PHILIP MORRIS against
             ANY OTHER CIGARETTE. Yes, try this test---BELIEVE IN
             YOURSELF – and you too will believe in PHILIP MORRIS,
             America's FINEST Cigarette!
             (Pause) And now, once again, here are Frances Langford
             and Lew Parker as John and Blanche Bickerson in "The
             Honeymoon Is Over."

THEME: (SOFT AND PLAINTIVE)

HOLBROOK: Well, even the persistent dripping water will eventually
             wear away a stone. So after seven years of cycloid insomnia,
             or Blaster's reaction, John Bickerson has finally yielded to
             Blanche's demands and consented to allow a specialist to

	relieve his condition. Outside his room at the Parkhaven Hospital, Blanche Bickerson has a last minute conversation with Dr. Rasper. Listen.
DOC:	He's all right, Mrs. Bickerson. The nurse is giving him a sedative now.
LANG:	Nothing can go wrong, can it, Dr. Rasper?
DOC:	He won't be in surgery over fifteen minutes and there's absolutely no danger whatever.
LANG:	What causes a man to snore like that, Doctor?
DOC:	Well, he's a mouth breather, very likely suffering from Kleinfeld's stertor, a respiratory disorder resulting from a post-pharyngeal condition. Does he drink anything?
LANG:	Anything. The operation won't hurt, will it?
DOC:	Not the slightest. All we have to do is take a stitch in his palate and shorten his uvula.
LANG:	I hate to bring this up now, Dr. Rasper – but how much will it cost?
DOC:	The fee will be fifty dollars with the anesthetic.
LANG:	How much is it without the anesthetic?
DOC:	I should say about forty dollars. But I wouldn't advise the operation without it.
LANG:	All right, Dr. Rasper.
DOC:	I think you better run along, Mrs. Bickerson – it's past midnight. He's got to get a good night's rest and you can come and see him in the morning.
LANG:	Well, I'll just look in on him now to make sure he's sleeping.
DOC:	Very well. (FADING) Goodnight, Mrs. Bickerson.
LANG:	Goodnight, Doctor. (DOOR OPENS AND CLOSES)
PARK:	(SNORES LUSTILY…WHINES…SNORES AND WHINES PITIFULLY)
LANG:	Sounds like he left one of his goats here!
PARK:	(SNORES AND GIGGLES)
LANG:	Isn't that awful!
PARK:	(SNORES AND GIGGLES MERRILY)
LANG:	Oh dear. I must see that he gets a good night's rest. John!
PARK:	Mmmm.
LANG:	Wake up!
PARK:	Wassamatter, Blanche? Wassamatter?
LANG:	How can you sleep like that?
PARK:	I cleaned the kitchen, I plucked the canary, I scaled the goldfish and I milked the cat! Everything's taken care of – lemme sleep.

LANG:	John, what are you talking about? We're in the hospital.
PARK:	Who's sick?
LANG:	Nobody's sick – you're going to have an operation. Dr. Rasper's going to shorten your uvula in the morning.
PARK:	Then what did you wake me up now for?
LANG:	The way you were snoring I was afraid you'd wear it off before he gets a chance to operate.
PARK:	I don't know why I let you talk me into this. (SOUND OF BED BEING CRANKED UP) Who made that broken down Dr. Rasper such an authority on ------------Stop cranking the bed up! What are you doing, Blanche?
LANG:	You weren't sleeping properly, and I'm supposed to see that you get a good night's rest.
PARK:	I was sleeping fine. Why did you tilt me like this?
LANG:	I was afraid the snore would roll down your throat and poison you.
PARK:	Oh, Blanche – will you please crank me down!
LANG:	(AS SHE CRANKS) You keep your voice down, John Bickerson – you're disturbing the other patients. And I still don't know why you have to have an operation to cure your snoring.
PARK:	I didn't want it! You've been working on me for seven years to do it!
LANG:	I'm beginning to think it's a waste of money. I could have used that fifty dollars. I'm still walking around in a short dress.
PARK:	What are you beefing about? Tomorrow I'll be walking around in a short uvula. Put out the lights!
LANG:	You mustn't excite yourself, dear. Open your mouth.
PARK:	What for?
LANG:	Just hand me that thermometer – I want to take your temperature.
PARK:	Blanche, they took my temperature eight different ways.
LANG:	Well, I want to check it again before we go to sleep.
PARK:	We? Blanche, what are you doing in your nightgown? You're not gonna sleep <u>here</u>, are you?
LANG:	Yes, I am. It only cost five dollars extra to have that cot moved in here and that silly night nurse gets ten dollars a day.
PARK:	What about it?
LANG:	Well, I'm going to take her place and save the money...Now open your mouth like a good boy...There...Keep that thermometer in there while I check your pulse.
PARK:	Mmmm.

LANG:	There isn't anything those nurses can do that I can't...There... Your pulse is normal – it's steady as clockwork.
PARK:	You've got your fingers on my wristwatch!
LANG:	Well, you shouldn't be wearing a wristwatch. Not good to have constriction when you're sleeping...Let me see that thermometer.
PARK:	Here...What does it say?
LANG:	Murphy's Bar and Grill! What was this swizzle stick doing in that glass?
PARK:	I had them deliver me a highball. And if you think that hot water bottle is full of hot water you're out of your mind.
LANG:	That bourbon! If Dr. Rasper knew about it he wouldn't operate on you.
PARK:	Why don't you tell him? I'd love it!
LANG:	Now please don't get excited, dear. It's my job to see that you get a good night's rest, and I'm not going to let anything disturb you.
PARK:	Well, put out the lights.
LANG:	I want to be sure that you have the right sleeping position... Stretch your feet out a little more...Move over to the center... Don't bury your head that way... There...Are you comfortable?
PARK:	Fine.
LANG:	Relaxed?
PARK:	Mmm.
LANG:	Will you be able to sleep well?
PARK:	Sleep well.
LANG:	That's fine. Now get up and unpack my bag.
PARK:	Unpack your bag! I thought you were putting me to sleep!
LANG:	I was just testing. Unpack my bag, John.
PARK:	Why don't <u>you</u> unpack it?
LANG:	I have to refill this hot water bottle.
PARK:	I don't need any hot water bottle!
LANG:	It's not for you, it's for me. I still have a little indigestion from those clams I ate for dinner. You always take me to those cheap restaurants. The whole dinner disagreed with me.
PARK:	It wouldn't dare!
LANG:	Now don't start getting irritable. I've done plenty for you, so you can do something for me. Unpack my bag, John.
PARK:	Aaaaaah! (GETS OUT OF BED) Where's my slipper? Did you bring my slipper?
LANG:	It's under the bed in that little foot bath.

PARK:	Footbath! Big nurse! (HEAVY OBJECT BEING DRAGGED) Look at the size of this suitcase. What did you bring it for? We're only staying one night.
LANG:	You never can tell. Put the stuff away.
PARK:	(OFF) There's no closet. Where'll I put these dresses?
LANG:	In the drawers.
PARK:	(OFF) Where do you want these drawers?
LANG:	In the dresser.
PARK:	(FADING IN) Listen, Blanche, I'm not gonna – Blanche!
LANG:	Crank me up, John.
PARK:	What are you doing in my bed? I'm the one who's getting operated on! You have no right to be in my bed eating fruit and candy! Maybe you'd like me to send you some flowers!
LANG:	No, but tell the floor nurse I can have visitors between two and four tomorrow. I'll feel better then.
PARK:	Am I supposed to sleep in that old wooden cot?
LANG:	Yes, It's easier to watch over you from here.
PARK:	There's nothing but a spring on this cot. Not even a mattress!
LANG:	Well, that'll keep you off your back and you won't snore tonight. Just crawl between the blankets. I want you to be well rested for the operation.
PARK:	(GETS INTO BED) Put out the lights.
LANG:	In a minute. Was everything all right at the house when you left?
PARK:	Fine.
LANG:	I would have checked things myself if I didn't have to prepare for your admission here. Maybe I should have stayed home?
PARK:	Mum!
LANG:	John, I'm worried about the house.
PARK:	Don't worry.
LANG:	I think I left the electric heater on in the bathroom. It might burn up the place.
PARK:	Won't burn.
LANG:	Did you turn it off?
PARK:	No.
LANG:	Well, how do you know it won't start a fire?
PARK:	I left the water running in the bathtub.
LANG:	John Bickerson!
PARK:	Oh, stop popping your topper. I checked everything.
LANG:	We should have taken all the animals with us. The poor little canary is locked in the cage – the cat can't get out of the

	house – and who's going to feed the goldfish? I'll bet they're terribly unhappy.
PARK:	Oh, they're not unhappy. They're having a fine vacation.
LANG:	They are not.
PARK:	They are, too. When I left the cat was fishing.
LANG:	Fishing? Where?
PARK:	In the goldfish bowl and he was using the canary for bait!
LANG:	What!
PARK:	Oh, go to sleep. The canary and the goldfish are fine – and I wish the cat would drop dead.
LANG:	Why are you so mean?
PARK:	I'm not mean. I'm full of those sleeping pills and I can't keep my eyes open. Now put out the lights.
LANG:	I'll be through in a minute.
PARK:	Blanche – why are you plucking your eyebrows at this time of night?
LANG:	I'm not plucking my eyebrows. I'm taking off my false eyelashes.
PARK:	False eyelashes? I didn't know you had bald eyelids!
LANG:	My eyelids are not bald. It's just that my lashes are short and they don't bring out my eyes. Lots of women use false eyelashes.
PARK:	Well, throw 'em away. You don't need anything to bring out your eyes.
LANG:	I do too!
PARK:	You do not. I'm satisfied with the way they bulge now! Are you going to let me get some sleep?
LANG:	Yes, dear – just close your eyes. I'm going to read the paper for a little while. (RUSTLES NEWSPAPER)
PARK:	(MUMBLES) Read the paper.
LANG:	There's certainly a lot of activity in Washington. What's all this tax reduction talk?
PARK:	Talk.
LANG:	Listen to what Senator ----
PARK:	Blanche, I read the paper – every word of it. Read it to yourself.
LANG:	Don't be so disagreeable. Dr. Rasper told me to keep you occupied so you won't think about the operation.
PARK:	All I'm thinking about is sleep.
LANG:	That's a good boy. You mustn't get nervous.
PARK:	Mmmm.
LANG:	You see what's happening to the stock market?
PARK:	It's going to pieces.
LANG:	Why don't we get a piece of it?

PARK:	Put away the paper, Blanche.
LANG:	What's the name of that stock you bought last year?
PARK:	I told you fifty times. Kentucky Saltpeter Mines.
LANG:	I can't even find it listed on the stock page.
PARK:	Look in the Help Wanted Column.
LANG:	Oh, listen to this! Here's a story about a doctor who left a pair of scissors inside of a ---
PARK:	Blanche, will you stop reading to me! I'm nervous and jittery about the operation and I can't stand the sound of your voice.
LANG:	I can just hear you making those insulting remarks to Gloria Gooseby!
PARK:	Now don't start with Gloria Gooseby!
LANG:	You wouldn't bite off her head like that without her squealing all over the place.
PARK:	I always bite her and she never squeals! I mean I hate the sight of Gloria Gooseby! And this is one night I don't want to hear about her.
LANG:	Oh, hush up and go to sleep.
PARK:	Go to sleep she tells me! In the morning they're going to cut out my uvula ---- steams me up ---
SOUND:	TELEPHONE RINGS
PARK:	What's that?
LANG:	It's the telephone. Answer it.
PARK:	Why don't <u>you</u> answer it? It's right next to your bed.
LANG:	I'm not supposed to be here. It might be the hospital superintendent, and I don't want him to find out. Go on and answer it.
PARK:	Can't even get any rest in a hospital…(GETS OUT OF BED. RECEIVER UP) Hello?
OP:	(FILTER) Mrs. Kimpert?
PARK:	Hah?
OP:	The maternity nurse asked me to call you. You can get ready now – they're bringing your baby in for his one o'clock feeding.
PARK:	What?
OP:	Isn't this room 43?
PARK:	I don't know what it is, but I'm not feeding any babies! (HANGS UP…GETS BACK IN BED) What kind of a hospital is this! I'm gonna get out of here!
LANG:	Now don't go getting hysterical. Just relax.
PARK:	How can I relax?
LANG:	Well, I'm doing my best to see that you get a good night's sleep. I'm so worried I won't be able to close my eyes tonight.

PARK:	What are you worried about? I thought you said it was only a minor operation.
LANG:	Oh, I don't care about that. I'm worried about Nature Boy.
PARK:	Who's Nature Boy?
LANG:	The cat. How's he going to get out tonight?
PARK:	What does he want to get out for?
LANG:	John – don't you know it's impossible for certain creatures to be shut up for the night?
PARK:	How well I know it! Why don't you go to sleep, Blanche?
LANG:	I can't sleep. I must find out if the cat's all right. Maybe you ought to call him, John.
PARK:	Okay – what'll I call him?
LANG:	No. I mean call him on the telephone.
PARK:	Have you gone stark staring mad, Blanche! How can I call a cat on the telephone?
LANG:	He'll know it's us, and the ringing of the phone will comfort him. Go on – call Nature Boy. It won't cost anything.
PARK:	(GETS OUT OF BED) Nobody would believe this! Calling a cat at three o'clock in the morning. (LIFTS RECEIVER)
OPERATOR:	(FILTER) Operator.
PARK:	Get me State 7-9970.
OPERATOR:	(FILTER) State 7-9970. Thank you.
PARK:	How much can a man stand of this sort of stuff before he cracks up!
LANG:	Oh, don't be so tragic. A lot of people call their pets up – any sound in the house to break the monotony makes them feel better.
PARK:	Sure.
SOUND:	(MUFFLED RINGING OF THE PHONE AT THE OTHER END)
OP:	There's no answer. Shall I keep ringing?
PARK:	Just a minute…How many times you want her to ring, Blanche?
LANG:	Are you sure she has the right number?
PARK:	Operator, are you sure it's the right number?
OP:	I'll try it again.
SOUND:	CLICKING…DISTANT RING…RECEIVER UP AT OTHER END
VOICE:	(FILTER…SLEEPY) Hello.
PARK:	Hello. Nature Boy?
VOICE:	Huh?

PARK:	Are you all right?
VOICE:	Fine.
PARK:	Good. I left a big dish of catnip under the sink. Don't touch the canary.
VOICE:	Okay.
PARK:	Goodbye. (HE HANGS UP) There. The cat feels fine and --- Blanche! Who answered that phone?
LANG:	I thought you were kidding. Did somebody answer?
PARK:	Must have been the wrong number?
LANG:	Do you think so, John?
PARK:	Of course I think so. Don't start making me believe that a cat can talk. Blanche, I can't stand any more of this. I'm going home!
LANG:	You get right back in that bed! Dr. Rasper will never forgive me if you run out on him.
PARK:	I don't care! I don't trust that doctor and I don't believe he knows what he's doing! I'm getting out of here.
LANG:	You are not! Everything's been prepared – the surgery – the nurses, the anesthetic. They'll think you're crazy, John.
PARK:	Blanche – it won't work, I tell you! There's no operation that can cure snoring – the guy's a fake! What's he charging you?
LANG:	Fifty dollars.
PARK:	Blanche – I appeal to your sense of economy. I'm a perfectly healthy guy – never been sick a day in my life. That snoring operation won't work and we'll be out fifty dollars.
LANG:	We won't be out a penny. I made a deal with Dr. Rasper.
PARK:	What deal?
LANG:	If the operation isn't a success, he's going to take out your liver and appendix for nothing!
PARK:	Goodnight, Blanche.
LANG:	Goodnight, John.
MUSIC:	BICKERSON PLAYOFF (APPLAUSE)
HOLBROOK:	Frances Langford and Lew Parker are standing by for a curtain call. In the meantime, for America's FINEST cigarette, here's another call well worth remembering....
JOHNNY:	CALL....FOR....PHILIP MORRIS.
MUSIC:	"ON THE TRAIL" THEME
HOLBROOK:	Remember: PHILIP MORRIS is definitely less irritating, definitely _milder_ than any other leading brand. Remember: NO CIGARETTE HANGOVER means MORE SMOKING PLEASURE – so...

JOHNNY: CALL...FOR...PHILIP...MORRIS!

HOLBROOK: And now, here are John and Blanche Bickerson as Frances Langford and Lew Parker.

LANG: Say, Lew, I was talking to your wife yesterday and she told me you just bought a big ranch out in the valley.

PARK: Well, Frances, you know my wife is a city girl and she doesn't know much about ranch life. But we'd like you to come out and see the place.

LANG: I'd love to see it, Lew.

PARK: It's only half an acre, but it's got good grass on it, and our livestock is thriving.

LANG: Livestock? What have you got – chickens?

PARK: No.

LANG: Pigs? Cows?

PARK: Oh, nothing like that.

LANG: Well, what kind of livestock are you raising?

PARK: Gophers.

LANG: Goodnight, Lew.

PARK: Goodnight, Frances....Goodnight, everybody.
            (APPLAUSE)

HOLBROOK: Be sure to listen next Tuesday night when PHILIP MORRIS again will present The Bickersons. And don't miss the PHILIP MORRIS Playhouse this coming Thursday night over this same station when PHILIP MORRIS will present Richard Greene and Francis L. Sullivan starring in "An Inspector Calls." That's Thursday night for the PHILIP MORRIS Playhouse, over CBS. In the meantime, don't forget to....

JOHNNY: CALL...FOR...PHILIP.......MORRIS!

MUSIC: UP
            (APPLAUSE)

HOLBROOK: The Bickersons came to you transcribed from Hollywood, California. John Holbrook speaking.
            This is the CBS....RADIO ....NETWORK!

"John the Shoplifter" is the 13th and last program in *The Bickersons* radio series, sponsored by Philip Morris cigarettes. By the early '50s, radio was severely wounded and was dying from the attack of that great beast, television. The Bickersons would no longer appear in that happy medium that made them huge stars, save for several radio commercial spots for various sponsors through the '60s and '70s.

THE BICKERSONS

BROADCAST: AUGUST 28, 1951

HOLBROOK: PHILIP MORRIS presents… "The Bickersons" produced, broadcast and transcribed, from Hollywood…….starring Frances Langford and Lew Parker.
MUSIC: THEME
JOHNNY: CALL… FOR…PHILIP…MORRIS!
MUSIC: (MUSIC UNDER:)
VOICE: BELIEVE…IN…YOURSELF!
HOLBROOK: Yes, BELIEVE…IN.. YOURSELF!! Compare PHILIP MORRIS, match PHILIP MORRIS----------judge PHILIP MORRIS against any other brand! Then….decide for YOURSELF which cigarette is milder…tastier…more enjoyable…BELIEVE IN YOURSELF…and you'll believe in PHILIP MORRIS, America's FINEST CIGARETTE!
JOHNNY: CALL…FOR…PHILIP…MORRIS!
MUSIC: (THEME UP TO FINISH)
HOLBROOK: They fight, they yell, they squabble and squawk, but they love each other as much as any married couple in the world – that's Frances Langford and Lew Parker --- stars of Philip Rapp's humorous creation – THE BICKERSONS. And here is John Bickerson himself – Lew Parker!
(APPLAUSE)

PARK: Thank you, ladies and gentlemen and good evening. Before Frances and I square off for our weekly Marital Mayhem, here is Miss Langford as her more lovable self – the GI's Purple-Heart Girl Friend…Frances!
          (APPLAUSE)
LANG: Thank you.
PARK: It's almost impossible to keep up with all the requests from the boys in the service, but I think we should attend to this one. It's from the gang at the Walter Reed Hospital in Washington, D.C. and they want to hear you sing "Falling In Love with Love."
LANG: Nothing would give me greater pleasure. So with the help of Tony Romano and the orchestra – this is for you, fellows.
LANG: SONG
          (APPLAUSE)
HOLBROOK: Friends, in a moment we'll have a look-in at the Bickersons… but first, I'd like to have a word with the <u>most important person in the world</u> when it comes to choosing a cigarette. That person, of course, is YOU.
          We of PHILIP MORRIS believe that no one's taste is more Important to <u>YOU</u> than <u>YOUR taste</u> – no one's judgement <u>is</u> more important to YOU than YOUR judgment That's why we ask you to…BELIEVE IN YOURSELF. That's why – unlike others – we of PHILIP MORRIS <u>never</u> ask you to test our brand alone. That's <u>no test</u> because it gives you <u>no choice</u>. We say…<u>compare</u> PHILIP MORRIS…<u>match</u> PHILIP MORRIS… <u>judge</u> PHILIP MORRIS against ANY OTHER CIGARETTE. Then make your <u>own</u> choice according to your <u>own</u> taste, your <u>own</u> judgment. In short, BELIEVE IN YOURSELF. Later, you'll hear an interview with an actual smoker – not an actor, not a paid performer, but a real person – who will make the only fair cigarette test, the PHILIP MORRIS nose test. I know you'll be interested – so stay with us, won't you? (PAUSE) Now, light up a PHILIP MORRIS and let's join Frances Langford and Lew Parker as John and Blanche Bickerson in "The Honeymoon is Over."
THEME: (SOFT & PLAINTIVE)
LANG: John!
PARK: Mmm?
LANG: Hurry up and drink your orange juice before it gets cold.
PARK: Let it get cold. I don't like hot orange juice, anyway.

LANG:	It isn't hot – I just warmed it a little to take the chill off. You know you have to be careful about what you eat with your sensitive stomach, John.
PARK:	Well, I don't want to eat anything. I just wanna get these sales reports finished before I go to work.
LANG:	Nonsense. I've already fixed breakfast for you and you're going to eat it. Why, even a horse eats before he works…Here. (DISH ON TABLE)
PARK:	What is it?
LANG:	Curried tapioca.
PARK:	Give it to a horse. I wouldn't touch it.
LANG:	What's the matter, John? Is business getting bad?
PARK:	It's always been bad – but now it's getting worse. Let me finish these reports, will you, Blanche?
LANG:	I don't know. For a man who doesn't make any sales you certainly do a lot of paper work.
PARK:	I make a lot of sales! Look at this – you see this big pile of papers over here? Well, half of them are orders.
LANG:	What about the other half?
PARK:	Cancellations.
LANG:	Cancellations?
PARK:	Yeah…I had orders for thirty-two hundred bowling balls all signed, sealed and delivered. Then some crackpot inventor came along with a bowling ball that makes mine obsolete.
LANG:	Obsolete? How can a bowling ball be obsolete?
PARK:	The one he invented has a <u>handle</u> on it! Says it does away with needing a carrying case. Did you ever hear of such a silly thing?
LANG:	I don't see anything wrong with it.
PARK:	You wouldn't.
LANG:	Is the handle detachable?
PARK:	No! The bowler's supposed to gallop down the alley, swing his ball like a polo mallet and whang the pins over! Of course it's detachable.
LANG:	Well, you needn't get hysterical. I wish you'd have thought of it.
PARK:	Forget it.
LANG:	Maybe you can invent something, John – you'll never get rich working. My uncle invented a printing press and made a lot of money out of it.
PARK:	Sure – but it's all counterfeit.
LANG:	It is not! And stop making my relatives out to be criminals – they're just as honest as yours.

185

PARK:	I know it – mine are all thieves! Hand me that eraser, Blanche – I made another mistake on this order.
LANG:	Well, why bother to correct it? It is a cancelled order, isn't it?
PARK:	Give me the eraser.
LANG:	Oh, here.
PARK:	Thanks…There – that does it…Books all balanced. Sales 5600 dollars – cancellations 5600 dollars.
LANG:	Well, I'll say one thing for you, John – you're the <u>neatest</u> failure I ever saw.
PARK:	Now don't start that again. I've got a steady job and that's what counts. Where's my hat?
LANG:	On the sideboard.
PARK:	Where's my lunch?
LANG:	In your hat. You'll be home early, won't you? John?
PARK:	I'll try.
LANG:	Never mind trying, just do it. We've got a long drive ahead of us tonight and I don't want to be late for the wedding.
PARK:	What wedding?
LANG:	Oh, come on, John! You know my cousin Agnes from Saugus is getting married tonight. I've got the invitation right here.
PARK:	This is the first I heard of it. I never saw any invitation.
LANG:	Well, it came two weeks ago. You told the mailman to take it back – you said the Bickersons didn't live here.
PARK:	I did? Let me see that envelope, Blanche.
LANG:	Here.
PARK:	Oh, no wonder! Your cousin's got the same handwriting as my dentist – I thought it was a bill!
LANG:	Well, it's a wedding invitation. We're going.
PARK:	I give up. If that fish-faced cousin of yours could hook a husband, no man in this world is safe!
LANG:	How can you say that, John? You know very well Agnes won a beauty contest last year at the canning factory.
PARK:	A fine beauty contest winner. Miss Imported Sardine of 1950! Skinless and Boneless division!
LANG:	Well, what do you care – you're not marrying her. You're only going to the wedding.
PARK:	No. I'm not.
LANG:	Of course you are, silly. I'm going to be the bridesmaid and you're the best man. Now be a good boy and buy a new tuxedo on your way to work.

PARK:	What's wrong with the one I've got?
LANG:	Oh, you can't wear that, John – it's out of style. Nobody's wearing seersucker tuxedos anymore!
PARK:	It's not seersucker, it's crimped sharkskin! All it needs is a pressing to cover up the shine in the coat.
LANG:	Well, a pressing won't cover up the hole in the pants. Don't be so stingy, John – you can pick up a nice second-hand tuxedo for under twenty dollars.
PARK:	I'm not stingy, Blanche – I just can't afford it.
LANG:	You can, too. If I can afford a brand new evening gown for 68 dollars you can certainly afford a second-hand tuxedo!
PARK:	I knew it! You only want to go to the wedding because you bought a.....Wait a minute! We can't go, anyway.
LANG:	Why not, John?
PARK:	I just remembered that I have to take inventory at the office tonight.
LANG:	Oh, John!
PARK:	(WITH A SMILE) Too bad. I would have loved going to that broken-down wedding, that's the breaks of the game...Take that dress back, Blanche!
LANG:	I can't. I've already had it altered.
PARK:	Well, give it to me – I'll take it back. I'm not throwing away sixty-eight bucks because you had it altered...Where'd you buy this dress, Blanche?
LANG:	At Fuller's. But John, can't you try to get off from work just for tonight?
PARK:	No.
LANG:	It's such a pity. You're the best man and the groom is depend-ing on you.
PARK:	What are you talking about? I never met the poor sucker in my life! Why should he depend on me?
LANG:	Well, he's very nervous and he's liable to call the wedding off if you don't show up.
PARK:	Oh. Well, in that case I've got no choice in the matter.
LANG:	You'll go?
PARK:	Of course not. It's the least I can do for my fellow man... Goodbye, Blanche! I'm gonna return this dress to Fuller's be-fore I go to work!
SOUND:	DOOR OPENS AND CLOSES
LANG:	John – Wait! You can't ----
SOUND:	PHONE RINGS...RECEIVER UP

LANG:	Hello...Oh, Clara – how are you?...I'm not so good...John's not going to the wedding...No – and he's taking the dress back to Fuller's.....What's that? I bought it at Plummers?... Good Heavens!....John!....John!.... John!
MUSIC:	HURRY BRIDGE
SOUND:	TELEPHONE RINGS...RECEIVER UP
MAN:	Fuller's Department Store, Adjustment Department, Grumper speaking ......Yes, madam?...I'm afraid you have the wrong department, you want alterations! (HANGS UP)
SOUND:	DOOR OPENS AND CLOSES
PARK:	Is this the Adjustment Department?
MAN:	That's right. Won't you sit down?
PARK:	Well, I'm in a hurry. I just want to get a refund on this –
MAN:	Certainly. Here at Fuller's, if you're not satisfied, your money will be cheerfully refunded.
PARK:	Fine.
MAN:	Yes, indeed, (CHUCKLES) cheerfully refunding money is a Fuller tradition handed down by our illustrious founder, just before he went into the hands of the receivers.
PARK:	That's very interesting, but about this refund ----
MAN:	That's what we're here for. At Fuller's your money is cheer-fully (CHUCKLES) refunded.
PARK:	Well, that's just (CHUCKLES MIRTHLESSLY) dandy!.....But if it's all the same to you, let's stop the cheerfulness and start the refunding.
MAN:	(NETTLED) Hmmmm. Well, let's fill out this form.
PARK:	Do we have to go through that?
MAN:	Purely a formality. Now then – reason for refund – doesn't fit perhaps?
PARK:	I don't know, I haven't tried it on.
MAN:	Well, then we're hardly being fair to the garment, are we?... Won't you try it on now?
PARK:	(SLIGHT PAUSE) I don't think so.
MAN:	Why not?
PARK:	Because blue evening gowns clash with my purple garters!
MAN:	(COOLY) Oh, it's a gown! How amusing.
PARK:	Isn't it.
MAN:	(CONTAINING HIMSELF WITH EFFORT) Now then – reason for refund?
PARK:	I want my money back.
MAN:	That's not a reason.

PARK:	Can you think of a better one?
MAN:	(ANGRILY) Look here – if we were to give a refund at the senseless and unreasonable whim of every crum-bum that comes in here -------
PARK:	What happened to all the chuckling?
MAN:	If you haven't a satisfactory reason for ---
PARK:	Just a minute! I happen to be one crum-bum who knows his rights. I don't have to have a reason for a refund!
MAN:	(GRIMLY) Very well. Give me your sales slip.
PARK:	I haven't got one.
MAN:	Then how are we supposed to know when this was bought? There are no refunds on anything after two weeks.
PARK:	I bought it yesterday!
MAN:	I have the files here. (OPENS FILE) Do you mind if I take a quick run through them?
PARK:	I don't care if you ride through them side-saddle, I'm going to get my money back! (FILES OPENING AND CLOSING UNDER THIS) You've wasted half the morning for me already with your silly questions, senseless grilling and idiotic chatter! Fine way to handle refunds! What you need here is somebody to adjust the Adjustment Department! And that somebody ought to have at least half a brain!
MAN:	(SLIGHT PAUSE) Are you – quite finished?
PARK:	Yeah. Now give me my refund, and I'll tell you one thing, you'll never find me in here again!
MAN:	You're right about that – at least, not for some time!
PARK:	What is that supposed to mean?
MAN:	We have no record of this gown being sold.
PARK:	Oh, you haven't.
MAN:	No...and you have no sales slip...somehow it all adds up.
PARK:	It does, does it? And what does it add up to?
MAN:	Shop-lifting! Oh, detective! (POLICE WHISTLE)
PARK:	Take your hands off me you ----
MUSIC:	BRIDGE
SOUND:	DOOR OPENS
LANG:	Excuse me, Could you direct me to ---
MAN:	(APPRECIATE WHISTLE)
LANG:	Well, thank you.
MAN:	Oh pardon me, Miss – I was carried away by that gown. What were you saying?
LANG:	I'd like to speak to John Bickerson.

MAN:	Bickerson – Bickerson – oh yes – cell thirteen. I was about to go back there. We just got an order to release him.
LANG:	Before you do, could you let me talk to him a few minutes? I want him to promise me something before he finds out he's released. It's – well, it's about a wedding.
MAN:	I understand, Miss.
LANG:	I doubt it. However, I haven't time to explain.
MAN:	Well, anyway, there's another little matter before he can leave. The bill.
LANG:	Bill?
MAN:	One pair of bent handcuffs, two back windows for the happy-wagon, and the sergeant's eyeglasses – forty-seven dollars. I'm afraid Bickerson wasn't very happy with us.
LANG:	Well, send him a statement.
MAN:	All right. (IRON DOOR OPENS) Third cell on the left – and good luck, Miss.
LANG:	Thanks. (FOOTSTEPS) Hello, John.
PARK:	(DISAPPOINTED) Oh, it's you. I didn't recognize you in that get-up.
LANG:	How's the food here, John?
PARK:	Dandy!...What are you doing here in that evening gown?
LANG:	Mr. Grumper at Fuller's was very apologetic when I explained it wasn't bought there.
PARK:	It wasn't bought there!
LANG:	No, I got it across the street. I'm sorry if my lapse of memory caused you any trouble.
PARK:	Mmmm.
LANG:	How do I look?
PARK:	Lovely.
LANG:	Sure, but what good are fancy clothes when you're the wife of a jailbird!
PARK:	I'm not a jailbird, and I'm going to sue that store for every nickel they've got for false arrest!
LANG:	You can't do that.
PARK:	Oh no? Give me one little reason why not!
LANG:	Because I signed a waiver releasing them.
PARK:	What'd you do that for??
LANG:	They were very sweet to me and let me pick out whatever I wanted in the store.
PARK:	So you sold me down the river for some worthless trinket! And what may I ask have you been doing to get me out while

	I languish in this Devil's Island, rotting away the best years of my life?
LANG:	You rotted away the best years of your life before I ever met you.
PARK:	That's beside the point. Have you hired a lawyer?
LANG:	No.
PARK:	Why not?
LANG:	Well, what do you ever do for me?
PARK:	What??
LANG:	I ask you to do one simple little thing, like taking me to my cousin's wedding, and you make up all kinds of excuses to get out of it.
PARK:	Those weren't excuses, I was supposed to take inventory to-night. Probably get fired for not even showing up.
LANG:	Well, it's too late to worry about that. But there's still time to go to the wedding if you could get a parole.
PARK:	What parole! I haven't been convicted of anything! If you'd just call that broken-down store and get them to drop the charges –
LANG:	Will you take me to the wedding if I do?
PARK:	Blanche! This is blackmail!
LANG:	Uh-huh.....Will you?
PARK:	To think that my own wife ---
LANG:	Will you take me to the wedding, John?
PARK:	Even if I said yes, where could I get a tuxedo at this hour?
LANG:	I've got one right here in this box – compliment's of Fuller's Department Store. Put it on.
PARK:	You thought of everything, didn't you?
LANG:	Uh-huh.
PARK:	I can't prove it, but I've got a sneaking suspicion you engineered this frame-up all the way down the line!
LANG:	Oh, John.
PARK:	All right, you win. Get me out of here.
LANG:	Rattle on the bars with your tin cup, dear.
PARK:	Ohh, what's the use. (RATTLES TIN CUP ON BARS) Hey, Screws!
LANG:	(PLEASED) Why, that's wonderful, John – you've adjusted to your environment perfectly.
PARK:	Thanks. Where is that guy?
MAN:	(FADING IN) Take it easy, I'm coming. Gonna let you out now, Bickerson. (KEY IN LOCK. HEAVY IRON DOOR OPENING)

LANG: About the wedding, John – I know how you feel, but believe me, you won't regret this decision.

MAN: So you finally broke him down, eh Miss? Gotta hand it to you – didn't even need a shotgun.

MUSIC: PLAYOFF AND APPLAUSE

HOLBROOK: (CHUCKLES) In a moment, we'll join the "happy" Bickersons. Right now, it's time to join our roving reporter, Bob Pfeiffer, for the story of his interview with an actual smoker in Louisville, Kentucky. Okay. Bob Pfeiffer!
(SWITCH TO INTERVIEW)
(BEATRICE ISAACS)
(RECORDING)

PFEIFFER: Hello there. This is Bob Pfeiffer. While we've been setting up our microphone here in the heart of Louisville, Kentucky, my assistant, Frank Higgins, has been interviewing passers-by on Fourth Avenue and has located a volunteer to try the PHILIP MORRIS Nose Test. All set, Frank?

FRANK: All set, Bob. I'd like you to meet Miss Beatrice Isaacs from Louisville, Kentucky. Miss Isaacs is not a PHILIP MORRIS smoker.

PFEIFFER: Thank you, Frank. How do you do, Miss Isaacs?

ISAACS: How do you do.

PFEIFFER: About the test, may I ask you one favor. For obvious reasons, we don't want you to refer to your present cigarette by its brand name. Is that OK by you?

ISAACS: Yes, it certainly is.

PFEIFFER: Now, let me offer you a PHILIP MORRIS, Miss Isaacs. Do you have one of your own brand handy you could take out for me?

ISAACS: Yes, I do.

PFEIFFER: Then we'll be all set to go. Fine. Now, which cigarette would you like to try first, Miss Isaacs?

ISAACS: I'll try my brand.

PFEIFFER: You'll try your brand first. All right, I'll give you a light, then take a puff, do not inhale and slowly let the smoke come through your nose. That's the way, Miss Isaacs. Now, that was your own brand – which I noticed was also one of the leading cigarettes. Now, let's try exactly the same test with the PHILIP MORRIS. Remember, I'll give you a light, you take a puff, do not inhale, and slowly let the smoke come through your nose. All right, Miss Isaacs, by your own choice you tried your brand first and then the PHILIP MORRIS – you made exactly the same test each time. What difference, if any, did you notice between the two cigarettes?

ISAACS:	Well, I think the PHILIP MORRIS is milder.
PFEIFFER:	The PHILIP MORRIS is milder.
ISAACS:	Yes sir.
PFEIFFER:	Miss Isaacs, you've just confirmed the judgement of thousands of other smokers who've also found that PHILIP MORRIS is milder. Thank you very much.
	END OF RECORDING
	LEAD OUT
	FROM COM #2
HOLBROOK:	Remember this…the test you just heard is entirely voluntary and no promise of any kind, no payment whatsoever, is made for any statement in the interview. Friends, the PHILIP MORRIS nose test is the only <u>fair</u> test for it allows you to compare, match, judge PHILIP MORRIS against ANY OTHER CIGARETTE. Yes, try this test – BELIEVE IN YOURSELF – and you too will believe in PHILIP MORRIS, America's FINEST Cigarette!
ANN:	And now, back to Frances Langford and Lew Parker as John and Blanche Bickerson in "The Honeymoon Is Over."
THEME:	(SOFT AND PLAINTIVE)
ANN:	The wedding of Blanche Bickerson's cousin Agnes turned out to be a big success… for cousin Agnes. For the Bickersons it turned out to be a long ride home. Too long. So, in a motel on Highway 99, in cabin number 13, the Bickersons have retired. Mrs. Bickerson tosses restlessly in her strange bed as poor husband John, victim of an obscure type of insomnia which attacks the patient only during the day, gives valid proof of his agonizing affliction. Listen.
PARK:	(SNORES LIKE A DIESEL TRUCK….WHINES….SNORES AND WHINES… BROKEN RHYTHM SNORE FOLLOWED BY A PITIFUL WHINE)
LANG:	Oh dear!
PARK:	(SNORES AND GIGGLES…SNORES AND GIGGLES AGAIN)
LANG:	I'd give anything to know what he's dreaming about.
PARK:	(SNORES AND GIGGLES MERRILY)
LANG:	John. John!
PARK:	Mmmm.
LANG:	Turn over on your side! Go on!
PARK:	(A PROTESTING WHINE) Mmmmmmmmmmm.
LANG:	I never heard such noises! You're giggling like a new bride. What are you dreaming about?

PARK:	New bride.
LANG:	What!
PARK:	What? Whassamatter, Blanche? Whassamatter?
LANG:	I hate this motel! We must have passed at least fifty others on the road. Why did you insist on stopping here?
PARK:	This was the only one that has a vacancy!
LANG:	The place gives me the creeps. I'm afraid to go to sleep, John.
PARK:	Oh, what's the matter with you, Blanche?
LANG:	There's all sorts of eerie sounds – and I swear I saw something moving outside the window.
PARK:	Probably the wind.
LANG:	No, it wasn't. I saw it distinctly. It was a terrifying shape with long ears and a head like a donkey.
PARK:	Woman's afraid of her own shadow! There's no donkeys outside the window, Blanche.
LANG:	Go and look.
PARK:	Okay. Put on the lights.
LANG:	The lights are on. Take off your sleep shade.
PARK:	Oh…(STUMBLES OUT OF BED)…You can think of more ways to keep me up… There's nothing outside the window… Nothing! Are you satisfied?
LANG:	I could swear I saw something.
PARK:	Put out the lights…(GETS BACK IN BED)…Goodnight!
LANG:	Goodnight… It was a wonderful wedding, wasn't it, John?
PARK:	Wonderful.
LANG:	Didn't my cousin Agnes look stunning in her wedding dress?
PARK:	Mmm.
LANG:	And didn't Willie look handsome in your tuxedo?
PARK:	Imagine that bum showing up for his own wedding in baggy blue jeans.
LANG:	They weren't baggy. They looked fine on you.
PARK:	Let me sleep, Blanche.
LANG:	I think they'll make a wonderful couple, don't you, John?
PARK:	Couple of what?
LANG:	I hope they'll be as happy as we've been.
PARK:	Mmm.
LANG:	In spite of all our little arguments you are satisfied with our married life, aren't you, John? Aren't you?
PARK:	What?
LANG:	Are you satisfied with our married life?
PARK:	Satisfied? I've had more than enough.

LANG:	You see. You're the one who always starts it.
PARK:	Blanche, I'm so sleepy I don't know what I'm saying...I have to get up at the crack of dawn, drive sixty miles and then go to work. Why don't you have some consideration for me?
LANG:	You're a fine one to talk about consideration. You're not even civil to me anymore. You come home from work, gobble your dinner, bury your head in the paper and you're asleep and snoring before you know it! You don't even like to say good-night to me!
PARK:	You're wrong, Blanche – I love to say goodnight to you. Good night!
LANG:	Sure – take the easy way out. Don't discuss things sensibly and try to reach a solution. Just go to sleep.
PARK:	Fat chance.
LANG:	I shouldn't talk to you at all after your behavior tonight.
PARK:	There was nothing wrong with my behavior.
LANG:	I suppose you thought it was all right to rhumba with Willie and hand the bride a cigar. Poor little Agnes. She cried so hard she ruined her bridal veil.
PARK:	She didn't need a veil. She could have combed her eyebrows straight down. First time I ever saw a bride with a crew haircut.
LANG:	You stop that! Agnes had a beautiful cropped bob. She may not be the prettiest girl in the world but she's got a lot of charm. The boy who married her got a prize.
PARK:	What was the prize?
LANG:	Don't be sarcastic. We had no right to leave before the ceremony was over in the first place. I don't know why you rushed me away from there.
PARK:	You know I have to be at the office at daybreak!
LANG:	You did it to embarrass me.
PARK:	I did not!
LANG:	You did too! Just because it was my cousin who was getting married. You've been to fifty weddings and always stayed for the ceremony. Did you ever regret it?
PARK:	Only once.
LANG:	Oh, that's too bad about you. You always make it sound like I got the bargain. I could have done better, I'm sure.
PARK:	I swear, Blanche, sometimes I wish you'd have married the first idiot who proposed to you.
LANG:	I did.
PARK:	Very funny. Put out the lights.

LANG:	All those promises you made when you were courting me. It makes me laugh to think of what you said when you proposed.
PARK:	It doesn't make me laugh!
LANG:	You were going to give me a life of luxury – twenty servants and a mansion. Did I ever doubt you? Did I investigate your bank account? No. Did I hire detectives to find out about your salary?
PARK:	No.
LANG:	Yes, I did.
PARK:	What?
LANG:	Yes, I did.
PARK:	What did you do that for?
LANG:	Because I didn't know what you were getting when you married me.
PARK:	Neither did I!
LANG:	I don't know how any man could be so cruel. Is it any wonder I'm getting old before my time?
PARK:	What time is it?
LANG:	You have a habit of making me feel unwanted – so small and insignificant. Sometimes I think I'm going to dissolve into nothingness and disappear entirely.
PARK:	You say it but you won't do it.
LANG:	So you've finally revealed your true feelings.
PARK:	I haven't revealed anything.
LANG:	You haven't loved me for years – if you ever loved me at all. Always answer me in monosyllables – never interested in anything I do – the only reaction I ever get from you is a shrug or a quick snort!
PARK:	Thanks for reminding me. (CLINK OF GLASS)
LANG:	What are you doing with that bottle, John?
PARK:	I'm having a quick snort.
LANG:	There's the answer to our problem! Bourbon!
PARK:	Now you're beginning to show some sense. How do you want it – straight?
LANG:	I don't want it at all. And if you hadn't had so much of it at the wedding tonight you'd have been able to drive me home!
PARK:	My driving never interferes with my drinking! I'm sorry I ever went to your broken-down cousin's wedding!
LANG:	You sure showed it, too! Everybody kissed the bride except you!
PARK:	Well, that proves I was sober!
LANG:	You wouldn't hesitate if it was Gloria Gooseby!
PARK:	Now don't start with Gloria Gooseby!

LANG:	I'll bet you'd stand in line if she was getting married!
PARK:	She's already married and I don't have to stand in line! I mean I hate Gloria Gooseby and the next time I see her I'm going to punch her husband Leo right in the nose!
LANG:	What have you got against Leo? He's a better husband than you are.
PARK:	And I'm sick of hearing that, too! Leo Gooseby is a cheap, chiseling bum!
LANG:	He is not. He's more generous than you.
PARK:	Generous? Would Leo Gooseby give you a new dress? No. Would he give you a new hat? No. Would he give you a mink coat?
LANG:	Would you give me a mink coat?
PARK:	No – why should I give you anything Leo wouldn't give you? Now let's stop wrangling and go to sleep.
LANG:	Our whole marriage started on the wrong foot. We should have had a real ceremony like Agnes – but you were in too much of a hurry.
PARK:	Mmmm.
LANG:	Well, you've got plenty of time now – and I want a real wedding with a big ceremony. I want you to marry me again, John.
PARK:	Mmmm.
LANG:	Is that such an unreasonable request?
PARK:	Yes. It isn't legal.
LANG:	Why not?
PARK:	A man can't be punished twice for the same crime.
LANG:	Oh, that's too bad about you. Well, for your information I've already sent out formal invitations to our wedding.
PARK:	Are you out of your mind, Blanche? I'm not having any formal wedding – and I'm not putting out a lot of dough just to feed your hungry friends and their squalling brats.
LANG:	There won't be any brats there at all.
PARK:	How do you know?
LANG:	Because it said plainly on the invitation. Mr. and Mrs. John Bickerson will be married September 12th. No children expected.
PARK:	Put out the lights.
LANG:	Not until you promise to go through with it. I want to wear a wedding gown and veil. Every woman's entitled to that.
PARK:	Oh, stop it – they'll throw us out of here.
LANG:	I wish they would.

PARK:	I never heard of such a thing!
LANG:	Oh, keep quiet and go to sleep.
PARK:	Go to sleep she says…Drags me 90 miles to see a crumb get married in my tuxedo…Makes me stay in a rat-trap over-night…wants to wear a veil…drives me crazy…go to sleep she tells me. I'll – never – sleep – another – wink – as long as --- (SNORES…PAUSE…PHONE RINGS) Hello? Blanche, the phone's dead – it's leaking!
LANG:	Put down that bottle of bourbon.
PARK:	Oh. (RECEIVER UP) Hello.
MAN:	(FILTER) This is the desk clerk. Are you the man that left a call for seven-thirty?
PARK:	Yes.
MAN:	Well, it's four o'clock.
PARK:	Well, what are you waking me now for?
MAN:	I'm going off duty. My wife'll call you at seven-thirty. Goodbye.
PARK:	(YELLS) DROP DEAD! (SLAMS RECEIVER) That's the last straw (GETS INTO BED) Put out the lights, Blanche.
LANG:	All right, dear. Goodnight.
PARK:	Goodnight.
LANG:	John.
PARK:	What is it?
LANG:	Are you angry with me?
PARK:	No. I'm just sleepy.
LANG:	Wouldn't you like to kiss me good night?
PARK:	I'll kiss you goodnight in the morning.
LANG:	Why can't you kiss me now?
PARK:	I'm not facing that way. Goodnight, Blanche.
LANG:	John, I have something important to tell you.
PARK:	Tell me tomorrow.
LANG:	Do you realize I'm the only woman in my set who doesn't have an engagement ring?
PARK:	You have too! I gave you a beautiful ring – fourteen-carat gold filled – and it had an enormous hole in the top for a diamond.
LANG:	I bought a diamond ring for three hundred dollars.
PARK:	Blanche! You didn't!
LANG:	I had to! After living with you for seven years, I was ashamed to face my friends. They were starting to talk.
PARK:	About what!
LANG:	About us. Everybody knows we're not legally engaged.

PARK:	Blanche! Are you insane? How can you squander three hundred dollars on a diamond ring?
LANG:	Don't scream at me!
PARK:	I deny myself everything! I've been cutting your bloomers in half and wearing 'em for shirt-sleeves – I've been using chicken-fat for hair tonic – my only bathing suit has a hole in the knee! I haven't spent a nickel on myself and she buys diamonds!
LANG:	You bought a sack of popcorn yesterday.
PARK:	What popcorn! That was my teeth – they fell out from malnutrition! Where's that ring, Blanche? Lemme see it.
LANG:	Here.
PARK:	There's no diamond in this ring! It's the same one I bought you!
LANG:	I didn't buy anything, silly! Why would I spend three hundred dollars on a diamond ring when we haven't got enough to eat? Who am I going to fool? My friends know we're paupers.
PARK:	Oh, they do, huh?
LANG:	Certainly. They laugh up their sleeves every time they see me wear that ring with the hole in it.
PARK:	Is that so? Well, I'll put a stop to that, honey. I'll take it to the jeweler's in the morning.
LANG:	John! Are you going to put a diamond in it?
PARK:	No, I'm gonna plug up the hole. Goodnight, Blanche.
LANG:	Goodnight, John.
MUSIC:	BICKERSON PLAYOFF
	(APPLAUSE)
HOLBROOK:	Frances Langford and Lew Parker are standing by for a curtain call. In the meantime, for America's FINEST cigarette, here's another call well-worth remembering…
JOHNNY:	CALL ....FOR ....PHILIP MORRIS.
MUSIC:	"ON THE TRAIL" THEME
HOLBROOK:	Remember: PHILIP MORRIS is definitely less irritating, definitely <u>milder</u> than any other leading brand. Remember: NO CIGARETTE HANGOVER means MORE SMOKING PLEASURE – so…
JOHNNY:	CALL...FOR ...PHILIP ...MORRIS!
ANNCR:	Now here are John and Blanche Bickerson as Frances Langford and Lew Parker.
LANG:	Oh, Lew – have you seen this package that arrived for you among the fan mail?
PARK:	No. What is it, Frances?

LANG:	It's a little gadget to encourage sleep. It's called an anti-snore ball.
PARK:	(CHUCKLING) Isn't that cute? Just because I snore on the program I guess people think that I actually snore at home.
LANG:	Well, do you?
PARK:	Of course not. I'm a very quiet sleeper...
LANG:	Well...Here's your snore-ball.
PARK:	Thanks...Who sent it in?
LANG:	Your wife. Goodnight, Lew.
PARK:	Goodnight, Frances. Goodnight, everybody. (APPLAUSE)
HOLBROOK:	Don't miss the Horace Heidt Show this coming Sunday night over this same station. That's Sunday night over CBS. In the meantime...don't forget to...
JOHNNY:	CALL...FOR...PHILIP...MORRIS!
MUSIC:	UP (APPLAUSE)
HOLBROOK:	The Bickersons came to you transcribed from Hollywood, California. John Holbrook speaking.

One of the best Bickersons routines, "Moving Day," is combined into this unperformed script written for television. Baby Snooks fans will recognize the trick-or-treat part of the script as being written for Fanny Brice's show, back before 1942 when Rapp wrote for Maxwell House's Snooks program. The old gags combine flawlessly into this new Bickersons situation.

It's only fitting to leave this book of scripts with a true rarity. This script was probably written around 1970 when the Bickersons was about to embark on its cartoon series. References to women's lib and a black Dr. Hersey also point this final entry in the direction of the early '70s. It's one of the last Bickersons scripts, if not *the* last, Philip Rapp ever wrote.

HALLOWEEN SPECIAL

(ESTIMATING SCRIPT FOR MG. PRODS.)

In this particular fabrication John and Blanche Bickerson are in the process of moving from what they continually referred to as their "one room goat's nest." Their new home is slightly more luxurious. Actually it is a two room goat's nest. The Bickerson furniture, with its old-time walk-in butcher's icebox dominating the tiny, cluttered kitchen, give mute testimony to their low profile financial position. The fact that the Bickersons are taking this gigantic step up the poverty ladder on the day of the Eve of Halloween furnishes the counterplot for this program.

FADE IN:

Establishing SHOT of extremely modest neighborhood. CAMERA PANS down street showing apartment houses, small stores, a market displaying pumpkins in crates and Halloween signs, more apartment houses, finally coming to rest on a moving van parked outside one particularly scruffy four storey building.

CLOSER ANGLE ON VAN

TWO MEN emerge from van. One is big and burly, the other is thin, small, and scrawny. It goes without saying that the big guy is carrying a tiny lamp, while the little one heaves a sofa on his breaking back. The big guy balances the lamp on top of the sofa, lights a cigar as his mate struggles into the apartment house with his burden.

                         BIG GUY
Steady, Oiving. Keep the fulcrum balanced
on your clavicle, and walk on the balls of
your feet. It's Apartment Thoiteen on the
fourth floor – The Bickersons, and the
stairs are very narrow. I shall follow with
the cushions.

                                              WIPE

INT. BICKERSON LIVING ROOM FULL SHOT

Blanche Bickerson, in her hat and coat, stands in the middle of the room,
supervising the placement of the furniture. Featured PROMINENTLY are
two large barrels apparently containing dishware, etc. Everything is in the
room, things that belong in the kitchen, bedroom, bathroom, all waiting to
be put in their proper place. The Little Guy staggers in carrying a stove, immediately followed by his colleague who daintily carries the broiling pan.

                       LITTLE GUY
                       (breathless)
Where do you want this, lady?

                        BLANCHE
                       (points off)
Right there in the kitchen – on the right
hand wall.

                         BIG GUY
Left hand wall, Oiving. There is no gas con-
nection on the right hand wall.

                        BLANCHE
Oh. I never thought of that.

                         BIG GUY
                     (elaborate bow)
It is my pleasure to do the thinking, madame. Oiving, my colleague, does the light
woik, like carrying stuff. Now, I think that
completes the moving operation.

Oiving re-enters, practically bent in half. Big guy hands him the broiling pan.

That goes in the oven, Oiving.

                       LITTLE GUY
                  (still bent over, mutters)
Never seen such a mess of junk in my whole life.

BLANCHE

I never realized we had so much stuff. I just
can't bear to throw anything away.

LITTLE GUY
(starting out)
All married people is like that.

BLANCHE

I suppose so – are you married?

LITTLE GUY

No, ma'am. I walk this way from carrying
heavy furniture.

He exits.

BIG GUY
(laughs)
Oiving is blessed with a great sensa yuma,
but no brains.

Oiving re-enters, carrying a stiff figure in what looks like a shroud.

LITTLE GUY

Where do youse want this mummy, lady?

BLANCHE

Mummy! That's my husband! Put him
down. John! John Bickerson!

JOHN
(as Oiving props him against wall)
Put out the lights, Blanche – I'm exhausted.

LITTLE GUY

He's exhausted! And I carried that bum up
four flights of stairs!

BLANCHE

I swear I never saw a man like you! You
can't be that sleepy – it's only nine o'clock
in the morning and you slept all night.

JOHN

Never closed my eyes. (climbs into barrel)
Put out the lights.

BLANCHE

You get out of that barrel this minute!

(SOUND of breaking crockery) Now look
what you've done. (she reaches in and pulls
out a broken dish) You broke my best chafing dish!

                    JOHN
Well, it was chafing me. Go to sleep,
Blanche.

                  BLANCHE
I will not. Besides, the beds aren't even
made up.

                    JOHN
Crawl in the other barrel.

                  BLANCHE
You're insane. I'd smother to death.

                    JOHN
Stick your nose thru the bunghole.

                  BIG GUY
Far be it from me to interrupt a domestic
scene, madame, but we have to consum-
mate the financial transaction.

                  BLANCHE
You get out of that barrel, John Bickerson,
and pay the man.

She exits, carrying stuff to bedroom. John wearily climbs out, eyes heavy-
lidded. We see now that the shroud-like garment he wears is actually pajamas, with the coat so long that the pockets are almost at his ankles. He is
also barefooted. He reaches in the neck of his pajamas and pulls out a purse
that hangs around his neck on a chain.

                    JOHN
          How much?

                  BIG GUY
Nineteen dollars and seventy five cents
with the tax.

John carefully opens his grouchbag, while the Big Guy peers over his shoulder for a closer look. John turns to him, then turns away, fishing in the
purse and hiding the contents. He comes up with a twenty dollar bill.

JOHN

All I got is a twenty dollar bill. You got change?

LITTLE GUY

Change!

BIG GUY

Quiet, Oiving! (to John) My dear sir, to this
new domicile of yours which is four flights
of stairs and no elevator, my colleague
and I have carried two beds, two trunks,
four cartons, one crate, one table and four
chairs, two barrels of crockery, a stove and
refrigerator, nine cases of bourbon and one
icebag. Our nominal charge is nineteen seventy five and you hand me a twenty dollar
bill and demand change. Is that correct?

JOHN

Yeah.

BIG GUY

I see. Well, I have no change but Oiving
here will carry the stove down and bring
it up again if you want us to work out the
extra quarter.

JOHN

Okay, wiseguy. Keep the change.

The moving men leave, shaking their heads. Blanche re-enters.

BLANCHE

Put some clothes on and help me get this
stuff put away.

She stares as he takes off his pajama coat and reveals a garter belt around
his waist from which are suspended twenty four bottles of bourbon.

BLANCHE

What on earth ----!

JOHN

Oh, quit staring and help me unhook my
bourbon girdle.

                    BLANCHE
That's the most ridiculous thing I ever saw.
All those bottles of bourbon hanging from
my old garter belt!

                     JOHN
Well, I wasn't gonna trust those moving
men with my life's blood.

                    BLANCHE
You trusted them with nine cases!

                     JOHN
A decoy. Those cases were full of empty
bottles.

                    BLANCHE
And we had to pay to drag them up here!
There's no deposit on the empty bottles is
there?

                     JOHN
If there was I could retire for life.

                    BLANCHE
Then what do you need them for? I can't
understand why you're so attached to a lot
of dead bourbon bottles.

                     JOHN
                 (fervently)
I was with 'em when they passed away!

He removes the girdle and bottles and exits. Blanche looks around at the
stacked furniture.

                    BLANCHE
                 (calling)
John, we've got to put the apartment in
order. I'll check the inventory to see if they
brought everything. Read off the list on that
pad. It's on the dresser.

               JOHN'S VOICE (O.S.)
Bunch of mustard greens, two fish heads, a
pound of chicken gizzards, cotton seed oil ---

BLANCHE
No! That's my shopping list.

JOHN
(entering, wearing shirt and shorts)
Shopping list?

BLANCHE
Yes, I'm going to bake a cake.

JOHN
I'm not eating any cake with chicken gizzards!

BLANCHE
Don't be silly. That's for Nature Boy.

JOHN
Who's Nature Boy?

BLANCHE
The cat. Get the other --- John! The cat!

JOHN
What about him?

BLANCHE
Where is he? He's lost and it's all your fault.
I begged you to take care of him and see
that he got here safely.

JOHN
He'll get here. They'll deliver him in the
morning.

BLANCHE
How do you know?

JOHN
I put him in a sack and dropped him in the
mailbox.

BLANCHE
John Bickerson!

JOHN
Oh, don't blow your stack! I didn't put him
in any mailbox. I guarantee that filthy cat'll
be here in the morning.

BLANCHE

What makes you so sure?

JOHN

Because I tied a label around his neck with
our new address on it.

BLANCHE

What good is that? He can't read.

JOHN

I know he can't read! But people can read
and somebody's bound to pick him up and
deliver him – heaven forbid!

BLANCHE

You hate Nature Boy, don't you?

JOHN

Who's Nature Boy?

BLANCHE

The cat! You hate him.

JOHN

I don't hate anybody. Now look, Blanche ---

BLANCHE

You'd get along with him fine if you just
show him a little kindness. All you have to
do is bring him a present once in awhile.

JOHN

Okay – I'll bring him a dog tonight! (point-
ing to his shirt, which has no tail) What
happened to my shirt, Blanche?

BLANCHE

Oh – that was Nature Boy.

JOHN

That stinking cat was wearing my shirt?

BLANCHE

No, he was sleeping on it and – er – had a
little accident. So I cut off the tail.

JOHN

It doesn't even cover my navel! How am I supposed to get it in my pants?

BLANCHE

Stop complaining. Just wear your pants higher.

JOHN

Higher! I'm wearing 'em so high now I have to unzip 'em to blow my nose! How am I gonna get to work?

BLANCHE

You can't go till later anyway. You have to stay here and help me with the furniture.

JOHN

Do you want me to lose my job?

BLANCHE

I don't care if you do. It's embarrassing to tell people my husband works in a cemetery selling graves.

JOHN

Plots, not graves, Blanche! Plots!

BLANCHE

All right, plots. Can't you find something a little better?

JOHN

I'm getting paid and that's all that counts. You squawk about every job I ever got!

BLANCHE

Well, why can't you get a regular job like other men. Last year you were a billiard ball salesman --

JOHN

Bowling balls!

BLANCHE

Don't yell! Before that you were a waitress feeler --

JOHN

(exploding)

I was not a waitress feeler! I was a mattress
filler! Kapok! I stuffed mattresses with kapok! Why do you take such a delight in raising my blood pressure, Blanche? I gotta get
out of here – where's my hat?

BLANCHE

In the icebox.

JOHN

Where's my lunch?

BLANCHE

In your hat!

He glares at her, goes to icebox, opens the door and Nature Boy flies out!
The diabolical cat runs to Blanche and hides behind her to avoid attack.

BLANCHE

So that's where you hid him! He could have
smothered to death!

JOHN

Never mind that – look what he did to my
lunch.

He removes a fish skeleton from his hat, holds it up. There is a knock at the door.

BLANCHE

Oh, that'll be Dr. Hersey. I asked him to
drop by.

JOHN

What's the matter? Are you sick again?

BLANCHE

It's that same pain.

JOHN

What pain?

BLANCHE

It's my head. I've had it off and on for two
weeks.

JOHN

Well, take it off now and tell him to beat it.

BLANCHE
(going to door)
I will not. And you be quiet, John – He's a
great doctor.

JOHN

Sure – no matter what's wrong with you he
says "Take two aspirins and lie down." You can
be dead and he says take two aspirins and --

BLANCHE

Oh, hush up! (she opens the door) Well, Dr.
Hersey. Do come in.

John exits. Dr. Hersey enters with his medical bag and removes his hat. He
is a tall, handsome black man.

DR. HERSEY

I'm in a bit of a hurry, Mrs. Bickerson – an
emergency at the clinic.

BLANCHE

Well, I just wondered ---

DR. HERSEY

I know. You told me your symptoms on the
phone. Just take two aspirins and lie down.

John enters, fully dressed.

JOHN

What did I tell you!

DR. HERSEY
(seeing him for the first time)
Oh, you still home, Bickerson? How's the
grave-digging business?

BLANCHE

He sells graves, doctor – he doesn't dig them.

JOHN

I don't sell graves I told you! I sell plots. (to
Hersey) And I'll be a millionaire if I can just
get all your patients! Goodbye!

He slams out. The door opens almost immediately and Barney, Clara and their son Ernie enter. Barney is a wisp of a man, his wife (who is Blanche's sister) is twice his size, and little Ernie is a fat little dollop of a kid around seven years old.

> BARNEY
> What's the matter with John? He almost knocked us down the stairs.

> DR. HERSEY
> (coldly)
> I'm sure he could never prove it was an accident. Good day, Mrs. Bickerson -- (to Barney) and to you and your wife and little Barney.

> CLARA
> It's little <u>Ernie</u>! You ought to know – you delivered him.

> DR. HERSEY
> So I did. He's seven now and I'm still waiting to be paid.

He exits.

> BARNEY
> That's a fine way you let that witch doctor talk to your own sister, Blanche.

> BLANCHE
> He's entitled to his fee for --

> CLARA
> He's entitled to nothing. He charged us sixty-five dollars for Ernie and he only weighed thirteen pounds.

> BARNEY
> Sure. That's more than you pay for a rump roast.

> ERNIE
> I'm hungry.

> CLARA
> Hungry! You just had four tuna sandwiches.

BLANCHE
Four sandwiches! Ernie, you'll get sick.

ERNIE
I am sick.

CLARA
Just give him something to gnaw on,
Blanche. Have you got a leg of lamb?

BARNEY
(who has been rummaging around in the cartons)
Here, give him this. And I'll have one myself.

He holds up two cans.

BLANCHE
That's for Nature boy! It's cat food.

CLARA
Won't hurt him. Probably make his eyes
shine in the dark.

Nature Boy tackles Barney, knocks him over and knocks the cans out of his hands. There is a mad scramble between the cat, Barney and Ernie as they fight for the cans. Blanche breaks it up, retrieves the cans and puts them back in the carton. Nature Boy skulks out, vengeance in his eyes.

BARNEY
(dusting himself off)
Well, tell her already, Clara.

CLARA
Yes. Well, we came over to ask you a favor,
Blanche.

BLANCHE
I thought you came over to help get the new
apartment straightened out.

CLARA
Barney – Ernie -- go on, help Aunt Blanche
put the things away.

Reluctantly they go to work clearing the room. Clara sits on the couch as Blanche works.

CLARA
About that favor, Blanche -- could Ernie
stay overnight with you and John?

BLANCHE

Oh, Clara – we've got so much to do and
you know how John feels about little Ernie.

CLARA

You'll have to help me. You see, Barney and
I have been invited to a Halloween Party at
his club, and --

BLANCHE

What club?

CLARA

It's the United Nations Pool Hall and Barney
is a charter member. We just can't leave little
Ernie alone – we'll be home so late.

BLANCHE

Clara --

CLARA

Look, John can have some fun with little
Ernie. After all, tonight is Halloween and
he can take the child trickin' and treating.

BLANCHE
(sarcastically)
I'm sure John'll just love that! I'm afraid, Clara --

CLARA

You can't turn down your own sister, can
you? And Ernie can be a perfect angel when
he wants to. Please?

BLANCHE

All right, Clara. But don't make a habit of this.

WIPE

The apartment is in some reasonable shape. Blanche stands surveying it
while little Ernie sits at a table devouring a whole chicken. John enters wearily. He takes two steps forward and Nature Boy trips him up.

JOHN

Blanche, you've got to get rid of that vicious
-- (stares at Ernie) Who's that?

BLANCHE

It's your nephew. Barney and Clara's little boy.
(to Ernie) Say hello to your Uncle John, Ernie.

ERNIE

(mouth full)
Chicken's too salty. More potato salad.

JOHN

(stares, mutters)
Now I know why tigers eat their young.

SPIN

Blanche and John are sitting on the twin beds in the bedroom.

JOHN

No, no, no! I won't do it, I tell you. I'm not
taking that little monster trickin' or treating.

BLANCHE

How can you be so cruel, John? Halloween
only comes once a year and the poor child
is in there crying his eyes out.

JOHN

He's in there eating my dinner!

BLANCHE

I'll get you something else. After you eat
you'll feel better. (reaches into night table
drawer and hands him a plate) Here. I hid it
so Ernie couldn't get his hands on it.

JOHN

(looking at plate)
What is it?

BLANCHE

Squid.

JOHN

Squid!

BLANCHE

Stuffed with kelp leaves and goat cheese. I
got the recipe from my mother.

JOHN

It looks like your mother. I don't want it,
Blanche. I don't want to eat.

BLANCHE
Well, what'll I do with it?

JOHN
Give it to the cat.

BLANCHE
You hate that cat, don't you?

JOHN
Don't start that again. I'm not gonna eat
that goop and I'm not taking Ernie out
trickin' or treating!

BLANCHE
You'll either eat this or take him out.

JOHN
(looks at the plate)
You leave me very little choice, Blanche.
(gets up, picks up plate) I'll take him out.

He exits and enters living room carrying the plate. Ernie is still stuffing his face.

JOHN
You wanna go out trickin' or treating?

ERNIE
(mouth full)
Sure.

JOHN
Then you'll have to eat this. It's stuffed squid.

ERNIE
Stuff it.

JOHN
You little heathen! Eat it or you don't go out.

ERNIE
(bawling)
Well, what'll I do with my funny mask?

JOHN
You can wear it when you get home.

ERNIE
I'm wearing it now.

JOHN

Okay, I give up. Let's go. And listen.
Tonight instead of playing jokes or doing
damage like soaping car windows or ripping off gates we'll have a different kind of
Halloween.

ERNIE

Like what?

JOHN

Like if we see any damage anywhere we'll fix it.

ERNIE

I'd rather eat the squid.

JOHN

You would! But maybe tonight I can teach
you a lesson in good behavior. And I don't
want you scaring the neighbors by wearing
that stupid mask now. Take it off.

ERNIE

I took it off already.

JOHN

Oh. Now I can see why Barney can't deny
he's your father. Let's go.

DISS.

EXT STREET NIGHT

John and Ernie go about repairing the vandalism caused by Halloween trick
or treaters.
1. John sees some cars parked in a lot with soaped numbers on the wind-
shields. He scrubs them off diligently only to be confronted by an irate used
car salesman who threatens him with a tire iron. It took the salesman half a
day to paint the prices on his used cars. John flees, Ernie tagging after him.
2. They see a gate that has been removed from a fence around a small house.
After a good deal of trouble because of Ernie's inept help they finally get
the gate hung. A woman comes out of the house and yells that she had the
gate taken off because it's going to be fixed. She demands that they take it
off again or she'll call the police. More trouble taking it off. As they are in
the process of removing it a cop nails them. John finally talks his way out of
trouble. While this is going on Ernie is mugging kids for their bags of candy
and other treasures.

3. John sees a bunch of kids turning in a fire alarm. He rushes after them but they get away.

> JOHN
> That's terrible, Ernie. Those kids! They
> turned in a false alarm.

> ERNIE
> How do you know?

> JOHN
> Can't you see the glass is broken? And they
> ran away, didn't they? If it was a real fire
> they'd wait here till the engines come and
> direct them.

By this time the fire engines have screamed up. John is apparently caught red-handed when he admits it was a false alarm. He insists he tried to stop some kids from doing it but they ran away. The Fire Chief is suspicious.

> JOHN
> (turning to Ernie for corroboration)
> Tell him, Ernie. Some kids broke the glass,
> pulled the alarm and ran away before we
> could catch them. Isn't that right, Ernie?

> ERNIE
> I didn't see nobody.

John is about to murder the little beast when the cop on the beat comes up and adds fuel to the fire. He caught this guy ripping off gates.

> COP
> Wait a minute – now I recognize this guy.
> He's wanted in Cleveland for arson.

> JOHN
> Arson!

> COP
> Yeah! I got your description right here on
> my hot sheet. You're Firebug Willie!

> JOHN
> You're insane! I'm not a firebug. (to Ernie) Tell
> him who I am, Ernie.

ERNIE
(chewing his stolen candy)
He's Firebug Willie.

The cop and firemen restrain John as he goes after Ernie.

FLIP

INT. JAIL CELL

John sits disconsolately on an iron cot. A jailer opens the cell door and Dr. Hersey comes in.

JOHN

Dr. Hersey!

DR. HERSEY

It took a long time to find you, but I finally choked it out of Ernie.

JOHN

(bitterly)
Oh, that little --

DR. HERSEY

I've cleared up the matter with the authorities and you're free to go home now.

JOHN

(grasping his hand)
Thanks, Doctor. That's mighty white of you.
(realizing his boo-boo) I mean --

DR. HERSEY

I know what you mean. Forget it. Your wife is plenty worried so get home as fast as you can.

JOHN

I'll do that.

DR. HERSEY

And – er – since you moved into that nice new apartment, I thought, well -- I left a little something for you on your night table.

JOHN

(all gratitude)
Oh, doc -- you needn't have --

DR. HERSEY
That's all right, Bickerson – you don't have
to pay it until the tenth. You can mail it in
with last month's bill.

He exits as John reacts.

FADE OUT

FADE IN BICKERSON BEDROOM NIGHT

John and Blanche are asleep in their twin beds, Blanche tossing restlessly.
As the ANNOUNCER'S VOICE comes over, FREEZE the SHOT.

ANNOUNCER'S VOICE
After an exhausting day of moving to a new
apartment, a fruitless day at the cemetery
selling graves – er – plots – a harrowing
Halloween Eve trickin' and treating with
Little Ernie, and a brief session in jail, John
Bickerson has finally retired.

(START FILM ACTION)

It is now three o'clock in the morning and
Blanche grits her teeth in anguish as poor
husband John, victim of diurnal insomnia,
or Thunderclap's Reaction, battles thru a
critical attack of the dread ailment.

JOHN
(Orchestrates the following)
SNORES LUSTILY....WHINES.....SNORES AND
WHINES PITIFULLY... A BROKEN RHYTHM
SNORE FOLLOWED BY A WHINE.

BLANCHE
(sitting up, putting on light)
It's like sleeping with a one-man band!

JOHN SNORES AND GIGGLES MERRILY.

BLANCHE
That's enough!...John!

JOHN
Mmm.

BLANCHE
Turn over on your side...Go on!

JOHN
(a protesting whine)
Mmmmmmmmmmmmmmmm!

BLANCHE
Stop it, stop it, stop it!

JOHN
(half awake)
Stop it, Blanche...Wassamatter?
Wassamatter, Blanche?

BLANCHE
That snoring and whining and giggling! It's
been going on for three hours. I wish you
could hear it!

JOHN
I hear it. Must be that fat guy in the next
apartment.

BLANCHE
It isn't any fat guy at all. It's you!

JOHN
Put out the lights.

BLANCHE
I will not. John, you've got to do something
about that awful snoring.

JOHN
Lemme sleep, Blanche – I'm exhausted.

BLANCHE
Dr. Hersey says you snore like that because
you have a long uvula and it flutters against
your palate.

JOHN
(sits up and stares at her)
Put out the lights.

BLANCHE
He says he can cure it with a very simple
operation.

JOHN
(settling back)
I'll go see him in the morning.

BLANCHE
You say it but you won't do it...Do it now!

JOHN
(sitting up)
Are you out of your mind, Blanche? It's
three o'clock in the morning and I'm not
gonna let that medical thief hack on my
uvula!

BLANCHE
He doesn't hack – he snares.

JOHN
I don't care if he knocks it off with a hockey
stick – nobody touches my uvula! Now put
out the lights and let me get some sleep.

BLANCHE
Well, I want to sleep, too. Go get me my
sleeping pills from the bathroom.

JOHN
(struggling out of bed)
Sleeping pills. Almost time to get up and
she wants sleeping pills. (starts searching
under covers) Where's my slipper?

Nature Boy is revealed under the covers. John flings him out.

BLANCHE
Under your pillow where it always is.

JOHN
(finds it, puts it on)
One slipper. Only man in the world with
one slipper. She wins a pair of slippers for
me in a raffle and has to be half on the
ticket with her stupid sister!

BLANCHE
Stop grumbling and get my pills before I
fall asleep.

He shuffles to the bathroom which has a swinging door. The cat trips him
as he approaches and he flies thru the door.

INT. BATHROOM

The swinging door returns and conks him on the head. He curses the cat as he gets up.

> JOHN
> (mutters)
> Fine apartment. A bathroom with a swing-
> ing door. (rummages thru medicine cabi-
> net, upsetting bottles, etc.,.) I can't find any
> sleeping pills.

> BLANCHE'S VOICE (O.S.)
> They're in the little green bottle, next to my
> shampoo.

John finds the bottle, exits bathroom.

INT. BEDROOM

As he enters with bottle. He stares at it.

> JOHN
> Are these sleeping pills?

> BLANCHE
> Of course they are.

> JOHN
> I've been taking three a day – I thought they
> were vitamin tablets.

He throws the bottle to her and tumbles into bed, hiding his slipper.

> BLANCHE
> How do you expect me to take a pill? Get
> me a glass of water.

He struggles out of bed again, retrieves slipper and shuffles towards the kitchen. In a trice he is out again carrying a glass of water which he hands her. Back to bed again, same business with slipper. Blanche takes a pill, sips some water, makes a wry face.

> BLANCHE
> John.

> JOHN
> Mmm?

BLANCHE

This water tastes funny. Did you let it run?

JOHN

No.

BLANCHE

Why not?

JOHN

Cat was sleeping in the sink and I didn't
wanna disturb him.

BLANCHE

Well, where'd you get the water?

JOHN

I dipped it out of the goldfish bowl.

BLANCHE

John Bickerson!

JOHN

Oh, don't get hysterical. I took it out of the
icebox. Now put out the lights.

BLANCHE

Not until you tell me what happened.

JOHN

I told you fifty times. That little son of a --

BLANCHE

I'm not talking about that. What happened
at work today? Did you sell any graves?

JOHN

Plots! And I didn't sell any. If you must
know I got fired.

BLANCHE

Why didn't you tell me before?

JOHN

Because I didn't feel like it.

BLANCHE

You never feel like anything. You treat me as
though I didn't exist. Like an old shoe. And
after I gave you the best years of my life.

JOHN

Were those the best?

BLANCHE

Never mind the sarcasm. I'm not taking
this kind of treatment any more. I'm joining
Women's Lib.

JOHN

(almost asleep)

Mmm.

BLANCHE

I'm sick of being just a sex object.

JOHN

Objection overruled.

BLANCHE

I heard that, John Bickerson. Now you just
apologize.

JOHN

Put out the lights.

BLANCHE

What have you got against Women's Lib?

JOHN

Oh, dear.

BLANCHE

What's wrong with women having their
own organization to stop being exploited by
men? Don't you believe in clubs for women?

JOHN

Clubs, baseball bats, sandbags, anything!
Just let me get some sleep.

BLANCHE

I won't stand for it. I'm getting old before
my time.

JOHN

What time is it?

BLANCHE
It's time you started paying a little more attention to my feelings. Here we are moving into a new apartment and you don't even carry me across the threshold.

JOHN
What carrying! We've been married eight years!

BLANCHE
What's that got to do with it? Why couldn't you carry me across the threshold?

JOHN
I can't carry a grudge that long.

BLANCHE
You didn't even kiss me goodnight.

JOHN
I kissed you last night, didn't I?

BLANCHE
Well, why can't you kiss me tonight?

JOHN
I'm not facing that way.

BLANCHE
You must really hate me.

JOHN
Oh, Blanche, I don't hate you! I'm just exhausted.

BLANCHE
Well, you don't love me.

JOHN
Yes I do.

BLANCHE
You don't, you don't, you don't!

JOHN
I tell you I do!

BLANCHE

Then why don't you say it?

JOHN

I love you! I can't live without you! I think of
you every minute of the day! NOW SHUT
UP AND GO TO SLEEP!

BLANCHE

That's no way to say it. I want you to say it
gently and with deep affection and really
convince me.

JOHN

Oh, Blanche – you know I love you so!

BLANCHE

So – what?

JOHN

That's what I say – the hell with it!

BLANCHE

Keep it up, John. You'll be sorry when I'm gone.

JOHN

Where are you going?

BLANCHE

Go on – make light of it.

JOHN

Put out the light.

BLANCHE

(tearfully)
How can a man be so unsympathetic – sick
as I am.

JOHN

(sitting up)
What's the matter, Blanche – are you really
sick? What is it?

BLANCHE

I get fainting spells all the time and Dr.
Hersey doesn't know what causes it. I know
I'll never recover.

JOHN

Don't be silly – you'll recover. You've got a
healthy constitution.

BLANCHE
(indignantly)
I have not!

JOHN

You have, too! You had pneumonia and you got
well, you had the flu and you got well, you had
the mumps and you got well – you've had sixty
diseases and you always got well. I never saw
such a healthy woman in all my life!...Go to sleep.

BLANCHE

I can't sleep. Not after what you did to that
child.

JOHN

He had it coming.

BLANCHE

Well, I don't think you should have dragged
Little Ernie back home. He was sleeping so
peacefully near the icebox when you came
back from jail.

JOHN

Don't mention his name.

BLANCHE

Was there anybody there when you took
him back?

JOHN

I didn't look. I just threw him on the sofa.

BLANCHE

And it was disgraceful the way you picked
him up and carried him out.

JOHN

Well, I used to be a bowling ball salesman.

BLANCHE

Get up and bring him back.

JOHN

What!

BLANCHE

Go on. I won't let you sleep until you bring
the child back here. And never mind your
coat – just put on my robe.

JOHN

(struggling out of bed, reaching for his slipper
– puts on her robe)
Nobody would believe this.

BLANCHE

And take a flashlight with you so you don't
wake Barney and Clara.

John grabs an object from a drawer and exits groggily.

EXT. STREET NIGHT

John, dressed in Blanche's robe, makes his way slowly, peering into the
darkness.

JOHN

Flashlight's no good – batteries are dead.

Cop walks into scene behind him. He holds John in flashlight beam.

COP

More Halloween tricks?

JOHN

Oh, hello officer. Shine that light around a
bit – I'm looking for number two fourteen.

COP

Live there?

JOHN

No – why?

COP

Not everybody walks around at three in the
morning wearing a pink negligee and carrying a bottle of bourbon.

JOHN

Bottle of bourbon! (now we see what it is)
No wonder it wouldn't light! Dear heaven, I
almost threw it away.

                           COP
          What's that?

                           JOHN
          I picked it up by mistake – I thought it was
          a flashlight. Well, it's not a total loss... Will
          you join me, officer?

He offers the bottle.

                           COP
          No thanks – I'm off duty.

John reacts.

                                                          SPIN

John is returning with a bundle wrapped in a blanket and walks right into
the same cop.

                           COP
          Pick up a friend?

                           JOHN
          It's my nephew – I'm bringing him home to my
          wife. It's a long story, officer, but I assure you it's
          nothing anybody would want to steal.

                           COP
          Uh-huh. Well, careful how you got that
          blanket wrapped around his head. He's li-
          able to smother.

                           JOHN
                      (hopefully)
          You think so? What a terrible idea!

He smiles broadly and moves on.

INT. BEDROOM.

John is just emerging from the kitchen as Blanche watches.

                        BLANCHE
          Is he sleeping?

                           JOHN
          He's sleeping. Now can I do the same?

                        BLANCHE
          I'm afraid not, John. It's just four o'clock.
          You'll have to get up.

                        JOHN

For what?

                       BLANCHE

You have to bank the furnace.

                        JOHN

What are you talking about? This is an
apartment house – the janitor banks the
furnace!

                       BLANCHE

John, how do you think I got this apartment
so cheap?

                        JOHN

That has nothing to -- oh no!

                       BLANCHE

Oh, yes – you're the janitor.

                        JOHN

I won't do it! I won't do it, I tell you. I kill
myself trying to make a buck and you're
gonna have me scrubbing floors and fixing
toilets! We're getting out of here, you hear me!

                       BLANCHE

Don't yell, you'll wake up little Ernie.

                        JOHN

Little Ernie can drop dead! I have to be a
janitor so you can have a fancy apartment!
I deny myself everything! I've been sewing
sleeves on your old drawers and wearing
'em for shirts! I don't even drink my bourbon any more. I just suck on the cork and
hit myself over the head with the bottle! I
never spend a penny on myself!

                       BLANCHE

You bought a tie-pin yesterday.

                        JOHN

What tie-pin! That was a hypodermic – I've
been selling my blood!

A small, sleepy figure emerges from the kitchen. He is clad in long underwear.

> BLANCHE
> (looking at him)
> Good heavens! John! Stop ranting for a
> minute and look.

> JOHN
> What – where?

He looks and sees the figure.

> BLANCHE
> You didn't bring back Ernie – you brought
> back Barney!

As John claps his hand to his head and falls back on his bed in complete defeat, we FREEZE on the tableau.

FADE OUT

THE END

THE BICKERSONS SCRIPTS
VOLUME I

by Philip Rapp

Edited by Ben Ohmart

ISBN: 0-9714570-1-8

$18.95

And now, here are Don Ameche and Frances Langford in Philip Rapp's humorous creation ... The Bickersons!

The Bickersons was one of radio's most popular and funniest comedy teams. Now for the first time ever you can read these never before published scripts. Included are full scripts from The Old Gold Show, the 1951 Bickersons series and other rarities. With an introduction by Phil Rapp himself!

Read just what the actors read!

❏ YES, please send me _____ copies of The Bickersons Scripts for just $18.95 each.

❏ YES, I'm interested in buying _____ copies of The Bickersons Scripts in bulk for my radio club, organization or store. Please send details.

❏ YES, I would like more information about your other publications.

Add $4 postage for up to 5 books. For non-US orders, please add $4 per book for airmail, in US funds. Payment must accompany all orders. Or buy online with Paypal at bearmanormedia.com.

My check or money order for $_____ is enclosed. Thank you.

NAME _____

ADDRESS _____

CITY/STATE/ZIP _____

E-MAIL _____

Checks payable to: Ben Ohmart * PO Box 750 * Boalsburg, PA 16827
ben@musicdish.com

THE BICKERSONS CDS
VOLUME 1 & 2

$11.95 each
or
Both Volume I & II for $19.95

Buy online at

bickersons.com

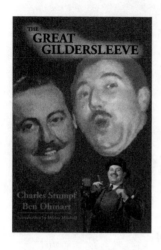

THE GREAT GILDERSLEEVE

by Charles Stumpf
and Ben Ohmart

ISBN: 0-9714570-0-X

$18.95

The Great Gildersleeve by Charles Stumpf and Ben Ohmart ranks as one of the best books on a radio program, if not the best. — Classic Images

Very comprehensive. A wonderful book! — Shirley Mitchell

It really takes me back to those delightful days on the show. — Gloria Peary

Give the gift of old time radio

❑ YES, please send me _____ copies of The Great Gildersleeve for just $18.95 each.

❑ YES, I'm interested in buying _____ copies of The Great Gildersleeve in bulk for my radio club, organization or store. Please send details.

❑ YES, I would like more information about your other publications.

Add $4 postage for up to 5 books. For non-US orders, please add $4 per book for airmail, in US funds. Payment must accompany all orders. Or buy online with Paypal at bearmanormedia.com.

My check or money order for $_____ is enclosed. Thank you.

NAME _____

ADDRESS _____

CITY/STATE/ZIP _____

E-MAIL _____

Checks payable to: Ben Ohmart * PO Box 750 * Boalsburg, PA 16827
ben@musicdish.com